Praise for Harold Coyle

"Coyle is at his best when he's depicting soldiers facing death. . . . He knows soldiers and he understands the brotherhood-of-arms mystique that transcends national boundaries." —*The New York Times Book Review*

"Harold Coyle is a superbly talented storyteller . . . the Tom Clancy of ground warfare." —W.E.B. Griffin

"When it comes to good military thrillers, Coyle is as good as it gets." —*Booklist*

"Harold Coyle has been dubbed the Tom Clancy of ground warfare and it's easy to see why. He focuses on the grunts because no matter how fancy the weapons are, eventually the military has to send in men to hold new territory." —*The New York Post*

"Coyle's attention to detail, his intimate knowledge of small unit fighting is remarkable." —Thomas Fleming, *The New York Times* bestselling author of *Washington's Secret War*

"With writers like Coyle standing watch over us, who needs Bruce Willis?" —*Kirkus Reviews*

BOOKS BY HAROLD COYLE

Team Yankee
Sword Point
Bright Star
Trial by Fire
The Ten Thousand
Code of Honor
Look Away
Until the End
Savage Wilderness
Dead Hand
God's Children
Against All Enemies
More Than Courage
They Are Soldiers

WITH BARRETT TILLMAN

Pandora's Legion
Prometheus's Child
Vulcan's Fire

HAROLD COYLE

DEAD HAND

FORGE®

A TOM DOHERTY ASSOCIATES BOOK
NEW YORK

This is a work of fiction. All the characters and events portrayed in this book are either products of the author's imagination or are used fictitiously.

DEAD HAND

Copyright © 2001 by Harold Coyle

A Forge Book
Published by Tom Doherty Associates, LLC
175 Fifth Avenue
New York, NY 10010

www.tor-forge.com

Forge® is a registered trademark of Tom Doherty Associates, LLC.

ISBN 978-0-7653-6387-9
Library of Congress Catalog Card Number: 2001018957

First Edition: May 2001
First Mass Market Edition: May 2002
Second Mass Market Edition: May 2009

Printed in the United States of America

0 9 8 7 6 5 4 3 2 1

To my mother,

Evelyn
1926–2000

She was more than a parent;
for me she is the personification of
Dedication, Sacrifice, and Love.

Prologue

Like the slow, steady pealing of a church bell announcing the death of a parishioner, the massive steel blast doors reverberated with each new explosion. Some of the more nervous officers and soldiers still at their stations jumped each time a new eruption shook the doors that separated them from the vicious combat on the other side. When the sound of one particularly violent detonation rippled through the launch-control center, even the steadiest of them dropped all pretenses of the calm demeanor that was a hallmark of the elite Russian Strategic Rocket Force. Comrades who had shared and endured so many hardships on the fringes of Siberia exchanged nervous glances. Now, with the rattle of small-arms fire growing closer and the acrid smell of cordite seeping into the room that controlled the ICBM fields of their regiment, one by one the mutinous soldiers turned to stare at the console where their commander should have been.

Unlike them, he was not at his assigned place of duty. His seat was vacant, as it had been since the first report that commandos, loyal to the government in Moscow, had managed to break into the subterranean complex where the control center was located. Nor was the deputy commander present. Knowing that he would never be able to idly stand by in the stifling confines of the control center and passively wait for the end, the deputy had abandoned his post to personally direct the defense of the complex. Nothing had been heard of him after the large blast door had been shut behind him. Only the growing sounds of fighting suggested that those mutineers tasked to defend the control center were losing ground.

It wasn't until the roar of battle was replaced by the sound of hushed voices just outside the blast door that the next-senior officer, a major, rose from his seat. Slowly, almost haltingly, the major made his way to the rear of the room, where the commander of the regiment sat alone in his office. Following protocol, the major knocked on the door before pushing it open and slipping into the darkened room. His colonel, who had led them into open revolt to protest the abysmal living conditions his men were forced to live under, was bent over his desk, holding his head in his hands. "Sir," the major announced, "it is time. I need the codes in order to—"

"To do *what*?" the colonel bellowed as his hands fell away and he glared up at the major. "Murder our fellow countrymen?"

Undaunted by this rebuke and spurred on by the ominous activities just outside the blast door, where he suspected the commandos were laying charges to blow it open, the major did not back down. Instead, he cleared his throat as he prepared to press for the codes the men waiting in the control room would need to launch their missiles.

The colonel, however, did not give him a chance. His blurry eyes, framed by a puffy, white unshaven face, was contorted by anger. "Or perhaps," the colonel sneered, "we should launch our missiles at the Americans and let them rain death and destruction down on our people for us."

"But our threats? Our plans?" the major stammered. "I fear the commandos are preparing to blast their way into here. If we don't act now—"

"Go away," the colonel moaned as he let his head drop back into the open, waiting hands as if his neck could no longer support it. "Close the door and let me be."

Determined not to leave until he had both the keys and the codes necessary to launch their missiles, the major snapped to attention and drew his pistol. "Colonel," he barked with as much conviction as his parched throat allowed, "we believed in you when you stated that you would force Moscow to honor its obligations to us and our families. We have endured three days and nights without sleep as we stood by and watched those bastards throw everything they had against us. Like myself, the others are prepared to carry out the just and righteous retribution that you yourself promised to deliver if our demands were not met. It is time to do so. I insist that you hand over the codes."

This time, when the drunken colonel lifted his head and looked into the eyes of the defiant major, he laughed. *"Ha!* The joke is on you, Major. I have no codes." As he leaned back in his seat, his right hand reached out and grabbed the bottle of vodka sitting on the desk before him. "Never had the bloody things. The deputy knew that. Why do you think he left to die out there?"

Stunned by this unexpected revelation, the major's jaw dropped open. Slowly, he lowered his pistol and looked around the room as if trying to collect his thoughts. When he finally turned back to face his commander, the colonel was taking a long, hard pull on the bottle. "This," the shaken major asked incredulously, "has all been a bluff?"

Finishing before he bothered to answer, the colonel pitched the bottle across the room, where it shattered against a world map that covered most of one wall. *"That,"* he yelled, "is all we're able to hurl at those bastards in Moscow who have starved our families and left us here to rot. *That's* all we ever had. You should have known that! We have no launch codes here! You're a fucking major, for God's sake! How could you have been so damned stupid? You know how the system works." Leaning forward, the colonel's expression became a scowl. "Now go away, you fool, and join the other fools who were gullible enough to stay with the colors while the crooks in Moscow broke promise after promise to us, while building dachas for themselves and sending the money that belonged to us to Swiss bank accounts. Go, and leave me alone. Perhaps," the colonel added, "if you're lucky, the commandos will kill you rather than take you prisoner."

Still stunned by the fact that he had gone into open rebellion against his own country, following the leadership of a man who had never intended to back his threats with action, the major turned and walked out of the office, pistol in hand.

Alone again, the colonel opened a lower desk drawer that contained two unopened bottles of vodka, a pistol, a hand grenade, and some ledgers. Reaching into the drawer, he pulled out one of the two bottles. As he twisted off the cap, he looked into the drawer at the pistol and the grenade. A smile crept across his face and he put the newly opened bottle down and bent over. Taking the grenade, the colonel firmly grasped it so that the spoon could not fly off when he pulled the pin. When he was ready, he gave the pin a firm yank with his free hand. Tossing the pin over his shoulder, he leaned over again.

Carefully he nestled the pinless grenade between the ledgers in the drawer with the last bottle of vodka. Keeping the spoon down, he slowly pushed the drawer in until he was sure he could release the grenade and the spoon would be held in place by the bottom of the drawer above. Then he slowly withdrew his hand.

Satisfied that all was set, the colonel eased the drawer in a bit farther until just the bottle of vodka, lying on its side, was visible. "There," he murmured with glee. "A gift for the victors."

With nothing more to do but wait, the colonel leaned back in his seat, retrieved the freshly opened bottle of vodka on his desk, and settled in to enjoy his last moment on earth. He had no desire to pray. His wife was the one infected by the wave of religious fanaticism that was currently gripping their staggering country. Nor did he intend to pen an excuse or an explanation of his actions for his former masters. They knew why he had done as he had. That was why they kept well-fed and well-paid men, like those preparing to force their way into the control room with orders to kill everyone in there, close at hand. Every commander in the Strategic Rocket Force knew that. Like his fellow regimental commanders, his only duty over the past few years had been to keep his people mollified as best as he could, no matter what happened, or suffer the consequences. There would be no compromise, no negotiations. He even suspected that the major who had been in his office had known what was coming. The only problem with the major was that he was still a bit too young. The system, or what passed as one nowadays in Russia, simply had not had enough time to squeeze the last vestige of hope from him.

While he waited, the colonel continued to do his best to drink himself senseless. He was well into his new bottle of vodka when a blast, just outside his door in the main room, announced that the commandos had penetrated the last barrier. As the sound of gunshots, exploding grenades, shrieked orders, and screams of pain filled the colonel's dark office, he suddenly had a funny thought. Looking down at the booby-trapped desk drawer, he smiled. "Well," he said, ignoring the sound of boots pounding their way up the concrete stairs that led to his office, "it seems I have created my own Dead Hand." Then, looking up at the partially opened door, he lifted his bottle in a mock toast. "I only wish those shits in Moscow could have been here to enjoy my last little joke."

Seconds later, it was all over—but for one last vengeful swipe by the dead.

1

Unable to ignore the leg cramps that were reducing his pace to a painful limp, the solitary Welsh guardsman came to a complete stop. Like a hunted animal in distress, his eyes frantically darted about the bleak Scottish landscape in a desperate search for a spot where he could hide. He had to find a concealed nook, a place that afforded him sanctuary. He badly needed to collect his thoughts, catch his breath, and sort himself out.

Nothing, however, seemed to fit the bill. Rather than offering safety, every rock outcropping and fold in the earth his eyes fell upon appeared ominous and foreboding, an ideal haven for his pursuers. Dejected, the Welshman drew in a deep breath before setting off again as quickly as his sore muscles would permit.

In the process of covering the next hundred or so meters, he noticed the sky becoming lighter. Yet the coming of dawn brought little promise that his agony and suffering would soon be at an end. Instead of a friendly, smiling sun to dry his clothes and warm his spirit, the night gave way to a dull, steel-gray sky crowded with low-hanging clouds heavily laden with moisture, which would add to his miseries and suffering. By the time it was clear enough to see the jagged ridgelines on either side of the valley, he was making his way through at a slow, laborious jog, Corporal John Jones's outlook was as bleak as the breaking day.

Placing his hands on his hips and drawing in deep breaths that formed dense, moist clouds when he exhaled, Jones forced himself to press on along the rock-strewn valley floor. With growing regularity, he scanned the barren mountain crest up ahead that stood out against the ugly morning sky. Every so often, he glanced behind. His failure to detect any sign of pursuers, which had been a blessing the night before, began to concern him. His state of mind, molded by the physical and mental punishment he and his mates had suffered at their hands on previous occasions, had twisted a healthy respect for his foe into a gnawing paranoia that hovered over him every waking hour. By now, he no longer saw the men who were hounding him as being part of the same human race to which he himself belonged. Rather than suffer from the adversities that sapped his strength, Jones fancied that they were growing stronger and more vicious at the very time his own abilities were ebbing. It was, of course, foolish to think like this.

Whether it was the hunger, the cold, or the overpowering exhaustion the likes of which he had never imagined possible, the twenty-three-year-old Welshman was finally coming to the realization that he was fast approaching the end of his rope. It was growing more difficult for him to maintain his pace, his focus, and even worse, his motivation. Panting, he again slowed until the pain in his legs brought him to a complete halt. Instinctively, he glanced over his shoulder, half-expecting to see the soldiers of the Rifle Brigade, fresh and unaffected by the rigors of the hunt, right there, ready to take advantage of his weakness. Capturing him would yield them a pass and put an end to his dream of becoming a member of the Special Air Service.

When he did not see them, Jones was struck by an odd thought. Rather than feeling relieved that they weren't there, the Welshman found that he was disappointed. He was almost sorry that no one was at hand to bring his suffering to an end. No sooner had that thought popped into his head than it was followed by a horrible realization. He had failed. It was all over. For the first time, he came to appreciate the brutal fact that he simply did not have what it took. Already broken in body, this failure of spirit was the last straw. Psychologically vanquished, he dropped to the ground and sat there, unsure of what to do next.

With his elbows planted on his knees, Jones allowed his head, too heavy for his overtaxed neck muscles to support, to drop down onto his chest. Though he was on the verge of crying, somehow he managed to hold himself together.

Suddenly a new fear sent a shiver down his spine. With a jerk, he threw his head back and frantically scanned the horizon. For a second, he imagined that he could hear the booming of the Welsh Guard's Regimental sergeant major thundering down from the top of a Scottish mountaintop: "Get your filthy ass off the ground, Jones. You're on parade." The sergeant major's voice resounded so convincingly in Jones's mind that he looked up, half-expecting to see the tall, barrel-chested sergeant major standing there, right in front of him, attired in his immaculate scarlet tunic.

But the uncompromising pillar of military correctness and decorum wasn't there. Only moss-covered rocks and brown winter grass stretching as far as he could see through the thick morning mist greeted his eyes. Again allowing his head to drop down, Jones cursed himself for trading in what he had thought was a living hell of shining brass and tedious days of guard duty in London for this. Sitting upright, he stuffed his hands into the pockets of his waterlogged battle-dress jacket in a vain search for something to eat. As his fingers rummaged about, he found himself longing for the warm, form-fitting wool tunic that he and his mates likened to straitjackets.

Jones wasn't paying attention to anything other than his memories of duty in London and the faint hope of finding something he had forgotten about to eat, when a blurred image popped up from out of nowhere. He didn't see the looming apparition for what it was. He didn't need to. Though he was still reeling from the surprise and desperately trying to brace himself for the coming impact, a voice in the back of his mind told him that his ordeal was finally over. Despite his best efforts, despite his determination not to give in to anything, his foes were about to prevail. Everything, from the well-nurtured feeling of paranoia that the antics of his tormentors had instilled in him, to the near-physical collapse to which the entire ordeal had taken him, told him that resistance was futile. Even in those few brief seconds before his body was bowled over into a helpless, twisted heap, John Jones accepted the cruel fact that he had been humbled.

Gnawing on an Army-issue biscuit, the SAS captain looked down at Jones without any feelings of mercy or pity. The man had been an idiot, Patrick Hogg told himself as he bit off a chunk of dry biscuit and slowly moved it about in his mouth until it was moist enough to chew. He entertained no thought of offering the SAS candidate something to eat or drink. Not that the man would have accepted. Even now, Hogg could see both defiance and loathing in the eyes of Corporal Jones, late of the Welsh Guard, as the hapless man lay on the soggy ground, tightly trusted and neatly gagged.

In the beginning, when he had run his first few groups of prospective SAS candidates through the hell that was his survival course, Hogg hadn't gagged those luckless souls he had personally tracked and subdued. In fact, he had often offered them something to eat. That all stopped one day when one particularly belligerent lad from Liverpool failed to show anything even remotely akin to gratitude. Instead, the bastard had spit the food Hogg had given him in his face and then launched into a tirade of oaths and blasphemies that Hogg felt were uncalled for. The twelve-year veteran of the British Army could have tolerated this. He had, after all, been subjected to far worse from experts. It was when the irate candidate started calling him a has-been, a washout who could no longer pull his weight in a real line unit, that Hogg snapped. Pulling the sweat-soaked scarf that he had been wearing around his neck, he had stuffed one end of it as far down the man's throat as he dare and used the rest to bind the gag in place. From that day on, Hogg made sure that he had something particularly nasty and odious in one of his pockets that could serve as a proper gag.

The sound of a helicopter making its way up the narrow valley brought an end to Hogg's silent breakfast. Tossing the half-eaten biscuit so that it came to rest inches in front of his prisoner's eyes, Hogg stood up and turned to face the approaching aircraft. Pulling a smoke grenade from his kit, he gave the pin a solid tug and let the safety spoon fly away. No longer held in place by the flat of the spoon, the cocked hammer was free to swing over and smash into the grenade's primer. But the SAS officer didn't throw the grenade when he heard the snap. Rather, he waited patiently, holding the grenade at arm's length, until the dense yellow smoke began to spew forth from either end of the grenade. Only then did Hogg casually toss it so that both he and his prisoner would be upwind from the billowing yellow cloud.

With an ease that came from countless hours of flying, the pilot sergeant of the helicopter came right up to where Hogg stood and, at the last second, flared out and lightly touched down so that the SAS captain had but a few yards to drag his prisoner to the waiting aircraft. This Hogg did without ceremony, without any apparent regard for the hapless candidate that he had managed to bring to bay.

At the door of the helicopter, Hogg was greeted by a smiling face. "And a fine cheerful morning to you, Captain," the red-haired senior sergeant sitting in the open door shouted above the noise of the chopper's engines.

Hogg gave Sergeant Kenneth McPherson a dirty look. "You know what you can do with your bloody Highland weather," Hogg shouted back as he took Jones and literally heaved the former candidate onto the floor of the helicopter next to McPherson's prisoner.

"I've been to Ireland, you know," McPherson countered. "I've seen that gloom you Paddies pass off as weather. I'm here to tell you, it isn't anything a sane person would be proud of."

For the first time, Hogg smiled as he climbed in and plopped down next to McPherson. "Now there you go, Sergeant," Hogg gloated, "confusing Irishmen with sane people. Next, you'll be telling me that Scottish lads coming of age can differentiate between the sheep they tend and the lasses."

While Hogg gave the pilot the signal to pull pitch, McPherson groaned as he poured Hogg a cup of hot tea the pilot had brought along for the instructors. "You're lucky you're an officer and I'm a proper and respectful noncommissioned officer," he shouted as he handed over the cup. "Otherwise, Captain, I'd be telling you a thing or two."

Hogg looked at the burly Highland sergeant with a genuine affection, one that he felt for all of his cadre. He enjoyed the casualness of the relationships shared by those in the Special Air Service, where rank meant nothing. Patrick Hogg had started, like most of the men in the SAS, in a regular unit. But life as a line officer in the Queen's Own Irish Hussars had been oppressive and confining for him. He needed something more from the Army than the routine of training, maintenance, and administrative duties that consumed an officer's life in peacetime. He had been born to be a member of the SAS. "That, Sergeant McPherson," Hogg finally replied after taking a sip of the wonderfully warm tea, "won't take too long, seeing that your intellectual capacity can handle but two."

"With all due respect, sir," McPherson stated with mock indignation, "bugger off."

The lighthearted banter between sergeant and officer had put Hogg in a better frame of mind by the time they reached the rally point where lorries waited for both candidates and cadre alike. Some lorries would take candidates who had completed the course to their next ordeal, a twenty-four-hour interrogation that was as brutal as military law would permit. Other trucks waited for those like Jones. He would be taken back to his barracks, where he would be given enough time to pack his kit and clear out before his triumphant companions returned to celebrate the completion of the selection process with a hot shower and a well-deserved sleep.

The usual assorted lot of support personnel was mixed in with the SAS cadre. The truck drivers congregated around the front of their vehicles, finishing off their morning coffee. The mess personnel stood ready behind steaming food pans, doing their best to look as miserable as they felt while spooning out hard-boiled eggs to cadre and support personnel as they wandered in. The medics, as medics do around the world, sat in the cab of their field ambulance, looking bored and praying that nothing happened to break that boredom.

Besides these assorted support personnel, Patrick Hogg noticed his superior when he and Kenneth McPherson hopped off the helicopter. Standing at the end of the mess line, Major Thomas Shields was chatting with several of Hogg's cadre. McPherson, busy giving an SAS sergeant major a hand hauling out the former SAS candidates, didn't notice Shields at first. When he did, he grunted. "God, I hope he's not out here to give us another one of his rousing speeches on the need to maintain the standards of the regiment."

Hogg, who had been looking at Shields and sipping tea from a battered mess cup, shook his head. "I don't think so."

When McPherson noted the circumspect exchange between the two officers, he guessed that there was something up between them. "Captain," McPherson stated in a tone that NCO's use when they are trying to tell an officer what to do, "why don't you run along and tend to business like a good officer and let me sort out these lads."

Taking one last look at Jones, Hogg felt his first pang of sympathy for the corporal of the Welsh

Guard. That poor soul, who was returning Hogg's stare with one that could kill, would be going back to rejoin his regiment at best. He'd be humbled by this experience. More than likely, the Welshman would be broken in spirit to the point to where a once-promising career was now all but impossible. While it was a shame that a good soldier such as Jones would be regarded as a failure because he hadn't measured up to the grueling demands the SAS held onto, Hogg knew there was nothing he could do about that. It was his job to sort out those who were merely good and those who had what it took. Without another thought, Patrick Hogg turned his back on the still gagged and bound Welshman and headed over to see what had brought the major out on a morning like this.

When he saw Hogg approaching, Shields excused himself, grabbed another cup of tea, and met Hogg halfway. "If you're after a bit of sun to add some color to your cheeks, you picked a hell of a day to do so," Hogg ventured, with a casual salute.

Shields smiled as he returned the salute and handed the second cup of tea he was carrying to Hogg. "If I was looking for the sun," the major countered, "this is the last place on earth I'd come."

The two men chuckled over this tête-à-tête, sipped their tea, and looked around at the comings and goings of the soldiers entrusted to them for several minutes. Hogg noted that the major kept looking over to where Sergeant McPherson was in the process of untying Jones and the candidate McPherson had run to ground. Hogg could see by the major's expression that he was displeased with Hogg's handling of Jones. But the major would say nothing. As long as life and limb were not too recklessly endangered, the commander of this portion of the SAS's selection cycle pretty much left the techniques used by his people up to them.

Like all members of the regiment, Shields had overcome every trial his instructors had thrown his way and accumulated an impressive operational record. But he was not at all like Hogg. The major's natural habitat was an office, sorting through the staff actions and routine paperwork that the Ministry of Defense and the Army took great pride in using to measure the abilities of the "less gifted" officers. For Hogg, having a superior like Shields was a blessing, for the major knew talent when he saw it and knew how to use it. He gave Hogg free rein when it came to operations and training and took on the task of keeping the paperwork beast at bay. Only on occasion, when he sensed that some of Patrick Hogg's techniques or his NCO's were getting, as Shields put it, "a bit rambunctious," did he intervene. And even then, the SAS major made his point by offering "suggestions" instead of directives.

Hogg decided to take the initiative rather than let his superior wander about on his way toward the reason for the unexpected visit to the field. "I take it you're here to talk to me about my pending request."

"MOD is after me again about you, Patrick," Shields stated. "They are not thrilled about your pending resignation. They think it's a mistake."

Hogg looked into Shields's eyes for a second. "And what do you think?"

The major didn't hesitate. "I agree." Lifting his cup, he waved it in the direction of McPherson and the two candidates, who were now on their feet. "I don't think that firm in London you're looking at is going to let you manage its personnel like you're used to doing."

Though Shields meant it as a joke, Hogg didn't respond, instead, after taking a long sip of tea, he looked away. "I'm honored that the lads at MOD think so highly of me. But you know I can't stay in."

"You're making a mistake, Patrick," Shields responded, with a frustration in his voice that he made no effort to hide. "Listen, I know what you're going through. God knows there has been many a day when I've asked myself why in hell I put up with all the crap the Army serves up. But you and I, Patrick, we're soldiers. While either one of us could walk into any company in the UK tomorrow and land a top job with an income that would put our Army pay to shame, we'd die. It's that simple. We need the Army just as much as it needs us. Maybe more."

"And Jenny?" Hogg asked in a quiet, almost plaintive, voice. "What about her?"

Though he was normally able to control his emotions, Shields let his anger break through the calm, businesslike demeanor that was his hallmark. "Damn it, Patrick! You know she'll never be happy with anything you do. I've seen this sort of thing too many times before. Though Jenny's a lovely girl, she doesn't appreciate who you are, or what you're doing. You're a bloody damned fool if you think leaving the regiment is going to make things right between the two of you."

If Shields had expected Hogg to respond in kind to his outburst, he was sadly disappointed. Instead, the SAS captain turned to his superior and looked into his eyes with a mournful expression. "But I love her."

This simple display of sincere emotion, so rare between two men such as Shields and Hogg, took the venom out of the major's argument. Instead, he placed his hand on Hogg's shoulder. "Look, Patrick," he said in a fatherly tone, "I don't doubt that you do. But these two loves of yours, Jenny and the SAS, are tearing you apart. Eventually something's got to give. I just don't want to see you getting hurt."

The first response that popped into Hogg's mind was to come back that he, Shields, didn't want it to go on his record that he had lost the services of one of the regiment's rising stars. But he thought better. There was no point in pissing all over your superior officer's boots when the issue didn't demand it. Besides, Hogg thought to himself, Shields really did care for him as a person and not just as a subordinate.

Forcing a weak smile, Hogg shook his head. "Look, now that this lot has been run through the mill, I'd like to take some leave. There're a couple of firms in London that have been badgering me to come down there for interviews. I thought that perhaps I'd take Jenny with me. While we're there, I'll have some time to talk to her."

This brought a smile to Shields's face. "Splendid! It so happens," he added, "you have quite a bit of leave stored up. Perhaps after you've finished in London, you could head over to Derry and spend some time with the family, away from all of this."

Though it was a well-meaning suggestion, Hogg knew that such a trip would be impossible. If anything, it would make matters worse. When Hogg had mentioned he was thinking about leaving the Army, his father had exploded. The Hoggs had a long tradition of serving both king and country. The elder Hogg had been the regimental sergeant major of the same regiment Patrick had belonged to before joining the SAS. And his only uncle had been killed in the line of duty by the IRA while a member of the Ulster Constabulary during "The Troubles." No, Hogg thought. Jenny would be enough to deal with.

"London will do," Hogg said, finally venturing to break the awkward silence and appease Major Shields. "Jenny's never spent any real time there. Who knows," the sad SAS captain said jokingly as he lifted up his battered cup in a mock toast, "perhaps

I won't need to do much talking to convince her that the big city isn't for us."

Satisfied that the major issue of the day had been put to rest, Shields turned to the discussion of operational matters and an upcoming inspection by the Prince of Wales. Neither man took note of the lorry pulling out of the line of parked vehicles. None of the SAS cadre or any of the administrative personnel supporting them took the time to say farewell to Corporal John Jones of the Welsh Guard and his bedraggled companions who filled the back of the nondescript Army lorry. That, after all, was not how things were done in the SAS. There simply wasn't time or energy to spare for those who could not keep up.

CORSICA
MARCH

Selection for membership in an elite organization is not an end to a soldier's trials. In many ways, it's simply the beginning. For once a soldier is awarded the cherished symbol of that unit, whether it be a beret or a badge, he accepts the responsibility of maintaining the heritage that those who went before him recorded with their own blood.

For Sergeant-Chef Stanislaus Dombrowski, this was normally not a problem. Like most young Poles, he had been conscripted into the Army as soon as he came of military age. Unlike many of his peers, he thrived as a soldier. Even before he finished the rudimentary training that passed as basic in the Polish Army, he knew that he had found his calling.

But it was a discovery tempered by the restrictive nature of Polish society and its institutions during the waning days of communism. Certain only that he would never be afforded an opportunity to test his newfound vocation if he remained in his native land, Dombrowski fled his chaotic country and headed to the one place where thousands of expatriates had gone for generations in search of adventure and a career as a soldier. At the young age of twenty, Stanislaus Dombrowski became a member of France's Legion Étrangère.

Once in the Legion, Dombrowski concluded that he would never be content with merely earning the *képi blanc,* or white kepi, that was as much a symbol of the Legion as the Green Beret was to the American Special Forces. Quickly bored by routine and ever anxious to prove to his fellow legionnaires that he was as tough as the next man, Dombrowski first earned his parachutist wings, then fought for the right to become a member of les Commandos de Recherche et d'Action dans le Profondeur, or the parachute regiment's commando team.

Known by an unfortunate acronym, these CRAP teams were the elite of the elite. Each CRAP team consisted of twenty-five officers and NCO's, divided into two ten-man subteams and a five-man command group. Trained to work with other units of the parachute regiment or alone, the CRAP teams were France's jack-of-all-trades. When operating as part of their parent regiment during large-scale conventional operations, they served as pathfinders and performed recon. More often than not, they were employed as commandos. As such, they could be used offensively to destroy enemy installations, covertly to gather intelligence in a hostile environment, or be dispatched to locate, safeguard, and evacuate French citizens abroad who found themselves in trouble. While each member of a CRAP team became a specialist in one area, all needed to master skills essential to the team, including combat first aid, demolitions, hand-to-hand combat, individual and crew-served weapons, communications, automotive mechanics, and the art of gathering combat intelligence. Dombrowksi's particular expertise was demolitions.

Yet as highly qualified and motivated as the Polish legionnaire was, he was never able to overcome a painful fear of heights. No matter how hard he tried or how many hours of free fall he logged, Sergeant-Chef Stanislaus Dombrowski's stomach always became roiled whenever the prospect of a jump loomed before him. And as if this were not bad enough, every member of his team knew it. As men of this type tend to do, they never let him live it down. Even now, as the French Air Force Transall C-160 climbed to altitude, his compatriots were conspiring against him. Seated next to the open door, the jump master for the team, Adjutant Hector Allons, leaned over and yelled out above the roar of air rushing into the Transall: "Franz, did you remember to bring plenty of barf bags for Stanislaus?"

Corporal Franz Ingelmann leaned forward and looked down the row of jumpers at the jump master. "Mon Dieu! I have forgotten them, *again!*"

"Damn you, man!" Allons thundered. "How could you? Have you already forgotten how slippery it can get when the good Sergeant-Chef Stanislaus Dombrowski deposits his breakfast on the deck?"

Feigning panic, Ingelmann tore the helmet from his head and offered it up to the adjutant. "Here, use this. I really don't mind."

Since he was seated between the two men yelling back and forth to each other, Dombrowski heard everything. He was, as he usually was at times like this, less than amused. Slowly turning his head, he mustered up the best killing stare he could manage under the circumstances and glared at Ingelmann. "Fuck you both," the Polish NCO groaned. "You can take that helmet of yours and shove it up your ass."

Sporting a puzzled look, Ingelmann came back at Dombrowski without missing a beat. "I do not see what good that would do either of us, Sergeant. I'm not having any problem keeping my bodily fluids contained, while it is obvious that you are on the verge of spewing."

In no mood to entertain his fellow team members by joining into the little play Allons and Ingelmann were staging, Dombrowski settled back in his seat, muttering a halfhearted, "Fuck you." Once he was as comfortable as his condition and his equipment permitted, he closed his eyes and began to pray that Allons would soon stand up and start issuing the commands that would bring his misery to an end.

How long it took before that moment came was hard for Dombrowski to judge. Forced to concentrate his entire attention on keeping himself together, he was unable to gauge the passing of time with any degree of accuracy. Rather than concern himself with what was going on about him, he was tightly focused on his struggle to preserve his dignity. So it wasn't until Ingelmann poked him in the side that Dombrowski opened his eyes. Towering over him, the Austrian legionnaire was grinning. "Do you plan on joining us, Sergeant-Chef? Or would you prefer that we instruct the pilot to make another pass over the drop zone when you are feeling more yourself?"

Though he was still in considerable distress, Dombrowski managed a cutting glare in response to the young Austrian's snide comment. This only caused Ingelmann's devilish grin to broaden. "Just asking."

Having made the trip this far without losing his composure or the contents of his stomach, Dombrowski took his time as he pulled himself up off the nylon jump seat to take his position in the line of paratroopers, known as a "stick." As he did so, no one offered their suffering comrade a hand. While the Legion is a brotherhood that commands a loyalty among its members that makes most blood kinship pale in comparison, there are certain rules and limits. One of the rules that has been a part of the Legion since its inception trumps all. That code demands that each and every legionnaire pull his own weight. It was essential, especially among parachutists, that every member of the unit be able to keep up and execute his assigned duties without fail. Only by doing so could the survival and success of the unit, whether it be a battalion or a small ten-man team, be assured. While it has been noble in Western literature to extol the virtue of honoring the sacrifice of the many for the good of the one, in combat, both leaders and soldiers must be as analytical and dispassionate as a mathematician. For combat abides by its own cruel form of arithmetic. Whether it is expressed by the amount of explosives required to achieve a desired degree of destruction, or in computing how much firepower will be needed to destroy an enemy unit, hard logic rules.

Dombrowski understood this. While legionnaires are indoctrinated to never abandon a wounded or dead comrade, the Pole knew that two men, or even one, could not be subtracted from the small unit's remaining complement of nine to care for one who was in distress. Ingelmann was not being unkind by refusing to offer a hand to his ailing friend. Rather, he was doing Dombrowski a favor. A soldier in a highly specialized unit such as CRAP who cannot keep up after being inserted deep behind enemy lines can be a lethal liability to all, as well as to the mission. To these highly trained professionals, it is duty, and not the man, that is everything. For the same code of honor that commanded them never to turn their backs on a fallen legionnaire also bound them to accomplish their assigned mission to its conclusion, regardless of the cost.

Mustering all his strength, the Polish NCO managed to take his place in the stick. Once on his feet, he shifted his equipment about so that everything would be where it needed to be when the long nylon cords of his deploying parachute snapped taut and brought his two-hundred-kilometers-per-hour free-fall plunge to an abrupt end. Only at that moment, when his body was jerked upright by a blossoming canopy, would Sergeant-Chef Stanislaus Dombrowski be free from his misery and able to turn his mind to the mission at hand.

He was in the process of yanking a strap on his harness back onto his shoulder to where it should have been when the shrill sound of the buzzer alerted him that it was time to go. Even before he looked away from his harness, his feet were in motion, moving along the swaying aluminum floor of the transport in rhythm with the other nine members of his team. Dombrowski could feel Ingelmann behind him, pushing him toward the door, just as he was doing to the man in front of him.

Exiting an aircraft as the member of a stick of paratroopers was always a blur for Stanislaus Dombrowski. So much was happening in a very confined space, in such a short period of time, that it was hard to take notice of any single image or event. This frenzied and confusing burst of activity was compounded by a rush of sensations, from the shock of facing the cold, stiff blast of air that came howling through the open door, to the feeling of being shoved from behind by a comrade as he moved along the heaving deck under his feet. As Dombrowski approached the door, the shouts of the jump master repeating his command, "Go! Go! Go!" mingled with the steady drone of the aircraft's engines, the annoying blare of the buzzer, and the screeching wind. All this served to heighten the Polish legionnaire's excitement, already brought to a feverish pitch by the flow of adrenaline coursing through his veins.

In these last few seconds before stepping out into thin air, all traces of the big Pole's queasiness disappeared. He no longer had to wrestle with his fear that he would lose his composure. All conscious thought was gone. Like the other nine members of the CRAP team to which he belonged, his body and mind responded as it had been trained and conditioned to do. Stanislaus Dombrowski was no longer a Pole far from home serving a country that was not his. He was no longer a man who had a particularly acute fear of heights and flying. He was a legionnaire, and as such, a highly skilled professional killing machine thundering through the open door of the C-160 transport without hesitation, without regard for personal consequences. When combined with the other members of his team, these men of the 2ème Bataillon Étranger Parachutiste became a force to be reckoned with.

2

From his seat against the wall, Major Andrew Fretello, United States Army, listened attentively as an Air Force lieutenant colonel answered questions that were being thrown at him by the bevy of generals and admirals seated around a conference table. Though the Chief of Staff of the Air Force was doing his best to deflect some of the more pointed inquiries concerning the plan the colonel had just presented, it was clear to Fretello that both the briefer as well as his proposal were on the verge of foundering. His solution to the problem under discussion contained little that was new. Anyone who regularly participated in these unannounced war games was familiar with the standard Air Force response to a crisis. That alone, Fretello reasoned as he watched, was grounds enough for the unmerciful pounding to which the briefer was being subjected.

A Naval lieutenant commander seated next to Fretello leaned over and whispered in his ear, "Stealth bombers and smart bombs. Stealth bombers and smart bombs. Doesn't the Air Force know any-thing else?"

Fretello pulled away and gave the Naval officer a funny look. "What does the Navy have to deal with in this situation that the Air Force doesn't?"

The lieutenant commander smiled as he tapped the Navy SEAL emblem pinned on his chest. "We have Demi Moore!"

As a longtime member of the Army's Special Forces, Fretello appreciated the joke. Rolling his eyes and shaking his head, he suppressed a groan. Without a word, he turned his attention back to the briefing.

As well as exercising DoD's Crisis Action Team or CAT, readiness tests and no-notice war games such as this gave talented officers like Fretello an oppor-tunity to engage in some high-speed exercises that were as exotic as they were intriguing. The face time before the military's most senior leadership wasn't anything to sneeze at either. That is, of course, pro-vided they liked what you were saying. In the case of the poor Air Force officer nervously twirling his laser pointer about as he waited for the next volley of questions, it was obvious that his briefing had fallen wide of the mark.

"Let me get this straight," the Army's Chief of Plans and Operations said as he shifted about in his seat. "The best *your* plan can deliver is a ninety-percent success rate."

The Air Force officer, standing before the gath-ered generals like a deer caught in the headlights of a speeding car, was quick to respond. "That's for the first strike only. The follow-up strike would, with-out doubt, eliminate those targets that were not neutralized by the initial attack."

Picking up the Army general's point, the Chief of Naval Operations leaned back in his seat and waved his hand about. "What makes you think the missiles that survived your first strike will still be there? The Russians, after all, also understand the principle of use 'em or lose 'em. I'm sure there isn't a man at this table who wouldn't be pounding down the President's door demanding he issue the release order if the Russians or Chinese had destroyed ninety percent of a key component of our strategic nuclear force." The admiral paused only long enough to see how many were shaking their heads in agreement before pressing on. "I'm afraid that no matter how you dress this solution up, Colonel, it isn't going to hack it. Our first strike will be our only strike. Though it is a trite old saying, 'Failure, even ten-percent's worth, is not an option.' "

The Chairman of the Joint Chiefs, having heard enough of the Air Force's plan, nodded in agreement. "Admiral Langsdorf is correct. The parameters set down for this exercise require not only a rapid and overwhelming response, but one that provides us with one-hundred-percent results, guaranteed."

Angered by this statement, the Chief of Staff of the Air Force threw his hands up in frustration. "Christ! You might as well ask us to deliver the moon and the stars." Pausing only long enough to rein in his anger, he continued: "We've all been involved in military operations. We all know that there is no such thing as guarantees when it comes to combat. Only a fool would make one."

After staring at the Air Force general for a moment, just to make sure that he was finished, the Chairman swiveled his seat around until he was looking at the Chief of Staff of the Army. "Well, Chuck. How's the Army's inventory of fools looking these days?"

Smiling, General Chuck E. Smith glanced over at Fretello. "Well, sir, if it's a fool you want, I've got one on deck, primed and ready to go." Turning back to face the other Joint Chiefs and their senior operations officers, Smith introduced the man who would present the Army's solution to the exercise problem the CAT was convened to resolve. "Major Andrew Fretello is a plans-and-operations officer at Fort Bragg. He's served with Special Force units in Central and South America, Europe, and Southwest Asia. Though still quite junior, his planning of and participation in several special projects, including last year's raid against the Iraqi chemical-warfare facilities, make him eminently qualified to deal with the situation at hand."

Taking his cue, Fretello stood up and quickly made his way to the front of the room. He carried no notes, no handouts. All of his briefing charts and diagrams were already in the hands of the NCO charged with operating the briefing room's audio-visual equipment. Fretello didn't even carry a pointer. In his opinion, they were a crutch used by weak or nervous briefing officers. By the time Smith was finished with the introduction, the Special Forces major, decked out in his greens, stood tall before the assembled general officers, straphangers, and fellow briefers. Having participated in numerous planning sessions, Fretello knew he could ignore just about everyone in the room. The only person he needed to be concerned with during the course of his presentation was the most senior officer present. He and no one else set the tone and pace. Having been afforded the opportunity to observe how the Chairman had handled those who went before him, it was clear that the man was using this exercise as a true working session. This, Fretello realized, allowed him greater freedom in the manner in which to proceed.

After finishing a hushed conversation with his aide, who was dutifully seated behind his boss, the Chairman of the Joint Chiefs of Staff twisted his seat about, locked eyes with Fretello, and gave him a nod. "Before proceeding any further, sir," Fretello stated crisply as he stood before the Chairman, "I wish to restate the parameters under which we are operating as set out in the initial planning guidance. The only criteria enumerated in the mission statement was one-hundred-percent destruction of the designated targets. To achieve this, the planning guidance stated that we can draw upon any national asset except special weapons. Nowhere was there any mention of limitations such as collateral damage, friendly casualties, or violation of the airspace of nations either affected by or not involved in the operation. I am therefore assuming that these factors are of no concern to us."

The Chairman nodded. "You are correct, Major. At this juncture, we are concerned only with an OPLAN that will achieve complete destruction of the targets."

With a slight nod, the Special Forces officer acknowledged the Chairman's confirmation of his assumption as he prepared to launch into his briefing. "Gentlemen, despite great strides in the modernization and digitalization of our munitions and weapons," Fretello stated boldly, "there is nothing yet in our inventory that matches the precision or reliability that can be achieved by a well-trained and disciplined soldier. While it is true that a soldier is vulnerable to enemy action, terrain, and other environmental factors, he is not susceptible to electronic spoofing or countermeasures. A soldier on the ground not only provides us with immediate and accurate damage assessment, he affords us an opportunity for an immediate follow-up attack, if necessary."

These statements, all of them directed at the Chairman, caused some of the other officers, both at the table and scattered about the room, to squirm in their seats. Some, Fretello noted, were clearly angered by his words. But none dared jump on him, yet. Their opportunity to pile on would come when the Chairman opened the floor to a general discussion and questions.

"First slide," Fretello stated quietly after casting a quick glance over to the sailor controlling the audio-visuals. "Operation Balaklava involves the insertion of U.S. and NATO Special Operations Forces on or near the missile sites that are to be attacked."

Clearing his throat, the Chairman snickered. "I'm not too sure I approve of the name you selected for your operation, Major." Those present who had a grounding in military history chuckled.

Fretello smiled. "Sir, my choice was intentional and, I daresay, accurate, given what happened then and what I anticipate would happen during this operation." He paused, letting his smile fade. "While we consider the comparison of a modern military operation with an event that most consider a blunder, let me remind you that the Light Brigade *did* succeed in seizing the Russian guns they were sent to capture despite the odds against them and the horrendous casualties they suffered. The only problem the British found after securing the guns was that they didn't have the means to destroy those guns. Our people will be far better prepared."

Fretello waited for all the chuckles and sneers to fade before he continued. "The concept of the operation is the same one used by the Germans on May tenth, nineteen-forty, to destroy the key Belgian fortress of Eban Emael. In that operation, a handful of German glider-borne combat engineers landed on top of that Belgium fort, placed shaped-charge explosives directly on top of the gun-and-observation turrets of the fortress, and neutralized the entire installation without having to enter it or overpower its garrison. The speed, the precision, and the results achieved that day rival, and I daresay surpass, those that the Air Force could hope for with its most sophisticated munitions. Next."

Behind him, the image of a standard Army cratering charge flashed onto the screen. "Given the time constraints, we will need to use demolitions that are suited for the task, on hand, available in sufficient numbers to accomplish the mission, and are man-portable. In this case, the munitions of choice is the standard forty-pound cratering charge. Not only is it easy to set up and very reliable, it is also a shaped charge designed to direct the bulk of its destructive power downward. Based upon the data we have on the nature of the silo covers, a number of these devices, placed directly over the missile, will not only penetrate the cover, but will generate sufficient fragmentation and shrapnel to disable or destroy the unarmored warhead of the missile below. Even if there are no sympathetic detonations due to the rupturing of the missile's fuel tanks, damage to the warhead will be sufficient to keep the missile from functioning properly."

As before, several officers around the room shifted and squirmed about in their seats. Fretello, however, was undeterred by this display of nervousness and displeasure. "Next slide." On the screen, a schematic showing the composition of the assault teams came up. "Three six-man teams will be assigned to each target. All will be fully self-contained and able to execute their assigned task independently. Each of these teams will be inserted separately and approach their target from different directions. All teams will be briefed that if discovered by Russian security forces, they will do their best to draw those forces away from the target, thus increasing the chance that one of the remaining teams will be able to reach the target and execute the assigned task."

Not waiting for any questions or reactions, Fretello pressed on. "Next." The new chart displayed the major Special Operations Forces of the United States, the United Kingdom, and France. Under each was listed the contribution each nation would be required to make. Next to each team was a designated target. "Because of the number of targets we are required to hit, the necessary redundancy the Chairman's criteria of success mandates, and the limited time we have to muster and deploy into the theater of operations, we will need to draw upon those Special Operations commands, both U.S. and NATO, that have trained personnel on hand and at the ready. As you can see, we will pretty much exhaust our appropriate national resources."

After permitting the assembled officers to digest the information on the slide, Fretello called for the next slide. "Upon completion of their mission, the teams will assemble at designated rally points. From there, they will either be extracted by NATO or directed to link up with Russian forces still loyal to the government in Moscow. Should our actions, or the overall political situation in Russia, result in a hostile environment that would rule out those alternatives, then the teams will be directed to either escape and evade, or to hunker down someplace safe until an Allied operation to extract them could be mounted."

Finished, Fretello gave the NCO in charge of the audio-visual equipment a nod. On cue, the last of the major's slides, one depicting the emblem of the Army's Special Forces and motto, flashed across the screen. "Sir," Fretello snapped, "are there any questions?"

Leaning forward, the Chairman of the Joint Chiefs removed his glasses and looked up at Fretello as he stood before the assembled senior officers at parade rest. "Is that all?" the Chairman asked.

"That, sir, is the concept of the operation," Fretello replied without hesitation. "The rest of my briefing covers the operational details concerning the actual loads each man would carry, locations for the marshaling of transports and teams, routes in and out for those transports, specific drop zones, and other sundry items, none of which I assume is critical at this juncture of the planning process."

After staring at the Army major for a moment, the Chairman looked over at General Smith. "A rather high-risk operation, Chuck."

The Chief of Staff of the Army understood what the Chairman was driving at. Turning to face him, Smith cleared his throat, throwing a quick glance in Fretello's direction. "Every member of the Army's Special Forces knows what's expected of him." Lifting his hand, he used his fingers to indicate each point of his case as he made it. "To start with, those people joined the Army of their own accord, many at a time when the nation's economy was booming and unemployment was all but unheard of. Most of them selected a combat branch when they enlisted. All elected to go airborne. And each and every one of them placed himself through hell to earn the right to wear that beret. At each step of the process, they were not only trained, they were indoctrinated in what membership in that elite band of brothers means. Let there be no doubt, if you say 'Jump,' each and every one will respond with a rousing, 'It's about time!' "

Dropping his fingers, Smith pointed at Fretello with his thumb. "While the people here in Washington have grown used to beating down our foes by remote control and on the cheap, those of us charged with preparing to wage war on the ground have never forgotten that the microchip cannot solve every problem. Men like the major there know that the time will come when we will come face-to-face with a situation to which there are no good alternatives, a crisis that will demand we ante up and pay, in blood, in order to remain king of the hill. While not everyone is as cavalier as Major Fretello, I assure you, they'll do their duty."

The Chairman sat and stared at Smith for several seconds after the Army general finished. He was about to open the floor to questions from other members of the Joint Chiefs when his aide, noting a flashing light on the phone at his side, picked up the receiver. Turning around, the Chairman waited until the aide, receiver at his ear, looked at his boss, then put his hand over the end of the receiver. "Sir, they're ready with that update you've been waiting for."

Though Fretello had no idea of who "they" were or what the update concerned, it was obvious that it was a showstopper. This was confirmed when the Chairman turned to his fellow service chiefs. "We're going to have to finish this at a later date, gentlemen." Then he looked around the room. "I appreciate your efforts and opinions. As you know," he added after a moment's hesitation, "exercises such as this are, ah, quite useful to us here. Though we may wear all the brass, we don't hold a monopoly on *all* the best ideas."

While a few of the briefers and straphangers acknowledged the Chairman's stab at humor with a cursory chuckle, none paused as they prepared to clear the room. Within seconds, only the five members of the Joint Chiefs and the Chairman's aide were left. "Okay, Gus," the Chairman muttered to his aide. "Tell them we're ready."

Two officers, an Air Force major general and an Army colonel, entered, using a door opposite the one through which the participants of the exercise had filed out. The colonel carried a thin folder from which he pulled prepared briefing slides. Quickly, quietly, he laid them out before each member of the Joint Chiefs. Even before he had finished, the Air Force major general began. "We are now reasonably sure that the events of the past few days have been resolved. The assault on the command-and-control bunker of the rebellious rocket regiment was successful. The ICBM's controlled by that facility have all been secured by troops loyal to Moscow and stood down."

The Chairman looked up from the annotated satellite photo he had been looking at and stared at the Air Force general. "How sure are you?"

The major general did not respond. Instead, he glanced down at his shoes, shrugged, and waved his right hand about at his side before looking the Chairman in the eye and responding. "We are as sure as we're going to be. Both the CIA and NSA confirm our conclusions. Everything, from satellite imagery to electronic intercepts, as well as analysis of operational traffic, seems to indicate this."

The chairman thought about this for a moment before he asked his next question. "What about the CIA's man in the Kremlin?"

Caught off guard, both the major general and the colonel looked at each other. The fact that the CIA had a contact who was a high-ranking member of the Russian government was one of those secrets no one dared mention, let alone discuss, not even among such high-ranking officers as the Joint Chiefs. That the Chairman would bring this up only highlighted the concern he harbored over the events in Siberia.

Nervously, the Air Force general cleared his throat. Even as he replied to his superior's pointed question, he could not bring himself to admit to the fact that such an agent existed. "Not all CIA sources have confirmed this, sir. They are awaiting additional data before they take this to the President."

While he mulled this over, the chairman looked through the package the colonel had handed out. As he was doing so, the Air Force major general interrupted. "We have been able to confirm that one of the missiles assigned to this regiment is part of Perimeter."

This announcement caused the Chairman to stop what he was doing and look up at the Air Force officer. Slowly, he turned to face the other members of the Joint Chiefs. "It would seem, gentlemen," he announced dryly, "that the little exercise we've been running this morning *was* justified."

As they nodded in agreement, the Chairman turned his attention back to the package before him, wondering when, and not if, he would have to give the men and women under his command the order to charge the Russian guns.

**MOSCOW
MARCH**

When the door of the conference room swung open, an Army colonel waiting in the brightly lit corridor snapped to attention. Unlike many of his fellow GRU officers, Colonel Demetre Orlov looked every inch a model soldier. There was no sign of flap or fat anywhere. Even the taut skin on his freshly shaved face was tan, showing that he spent far more time outside doing, instead of hiding away in a vault theorizing. The colonel's uniform was tailored to complement the slim, muscular physique, the kind that cannot be acquired by generating intelligence reports.

Any doubts about what sort of soldier Orlov was were dispelled by the ribbons, medals, and qualification badges he wore riveted to his chest. The collection of decorations he proudly sported was an unusually robust one. A person able to decipher the special code that the colored ribbons represented could have discerned that this man had been everywhere. Everywhere, that is, where there had been "active" operations. No one, of course, could tell that he had also been involved in operations for which a medal would never be struck.

One man emerged from the room Orlov stood facing. Had the person in a rumpled, dark-blue suit been a younger man, he would have stood a good quarter meter taller than he did. But years of working in the old Communist party, and then for a dizzying rotation of Ministers of Defense, had taken their toll on this man. Both the verbal beatings he had been subjected to over his long career in Russia's byzantine system and the insoluble problems he faced day in, day out, left Yuri Anatov's head perpetually bowed between his sloping shoulders.

This morning was no different. Orlov could see that his superior's head was bowed just a bit lower as he emerged from a long meeting with the current President and the pack of jackals who served as his advisers. Anatov had been called forth, alone, to account for the incident east of the Urals that had paralyzed the Kremlin. Finished now, he was in a hurry to put as much distance between himself and the President as quickly as his short legs could carry him. Without a word being exchanged, Orlov fell in on his superior's left and accompanied him down the hall. The staff and lesser lights moving along the long corridors did not step aside out of respect or fear of the wizened old man who was supposedly one of the most powerful men in the government. Rather, they parted and let the odd pair pass because of Orlov, a man with the charm and demeanor of a trained attack dog, an analogy the GRU colonel intentionally cultivated.

Only when they were outside of the building did they exchange words. "So," Orlov stated crisply, "you have survived yet again!"

The minister of defense stopped abruptly on the steps and stared at the colonel. "Is that what you think this is all about? My personal survival?"

The colonel paused and looked back at the balding man and smiled, unapologetically. He waved his hands in the air. "That is not a bad thing, Minister. Your survival means that others, such as myself, survive."

"Since when," Anatov asked coldly, "did you depend on anyone besides yourself for survival, Colonel Orlov?"

Turning, the colonel continued down the steps, speaking over his shoulder as he did so. "These are very difficult times, Minister. We must depend upon each other if any of us are to live to see better days."

Anatov did not respond or move. Rather, he looked down at the self-assured colonel who had, just days before, "cleaned up" the unfortunate mess that a rebellious colonel in command of a regiment of ICBM's had created. It seemed to the aging bureaucrat that men like himself were always finding themselves dependent upon men like Orlov to bail them out of embarrassing situations.

Yet the cruel realities of the post-Communist Russia they ruled often left them little choice but to force some portion of the population to suffer in order to keep another, more volatile portion of the same population from going under. Sometimes, in the day-to-day running of the government, things slipped through the cracks. Resources diverted from here to help over there were not replaced. What started as a temporary sacrifice quickly became routine. When the affected portion of the population was one with little clout, the noise of more pressing concerns drowned out their cries. But when, as with the mutinous Strategic Rocket Regiment, these demands for restoration were backed by a real and viable threat, quick and decisive action must be taken.

Hence, the need for men like Orlov. As long as he and the crack commandos under his command remained loyal to the government, promises could be fudged and errors in judgment "corrected." Anatov's chief problem in dealing with issues in this manner was the cold fact that men like Orlov could be depended upon only up to a point. "Patriots wed to the silly notion that they owe all to Mother Russia and nothing to the system that gave them their power," the old man had told his political masters in the meeting he had just left, "are dangerous. The people we send to deal with those who wish to discredit us may, one day, decide that we, and not those they were sent to eradicate, are the problem. When that happens, they will ride into Red Square with our heads upon their lances."

"By the way, Minister," Orlov asked innocently as he paused before reaching the bottom of the steps, "did the issue of Dead Hand come up?"

Anatov's expression turned from one of concern to that of anger. Nervously, he glanced to his left and right before he descended the remaining steps until he stood toe-to-toe with Orlov. "No one in Moscow is to know about that. Do you hear? *No one.*"

It took all of Orlov's strength to keep from smirking. His mention of the Perimeter system, using the code word "Dead Hand," had achieved the desired effect on the Minister of Defense. Few in the Russian government knew of the existence of Perimeter, a system designed to respond to a first nuclear strike.

The entire system was dreamed of and built during the Soviet era when the Kremlin was acutely aware of the growing precision of the United States' overwhelming nuclear arsenal. Unable to match the Americans' technological edge, the Soviet leadership searched for a system that would dissuade the Americans from launching a deadly accurate first strike against them.

Since military planners assumed that an American first strike would disrupt their strategic command-and-control, perhaps even eradicate their national political and military leadership in the process, they appreciated the fact that they, or their successors, might not be able to launch their own counterstrike. While such an event was in of itself terrible to contemplate, this assessment was made worse by the idea that they would be unable to respond in kind. Mother Russia and her brand of communism would be wiped from the face of the earth, leaving capitalism and America unscratched and triumphant.

This line of thinking led to a system that was meant to be robust, redundant, self-contained, and to the greatest degree possible, self-initiated. Put simply, it was an automated means of retaliation, a sort of doomsday system. Called "Perimeter," it was better known within the Russian military as Dead Hand, for obvious reasons. Of all the remnants of the old regime and the Cold War, Perimeter was one of the best-kept secrets, and most-feared element, of the Soviet Union's nuclear arsenal.

At the core of Perimeter were fields of sensors located at strategic points throughout Russia and parts of the former Soviet Union. These sensors were designed to detect major and unnatural disruptions of the earth's surface, like those created by a nuclear attack, as well as unexplained disruptions of the military's command-and-control channels. If enough cues were picked up by Perimeter's sensor fields, selected missiles would automatically be activated and prepared for launch. These designated missiles, unlike those they were collocated with, carried a transmitter instead of a nuclear payload. Once alerted that a Perimeter missile was set, the commander of the regiment to which it belonged simply had to confirm the circumstances that had triggered the activation. If he could not contact his superiors in a reasonable amount of time, the regimental commander was authorized to enter a code from his location to complete the launch cycle. After that, everything happened automatically.

Each Perimeter missile had a set program and flight path that took it on a low-level trajectory over the missile fields belonging to other regiments of the Strategic Rocket Force. Once launched, the Perimeter missile would transmit a special launch code to selected missiles that were tied into the Perimeter system. Unlike the initial Perimeter missile, these second-tier missiles were nuclear-armed. And unlike the initiating missile, they would launch without any further input, either from the regimental command-and-control bunker in the missile field in which they were located or the National Command Authority.

Anatov glared at the GRU officer. The Minister of Defense hated it when a man such as Orlov made a comment like that. Without saying so, Orlov was telling his superior that he, Orlov, had information that, used properly, could ruin him. How willing Orlov was to play this particular hand or any of his other well-kept secrets was a matter of speculation. That the military man would, under the proper circumstances, use his information was without doubt. Orlov had, after all, been given barely enough time to wash the blood of his fellow Army officers from his hands before returning to Moscow to report on the situation in person. That those same hands could be turned on him, or on any other government official the military deemed unworthy, was a cold fact never far from Anatov's thoughts.

Sensing that he had gotten the minister's attention, Orlov turned and continued on down the steps. When he reached the car, he opened the door but waited to get in. Looking back, he studied the old man glaring down at him. It gnawed at Orlov that he had to serve a man such as this. In the night, the screams of those he had murdered to protect the lumbering government in Moscow robbed him of his sleep. The voices of his victims called for atonement. They pleaded with him in his nightmares for justice. But Orlov was a realist. He knew there could be no justice in this world as long as the people of Russia cowered like sheep before men such as Anatov. Until someone with a vision, a proper one, for Russia came forth, he and others like him could only do what they could to hold things together.

Turning, Orlov looked out into Red Square. For a brief moment, the image of Marshal of the Soviet Union Georgi K. Zhukov, leading the victorious Red Army while mounted on a white horse in defiance of Stalin, flashed through Orlov's mind. "Perhaps," the GRU colonel whispered, "another such as he will step forth and save Mother Russia."

3

Few would debate that the members of the military are the most visible guardians of their respective nations. But they are not the only ones. As the world becomes a more complex place, many of those who stand watch while their fellow citizens go about their daily routines never touch a gun, let alone step out of an airplane at an altitude of thirty thousand feet. Most do not wear a uniform of any type. The vast majority of them would be taken aback if someone were to lump them together with the military. Yet all are just as dedicated and skilled in their respective fields as are Captain Patrick Hogg, Sergeant-Chef Stanislaus Dombrowski, Major Andrew Fretello, and Colonel Demetre Orlov. Some of these sentinels without uniform are physicians and lab technicians at the Center for Disease Control, standing ready to repel a biological invasion of the United States by microscopic pathogens. Others belong to the twenty-something generation of computer hackers in the service of Great Britain's MI 5, where they continue the traditions of World War II's Blenchly Park by monitoring links to the worldwide Web and laying traps for their malicious counterparts. Though few recognize their roles as such, these men and women are no less vital to their nations as are the men who wear berets.

One of the more obscure groups that fit into this class are the Near-Earth Object Discovery teams. Though they hail from many countries, astronomers who participate in NEO projects have but one purpose: to search the night skies for objects that pose a threat to planet Earth. From observatories around the globe, these teams scan the heavens, using an instrument called a "charged couple device," or CCD. Similar in purpose and function to a camcorder, CCD cameras digitally record several images of the same region of the sky over a period of time, usually an hour. The images are then analyzed by computers to determine if any object captured by the CCD has systematically moved in relationship to known stars, which tend to remain fixed in place. When a suspect image has been identified as something other than a star or planet, it is studied in order to ascertain its precise location, size, and, most important, its projected trajectory.

If, as a result of this closer examination, it is determined that the newly discovered object and its orbit may place it in close proximity to the earth, it is classified as a near-earth object. Given a name, the newly discovered NEO is added to a list of known NEO's and monitored. If a NEO's travel through space will bring it to within what is called an earth "minimum-orbit intersection distance," or MOID, it is classified as a potentially hazardous asteroid, or PHA, PHA's, quite naturally, receive special attention. By the end of the beginning of the third millennium of the Common Era, there were over seven thousand known asteroids, with several times that number yet to be discovered.

Asteroids come in many sizes and shapes. The largest known asteroid is 1 Ceres, measuring some 933 kilometers in diameter, or somewhat greater in width than the distance between Washington, D.C., and New York City. The smallest are measured in inches. The asteroid that is credited with bringing the age of dinosaurs to a close, known as the KT Event, was estimated to be 12 kilometers, or 7.2 miles in diameter. When it plowed into the earth some sixty-five million years ago, it gouged out a primary crater 180 kilometers wide. This single event created so much havoc to Earth's climate and environment that it is estimated that two thirds of all species in existence at the time passed into extinction.

An even more spectacular event, if one can use that word to describe such a catastrophic occurrence, led to the creation of Earth's moon. Today it is generally believed that an object the size of Mars, which measures some 6,800 kilometers in diameter, collided with Earth, which is 12,753 kilometers in diameter. The resulting impact threw tremendous amounts of debris into space. In time, this rubble was drawn together to form the moon. That particular cosmic event and its results are credited with creating Earth as it is known today.

The discovery of this geographic history has given the study of asteroids a greater sense of urgency and importance. While the time span between planet-killing events such as the KT Event is measured in millions of years, the fact that astronomers have been unable to identify all but the smallest number of these unwanted visitors has engendered a degree of paranoia among some of those who specialize in this area. For them, it is not a question of "if." Rather, they endeavor to prepare for the time "when" Earth will be struck by an extinction-level event. Like other professionals, the men and women who are part of various Near-Earth Object Discovery teams are committed to searching the skies, waiting, watching, and hoping that somehow their efforts will provide the time necessary to do something about any potential threat.

This effort is not an easy one, for not all asteroids are alike and their travels are often less than predictable. The pull of gravity by the sun and other planets, the weight and shape of the asteroid, not to mention random collisions with other asteroids, influence the path of an asteroid. All of these calculations include some high-speed guessing. To start with, the exact weight of an asteroid cannot be precisely measured. Unlike planets, asteroids are not round. Some look like peanuts. Others bear a striking resemblance to potatoes. Besides their irregular shapes, the exact composition of an asteroid is difficult to gauge. By far, the most numerous are C-type asteroids. Accounting for seventy-five percent of all known asteroids, they tend to be dark. C-type asteroids have the same chemical composition as the Sun, minus hydrogen, helium, and other volatiles. The next-largest class are those of the S-type. S-types are made up of a metallic nickel-iron, mixed with iron and magnesium silicates. These are considerably brighter in appearance.

Most asteroids that come into contact with Earth never make it to the earth's surface. Instead, they fall victim to the atmosphere, much as a dead man-made satellite does when gravity finally reclaims it. This is what happened in 1908 when an asteroid measuring fifty to sixty meters in diameter was pulled off its path and onto a collision course by Earth's gravity. Traveling at a speed of twelve to twenty kilometers a second, this stony asteroid exploded approximately six kilometers, or twenty thousand feet above the Tunguska region of Siberia with an estimated force of at least twenty megatons.

Had this event taken place over a populated section of the world, say Western Europe instead of the barren wastelands of Eastern Russia, it would have been listed as the greatest natural disaster in recorded history. Knowing full well that the next visit by such an alien force may not be so obliging, the NEO teams watch, plot, and project the travels of a threat few of their fellow human beings concern themselves with.

One of these tireless guardians was a middle-aged astronomer by the name of Frederick Kellermann. As part of the joint French and German OCA-DLR Asteroid Survey Team, it was his task to review the data at the Institute of Planetary Exploration in Berlin, Germany, that was gathered by the Observatoire de la d'Azur, located in southern France. A sickly child, Kellermann had spent much of his youth in clinics and hospitals. Though the quiet orderliness of those institutions appealed to him, the suffering he endured while confined in them prevented him from pursuing a medical career.

Instead, he opted to pursue another field of study that was just as orderly, and even more sedate: astronomy. Throughout the years when he had few friends and little freedom to wander about this earth, Frederick Kellermann was drawn to the distant heavens. They were boundless, yet orderly. Always in motion, but quite predictable. And above all else, they were silent. Whether it was in the dimly lit office where he spent many an hour hunched over his computer, picking his way through digitized information forwarded to him, or perched behind a telescope under the cavernous dome of an observatory, the German astronomer cherished the reserved world in which astronomers existed. What thoughts and words filled his head were his, and his alone. He could dwell on them and organize them as he saw fit, just as he sought to establish an orderliness out of the marauding chunks of rock and iron that threatened planet Earth. Perhaps one day, Kellermann dreamed, there would be a way of controlling these menaces just as effectively and efficiently as he did his own thoughts and words.

On this particular night, Kellermann was reviewing data on a number of PHA's, potentially hazardous asteroids, that were coming around for another encounter with Earth. None were expected to be of any great danger. All had been identified, analyzed, categorized, named, and listed. Since their travels were predictable, the computer that maintained the list spit out their names when they were about to reach their projected earth minimum-orbit intersection distance so that NEO teams could turn their attention to them, analyze their current activities, and update the data they provided.

Among the PHA's that Kellermann was studying on this night was one bearing the designation Nereus 1991 HWC. It would be making a close pass to Earth shortly, coming to within .0032 AU's, or astronomical units. An AU is equal to the distance of the earth to the sun: 150 million kilometers, or 93 million miles. Since the distance between Earth and its moon is .0027 AU's, that means that Nereus 1991 HWC would, for a period of time, be right there in the neighborhood, so to say. During close encounters such as this, an asteroid is monitored with greater frequency. In the case of Nereus 1991 HWC, its angle of attack and the rotation of Earth itself put the Observatoire de la d'Azur in the best position to track it.

Measuring less than one hundred meters in diameter, Nereus 1991 HWC was definitely not a planet killer. But it was still a threat, one that Frederick Kellermann was charged that night with inspecting. From file data, the German astronomer knew that Nereus 1991 HWC was a small S-type asteroid that tumbled about the inner solar system, which meant that it was close enough to the sun to be stripped of most of its gases and liquids. Asteroids, sometimes referred to as comets, that spend most of their time in the far reaches of the solar system retain many of the gases and liquids that are part of their formation. It is only when they come close, relatively speaking, to the sun that these gases and liquids are heated and shed, creating the long tail that characterizes them. Lacking this cosmic signature, and due to its small size and dark profile, Nereus 1991 HWC was a bit more difficult, but not impossible, to track.

In combat, routine can kill. Soldiers who follow a pattern, who execute their duties in a predictable manner, often set themselves up for disaster. An enemy who is aware of his foe's habits can exploit those routines in many ways. The most obvious is to lay an ambush. But that is only one way of exploiting a pattern. An opponent can hide what he chooses from an enemy when the "scheduled" enemy patrol is due to arrive. This technique is used on a strategic level by nations that are concerned about satellite surveillance by a foreign power. Since the orbit of a spy satellite can be predicted, a foe can cease certain activity while it is overhead. This can be used at any level. An opposite approach can be equally effective. Called a ruse, one side deploys false emplacements, dummies, or stages mock maneuvers so that his foe's intelligence community will generate a false picture of their opponent's capability, activities, or intentions. This is what the Allies did in World War II before D day, when George S. Patton was placed in command of an army group consisting of plywood tanks and empty troop camps.

In the world of science, however, routine is cherished. This is especially true for astronomers, who often find themselves dealing with phenomena that are as predictable as the stars. The scientist must be most meticulous and precise when tracking and dealing with objects that appear, even when enhanced, as little more than pinpricks in the night sky. Entities as small as Nereus 1991 HWC can be tracked only with the use of computer programs that generate an image a human would not otherwise be able to view. Yet even the most sophisticated computers have their limits, especially when it comes to detecting things that are smaller than a fraction of a pixel.

On this night, Frederick Kellermann had a number of PHA's to look at. He took them in the order of the priority that his superior at the Institute of Planetary Exploration had established for him. Kellermann reviewed the latest images captured by the CCD at the Observatoire de la d'Azur. Next, he ran this information through a program that matched the new data with that which had been previously generated to see if there were any changes or variations in the projected trajectory of each PHA. Since asteroids are small, the gravitational pull of larger planets and moons, including Earth's can affect them. The same invisible force that holds the moon captive can, and on occasion does, draw other celestial objects toward Earth. This is where the great danger comes from in regard to PHA's. Like a steel ball-bearing rolling about in a maze of magnets, the path of an asteroid can be bent this way or that whenever it comes close to a planet. Since Nereus 1991 HWC's travels also took it close to Mars, there was concern that the pull of Martian gravity would alter the asteroid's trajectory. A quick comparison of the computer-generated plot with the historical data satisfied Kellermann that this had not happened, not this time.

Next, the German ran the program that factored in the moon's potential impact on the incoming visitor. Since the moon would be hidden behind Earth when Nereus 1991 HWC swept in and made its pass, the moon would be unable to influence the asteroid. The final check was to do the same for Earth itself, for the very planet that the NEO teams were trying to protect had the potential to draw in a fatal asteroid with a blind determination not unlike that which a disgraced samurai warrior relies upon when he plunges his own sword through himself.

When all these checks had been made, using the same techniques and routines used to analyze each PHA, Frederick Kellermann leaned back in his seat, lifted his hands above his head, and stretched. As he did so, he stared at the image of Nereus 1991 HWC for a moment. Like all the other PHA's he had studied and would see before this night was out, Nereus 1991 HWC was behaving as it should. It afforded him no surprises and generated no concern. It was adhering to the routine that Kellermann had come to expect, in a manner not at all unlike the one Kellermann himself was following.

Glancing at his watch as he lowered his hands back to the computer's keyboard, the German astronomer saw that time was slipping away. He still had a dozen more targeted PHA's that he needed to look at before his shift was over. Without another thought, he reached out and automatically closed the file on his screen, never once suspecting that another object, a tiny, dark C-type asteroid was fast closing on Nereus 1991 HWC. Too small to be detected by the CCD at the Observatoire de la d'Azur, this unnamed chunk of space rock was on a collision course with Nereus 1991 HWC. Out of sight of the seven billion inhabitants of Earth, this rock, measuring less than five meters in diameter, slammed into the larger asteroid and set in motion a chain reaction that would create a crisis unlike anything seen on Earth since the KT Event.

4

Having finished rereading the chapter that covered the Battle of Canne, General Chuck E. Smith closed the book on Hannibal, set it down in his lap, and looked around the room. As he did every evening before heading off to bed, he read from one of the hundreds of history books that lined the shelves of his small study. This was the only time of day that he was free to enjoy the quiet, to indulge his own thoughts, and to ponder personal issues that needed sorting out. As Chief of Staff of the Army and an integral part of the National Command Authority, opportunities such as this were quite rare.

On this night, the personal issues that Smith found himself mulling over were disquieting. As March gave way to April, the fact that he would be retiring within three months could no longer be ignored. After thirty-five years of service to his nation as a soldier, he would be forced to stack arms and walk away from the only profession he knew. On the last day in June, after an appropriately dignified ceremony, he would be tossed from the secure embrace of the United States Army and out into a world about which he knew very little.

Not since his plebe year at West Point had Smith been so gripped with such an all-pervasive apprehension and loathing of the unknown. For Smith, the Army had been a sanctuary, a place where honor and traditions meant something. To him, the nation he had been charged to defend bore no resemblance to the well-ordered machine that he had come to command. The world outside the perimeter fence was populated by ruthless corporate CEO's, cutthroat lawyers, clueless twenty-something professionals, immoral politicians, and godless sodomites.

As disquieting as such thoughts were, there was no escaping the inevitable. It was time to make a decision as to what he would do with the rest of his life. This was no easy task. During his tenure as Chief of Staff of the Army, there had been no world-shaking events, such as a minor ground war, in which he had played a pivotal role. That meant he was not a good candidate for the rubber-chicken lecture circuit or a lucrative book deal. Teaching at a university was out. The idea of wasting his time trying to educate undergraduates who were convinced they knew more than their professors was almost as repugnant to Smith as the thought of associating with ultraliberal colleagues. Even the option of throwing his lot in with one of the defense contractors who provided a safe haven for many a retired officer was less than attractive. To Smith, that would be like selling his soul and his reputation at a public auction.

That pretty much narrowed his options to an offer from a think tank that specialized in military affairs. He was, after all, more than qualified for it. But even this left Smith cold. He found it difficult picturing himself stuffed away in an office, day in and day out, working with other retired generals discussing world events that they were unable to influence. Looking up at the bookshelves across from him, the weary old soldier stared at the cluster of books on George S. Patton. In the end, Smith thought to himself, Patton had gotten it right. Although his death had been the result of an accident, when the alternatives were considered, the Fates had been most kind to Old Blood and Guts.

Slowly, almost subconsciously, Smith ran his hand across the cover of the closed book in his lap. He had often thought about taking up writing. He loved history. Throughout his life it had been a constant, a friend to whom he could turn. Whether he would be able to make a living out of recounting events that had been discussed and debated countless times before didn't matter. After having been in the Army for so long, he was used to doing things because he believed in what he was doing, and not simply for material gain.

Smith was in the midst of these deliberations when he heard the phone ring. Slowly, he turned his head and gazed at the extension on the table next to him. Years ago, he would have bounded out of his seat without a second thought, snatching up the receiver and dutifully answering the call to arms. As of late, however, with the end of his long career so clearly in sight, his response to these late-night intrusions was something less than automatic. Soon, he told himself as he listened to the second ring fade, he'd be out of the loop, just another old soldier who had been ridden hard and long before being put out to pasture and forgotten, like so many before him.

When the phone didn't ring again, Smith knew that his wife had taken the call. Perhaps, he found himself hoping, it was one of their kids calling their mom to fill her in on the latest accomplishments of their own children, or seeking counsel on an issue that threatened to overwhelm them. Even as he tried to guess who was calling at this hour, he found himself envying his wife. Her role in the world would hardly change. While he would be demoted from the most senior officer in the United States Army to a retired old geezer overnight, she would remain a wife to him, a mother to a son and two daughters, and a grandmother of six. No matter where they went, no matter what he did with the rest of his life, she would find a church to attend, would volunteer with the local Red Cross, and knit together a gaggle of friends with whom she could share a cup of coffee and gossip, just as she had done a dozen or more times as they had traveled the world, moving from one assignment to the next.

From beyond the dim light of the study, a voice called out, "Chuck, it's for you. The duty officer at the war room."

Before moving, the tired old general looked at the clock on the wall. Out of habit, his mind automatically computed Greenwich mean time as well as the current time in Moscow, Riyadh, Seoul, and the Taiwan Straits. After laying the history of Hannibal aside, he reached over, picked up the phone and growled into the receiver. "Smith here. Who's rattling his cage tonight?"

On the other end of the line, the duty officer took the general's gruff response in stride. "Sir, it's not a who. Rather, it's a what. It seems that NORAD's deep-space radar has picked up a hither-to unknown object that is on a collision course with Earth."

"A meteor?" Smith asked as he rallied himself out of his funk and began to slip back into his role as Chief of Staff of the Army.

"The Air Force is calling it an asteroid, but I don't think they know for sure yet. As of five minutes ago, they had yet to contact the Near-Earth Object team over at NASA to confirm this. Until they do, the Air Force is labeling it an unknown object."

"Has the Chairman called a meeting?" Smith fired back.

"No sir, not yet. But the duty officer in the Joint Operations war room expects that he will be doing so shortly."

"What makes you say that?" Smith asked curtly.

"Well, sir, if the initial calculations from the tracking team at NORAD are confirmed by NASA, whatever it is that's out there will reach us in four days."

The duty officer didn't need to say another word. In an instant, General Smith realized that within the hour, every man and woman who was considered a key player in the federal government would be manning their respective command-and-control centers, waiting for hard information and preparing plans for a contingency that no one, as best as he knew, had ever thought seriously about.

"Okay," Smith replied to the duty officer. "Notify the Joint Ops Center that I will be in directly. Activate our own Crisis Action Team and pass the word on, as you get it, to all major commands. Advise Forces Command, as well as Seventh Army, to put their CAT's on a short string."

Smith hung up the phone without waiting for a response. As he rose from his chair, leaving his book on ancient history behind, a strange thought popped into his head. "Perhaps," he found himself thinking, "I won't have to settle for rewriting someone else's history."

**MOSCOW
APRIL**

Panicked calls by junior officers who were ignorant of even the barest facts were not new to Demetre Orlov. Nor was waiting in the outer office of the Minister of Defense. In fact, he had become such a fixture there that he even had a favorite chair that was automatically vacated by whomever occupied it at the moment Orlov entered the room. It was less a point of respect than one of fear, for everyone associated with the Ministry of Defense knew who Orlov was. Though no one talked about it, all knew what his very special skills were used for and that his presence meant that they would soon be employed.

On this day, the colonel who commanded Russia's elite special-response team didn't have to wait long. In fact, he was still in the process of settling into the overstuffed leather seat that he preferred, when the Minister's doors flew open. Like a locomotive under a full head of steam emerging from a tunnel, Yuri Anatov plowed through the crowded waiting room, head down as usual, and made straight for Orlov.

Surprised, Orlov barely had enough time to come to his feet before the Minister reached him, grabbed his arm, and escorted him out of the anteroom and into the bustling corridor. This neither surprised Orlov nor anyone else who had been waiting for their moment with the Minister. Like everyone connected to the government, Anatov had no doubt that his office was bugged by at least one agency, perhaps more.

Once in the flow of the traffic that always seemed to be going this way and that but never getting anywhere, Anatov began to speak in hushed tones. "I want you to pull together as large a team as you can, as quickly as you can, and be ready to go when I give you the word."

Orlov raised an eyebrow. "So, it has been confirmed? It *will* hit Russia."

The Minister of Defense sighed. "Yes, again." There was a silence as the two walked briskly down the hall. Everyone who saw them coming parted for them, as much out of fear for Orlov as for respect for their superior. This was good, for the tired old man who was charged with defending Russia's faltering regime was staring vacantly at the floor as he marched on. When he finally did speak again, there was a hint of anger in his voice, mixed with a bit of frustration. "For the second time in one hundred years, we are going to be hit by a meteor." Looking over at Anatov, the colonel could see the concern in his expression as he continued to mumble: "The mystics and the fringe have already latched onto that little coincidence. I'm sure you've seen them in the streets and on the bloody damned television, sprewing their prophecies of impending doom."

Without commenting, Orlov nodded. The comparison between the Tunguska event and the political turmoil in Russia that followed less than nine years after that had been seized upon by more than one group in opposition to the current regime. The similarities between the corruption that was rampant in czarist Russia and the state of affairs in modern Russia were far too obvious to ignore. Hence, the connection between the devastating event of 1908 and the revolution that followed in 1917 was being viewed as a blessing from the heavens by those who sought to stir the people of Russia to rise up and sweep away the government in Moscow.

These thoughts led Orlov to his next question. "Is there a particular target of interest that you would like me to concentrate on?"

Yuri Anatov hesitated before answering. He knew that Orlov was politically astute. To survive as long as he had in his profession, particularly in the position he held, one needed to know who the players were and how to stay afloat in the swirling tides of intrigue that were part of Russia's political system. From the way the colonel had framed his question, the minister of defense suspected that he knew who in the regime in Moscow he was most concerned with. "Yes," Anatov stated bluntly. "General Likhatchev."

Stopping, Orlov stared at his superior with an expression that was as much one of anger as surprise. Being dispatched to the far reaches of Russia to deal with an officer who had stepped out of line was one thing. To be ordered to go after a man whom many considered to be the last true patriot in all of Russia, a man whose only crime was that he had dedicated his entire life to the service of their Motherland, was quite another.

Caught off guard by Orlov's sudden stop, Anatov hesitated, turned, and looked back at the silent colonel. "Is there a problem?"

Unsure of where he stood on the issue, Orlov chose the course he normally followed. Gathering himself as quickly as he could, he allowed his face to assume its usual dispassionate expression. "No, Minister. Not at all."

"Good," Anatov snapped. "Now, let us continue. I have much to do and so little time." Orlov acknowledged with a mumbled response that the Minister of Defense did not hear. General Igor Likhatchev was an ultranationalist who had barely been beaten during Russia's last presidential election. That he intended to have that position, one way or the other, was not a state secret. The General took every opportunity he could to promote himself and to criticize the current president. It came, therefore, as no surprise that Likhatchev would find a way to use the pending disaster to his advantage.

After moving along the corridor in silence for several seconds, the Minister picked up where he had left off. "If projections are correct, the resulting impact of the meteor, though not catastrophic, will have the same characteristics of a nuclear detonation. It is believed that the disruption of normal communications as well as the seismic signature of the impact will be enough to trigger a fully functional Perimeter. Therefore I issued an order last night to all elements of the Strategic Rocket Force to disable the Perimeter system." After a moment's hesitation, Anatov glanced up from the floor in front of him and over to Orlov. "This morning, when it became obvious that this order was being ignored, it was repeated. An hour ago, every regimental commander in Likhatchev's province responded that they would not comply."

"The launch officers at the individual sites must still initial the final sequence," Orlov stated briskly. "They, and not General Likhatchev, are the key to Perimeter."

"Ordinarily, that would be true," Anatov countered. "But it seems that General Likhatchev has managed to subvert the normal chain of command. As you know, he took extraordinary steps to ensure that key military units and personnel in his province were well taken care of in an effort to cultivate their loyalty."

This came as no surprise to the colonel. Likhatchev's efforts to generate a base loyal to him and him alone was well known throughout the military. Even officers in Orlov's own handpicked command had been courted by representatives of the General.

"What makes you think that removing General Likhatchev will make a difference?" Orlov asked.

This time, it was Anatov who stopped in his tracks. "Damn it, Colonel. I do not have time for this! What is and is not possible on the political level is not your concern. You are a soldier, I give the orders, you execute them. Is that clear?"

Orlov hesitated before answering. While none of his missions could be described as ordinary, this one was quite different. The other targets Orlov had dealt with had meant nothing to him. General Likhatchev, on the other hand, did. In his heart, Orlov had long ago suspected that it would take a man like the General to save Russia. Perhaps, Orlov thought to himself as Anatov droned on, the general is the one, the man on the white horse who has come to save Russia.

"Colonel," Anatov snapped. "You *do* understand what you must do?"

Suddenly aware that his mind had been wandering, Orlov managed a crisp "Yes, Minister, of course."

Satisfied by this automatic response, Anatov resumed his brisk pace. Without another word, the colonel fell in, like a good soldier should, to the left of his superior. As they continued down the corridor and Colonel Orlov listened to the Minister's special instructions, he began to formulate his own plan of action.

5

Each of the plans-and-operations officers assigned to the 22nd Special Forces Group had a unique specialty. Major Kevin Spatlett, for example, was the master when it came to dealing with antiterrorism issues. Captain Jon Ellison, a quiet and studious type, had proven himself unparalleled in the fine art of setting up training programs for the military of third world nations. Armed with a fertile imagination and a flair for hatching flawless raids, Captain Tony Jones had earned the nickname of "Indiana Jones."

To most, however, Andrew Fretello reigned supreme within the realm of Special Forces plans and operations. A graduate of Leavenworth's School for Advanced Military Studies, he was known throughout the group as "The Wizard of Weird." This title derived as much from Fretello's ability to deal with the unusual as from his habits while doing so. When handed an off-the-wall task in hand, Fretello would slip away to a dark corner of the group's oversized walk-in vault. Sequestered from the hustle and bustle that characterized the Group's operations section, he would conjure up a concept of dealing with whatever contingency or mission he had been assigned. Though his solutions were often unconventional and his plans frequently controversial, few could match his ability to pull together all the diverse elements that went into a Special Forces mission as quickly as he could and weave them into a clear, coherent operations order.

It was this ability that had caught the attention of the Deputy Chief of Staff of the Army for Special Operations Forces, who had drawn him into exercises at the Pentagon, much to the annoyance of Fretello's immediate chain of command. A man of uncompromising beliefs and the personification of the term "type A personality," Colonel Robert Hightower made sure that Fretello was aware of his displeasure each time the ambitious young major was called away to Washington. "A man cannot serve two masters, Major," Hightower had warned Fretello after he returned from his latest exercise in D.C. "You're going to have to make a choice, soldier. I can't afford to have my staff gallivanting off to Washington every time those folks want to play a war game."

Attuned to the internal politics of the Group, as well as to the personal animosity Hightower felt toward the Deputy Chief of Staff of the Army for Special Operations Forces, Andrew Fretello took the warning quite seriously.

Still, even Colonel Hightower understood that there was little he could do. Like the people in the Pentagon, the Group commander saw Fretello's potential and value. To punish a subordinate for simply doing his duty was not an option. It would be both mean-spirited and unprofessional, something that Hightower was not. So the colonel ignored the

special taskings that robbed him of his most talented
staff officer as best he could.

On occasion, however, Fretello's activities in one
world collided with the other.

Orders for the Group to stand by for immediate deployment came down the chain just as the news media broke the story about the impending encounter
with the rogue asteroid. As was the practice in the
Group's operations section, a TV was wheeled in
and tuned to CNN. The value of that network as a
source of information and intelligence, long ago
confirmed during the First Gulf War, could not be
ignored. In many ways, CNN made the task of the
American military easier by providing an overview
and a background of a developing situation and
thus allowing higher headquarters to skip some of
those details when passing orders down to major
subordinate commands. It also permitted those
commands concerned with operational security and
the running of deception plans to gauge the success
of their efforts. Though the media types tended to
become self-righteous and somewhat enraged when
they were accused of being unwilling accomplices in
the dissemination of government-planned disinfor-
mation, the manner in which they conducted their
business made them the perfect dupe in the dark
and murky business of illusion and lies. For those
like the operations-and-plans officers of the 22nd
Special Forces Group, who knew what was fact and
what was fantasy, it was a hoot to see which reporters
were hitting near the mark and which ones were
making asses of themselves.

At times like this, news shows also served as a diversion. With nothing but a very ambiguous warning
order in hand but no specifics, the officers of the
operations section had little to do but wait until they

received definitive planning guidance with which they could work. This uncomfortable period, the time that existed from when they knew they would soon be receiving orders but didn't know what those orders entailed, could be very unnerving. With each ring of the phone, all eyes would turn from the TV screen or whatever busy work they had been pursuing and glance over to the ops sergeant, who took all incoming calls. When the call turned out to be from nervous battalion staff officers, calling on behalf of their impatient commanders or just trying to get a head start on their own planning process, each of the anxious staff officers would go back to what they had been doing. When a summons from the Group commander's executive officer finally did come, it was greeted with a palpable sense of relief.

It surprised no one that Andrew Fretello had been the one tagged to report to the Group commander, where the Group operations officer was already waiting. While Fretello gathered himself and his notebook, his fellow officers threw witty comments his way in an effort to cut some of the tension. From the desk that sat butted up against Fretello's, Kevin Spatlett turned away from the TV toward Fretello. "Hey, Andy, what course of action are you going to go for? The one using astronauts to plant nukes on the asteroid, or the one using a gang of roughnecks?"

Since the asteroid story had broken, the TV had been awash with scenes taken from popular movies about just such an encounter. To Fretello, the reliance by supposedly serious journalists on Hollywood's view of the forthcoming real-world disaster was a bit disquieting. It did, however, provide practitioners of graveyard humor such as Spatlett a great source of comic relief from an otherwise ominous event.

Playing along with the theme, Fretello looked at

his fellow officer with a shout of deep concern on his face. "I'm not sure. A lot, I imagine, depends on how much we have left in the Group's annual budget for hiring outside contractors. We may find that we have no choice but to task this week's duty unit with the responsibility of saving the world."

From his little corner across the room, Captain Tony Jones called out to Fretello as he was headed out. "Hey, Major. Just be sure when it comes time to make the movie about this that you hold out till they agree to cast Tom Hanks as you."

Fretello paused at the door, turned, and was prepared to reply to the young captain when Spatlett cut in. "No way Hanks is going to go for that," the major sneered. "An actor like that would never consent to play a bit part in such a major production."

Rather than seeing the humor in this remark, Andrew Fretello was stung by the inference that what he did was, in the greater scheme of the universe, nothing more than a supporting role. Without another word, the miffed plans-and-operations officer stepped out of the crowded office and made his way down the corridor to where his boss and the colonel awaited him.

With no details to mull over and nothing to distract his mind, Fretello was left to reflect upon his personal thoughts and feelings. It annoyed the Special Forces major that neither superior ranking officers outside of his immediate chain of command nor historians recounting this episode at some later date would give him due credit for whatever plan he was about to generate. Outside of one or two sentences on his next officer's evaluation report, his talents, skills, and labors would go unnoticed. That this was the normal lot of the staff officer was taken in stride by most professional soldiers. It was part of the game, an unwritten rule in the Army stating that a staff officer's primary function was to make the commanding officer he served look as good as possible. In turn, the staff officer could expect to be rewarded with glowing evaluation reports and, if luck smiled on the superior officer and stars one day graced his shoulders, elevation to higher rank and positions of great responsibilities for all the little people who had made that possible.

But it went against Andrew Fretello's nature to wait patiently for a ride on another's coattails to fame and glory. Such a course of action left too much to chance, too much in the hands of others over whom he had no control, no influence. Fretello was the sort of soldier who wanted to be the master of his own destiny, his own future. That he was about to be a participant in what could be the single most important operation that the Army engaged in during his entire career was quite clear to Fretello. That he had to do something to capitalize upon this for himself was equally beyond dispute. As he turned the corner and entered the outer officer leading to the group's conference room, Andrew Fretello straightened up, banished whatever thoughts he had concerning his own ambitions, and prepared to do his duty as all good little staff officers were trained to do.

Colonel Robert Hightower lost no time in accosting Fretello. Even before the major had an opportunity to lay his notebook on the long, well-polished table, the group commander started speaking. "Major, do you have any of your notes from that little jaunt you took to Washington last month?"

Ignoring the fact that Colonel Hightower spit out the word "Major" as if it were an annoying bone that had been caught in his throat, Fretello found himself trying to make a connection between the subject of the war game in which he had participated at the Pentagon and the coming disaster. It took him a moment to appreciate the fact that the Russian early warning system might not be able to recognize the impact of an asteroid, which bore an uncanny resemblance to the man-made nuclear horror. Shaking his head, as if clearing a child's play slate, the planning officer looked his commander in the eye. "As is their custom, sir, the staff of the Deputy Chief of Staff for Special Operations retained all my notes and briefing papers. I was also required to sign a statement that I would not discuss the subject of that exercise with anyone who had not been involved in it."

Having expected this from his high-strung subordinate, Hightower picked up a paper and flung it across the table toward him. "Here's your authorization. Now take a seat and tell us everything you know. And remember, Major," he added, "the clock is ticking."

In the time it took him to take his seat, Fretello had managed to merge what he knew about the pending disaster and the mission he guessed he was about to be tasked to plan for. Without waiting, he began to push for more information. "What does that give us? Two days to prepare, coordinate, and war-game an operational plan?"

Hightower's eyes narrowed. "Wrong, mister. As of noon today, we have twelve hours to be wheels-up and headed for our overseas staging areas. So how about we get down to the issue at hand."

LONDON, ENGLAND
1520 HOURS ZULU, APRIL 3

As much as Patrick Hogg wished he could duck into another room while taking the call from Thomas

Shields, he was trapped. With his wife glaring at him from across the small London hotel room, Hogg turned his back on her and did his best to speak as softly as he could. "But sir," he pleaded, "I did leave an address and phone number with the duty officer before I signed out."

Hogg could almost see on the other end of the line the pinched expression on his commanding officer's face as he fumed. "Yes, yes. I'm sure you did. But right now, I don't have time to sort out how this got messed up. Nor have I time to go into any specific details as to what we've been ordered to do. The bottom line is that I need you here, right now, no questions asked."

Hogg paused as he tried to figure out which option would be best-suited for this sudden and unexpected recall: train or plane? When he had decided that catching a flight would probably be the faster way out of London, he announced this decision to Shields, followed quickly by the caveat that it would take some time to make the arrangements.

"Don't bother," Shields snapped. "As we speak, the sergeant major is on the line to MoD there in London. The arrangements to get you back here will be handled by them, including a lift to the airport. Just make sure, Captain, that you're standing in front of your hotel, ready to go, in ten minutes."

Though Hogg knew better, he had to ask about his wife. "Sir, what about Jenny? She's here with me," he whispered.

Already flustered by the complexity of the mission he had been given, and the ludicrously short time in which to prepare for it, Shields snapped, "Patrick! Jenny's a big girl. Neither you nor I have time to tend to such trivial concerns, not when we have been handed the mother of all nightmare scenarios and not near enough time to prepare for it. Now, get down to the street and back here. Understood?"

Realizing that the situation had to be critical, for Shields seldom lost his temper over anything, Patrick Hogg murmured a quick, "Yes, sir," and hung up.

For several long seconds, Hogg stared down at the phone. That this emergency recall was related to the news that had been blaring from every source for the past few hours was without doubt. What he and his NCO's could do about it was quite beyond him. Riot control, perhaps. Or more likely than not, they would be sent in to deal with the nut cases that saw this as a biblical Armageddon and went off the deep end. Already, half a dozen hostage scenarios, from storming Westminster Abbey to abducting the Archbishop of Canterbury were running through Hogg's troubled mind.

From behind him, the impatient tapping of a shoe on the thin hotel carpet reminded the SAS captain that he had a more immediate problem. He had no idea of what he would tell his wife, who was already seething in a silent rage over this untimely interruption. Unable to delay the inevitable, Hogg turned to face Jenny.

With all the practice of a woman who has endured the abrupt termination of far too many private moments by a phone call, Jenny Hogg all but growled, "Well?"

Patrick Hogg was a professional soldier, a member of Britain's elite Special Air Service. He was known as being tough and uncompromising, characteristics that had earned him a slot at Hereford. Prior to that, his knack for making the tough jobs look easy had placed him in high demand and led to frequent overseas deployments. Even when he wasn't engaged in an active operation, the training cycle of the SAS meant that he was in the field more often than not. While he was quite content with this sort of life, Jenny found it intolerable. Had Patrick

Hogg been a barrister or a corporate type, tied to a more traditional community and a schedule honoring the conventions that saw him working by day and at home at night, their marriage would have been the stuff that generations of English poets romanticized about. But Patrick Hogg was not cut out to wear a suit and tie, or to lead a well-ordered, time-clock life, no more than Jenny had been raised to be a soldier's wife.

"You can't say no, can you?" she snapped.

Though he had expected a scene, he was quite taken aback by this sort of thinking on the part of a woman who knew better. "For God's sake, Jenny, I'm a soldier."

"And I'm your wife!" she countered. "I wouldn't mind if the times you had to drop everything and run out were disproportionate. Christ, I'd be bloody happy if I managed to win one conflict in ten. But I've never won, Patrick. Never!"

Like a fighter who has been hit too many times and finds that he no longer has the strength to lift his fists to protect himself, Hogg's shoulders drooped as he looked over at his wife with sad, sheepish eyes. He wanted to plead with her to be patient one more time. He wanted to implore her to try to understand that this mission was important, that he couldn't possibly turn his back on his regiment. He so wanted to cross the space that separated them and to embrace her, to tell her that everything would be different after this, that he would never again leave her side. But he couldn't do that. It would be a lie. And while he had lied to his wife on numerous occasions before, he found that he no longer had the will to do so again.

"Jenny," Hogg finally muttered, "I've got to go."

When he offered no excuse or made no effort to offer up a lie, Jenny knew she had lost. As she took a moment to control her breathing, her chin dropped down and her expression of rage fell away. "I know that you love me, Patrick," she whispered with a gentleness that surprised Hogg. "Maybe even more than I love you. But I'm just not cut out for this sort of thing. I need more than a picture on a mantel and a ring on my finger to remind me I'm married." Looking up, Hogg could see tears welling in her eyes. "I know now that you were never mine. Perhaps I've known that for a long time. For years, I thought I could beat the Army, that I could win out over this obsession that possesses you. But I was wrong. You're not my husband, not really. You're Captain Patrick Hewitt Hogg, of His Majesty's Special Air Service. Though I've tried, I simply can't trump the sort of odds the Army's thrown at us. So I'm not even going to try anymore."

There was an awkward silence as the two looked at each other from across the room. Jenny, on the verge of crying, stood her ground. And Patrick Hogg returned her stare with nothing more than a blank expression. After a while, when it was clear that she had finished her say and he found that he was unable to meet her eyes any longer, Hogg looked down at the floor. "Will you be there when I come back?" he asked, more afraid to hear the answer to this than of anything he had ever had to face before.

"No," she responded without hesitation. "Not this time."

It was more the tone of her response than the promptness with which it was delivered that told Hogg there was no point in pursuing the issue.

Without another word, without even looking over at his wife, he gathered his jacket from the chair it was draped across, walked past Jenny, and left the room.

Even a force as renowned for its thoroughness

and toughness as the SAS could not prepare its men for every contingency.

CALVI, CORSICA
0315 HOURS ZULU, APRIL 4

With the hands on the clock dipping low, Stanislaus Dombrowski found that he was having to slow down lest he make a mistake. Pausing, the Polish legionnaire straightened up on the small stool he was perched upon and examined the oversized shaped charge on which he was working. With great deliberation, his eyes followed the wire from one of the detonators along the outer frame of the charge to the junction where it would be joined to the wires from other detonators and the timer.

A shaped charge is a useful military tool. Though the principle behind it was discovered accidentally at the end of the nineteenth century, it wasn't until the Second World War that it began to appear on the battlefield. In the beginning, this wonder of technology was employed by combat engineers during special operations. The Germans who stormed the mighty Belgian fortress of Eban Emael in May of nineteen-forty were not crack commandos, as thought of today, but glider-borne engineers equipped with small arms and shaped charges. In less than a half a day, something like eighty of these *fallschrimjager* pioneers unhinged the entire defense of Belgium. Later in the war, the clumsy shaped charges in use for cracking the gun turrets of that

Belgian fortress were modified so they could be packaged as warheads. In this role, they proved very effective as an antitank round and became the heart of the American bazooka, the German *panzerfaust* and *panzerschreck*, the British PIAT, and the Russian RPG.

Toward the end of the war, the idea of shaping an explosive charge so as to direct and magnify its force reached its ultimate refinement when the plutonium core of a bomb called "Fat Man" was encased in highly refined explosives. When triggered, the conventional munitions literally crushed the sphere of plutonium for the briefest of moments. But that proved more than sufficient to generate the critical mass necessary to initiate a chain reaction and devastate Nagasaki. After the war, the shaped charge continued to evolve, both as an antitank weapon and as the triggering agent for the world's nuclear arsenals. In a strange way, the jerry-rigged shaped-charge device being assembled by Sergeant-Chef Stanislaus Dombrowski to destroy Russian nuclear warheads was poetic. The crudest and earliest form of that principle was being employed against its most modern and sophisticated refinement.

Everything had to be exact, everything perfect. There could be no slack, no fudging anywhere. While the nature of the explosion was almost immaterial, the shaping of the explosive cone and the placement of the detonators to trigger the explosives were critical. If the lead from one detonator was even the slightest bit shorter than those of others, the electric current would prematurely reach the blasting cap to which it was connected. This would result in the initiation of the explosion on that part of the device first, rather than in synchronization with the rest of the package. So instead of generating a single, concentrated jet stream aimed with the precision of a laser beam against the desired point of impact, the entire device would turn into a shapeless, low-yield explosion that had no chance to burn through the concrete-and-steel cover it was designed to penetrate.

Done correctly, however, the bulk of a shaped charge's explosive force is directed in whichever direction the hollowed-out cone is aimed. This generates a jet stream capable of exerting over 100,000 foot pounds of pressure per square inch. Anything in the path of this jet stream with a tensile strength of less than that is penetrated. This penetration is not achieved by burning, as is popularly thought, but by the displacement of the target's molecules, which are either pushed aside or become part of the jet stream. It is the same principle that allows a person to place a finger into a glass of water. The denser finger easily penetrates the surface of the water by displacing the less-cohesive water molecules.

Destruction of most targets occurs when this jet stream makes contact with a target that is either flammable, such as fuel and hydraulic fluids, or propellants, like those found in the rounds stored on tanks. This secondary detonation, inside the confined space of the object being attacked, is what does the bulk of the damage. There was little danger that the devices being prepared for use against the Russian ICBM's would initiate a nuclear detonation. The same was not true of the rocket fuel. The thin-skinned rocket just under the concrete cover sat confined in a very tight silo. Once the cap of the silo was penetrated, there would literally be nothing of substance between the all-powerful jet stream and thousands of gallons of volatile fuel.

Satisfied that all was in order with the device before him, Dombrowski closed his bloodshot eyes, rubbed his face, and yawned. Allowing his arms to fall away, he opened his eyes and again gazed upon the shaped charge sitting on the table. Blurry-eyed, he waited until his vision cleared before proceeding. It definitely was not pretty, the Pole thought to himself. In fact, if one of his fellow legionnaires had thrown this monstrosity together as part of a training exercise, Dombrowski would have ordered the entire thing pulled apart rather than risk removing it to the demolitions pit for immediate destruction.

From behind, Dombrowski heard footsteps. Turning, he peered into the darkness that engulfed the isolated workshop where he worked alone, perfecting his trade as the demolitions expert for his team. "I came by to see how you were doing, Stan," his captain called out. "And to bring you this. I thought you could use it."

As he emerged from the shadows, Captain Jules Pascal, Dombrowski's team commander, was holding two cups of steaming coffee before him. "If it's that used motor oil the French drink, *mon capitain*, then you are doing me no favors."

Stopping within arm's reach of the weary NCO, Pascal smiled and offered him the cup in his right hand. "No, I would do nothing like that to you. I know how much you enjoy that cow piss the Americans laughingly call coffee."

Taking the cup, Dombrowski lifted it slightly, as if making a toast. "*Merci.*"

Together, each man took a long, almost ceremonial, sip of his respective brew, then paused for a moment to silently savor his drink, and enjoy this brief moment of calm in what had been a most hectic day, even by the standards of the Foreign Legion.

Finally, Pascal turned his attention to the device Dombrowski was working on. "Not very elegant, is it?"

The Polish NCO turned to face the object of his

captain's comment, chuckling as he did. Only a professional soldier could judge an explosive apparatus capable of ripping flesh and concrete apart as an object of beauty. "No, it is not," Dombrowski responded. "But if this is a case where function is the sole concern, then it will work, and very nicely, I daresay, to take out the target it was designed for." Then, turning toward his commander, Dombrowski looked him in the eye. "And just what target, *mon capitain*, do our American friends envision using this thing against? Or should I say, on?"

A small smile crept across Pascal's face. "As I told the rest of the team, we will be informed of that at the appropriate time, Sergeant."

Not willing to be so easily turned away, Dombrowski took a sip of coffee before he launched into his discussion of the subject. "The sergeant major instructs us to prepare our arctic gear. The adjutant comes by, while I am in the midst of my efforts here, and asks me how my Russian is. On my last trip over to the riggers, when I went to deliver a completed device, a load master on one of the transports we will be using asked me why we were taking these to an RAF base in Scotland. And the special instructions detailing how these particular shaped charges are to be assembled, which no one had time to translate from English to French, referred to a diagram of a standard silo cover, which I was not given."

"And your conclusion?" Pascal asked, waving his free hand about.

Again, Dombrowski took a sip of his coffee, watching his captain's expression as he did so, trying to decide if he should continue or not. Finished for the moment with his coffee, the Polish NCO began to lay out his case. "This asteroid is going to hit eastern Russia in a region where many of their older missile silos are, the ones that the current regime never seems to get around to disabling. That region is also where that ambitious ex-general who is anxious to revive the former glory of the Soviet Empire is exiled. My guess is that the general plans on using the missiles he has in his own backyard to blackmail someone. If that is so, I suspect that we are going to be sent in with the mission of punching holes in those silos with these little beauties and disarming him before he has a chance to make mischief."

Looking down into his half-empty cup, Pascal did not immediately respond. Instead, he swirled his drink and watched it as if he were deep in thought. Finally, he looked up at the clock on the wall across from him, then pointed at the oversized shaped charge on the workbench. "I expect that the riggers are waiting for this one. How soon before you are finished with it?"

Realizing that his commander wasn't going to comment on his assumption one way or the other, Dombrowski turned and looked at the device. "It is ready now, *mon capitain.*"

"Good! I will go over to their area right now and send a couple of men to pick it up. That will leave you free to get started on the last of them."

Though he was tired and wanted so badly to ask that he be allowed to take a break, Dombrowski knew better. Pascal was a good commander, a man who knew when he needed to push his men and how far he could go. The Polish NCO suspected that they had little time, so he made no protests, no further comments. With nothing more than a simple "*Oui,*" Dombrowski turned his full attention back to his assigned duties. In time, he and his companions would be told all they needed to know. Until then, he could only do as he was told and trust that his superiors, and the Americans who seemed to be behind this operation, knew what they were doing.

6

The sight of General Eric Shepard, Chairman of the Joint Chiefs, walking side by side with the Chief of Staff of the Army in and of itself was unusual enough to raise eyebrows. To be together in the Army's wing of the Pentagon was downright strange. Though he was proud of his parent service and what it had achieved during his years as a junior-grade officer, Shepard felt he needed to distance himself from the Army in order to escape the impression that he favored one branch of the armed forces over the others. While this was laudable to some, Chuck Smith often found himself reminding his superior and longtime friend of what color his uniform was, especially when the two were on opposite sides of an issue.

That the two officers were at odds was clear to Smith's staff as the pair moved through the outer suite of offices and straight into Smith's at the double-quick. Smith's only comment to his staff was a short, gruff "No calls" to no one in particular as he went blitzing by.

Once the door was closed, the Chairman of the Joint Chiefs turned and faced Smith. "Just what in hell are you doing, Chuck?"

Having expected something like this, Smith was not bothered in the least. Moving to a sofa, he undid the last two buttons on his blouse and sat down before answering. When he did, his voice was calm and relaxed. "General, I'm just doing my job. Nothing more."

Rather than satisfying him, the tone of Smith's voice as well as his patently evasive manner only stoked Shepard's rage. "Dammit, Chuck. Your conduct during the meeting with the President went beyond the pale. You all but accused the Air Force of being incompetent and impotent."

Still unruffled, Smith shrugged. "But it's true, Eric. You heard Wagner's own assessment. Even if the Air Force had sufficient ordnance available to handle the task, they have neither the aircraft nor the conventional cruise missiles to take out the Russian missile silos in a single, swift strike." Pausing, Smith's expression hardened. "The Commander in Chief himself set the criteria for this operation at the very beginning of the NSC meeting this morning. One," Smith stated crisply as he held his right hand up and lifted a single finger, "given the nature of the Perimeter system, the targets must be neutralized with a single, swift strike. Two," he continued, raising another finger, "the strike force has to be under positive control at all times, with the decision to execute or abort delayed until the last possible moment. And three," he emphasized with the addition of a third finger, "the end result, the total neutralization of the Perimeter system, must be guaranteed."

Dropping his hand, Smith locked eyes with Shepard. For several long seconds, the two most senior officers in the United States Army glared at each other. Finally, Smith broke the silence. "The option the Air Force offered couldn't meet a single element set forth as being crucial to success."

Though Smith's oratory took some of the venom out of Shepard's, the Chairman was still far from pleased by what had happened at the White House. "There's more to this than simple, blind professionalism. I know you too well."

Smith did not respond right away. Rather, he looked over to the Army flag and the seal of the United States Army that adorned the wall behind his desk. "I have spent my entire adult life in the Army, just as you have," he stated, glancing over at Shepard for a moment. "We joined this man's Army while it was in the throes of pulling itself together after Vietnam. In later years, we thought we had seen rock-bottom. We thought things couldn't get any worse."

Smith paused when his eyes fell upon one of the many plaques that adorned the walls in his office. This particular plaque had been his first, received when he was a platoon leader. It was an award for being part of the best tank crew in the battalion during annual tank gunnery. "The day I reported in to my first unit, three of the five tanks in my platoon were deadlined. Our motor pool was mostly on dirt, which became a sea of mud the second it rained, which in Germany during the winter is often." A fond smile crossed Smith's face as he looked over at Shepard. "You know, the first time I saw my own tank, it was sitting in the middle of that muddy mess, its engine on the ground behind it. I had never seen a tank with its engine pulled before. All sorts of cables and hoses were running from the haul of the tank to the engine." As he spoke of that long-ago day, the old general made motions with his hands. "In the haul, looking as miserable and nasty as the weather, stood a bedraggled mechanic hooking up more hoses. I looked over into the haul and watched. Finally, I managed to muster up the gumption to ask, 'What's wrong?' Well, without looking up, the mechanic flapped his arms about and mumbled, 'Fuck! I don't know.' "

For the first time that day, Shepard laughed, as much from the recollection of his own faux pas when he was a young second lieutenant as from Smith's little story. Feeling a bit of the oppressive burden he had been shouldering all day slip away, the Chairman followed Smith's example by unbuttoning his blouse and easing his tall frame into one of the overstuffed chairs behind him. "Back then," he stated blissfully, "I can remember asking, 'Dear God, what have I gone and gotten myself into?' "

Having both pondered that thought at one point in their careers, the two senior officers laughed. Then, in unison, they looked away from each other as the burdens of their offices and the train of thought that Smith had set in motion began to play out.

"For a while," Smith continued, "this Army really amounted to something. We had a mission, the capability of executing that mission, and leadership with the courage to see things through. Now," he stated sharply, making no effort to hide the bitterness in his voice, "we're thrown hither and yon as peacekeepers, with no objective other than short-term political gain for the current occupant of the White House. Instead of training and maintaining combat readiness, we participate in social engineering. I'm here to tell you, Eric, if things don't turn around soon, this Army of ours will be a basket case."

Shepard studied his friend and fellow officer for a moment. Leaning forward, the Chairman brought his hands together, resting his elbows on his knees. "Is this what all your posturing is about? Grab this mission and run with it so that we can justify our existence? Throw our troops into Russia to prove that we can still be bad?"

The manner in which the Chairman of the Joint Chiefs put his question tended to make what Smith was trying to get at sound both sordid and illicit. But that was Shepard's way when he was dealing with tough issues. So Smith pushed on without mincing words. "Why the hell not! The Air Force has been doing it for years. You remember their BS after the First Gulf War in ninety-one, and again after Kosovo."

"Chuck, even you have to admit that it was the decisive element in both those wars."

Lurching forward, Smith quickly countered, "But only because we had a viable ground threat that we used in the Gulf and finally got around to threatening to use in Kosovo. Without that arrow in the quiver or the will to use it, our entire posture as a military power is less than credible to many who would oppose us. So you see, using the Army here, when we *are* the best choice for the job, makes our deterrence that much more meaningful in the future." Finished, Smith eased back onto the sofa.

Looking down at his clutched fists, Shepard considered Smith's position. After several moments of silence, when he spoke, his tone was uncharacteristically soft. "No matter how well this thing unfolds, we are going to lose a lot of your people, Chuck."

The expression on Smith's face hardened. "So be it. Far too many people, especially those who view this country as their next major enemy, don't think we have the stomach to shed the blood of our youth to achieve our national goals. Even worse, an entire generation of our own politicians and fellow citizens have grown up thinking that we can wage war on the cheap. Eric, as cold and as terrible as this sounds, we must teach all of them that they are wrong."

As he listened to Smith's justification, a chill ran down Shepard's spine. While he had entertained many of these same thoughts, to be faced with such a decision was quite sobering. Standing up, he started to button his blouse in preparation to leave. Taking his cue, Smith also rose. "Well?" he asked, after giving Shepard time to consider the issue.

The Chairman of the JCS looked into Smith's eyes. Rather than anger, Smith could see the pain his superior was feeling. Finally, Shepard bowed his head and shook it. "I'll call the President and inform him of our decision." Then, looking up at Smith one more time before turning away to leave, he added, "And may God have mercy on our souls."

**MOSCOW, RUSSIA
1200 HOURS ZULU, APRIL 4**

For an officer such as Demetre Orlov, time was a valuable commodity. As the commander of an independent unit operating outside the normal military chain of command, it was up to him to arrange for every detail of his unit's deployment or to see to it that the subordinate chosen to execute that task was doing so promptly and in accordance with Orlov's concept of operations. All of this was complicated by the fact that Orlov never committed his plans to paper and never articulated the entire scheme to any one man in his unit. Even his deputy, Major Gregory Petkovic, was provided only with information that would be needed in order to arrange for the transportation required during the operation.

Such precautions are part of what is known in American military circles as "operation security." These are measures taken to ensure that a foe does not become aware of one's plans. Few bothered to argue that Orlov's approach to this concern was too draconian. Every man in Orlov's elite special-action unit understood that no one, not even their comrades, could be trusted completely. The simple fact that the unit was often used to bring dissident elements of the Russian military back into line made this concern even more acute. Orlov had no way of knowing when one of his handpicked paratroopers would decide that his loyalty lay not with his current comrades, but with those they were being sent against. The founders of the Red Army, after all, were the same men who had entered the ranks of the old czarist army and fermented the revolt that led to the Revolution of 1917. While their efforts were revered in the mythology of the Army even after the collapse of the Soviet Regime, what they did was never forgotten.

In a way, the soldiers of the special-action unit preferred it that way. It was one less thing they needed to worry about, one less thought bouncing about in their fertile minds as they prepared their weapons and equipment for their next mission. Within the unit, Orlov's men saw that they had all the specialized skills needed to handle just about any tactical situation they could possibly face in the field. In addition to being lavished with the best ordnance available, each soldier was afforded ample time and munitions to hone his skills and marksmanship to near perfection. Even when it came to family housing, nothing was overlooked. So it was easy to live with Orlov's particular idiosyncrasies when it came to keeping his own council and running the unit. Every man understood that when the time came, he would be told what his target was. All that was required of him was absolute trust in his officers and a willingness to do whatever he was ordered to do, without question.

To prepare himself for his coming ordeal, Demetre Orlov conducted a routine that bordered on ceremonial. As he did before all operations, he followed a ritual as measured and reserved as the dressing of a matador. The centerpiece of this ceremony were the Russian colonel's pistol and assault rifle. After issuing a stern warning to the enlisted soldier who served as his secretary that he was not to be disturbed, Orlov closed the door of his office. A few measured steps took him to the locker where he kept the box with the cleaning kit for his weapons. Taking it in both hands, he moved over to a metal table that served as a work space and conference table. There he placed the box in the same spot he always did. Before taking his seat, he looked across the table to where his two weapons sat. Only after he saw that all was ready did Orlov take a seat and begin.

From the top of the metal box he lifted a neatly folded, thin, off-white cloth and spread it out on the table before him. Like a priest preparing an altar for High Mass, Orlov took a moment to flatten the cloth and square it up with the edges of the table. Next, he retrieved the various items he would need for cleaning his weapons. Since there was insufficient time to do more than field-strip them, he didn't pull the small container that held his special tools out of the metal box. Instead, he fished out the appropriate bore brushes, cleaning rods, patches, oil, and extra-fine steel wool, all of which he laid out across the top of the white cloth in the order in which he would use them.

When all was set, Orlov reached across the table

for his assault rifle that had been sitting there like a loyal dog waiting for its master. As with everything else in his life, he took things in priority. Though he didn't anticipate any interruptions, a man in his position could never be sure of when a priority call or an unexpected development would force him to drop what he was doing and rush off to deal with a new crisis.

The weapon before him was an AKR submachine gun. This particular weapon was a derivative of the AKM, which itself is a modified AK-74. All of these weapons were descendants of the infamous Kalashnikov AK-47. The latest reincarnation of this legendary assault rifle fired a 5.45mm cartridge that was noted for causing particularly nasty wounds. Unlike the standard AKM, Orlov's weapon was quite stubby. Its barrel was all but nonexistent. The Y-shaped metal folding stock, which Orlov never used, was almost as long as the submachine gun itself.

This reduction in barrel length, as can be expected, affects the accuracy of the AKR. But marksmanship was not a primary concern for the Russian colonel. Reliability and cyclic rate were what held his interest. As the senior officer of a unit, his primary function was command and control. To carry out these critical tasks, he had to refrain from engaging in combat. A soldier firing his weapon tends to focus on his target, resulting in tunnel vision and a reduction in situational awareness. Since the type of operations Orlov's unit participated in moved with a speed almost incomprehensible to ordinary people, he could not afford a lapse in his ability to view and assess the overall tactical situation. So he always placed himself where he could look, quite literally, over the shoulders of the men under his command, who were the designated killers.

Still, those same missions placed the Russian colonel in situations that had the potential of going south in a heartbeat. He needed to be prepared to either defend himself or, if the occasion really went to hell, step up onto the firing line himself and finish the job his unit had been dispatched to execute. That's why Orlov preferred the AKR. It had a good volume of fire, it used the same cartridge as his PRI pistol, and it was small and light, allowing him to easily sling it over his shoulder onto his back and out of his way.

Carefully, he broke his submachine gun down into its primary functional groups. As he removed each component, he placed it upon the cloth in the order in which he came to it. By the time he was finished with field-stripping the weapon, his mind was already turning toward other issues.

In the West, the question of loyalty to a unit commander or the nation is seldom a concern of a commanding officer. Part of being a professional soldier is commitment, without question, to the country and the organization to which the Western soldier belongs. Even in the Legion, a unit composed entirely of non-French, there is a dedication to the unit and a legionnaire's comrades that is beyond question. A member of a special-operations unit in the United States, Britain, France, or any other NATO nation, may not always agree with the mission to which he is assigned, or may not get along with the officers selected to lead it, but his reliability is never suspect.

The same could not be said for the armed forces of the Russian Republic. Though the end of the Cold War swept away the old Communist government and many of the systems that had run the country since the 1917 Revolution, there was never a break in the continuity within the Red Army. Everything, with the exception of the flag under which it served, remained as it had. What changes were introduced, such as uniforms, organization of combat units, and unit designations, were implemented by the same officers, operating within the existing framework that was built upon the traditions, customs, and practices of the once-proud Red Army. Some critics of the present Russian regime were fond of drawing a parallel between the current conditions in Russia and the German Weimar Republic of the 1920's and its Army. There were some who even whispered that given time, General Igor Likhatchev would legally assume power in much the same way Hitler had.

The concerns that kept many a politician in Moscow awake at night made Orlov's task of commanding a unit used to dealing with internal disorders a nightmare. On more than one occasion, the special-response team that Orlov led had been sent to deal with insubordinate or rebellious units from which many of his own men had been recruited. It was not at all unusual for a member of his command to have served under the very officers they were ordered to eliminate. This created tension within the unit over and above that normally associated with combat operations. Even more important, however, was the stress that it created between Orlov and his men, and even between the soldiers in the ranks themselves. Though he never spoke of it to anyone, the Russian colonel often wondered if the day would come when one of his own would turn in the midst of a firefight or at a critical juncture of an operation and declare for the opposition. Hence the necessity of keeping his personal weapons, designed for close-in work, well cared for, functional, and ready for any contingency.

Finished with the receiver group of his AK, Orlov returned it to its proper place on the off-white cloth and picked up the bolt. Before he did anything else, he wiped away the light coat of oil that remained on it from its last cleaning. Lifting it up, he carefully studied the assembly. Turning it this way and that, Orlov inspected every square millimeter of the bolt for rust, wear, and damage. Though all was in order, he lowered it back down to table level. With his free hand, he picked up a small clump of extra-fine steel wool and began to gently work on an imaginary blemish on the side of the bolt. All the while, he looked over at far end of the table, where there was a pile of maps, diagrams, copies of messages, and intelligence reports.

Nowhere in that pile was there any sort of directive assigning Orlov and his men the mission they were preparing for. The Russian colonel never received written orders for any of his missions. While the Minister of Defense explained that the reason for this was in the interest of operational security, since written orders could be copied or read by unauthorized personnel. Orlov knew better. Written orders needed to be prepared by someone. Should the operation that those orders launched go bad, or actions taken by those executing those orders prove to be unpopular, the government official who originated them would be held accountable. Without such orders, the only person who could be held accountable was the one who actually led the action. In operations that required the use of the special-response team, this meant Demetre Orlov.

While this added another element of risk to every mission he was given, Orlov preferred working without hard orders. It gave him a greater degree of freedom than he would have otherwise had. It also gave him an out should he be brought to account for his actions later. The blame game, after all, could be played both ways.

None of this meant that the Russian colonel didn't lack for guidance or advice from his superiors on how to accomplish his mission. The Minister of Defense had wanted Orlov to deploy his team to

Siberia before the impact of the asteroid so the outfit would be in place and ready to respond as soon as General Likhatchev made his move against the government in Moscow. Colonel Orlov, however, did not care for this idea. When he pressed the team of scientists and experts who were advising the government on the technical aspects of the pending collision between Earth and asteroid, he had quickly come to the conclusion that no one knew for sure what exactly would happen when the moment came. Some believed that the asteroid would burn up as it hit the atmosphere. Others felt that it would skip off the dense layer of air that surrounded the planet like a stone across water. A few, after studying the object as it grew closer, thought that the asteroid would break up, just as Shoemaker-Levy did before hitting Jupiter. To a man, none could muster up the nerve to state categorically where in Siberia the thing would actually impact. "There is," one frustrated astronomer confessed, "no way of knowing for sure what will happen. There are simply too many variables and not enough facts."

Given this sad state of affairs, Orlov was successful in resisting pressure from the Minister of Defense and others to deploy his unit. "Without knowing the precise location of impact," he explained, "it would be foolish to place my men on the ground, especially since we would have no shelter to protect us from the horrific effects of the asteroid if the worst-case scenario is realized. Besides," Orlov went on to point out, "the general will undoubtedly sit out the event in one of the military command bunkers scattered throughout his province. Only after the asteroid has struck will he come out. And when he does, he will need to rely on radio and satellite communication to reestablish his authority in the region, as well as to negotiate with the government in Moscow. This means we will be able to track his movements and pinpoint his location. In addition," Orlov went on when Yuri Anatov made no effort to counter his argument, "the resulting chaos throughout the region, with relief flights coming and going, will provide us with the perfect cover for our insertion. We will simply join the flow of aircraft rushing into a devastated area, where the ability of security forces to protect the General, as well as the missiles, will be thoroughly compromised."

Though Anatov disliked the idea of waiting until the gun pointed at Moscow's head was loaded and cocked, as the Perimeter system would be after the impact, the tone with which Demetre Orlov delivered his proposal left no doubt that there was no room for discussion or disagreement. Since Orlov's loyalty to the government in this particular matter was already suspected by some, it would have been foolish to push him into accepting a course of action that he vehemently opposed. Besides, there was no one in a better position than Orlov to know what Likhatchev would do in this sort of situation. After all, Demetre Orlov had once served General Likhatchev as his Chief of Staff.

7

One of the popular modern myths concerning the military is that the warrior, marching off to battle, is somber and dispirited by the stress of leaving home and sallying forth into the great and dangerous unknown. Though few would ever admit it to anyone who hasn't "been there," many veterans find themselves looking forward with great anticipation to their deployment into an active theater of operations.

Going to war has always been, and still remains, an adventure of unparalleled complexity and excitement. It is the ultimate ride of terror, one in which there is no safety net, no fail-safe brake system. For the individual, it is also a test of skills, courage, and stamina. No modern sporting event can come close to equaling the challenge or danger that a man going into combat must face. Though sportswriters and promoters may wax philosophical about "do-or-die" contests between teams and speak of "smash-mouth football," "sudden death" overtimes, or a team's "devastating" offense, every one of the players involved in such contests knows that at the end of a prescribed time, the "combatants" of both teams will be able to shake hands, retire to a warm locker room, and enjoy a hot shower before heading off to their respective homes.

The same cannot be said of the combat soldier. Battle is not limited to four quarters. There are no time-outs. Refs do not stand ready to halt the action when there is an infraction of the rules of war. Nor is a soldier given a guarantee that when he completes his current mission, there will not be another, perhaps a more dangerous one, waiting for him. In war, only death is a greater unknown. And sometimes the two, death and combat, become one and the same for those who are unwary, or just plain unlucky.

When the orders calling selected special-operations units belonging to several NATO nations went out, the men tagged to participate in what was being dubbed "Operation Tempest" embraced it with enthusiasm. This does not mean that those with families were not troubled by having to leave their loved ones under the circumstances, or that they were insensitive to the suffering and devastation that the asteroid would soon inflict on so many. To be faced with the alternative, however, would have been unbearable to these highly trained professionals. While Andrew Fretello penned the order that would translate his concept into a coherent plan of action, Patrick Hogg rushed back to his home station, and Stanislaus Dombrowski put the finishing touches on his infernal machines. Those who were not part of Tempest stood off to the side and out of the way, idle and waiting for orders. For the majority of NATO units, the only guidance they received started with soft phrases such as "Be prepared to—" or "On order, execute the following tasks," which, loosely translated, mean, "Don't call us, we'll call you."

This placed the poor souls in those organizations in the same predicament as the civilians whom they were charged with defending. Psychologists who study people involved in crisis situations generally agree that those who are unable to do anything to help themselves, or who are not involved in some sort of physical activity aimed at fending off a pending disaster or recovering from it, are prone to suffer distress, depression, or anxiety. Busy work, even if it is not directly related to the disaster at hand, is a means of coping with these degenerative conditions. This explains why so many people labor long hours, under horrific conditions, to build sandbag levies to fend off the rising waters of a flood, or immediately rush off to help a neighbor whose home has been devastated by a tornado, even when they themselves have suffered from it. By engaging in an activity that is familiar or seems to be beneficial, the mind is kept from contemplating the unthinkable and gives the participant a sense of control in an uncontrollable situation.

This does not mean that the soldiers, sailors, marines, airmen, and legionnaires marshaling at an obscure RAF base in northern Scotland did not harbor their own concerns over the story that the media was describing as "the cosmic event of the new millennium." These unwelcome interludes were accentuated by the barren landscape surrounding the base and the gloomy weather that matched the bleak predictions spewed out by twenty-four-hour news programs lacking factual information with which to fill their airtime. Like an annoying guest, televisions and radios were peppered about everywhere on the base. Seeing as how the collision of an asteroid of respectable size with Earth would be the single most historic event that the majority of the men and women at the RAF base would live through, no one wants to comment about it very much.

For the planners and those charged with maintaining operational security for Tempest, the diversion that the asteroid provided to the troops under their control was a blessing. Due to the intrusive nature of Tempest and the targets that would be attacked, the exact nature of their mission was a taboo subject for the rumormongers. So whatever free time was not being taken up by sleep or personal needs was dedicated to ongoing speculation about the asteroid. Like the talking heads on the tele, the gathering soldiers, sailors, marines, and airmen wondered aloud how they thought it would affect them, their immediate families, and their respective nations. The arrival of each new contingent brought a set of fresh ideas and thoughts to this disjointed forum.

This gave rise to a curiosity and an interest that occasionally bordered on the morbid and macabre. Along with the more mundane subjects kicked around by the impatient commandos were topics such as casualty projections and the equivalent nuclear yield of the impact. These and other asteroid-related trivia were discussed, and even bet on. For those who enjoyed placing a wager or two, there were a variety of pools run by enterprising young men who had nothing better to do with their time and sought to keep their minds off the collision and the operation that would follow. Anything, from the exact time of the impact to the exact location, could be bet on, using dollars, pounds sterling, francs, deutsche marks, or euros.

By far, the greatest concentration of these exchanges took place in the areas set aside for the officers' and NCO's messes. Like so many other NATO installations, the end of the Cold War had

seen a decline in the need for bases such as the one
being used to marshal the Special Operations Units
assigned to Tempest. This particular RAF base had
been relegated to a caretaker status, meaning that
the primary mission of the small garrison assigned
there was to maintain the facilities and infrastruc-
ture so that the site could be used in an emergency.
On occasion, a local territorial unit would conduct
a weekend drill there, or an RAF squadron would
use the airfield as a target to hone its ground-attack
skills. Patrick Hogg and the 22nd SAS Regiment had
even used this particular base on occasion while
practicing a number of contingencies. Otherwise,
the sleepy little relic of the Cold War and its tiny
garrison marooned on the Scottish moors was left
in peace.

The cumulative effect of this was that the entire
facility, save for a few administrative offices, barracks, and personnel-support buildings, was run-
down and rather seedy. Everything was in need of a
thorough refurbishing and a coat of paint. This was
particularly true of the recreation facilities, areas
that had been rather low on the list of things to
keep up to snuff. Since the base was going to be
used only to marshal the Tempest units before cat-
apulting them into Russia, no one saw the sense in
wasting valuable time in establishing separate clubs
or messes for each of the various grades. Few of the
base's new residents saw any problem with this. Special Operations Units, by their very nature, are close-
knit organizations in which differences in rank are
viewed as nothing more than a functional concern
rather than as a class distinction. All that mattered
to most of the troopers who gathered in the ad hoc
lounge/snack bar was that they could get a beer,
something to eat other than mess-hall food, and
find a place where they could go other than to their

overcrowded barracks rooms or bustling work spaces.

Of course, soldiers would not be soldiers unless they were complaining about something. The haste with which the lounge, dubbed the "Red Devil's Pub" by the first British unit that arrived there and opened it, provided the patrons with plenty to complain about. In no time, the Americans were unanimously viewed as the biggest whiners. Their genetic inability to tolerate warm beer, and a habit of making their displeasure about having it served to them that way, was always met with a snide comment from one of their European counterparts, who saw the chilling of the brew as something akin to sacrilege and perversity.

But the warriors from across the Atlantic were not the only ones vocal in their disparagement of the Red Devil's Pub. French commandos and legionnaires ran a close second. Over his years of service in the Legion, Sergeant-Chef Stanislaus Dombrowski had led a simple life. He had his duty, the Legion, his comrades, and not much else. As a result, the few pleasures he bothered to indulge in had become important to him. Chief among these was a taste Dombrowski had acquired for the national beverage of France. Like many of his compatriots, the drinking of wine was an occasion to be savored. So when the big Pole and his companion saw that they were about to be served wine from bottles with screw caps, they recoiled in horror.

"What is this?" Dombrowski bellowed, causing a number of other patrons to interrupt their conversations as they turned to see what the problem was. "I asked for wine, not fruit juice."

The RAF airman who had been dragooned into tending bar was taken aback by this unexpected rebuke. With confusion on his face, he looked down at the bottle he had offered to the burly legionnaire.

After satisfying himself that he was holding the correct product, he looked back at Dombrowski. "But this is wine!" he exclaimed, thinking that perhaps the Frenchman couldn't read the English label on the bottle. "It's called a mir-lot."

Bug-eyed, Dombrowski leaned over the counter. "A what?" he asked in amazement.

Convinced now that the big legionnaire was having a problem with the English language, the RAF airman raised the bottle to show Dombrowski the label. Pointing out the word "merlot," the airman did as most folks do in an effort to make themselves understood by a foreigner, he spoke louder and slower. "I said, it is called a mir-lot. It's a red wine. See?"

Franz Ingelmann, unable to hide his smirk, turned away from the scene and shook his head. "And these," the Austrian legionnaire whispered to Dombrowski in French, "are the people who once ruled the world?"

Unsure of what infuriated him more, the offer of such a cheap excuse of a wine, or the manner in which the RAF airman was treating him, Dombrowski stood rooted to his spot, fuming as he glanced back and forth between the airman and his Austrian companion, who was by now laughing out loud. "Shut up, you moron," the big Pole snapped as he looked down at Ingelmann, who doubled over in the agony of sheer delight. "If you had any pride as a legionnaire, you'd be just as indignant as me at this travesty."

Using one hand to cover his face, the Austrian grabbed Dombrowski's arm with the other and gave it a friendly squeeze. "My friend, you are doing a magnificent job of defending the honor of France without my help."

Forgetting the cause of his anger, the Polish legionnaire now turned his entire attention on his comrade, who was enjoying the incident a bit too much. "What the hell do you know about honor, you beer-drinking peasant?"

Rather than infuriate the easygoing Ingelmann, Dombrowski's attitude only spurred the Austrian on. Between his efforts to stop laughing and catch his breath, he managed to spur his Polish companion on. "Perhaps," Ingelmann continued in French, "we can convince the captain to haul this fellow out behind the hangar and have him guillotined for crimes against grape pickers."

Unable to understand what was being said between the two legionnaires, the RAF airman had continued to hold the bottle of wine up before Dombrowski's face. Not sure of what to do, the airman cleared his throat. "Ah, excuse me, but do you want this one, or would you rather have a bottle of the white stuff they have here?"

Though he was tempted to tell the RAF airman what he could do with the bottle of wine he was holding, Dombrowski held his tongue in check and turned away from a delirious Ingelmann, who had by now collapsed on the floor with uncontrollable laughter. Storming through the crowded room and out the door, the big Pole all but bowled over an American major who was headed into the lounge.

From his seat, Patrick Hogg had watched the confrontation between the big legionnaire and the bewildered airman. Under ordinary circumstances, he enjoyed such antics. Unlike their counterparts in line units, the men who belonged to the Special Operations Forces tended to be less constrained, more apt to let their emotions show, whether it was inventing their anger or enjoying a good laugh. He himself enjoyed participating in activities that would be grounds for disciplinary action in any other unit.

Such was his mood this day, however, that even the unrehearsed Punch-and-Judy show that had just transpired over the bottle of wine was wasted on him. Looking back down at his half-empty beer, Hogg slowly rotated the bottle. Enjoying a beer or two at the unit's mess was nothing unusual for the SAS captain. Like dress parades or the trooping of the colors, it was part of an officer's life in the British Army. Doing so alone, in the middle of the afternoon for no good reason, however, was not.

Hogg tried to collect himself as he toyed with the bottle he held. He had a good reason, a bloody good one. It hadn't been until he was on the military transport, headed north from London, that the full impact of what had happened between himself and Jenny hit him. No matter how this operation came out, no matter what he did from that moment on, his personal life would never be the same. While the conflict between his chosen profession and his wife was an unending source of conflict within him, he had always managed to keep the faint hope alive that maybe, somehow, things would sort themselves out. Like a mariner clings to the mast during a storm, Hogg had held onto the dream that one day, all would be made right.

That this dream was now dead was crystal-clear. Again and again, he went over her final remarks to him and the way she had delivered them. Every so often, as he stared at the bottle he was mechanically turning, the words "She's gone" drifted through his mind. When they did, Hogg would grip the bottle firmly in his hand, lift it to his lips and take a long sip. For the briefest of moments, the warm beer making its way down would vanquish all thoughts of Jenny. But only for the briefest of moments.

*   *   *

Having again worked through lunch and unable to wait for whatever food substitute the Brit mess teams had chosen to serve that night, Andrew Fretello opted to try his luck at the Red Devil's Pub. That he might have made a bad choice occurred to him as he was all but knocked down by an angry legionnaire barreling out of the place just as he was preparing to enter it.

Once inside, Fretello sized up the situation to determine if he wanted to stay or trust his luck and stomach to the mess hall. A quick scan of the crowd yielded nothing more noticeable than a single French legionnaire, over at the bar, struggling to his feet. This did not surprise the American major at all. Such antics, including toppling over dead drunk in the middle of the afternoon, were to be expected from enlisted men, particularly those belonging to foreign units.

After deciding to stay, Fretello made his way over to where sandwiches were served. There he picked up something that looked both familiar and safe. After paying for it and a warm coke, he turned and headed off into the crowd in search of a place to sit. When it became obvious that there were no open tables anywhere in the room, he began to seek out a table where there was someone who, like himself, was not interested in swapping stories or jabbering about the asteroid. Finally setting his sights on a seat across from a lone SAS captain, Fretello made his way forward.

"Excuse me, but do you mind if I join you?"

Looking up from his beer bottle, Patrick Hogg stared at the American for a moment before nodding. "Be my guest."

Using his foot to pull a chair out, the American set his plate and drink down and took a seat. Hogg paid him little attention as he went back to vacantly staring at the bottle that was now better than three-quarters empty. For his part, Fretello threw himself into consuming his first substantial meal of the day.

Eventually, Patrick Hogg managed to look up from the bottle that had been the object of his attention for the better part of an hour and across the table at the American major who was wolfing down a sandwich as if there were a time clock on him. "In a bit of a hurry, I see. I envy you."

Fretello, who had been lost in his own thoughts, was startled by this sudden comment from his table mate. Even before he finished swallowing the food in his mouth, the American shook his head. "Gotta get back to work. The Air Force doesn't think it's going to be able to pony up the number of aircraft we requested. If that happens, we're going to have to reshuffle the loads."

"Whose Air Force?" Hogg asked, more out of a desire to keep the conversation going than in finding out the answer to his question.

Before taking another bite, Fretello looked at Hogg and hesitated. "Don't know. NATO, in Brussels, is handling all the air taskings. We just submitted our requirements to them."

While his harried companion tore off a good size of sandwich and proceeded to grind away at it, Hogg's somewhat impaired mind considered this piece of information. From what he had seen so far, the airlift on hand was already more than sufficient to handle the number of Special Ops teams that he had seen wandering around the base, provided the aircraft were loaded to capacity. His curiosity peaked, and anxious to address something other than his own personal issues, Hogg decided to pursue the matter. "So, we're going to be scattering a lot of little teams all over Hell's Half Acre in a short period of time, going after hardened sites that all have the exact same characteristics. Russian missile silos, I would imagine. Wouldn't you?"

Though he had done his best to discourage a continuance of the unwelcome chatter by concentrating on eating and getting out as soon as he could, the SAS captain's last comment dismayed Fretello. With his sandwich suspended midway between his plate and his gaping mouth, the American gazed bug-eyed across the table at Hogg.

Realizing what the problem was, Hogg chuckled. "Sorry, I didn't mean to shake your tree, Major. But it's bloody well obvious what we're all here for, though I daresay there's a great deal of speculation as to why we're going at a time like this."

Slowly, Fretello lowered his sandwich back onto the plate, glancing this way and that, as if looking to see if anyone around them was paying attention to what the SAS captain was saying. Because of the nature of the targets, and the inevitable political ramifications that the operation would set in motion, a decision had been made to maintain the tightest possible lid on Tempest. In selling the idea of withholding information until the last possible moment, Fretello himself had pointed out that the actions of the teams were to be rather straightforward and simple. "They'll be dropped at a location within easy striking distance of their respective targets," he had briefed before leaving for Scotland. "The aircraft themselves, each making individual penetrations of Russian airspace and following different egress routes, need only know the drop-zone locations for the teams they are transporting. For the most part, all we need to do is to provide the teams themselves with the location of their designated targets. Since they are all highly trained specialists and the silos are stationary and quite obvious, there's little need for detailed instructions on what to do when they get there. As to what they do when they're done . . . well, again," Fretello stated with more confidence than many in his audience felt, "we will be able to rely on their intelligence and expertise to see them through." Though it was pointed out that in this line of thinking there were gaping holes that would allow the passage of a fleet carrier, the situation was such that words like "hoped" and "anticipated" were weak substitutes for definitive guidance.

Sensing the discomfort that the American was laboring under, Hogg managed a smile. "Don't worry, old boy. All this is pretty much common knowledge. After all, one doesn't gather a collection like this," he went on, waving his right hand in the direction of the crowded tables, "without a healthy amount of speculation as to 'why.'"

Recovered somewhat, Fretello folded his hands on the table in front of him, pushing the half-eaten sandwich away as he did so. Like so many other plans officers, he often forgot that the units listed in his operations orders were comprised of living, breathing human beings filled with all the natural curiosities that any normal person possesses. If anything, members of Special Operations commands are, on the average, a bit more intelligent, have greater curiosity, and are decidedly bolder than their fellow citizens. So the idea that there were all sorts of discussions as to "why" and "where" should not have come as a surprise to Fretello.

Still, the Special Forces officer felt that he could not ignore the breach of security he had just been party to. "That may be so, *Capitain*," he stated crisply, accentuating the word "*capitain*." "But it does not mean that we officers need to add our voices to that sort of thing. If anything, I would expect an officer would do his best to discourage violations of operational security."

Already in a dark mood, the smile on Hogg's face faded. "There's one thing that I am in no need of, Major," he replied in a low, menacing tone, "and

that is a lecture on what my duties as an officer are."
He was about to add "especially by an American,"
but decided that would be a bit too much. "As an
SAS officer," Hogg went on as the American stared
at him in stony silence, "my men expect me to make
informed decisions and show them the same sort of
trust they show when they salute smartly and follow
my orders. While things may be different in your
Army, in this regiment, simply telling the men that
they have no need to know doesn't cut it." He was
about to leave it at that, but Patrick Hogg was not
one to drive the knife in without giving it that last
painful twist. Leaning forward, he looked into Fretello's eyes. "Perhaps, Major," he whispered with a
sinister smile, "if you spent a bit more time with your
feet in the mud where the real soldiers are and less
time parked behind a keyboard pounding out directives and plans that brief well, you'd understand
that sort of thing."

Flushed with anger, Fretello jumped to his feet,
knocking his chair over as he did so and into one
being occupied by a German belonging to Grenz-
schutzgruppe 9. This commotion brought an abrupt
halt to a dozen conversations that had been going
on in the crowded lounge. It also placed Andrew
Fretello in an awkward position. Though he wanted
to respond to the SAS captain in the most decisive
manner that reason would permit, to do so in public
would have serious consequences, consequences
that the American staff officer was not prepared to
pay. Opting to choose discretion over personal satisfaction, Fretello turned and stormed off through
the crowd, which parted before him like the Red
Sea for Moses.

He had almost made it to the door when, from
behind, he heard the Irish drawl of the SAS captain
call out: "Major, you've forgotten your dinner.
Would you care for a doggie bag?" As bad as this

was, the chorus of laughter that followed pierced him like an arrow. With nothing by way of a reasonable response open to him, Fretello clenched his fists and kicked open the door, almost hitting the same big legionnaire he had run into when he had entered.

Quickly stepping aside and out of the way of the infuriated American officer, Stanislaus Dombrowski watched him go before turning and entering the pub. As he did so, he noted that everyone in the place was looking at him. Stopping, the big Pole asked, quite innocently, "Did I miss something?"

This brought about another wave of laughter before everyone got back to whatever they had been doing. At his table, a self-satisfied Patrick Hogg hoisted his beer and took the last of his brew down in a single gulp. Finished, he slammed the empty bottle on the table and smacked his lips. "I think I'll have another," he shouted to no one in particular as all thoughts of his Jenny had faded, for the moment.

8

Looking up at the pale blue sky, whatever doubts Tim Vandergraff had been harboring over entering the asteroid's footprint to cover this story were quickly forgotten. The "footprint," as the journalist of his tiny TV news team explained to the audience back home, was the zone in which the particles that had once been asteroid Nereus 1991 HWC were expected to enter Earth's atmosphere and impact. Though continuous observation and an analysis of data gathered from it had shrunk the footprint to an area of only several hundred square kilometers, no one was willing to pinpoint where the asteroid would actually impact, if indeed it did. Laborious and often heated debate between the experts, both on camera and in hundreds of closed meetings, as to what would happen at 05:34 Greenwich mean time tended to create more doubts than answers.

It was as a result of this climate of uncertainty that Tim Vandergraff decided to risk crossing over the imaginary line to cover the biggest story of his career. "You know how those government and civil-defense types are," he explained to journalist Anna Roberts when she voiced her concerns. "When faced with a situation like this, they go overboard. They evacuate twice as many people as is necessary and build a margin of safety into their projections that borders on the ridiculous. I'm sure that if he had his way, General Likhatchev would empty all of Russia east of the Urals just to be sure." Though still concerned, Anna Roberts and Antonio Halbas, cameraman and sound tech, went along. Only their official guide, a Russian from the State Information Bureau, had no doubts that what they were doing was tantamount to suicide. It had taken a bribe four times that normally budgeted for use in "persuading" Russian officials to convince the guide to abandon common sense and cooperate.

Using the projections that NASA had generated, Vandergraff took his intrepid little team of Americans to a spot that was just off the anticipated glide path of the asteroid. Located on the north slope of a heavily wooded ridge overlooking a river, Vandergraff hoped to catch sight of the incoming projectile as it first hit Earth's atmosphere southwest of where they now stood. If their luck held and the folks at NASA were even close to being right, Halbas would be able to track Nereus 1991 HW.C as it sliced through the increasingly dense air that it encountered. The heat created by the friction generated as air passed over the irregular surface of the asteroid would reach several thousand degrees Fahrenheit within seconds. The entire asteroid would become a fireball as the silicate rock and iron that it was made of melted. Vandergraff was told that this phenomena would create a spectacle that would stand out against the bright, early spring sky. And though he expected to lose sight of the asteroid as it disappeared over the southeastern horizon, the TV camera would be able to pick up the flash and resulting mushroom cloud as the alien intruder finally made contact with Earth's surface some one hundred kilometers away. "I'm not guaranteeing you the Pulitzer prize," he told his fellow journalists as he made his pitch to ignore the published minimumally safe distance, "but what we record tomorrow will rank right up there with the film clip of the *Hindenberg* and man's first step on the moon."

Neither Roberts nor Hables were fools. Both were veteran correspondents who had covered more than their fair share of natural and man-made disasters around the world. Anna Roberts had earned her spurs reporting in the Balkans and covering the Second Gulf War. Hables had honed his skills in the camps of Colombian guerrillas and covering the Mexican drug wars. Individually, each entertained doubts about the wisdom of crossing over into the footprint of the asteroid in the off chance that they would find the perfect spot, one that was both safe and ideal for viewing its descent. Yet such was the challenge of the chase, not to mention their pride as journalists willing to hang it all out in pursuit of a story, that they kept their concerns to themselves.

Once committed, all thoughts of any dangers associated with their decision were pushed aside as they prepared themselves and their equipment for an event they would have only one opportunity to capture. Besides technical matters, such as establishing a good satellite uplink and a location in the Siberian wilderness that would provide them an unobstructed, panoramic view of the southern sky, there were more aesthetic concerns that needed to be addressed. Though the primary focus would be on the asteroid itself, a suitable spot where Anna Roberts would stand and deliver her commentary was necessary. Tim Vandergraff was an absolute genius when it came to that sort of thing, which was why he was there.

In short order, he had found a site that was ideal. From a ledge on a ridge that was slightly higher than where Anna stood, Hablas would be able to capture, as background, the river below them, the southern ridge of the valley across the way, and the horizon while Anna was addressing the audience. When the time came for the asteroid to make its appearance, all Hablas need do was to tilt his camera up a bit and angle it slightly to his right. With luck, he informed Vandergraff, he would even be able to catch Anna as he tracked the course of the asteroid across the southern sky by zooming out at the right moment. "For a few seconds," he warned the female journalist, "you will be in the same frame as the fireball. So make sure you're wearing a suitable expression." Just what sort of expression would be appropriate for such an occasion was beyond Anna. But, trusting her instincts, she had no doubt that she would be able to make a good show of it when her moment came.

Following the practices normally adhered to when covering this sort of event, Vandergraff's team beamed a continuous feedback to their network's studio. There, a production manager synchronized reports and feeds being sent to him by a number of other teams located around the world. From his darkened control room in New York City, this production manager coordinated his teams, prompting them when he would be cutting to them and what he wanted each to address during their next on-air segment. In turn, the on-camera member of each team was privy to both image and audio that were being put out over the air. This permitted them to chat with each other as if they were in the same room, or to pick up a train of thought that had been initiated by someone else on the other side of the globe.

Besides Vandergraff's team in Siberia and the program anchor in New York, there were a noted astronomer, a professor of geology, and a Nobel-winning physicist in the New York studio with the network's own science-and-technology correspondent. From her office in Pasadena, an astronomer who worked for NASA provided an official view of the event. Elsewhere, various reporters with assigned beats such as the Pentagon, the White House, the UN, and other seats of authority stood ready to chime in should any statements of note at their location be released. And, of course, no coverage of a major event would be complete without the ubiquitous "man-on-the-street" interviews. In the case of this network, there were correspondents on the streets in New York City, Los Angeles, London, Moscow, and Tokyo, as well as in an auditorium at a local university and a high-school science class.

Vandergraff followed all of this from the monitor that was part of his electronics gear. Though he understood that his team was but one of many, he also appreciated the fact that if the Fates were kind to him, they would be the undisputed center of attention not only during the event, but later as fellow media types in search of people to fill airtime scrambled to interview him and his intrepid little crew. Not only were they part of the handful of trained observers who had "been there," but they were fellow media types in a nation where news anchors had become cult heroes and celebrities.

From the small earpiece that fed him audio, Vandergraff heard the production manager's cue: "Cutting to Siberia in five."

Quickly turning, the producer pointed to Roberts, then held five fingers up, dropping one almost instantly as he began his countdown. "In four, three—" The last two counts were silent hand signals.

When the image of Anna Roberts flashed on the screen of the television sitting on the bar of the Red Devil's Pub, she was a picture of composure. "Do you suppose she'd look as calm as she does," an American Navy SEAL asked his buddies, "if she knew we'd be descending upon the spot she's standing on in a few hours?"

A ripple of laughter went through the room that had been, for the most part, quiet. Few of the Special Ops types who had been assembled in Scotland for Tempest found they were unable to stay away from the television or radio now that the moment was at hand. Even those who could were unable to remain in their sleeping bags during the appointed hour, opting instead to work off their nervous energy by running laps around the quiet runway despite the cold, predawn drizzle that swept the RAF base.

By way of response, a Dutch marine belonging to the Amfibisch Verkennings Peloton snickered. "If you were getting what she's paid to be there, you'd be smiling, too."

With a Scottish accent that almost defied comprehension, a Royal Marine of the SBS, sitting next to his Dutch counterpart, called for silence. "I've been listening to you lads for days now. I'd like a chance to hear what the lass has to say. We might learn something."

Unable to let this go by without comment, an SAS sergeant took a parting shot at the red-haired Scotsman. "The only thing you're interested in learning from her, James, is her phone number."

Though this last was followed by a few chuckles, most of the men assembled in the Red Devil's Pub were concentrating on what Anna Roberts was saying: "As you can see," she stated loudly in order to be heard over the cold Siberian wind that whipped past her open mike and caused the ends of her scarf to flutter about, "there's not a cloud in the sky. I'm told that even if the asteroid does not follow the exact course that NASA has projected, we'll be able to see it."

Cutting back to the studio, the image of an immaculately dressed and well-polished man, seated behind the anchor's desk, flashed across the screen. "I can clearly see that you're being buffeted by the wind where you are. Just how cold is it there?"

Though she understood that the anchor was simply marking time until the asteroid began its final approach, his insipid question bothered Roberts. She was there to cover the story of the century, she told herself as she hesitated, not the local weather. Still, she did her best to hide her annoyance, to muster up the best smile she could, and to deliver an appropriate answer. "I was told, as we set off this morning to reach this site, that the thermometer was well below freezing, with little prospect of rising much beyond that throughout the course of the day. That means that a great deal of this past winter's snow is still on the ground, giving Russian officials here a great deal of concern."

"How so?" the warm, comfortable anchor in New York asked, trying to make it sound as if he really cared.

"In advance of the shock wave that the impact of the asteroid will generate," Anna stated matter-of-factly, "a heat wave will sweep over an extensive area at the speed of light. I am told that this phenomenon will be capable of igniting trees as far away as twenty miles or more from ground zero. This could result in flash floods throughout this region, not unlike those that the residents of the State of Washington experienced after the eruption of Mount Saint Helena." Pausing, Anna Roberts motioned toward the river below. "As turbulent as that river is now," she stated, "by this afternoon, it will be many times as wide, and choked with debris and shattered trees."

Cutting back to the New York City studio, the production manager caught the anchor making an expression that showed concern. "I hope," the well-polished anchor stated with as much sincerity as he could muster, "that you will be safe where you are."

Anna gave the camera a brave smile as she turned to face it. "I can assure you, Jerry, we will be out of harm's way long before there may be any danger."

The New York anchor was about to launch into a new series of burning questions when he was cued that the time had arrived. "Anna," he announced in a deep voice, "I've just been told that the asteroid is about to come into contact with the upper atmosphere. Can you see anything yet from where you are?"

By the time the production manager switched the views being sent out to the TV network's audience, Antonio Hablas had already pivoted about and trained his camera on the point in the sky where Tim Vandergraff had been told the asteroid would first become visible. The moment of truth, for so many people in so many different ways, was at hand.

Turning toward the southwest, Antonio Hables zoomed his camera out so he would have the widest possible field of vision while he searched for the asteroid through the panoramic lens. For her part, Anna Roberts turned to her left and watched, ever mindful that at any moment she would be part of an image beamed around the world to countless millions of television viewers. Tim Vandergraff, who had selected the site and had done so much to convince his superiors that his team was going to be the one for viewers to follow, stood next to their vehicle, nervously waiting. For the first time in hours, the headphones he wore over one ear were silent as journalists, editors, anchors, experts, and everyone who was on the World News Network loop held their breath.

From the studio in New York, one of the astronomers looked up at the clock across from him and cleared his throat. "If our calculations are correct," he stated in a guarded tone, "the asteroid should already be cutting into the upper layers of the atmosphere."

This statement caught the production manager off guard. Scanning the row of monitors before him, he saw nothing. "Vandergraff," he snapped. "Do you have anything yet?"

Anxiously, Vandergraff looked over at his cameraman. Having heard the same question in his earphone, Hablas glanced over his shoulder at Vandergraff. With a shake of his head, Hablas indicated that he was seeing nothing. Despite the cold, Tim Vandergraff now began to feel sweat running down his forehead. Had he erred, he began to wonder.

Like all projections and estimates, the incoming track of Nereus 1991 HWC was little more than an educated guess. It was a well-studied and frequently revised prediction, but it was still a guess, using calculations based upon measurements that were in themselves only guesses.

As so often happens when man attempts to define something as random and chaotic as nature, Nereus 1991 HWC did not cooperate with the earthbound experts. Like a stone hitting a smooth millpond, a major chunk of the shattered asteroid ricocheted off the upper layer of the atmosphere. It wasn't a very big hop. Rather, it was more of a burble. But it was enough of an interruption on the otherwise smooth and steady flight to alter the asteroid's angle of arrival and its speed. The new track, occurring as the asteroid traveled at a rate of twenty kilometers per second, took every astronomer who was watching by surprise. And though they endeavored to record, analyze, and input this new data into revised predictions, the speed of events outpaced their abilities.

While he had seen the computer-generated images of what the asteroid would look like as it bore down on planet Earth, Hablas was still unsure of what, exactly, to look for. Vandergraff wasn't much help here, having been born and raised in a city where flickering streetlights and not twinkling stars decorated the night sky. From her spot, Anna Roberts joined in scanning the southeastern sky. But her assistance in this search was limited since she needed to keep one eye on the camera at all times, just in case it turned on her. Not even their Russian guide, a native of the region, was of much help at the moment, though his problem was more a result of the vodka he was all but inhaling rather than his lack of visual-acuity skills.

Back in the control room in New York City, where it was just after midnight local time, the production manager was feeling the effects of stress and uncounted cups of coffee. "What in hell is going on out there?" he snapped. Though he didn't preface this question with the name of a site as he usually did, no one had any doubt that he was directing the inquiry to Vandergraff. When his team leader in Siberia said nothing and he saw no indication of anything even remotely looking like an asteroid on the screen labeled "Siberia," the production manager pivoted about and began to pace in the close confines of his small domain. "Does anyone have anything?" he pleaded over his open mike.

Had he been paying attention to his monitors, the harried coordinator of the live news show would have noticed that the chair in which the NASA expert in Pasadena had been seated was shoved to one side and empty. An even closer examination would have revealed a flurry of activities in the background, where a number of NASA astronomers were scrambling to sort out the alarming new data that was flowing in.

In Siberia, Anna Roberts felt a sudden chill, the kind of chill brought on by an inexplicable feeling of insecurity stemming from a danger that is perceived but not yet visible. Though ever conscious that she was standing in front of a live camera, she slowly turned her head this way, then that, in an effort to see if she could find the source of her vague uneasiness. While Vandergraff and Hablas scanned the distant southwestern sky, Roberts searched the area around them.

With the exception of the Russian guide, who was far too drunk to pose anything resembling a threat, Anna saw nothing amiss. This immediately caused her fertile imagination to conjure up all sorts of threats, ranging from Russian internal-security forces creeping up on them, to predatory animals in search of their next meal. It was only when her body's natural responses overrode her sophisticated logic that the source of this inexplicable discomfort became obvious.

Craning her head back ever so slightly so as not to look silly on the camera should she be in its field of view, the veteran TV journalist stared out along the crest of the ridge they were on and off to the west. It took her only a moment to realize that the glowing orange ball hanging in the sky above the ridge was, in fact, the very asteroid they had been sent to watch. It took another second or two for her to realize that the aspect of the asteroid, as she had been prepared for, was all wrong. For one thing, there was no tail, no long streak of burning gases and molten material trailing the intruder. Only bits and pieces peeled away from its surface as it sliced through the ever denser atmosphere. And the object didn't seem to have any apparent motion, not at first. It simply appeared to be hanging there, like the gigantic glowing ball that hangs over Times Square on New Year's Eve. It was all very odd to the journalist, as well as disconcerting. Still, she managed to find enough of her voice to warn her cameraman. "Pan right, Antonio," she whispered. "To your right and—"

At that moment, as the cameraman was in the act of complying with her order, Anna Roberts knew why things weren't making sense. What she was watching was not an asteroid harmlessly streaking through the sky in the distance. Rather, the ever-expanding ball of fire before her eyes was the very object they had been sent to capture on live TV, now bearing down on them with all the relentlessness of a locomotive.

Back in New York, a vigilant member of the production staff saw the camera held by Antonio Hablas in faraway Siberia suddenly swing about to the right, then fix upon a tiny red dot in the sky. Even before the cameraman was able to zoom in on the object, the staffer switched the feed going out to the audience to the one he himself was watching. "That's it!" someone yelled, catching the pacing production manager off guard.

"What?" he shouted as he turned to see what everyone about him was jumping up and down about. "Who told you to send that out?" he demanded before he took the time to consider what his staff was looking at.

"Vandergraff's team!" an excited assistant editor

answered. "They've got it! They're tracking the asteroid!"

Relieved and thinking clearly now, the production manager swung into action. "Okay, boys and girls, we're in business. Is everyone seeing this?" he asked, fighting the excitement that gripped everyone around him. "Anna!" he all but shouted into his mike, "say something. Start talking."

On the other monitors, anyone who cared to look would have seen the New York anchor, the experts in the studio, and countless others scattered about the globe who had a World News Network camera on them, turn away from the camera before them and cast their eyes upon the nearest TV monitor. In silence, they watched as the asteroid grew larger, more distinct, and ominously closer with each passing second. Only in the control room of the production manager did anyone speak. "Harry," the manager snapped, "check the audio. Make sure we're getting a good feed from Siberia."

With a quick scan, the audio tech in New York saw that all was in order at his end and in Siberia. "All systems are go and live, boss," he replied as he fought the urge to turn away from his own battery of instruments and join in watching the descent of the asteroid.

Again the production manager barked into his mike. "Anna. Vandergraff. Someone say something. Anything!"

For the longest time, the production manager heard nothing over the earphone of his headset that fed him audio from the various journalists, experts, and people chosen to be interviewed. There was not even the crackle of static. Just an unnerving silence as everyone held their breath and watched.

From one of the live feeds, the words, "Dear God in heaven," finally broke the silence. No one knew who had spoken those words, but the sentiment expressed by that one person reached several of the experts almost simultaneously.

Not yet attuned to what those experts were seeing, the production manager turned to an assistant. "What? What's going on?" he called out, first to those around him, then to people scattered about in various locations. "What's going on? Anna? Tim? Anyone? What's going on out there?"

Though the team in Siberia heard the frenzied words of the production manager, none of them replied. Anna, now totally unconcerned with what Antonio was doing with the camera, reached up and pulled her earphone out without taking her eyes from the growing fireball that was growing nearer. The cameraman, who had always asked himself the question of what he would do in a no-win situation, struggled to maintain his composure as he tracked the progress of the asteroid now bearing down on him. For his part, Tim Vandergraff stood transfixed. The thoughts that passed through his mind before he died would never be known, but winning a Pulitzer was probably not one of them. Only their Russian guide, far too inebriated to appreciate what was going on, met death with anything resembling serenity.

In the Red Devil's Pub, the sudden loss of picture announcing that a large chunk of the asteroid had impacted was met with a stony silence. As at the news network itself, several seconds passed before anyone in the room managed to speak. "Well," a solemn Navy SEAL quipped, "looks like the media pool just got a little less crowded."

Though every man gathered in Red Devil's had seen people die, and reveled in the graveyard humor they all used to soften that brutal experience, no one laughed, no one offered a retort. Instead, one by one, each of the highly trained killers stood up, turned his back on the blank screen and walked away, wondering if he would be the next to be called upon to face death.

9

For twelve hours after the primary impact of Nereus 1991 HWC, the remnants of the asteroid continued to rain down on central and eastern Siberia. Like the first major chunk of cosmic debris, those bits and pieces that followed refused to adhere to the predictions of the experts, leaving the Russian leadership in a quandary.

The shock wave generated by the fragment that had killed the World News Network crew had not yet finished running its course before a lively debate in Moscow broke out over what to do. Some members of the Russian security council favored additional evacuations of civilians from the area, now defined by an expanded footprint. Others pointed out that the means to organize and effect those evacuations didn't exist. Even if they did, as the Minister of Defense pointed out, there was no way of knowing for sure if the people they reached were being moved away from danger or being placed in harm's way. In the end, the paralysis created by this debate ate up what little time authorities on the spot had, leaving them no option other than to simply urge the populace in that new danger zone to seek the best shelters available and ride out the storm.

Not everyone in Moscow was dumbstruck into inactivity while the rest of the nation was reeling from the disaster then unfolding in the eastern province. At a military airfield chosen for its remoteness, Colonel Demetre Orlov slowly made his way down the line of commandos who stood at attention in full combat gear, patiently awaiting inspection by their commanding officer. At a time when most units within the Russian Army had no discipline to speak of, Orlov insisted on maintaining the most rigid standards that he dare impose. Though this created a palpable degree of coolness between him and his men, it left no doubt in anyone's mind as to who was in charge. Besides, Orlov found that the gulf that separated him from his men due to his policies and manner permitted him to view both their abilities and loyalties objectively. Far too often he had watched as senior officers found themselves in difficult straits because they had allowed feelings of camaraderie with subordinates cloud their judgment. Faced with the sort of missions that were routinely assigned him, as well as his concerns over individual loyalties that were never far from his mind, a lapse in judgment, for any reason, was the last thing the Russian colonel needed.

The aloofness that Orlov jealously guarded did not leave him lacking in an understanding of the men under his command. He knew which of his soldiers were crack shots, and who were the most nimble. He knew who had to have everything expected of them explained in great detail, and who had the mental agility to grasp complex situations and concepts quickly. As he slowly went from man to man, Orlov regarded each of his soldiers with the same critical eye. Yet there were some he passed with nothing more than a quick once-over and a nod, while stopping before others and checking their every piece of equipment and weaponry. No one complained about this inequity. That was not because complaining in this unit would do no good, which was true. Rather, each of the men Orlov was looking at understood that they were only a piece of the whole, a single cog in a complex machine. They also understood that not every man was the same, that there wasn't a man among them who had at his command all of the talents necessary to deal with every situation they were expected to face. So a man who was a bit slow mentally was tolerated because he had the brawn to shoulder the heaviest loads. And no one made fun of the man who wore glasses but was an absolute whiz when it came to dealing with electronics.

Pausing before one of his more outspoken soldiers, Orlov took time to tighten a strap on the man's harness that he thought was too loose. As he retained his ramrod posture of attention, the soldier gazed over his commander's shoulder off into the distance. Though the sun had disappeared below the western horizon hours before, the eastern sky still glowed with bright hues of red and orange. This caused the soldier to smile. "It has always been said that you would one day lead us all straight to hell, Colonel. I just never thought that day would actually come."

Without looking up from the strap he was adjusting, Orlov replied, "You are an atheist, Stephonich. What could you possibly know of hell?"

"I am a practical man, Colonel. I know that on this earth of ours, there are some places that are said to be paradise, and other places that are not so nice. While I never expected to visit the paradise so many of our leaders promise they will one day lead us to, I was hoping to avoid those other places."

Finished, Orlov stood upright and faced the soldier. "If that is so, why did you volunteer for this unit?"

This caused the Russian commando's smile to broaden. "I suppose I am a bit insane."

"Yes, well, if you must know, I think we are all a bit touched," Orlov remarked as he turned away.

"Tell me, Colonel," the soldier said, not letting the terse conversation end there, "are we being sent by the chief inmates of our asylum to kill other wretched souls like ourselves? Or have the sane people out there gotten out of hand?"

Unable to pass up this challenge, Orlov backpedaled and faced the soldier again. "Be sure to watch your step when we leave here, Stephonich. It is a dangerously narrow line that you will be walking."

The commando locked eyes with his commander. He knew that the colonel was not speaking of those hazards that are normally associated with an active military airfield. Realizing that he had pushed his luck as far as he dare, the soldier nodded. "Yes, sir. Of course, sir."

As he continued his inspection, Orlov was haunted by the analogy that Stephonich had chosen to use, for even the most dedicated officer he knew considered their struggle to protect the current regime to be illogical. "While we mock those in the Kremlin and call them clowns," a general had casually remarked to Orlov during an unguarded moment, "I believe it is we who are the fools. After all, are we not the ones who are keeping them in power?" Orlov himself entertained such sentiments, making his current mission all the more difficult since he was being sent to eliminate the one man whom soldiers like himself considered to be Russia's last best hope for salvation. Hesitating before continuing his precombat inspections, he looked off at the red eastern sky. Red had always been the color of revolution. It had always been his favorite color. Was this, he wondered, a sign? Perhaps the doomsayers were right. Could it be that the advent of the asteroid was not a disaster, but rather, the harbinger of a second coming, the beginning of a new era of revolution and a rebirth of the Soviet Empire? What a shame, he found himself thinking, to be on the wrong side of that monumental event.

Bowing his head, Orlov tried to clear such thoughts from his mind. This was not the time to entertain foolish speculation, he told himself. He had a mission. He had his orders. But as he straightened up and glanced off into the east again, he found that none of his doubts had subsided. Perhaps his mission and his orders were not one and the same. Perhaps the paradise Stephonich spoke of in a half-joking manner lay just beyond the hell into which he would soon be going. Perhaps all that was necessary to reach that paradise was the courage to do what was right, and not that which was expected.

SCOTLAND
18:05 HOURS ZULU, APRIL 8

By early evening, it had become obvious that the worst-case scenario the American Central Intelligence Agency and the British MI 5 had feared was in play. Both agencies, through their contacts within Russia and via electronic surveillance of the Russian strategic command-and-control nets, independently came to the same conclusions.

The impact of the primary asteroid at 05:34 Greenwich mean time, followed quickly by a succession of blows delivered to the Siberian region of Russia by fragments of Nereus 1991 HWC, had alerted the Perimeter sensors to the fact that the Motherland was being rocked by a cataclysmic event. This, coupled with a disruption of the national command-and-control network, had initiated the sequence of events that freed field commanders within the Strategic Rocket Force from the fail-safe system controlled from Moscow.

Though military communications had not been affected to the same degree as the civil system had been, the resulting disarray caused the leadership in Moscow to resort to radio and satellite communications rather than to use the more secure landlines that most senior officials in Russia preferred. This reliance on networks that broadcast over the airwaves gave intelligence agencies in the West a glut of information on just about everything that was going on both in Moscow and in Siberia. In some cases, the speed of the CIA's decryption equipment was able to pass messages intercepted and decoded to their analysts before the addressee in Russia was privy to it.

Intelligence, of course, is not an end in itself. It is only a window through which one can freely view the actions and activities of another. More often than not, the picture generated by these captured bits and pieces is not complete. Almost always, the actual intent of the parties observed from afar by electronic means is obscure. It is like walking into a conversation concerning a matter you have no first-hand knowledge of, and having to leave before the parties involved have come to a resolution. It is left up to the analysts to fill in the pieces that are missing and place the pirated message within its proper context and purpose. Quite naturally, the skill of the analyst and the willingness of his superiors to accept the conclusions he derives from the puzzle pieces handed to him for interpretation are critical to this process. In the end, it is the person who has assumed the mantle of command, whether he be a battalion commander in the field or the current occupant of the Oval Office, who must decide how to use the information at his disposal.

Intelligence provides the reason and the target. Plans define the means and the mechanics. But, unlike a machine, these plans never remain fixed or static. This is especially true of plans that are thrown together on the spur of the moment. No matter how gifted the creator of the original draft is, even the best plan can be improved upon. In addition, it is often necessary to make concessions when dealing with allies. Some ideas brought to the table by non-U.S. participants were, in the overall scheme of things, quite beneficial. Others were included in Tempest for no reason other than to gain the support of those nations being asked to pony up some of their best troops for the operation.

As a seasoned staff officer, Major Andrew Fretello understood the rules of the game. He knew that as soon as other NATO planners were brought onboard, they would insist on putting their own imprint upon the plan. In the name of maintaining peace among the world's foremost warriors, Fretello would have to accept a certain amount of give. Thus he found himself engaging in ceaseless revisions to Tempest as a blizzard of changes and alterations were handed down to him by his superiors.

One of the first changes to his plan came as soon as the NATO tasker for aircraft was put out. In Fretello's original plan, each team being inserted would have its own aircraft. This wishful bit of thinking was turned down without a second thought. As an alternative to one aircraft per team, Fretello suggested that the three teams assigned per target would share an aircraft. While this would require the pilot of the transport to make a series of quick turns in a very short period, it would reduce the number of aircraft required for Tempest by two thirds.

This change had no sooner been agreed to by the Military Airlift Command and penciled in by Fretello, when a representative of the intelligence staff pointed out that aircraft slated to carry relief aid into Russia could be used to drop the Special Ops teams as part of their deception plan. In this way, the intelligence officer pointed out, NATO would not be in the difficult position of justifying unscheduled overflights to the Russians. Though the staff judge advocate assigned to the joint planning staff for Tempest worried that using medical supply aircraft as troop carriers could be considered a violation of the Geneva Convention, his concerns were overridden. This change now meant that Andrew Fretello and the Air Force major working with him had to plot new air routes from Scotland into Russia that would permit the dual-purpose transports to overfly their special targets before continuing on to an airfield where relief aid was being sent, without raising undue suspicion.

Not every change to Tempest was greeted with a collective groan by Fretello and those working with him to keep the plan from becoming any more complex and risky than it already was. One addition to the plan actually turned out to be to his liking.

While it is quite easy for the chair-borne warriors who populate the Pentagon, as well as for the planning staffs, to be cavalier when it comes to placing the soldiers of their armed forces at risk, the commanding officers of the units from which those men and women come are far less sanguine about putting their people in harm's way without a well-defined plan of extraction. The original concept of having the Special Ops teams make their way to un-defended rally points on their own after executing their tasks was met with a unanimous outcry from every troop commander as soon as he saw it. General Gérard Rougé, commanding officer of France's Commandement des Opérations Spéciales, demanded that command-and-control teams be included in the plan. "The days of dropping French soldiers behind enemy lines without a practical means of extracting them," he stated with a firmness that left no doubt that his point was nonnegotiable, "ended with the fall of Dien Bien Phu." Rougé pointed out that these command-and-control elements were necessary to give his soldiers, as well as those being sent by other NATO nations, a fighting chance to survive once their targets had been destroyed. Under his plan, these command-and-control elements would serve as rally points for the teams, coordinate impromptu actions to assist teams that found themselves in trouble, and coordinate the extraction of the teams from their assigned area of operations.

Without exception, this sentiment was echoed by every senior commander tasked to provide troops for Tempest. It was, as were many of the operational details, left to Fretello to come up with a way of satisfying this new requirement without creating a top-heavy command structure. His guidance for tackling this particular change was simple. "Come up with an organization that can get the job done with the fewest possible number of people using the least amount of equipment."

As a practical matter, Fretello recommended that the personnel needed to populate these command-and-control teams be drawn from the staff already gathered at the RAF base in Scotland. This had several advantages that he knew would appeal to his superiors. First, it would save time, a consideration that was always critical in military operations. Second, it would use people already dedicated to Tempest as support personnel. "Once the strike teams are airborne," Fretello pointed out, "everyone left back on the ground in Scotland is out of a job." That this included himself was not overlooked by the young major or his superiors. This provided the third, and by far the most important, reason to Fretello for using on-hand personnel.

While he didn't expect to have a great deal to do as the executive officer of one of the forward operation's command-and-control teams, or FOCCT's for short, at least he would finally participate in a combat jump. When this matter was brought up by Colonel Hightower, who was serving as both the senior U.S. Army troop commander for Tempest and chief of the combined Special Operations staff, Fretello appealed to his warrior ethics. "For fifteen years, sir, I have accepted every assignment and duty without hesitation or complaint. When I was not tagged to go to the Persian Gulf in ninety-one, I did not despair. When I was told that it was more important for the Army that I stay at Leavenworth and finish my course in advanced military studies while my contemporaries were being rushed off to defend Taiwan, I swallowed my pride and soldiered on. To miss this opportunity to earn my pay as a soldier would be intolerable."

Hightower patiently listened to Fretello's plea. "You realize, Major," the colonel finally replied, "that officially, this operation will never have taken place. If this goes off the way you've planned it, there will be no campaign ribbon for it. No one will be awarded a medal, a citation, or even get credit for his role in Tempest on his next evaluation report. So as far as your career is concerned, this will be little more than a shadow, nothing more."

Though he hoped that this wouldn't be true, Fretello understood what his commanding officer was saying. "If nothing else, sir," he acknowledged, "I'll be able to prove to myself that I have what it takes. Though that may sound selfish, not to mention a tad bit clichéd, it's how I feel."

Having experienced his share of disappointments during his own military career, Hightower nodded. "You understand," the colonel grumbled, "that this new assignment you've managed to create for yourself in no way relieves you of your current duties and responsibilities as the chief plans officer for the operation. You have a final briefing for all group and team commanders in less than two hours. So plan accordingly."

Though he tried hard not to, Fretello found himself smiling. "Yes, sir. Of course, sir," he responded out of habit. "Rest assured, everything is in order and ready to go in regard to the briefing."

In past training exercises, it had been the practice of Hightower to cool the ardor of his subordinates when they made bold claims such as this by responding with a terse comment such as, "It damned well better be," or "We'll see about that, *Major*." Colonel Hightower, however, was not in the mood for such theatrics at the moment. He would be making what he expected to be his last combat jump. Within a year, he would be relinquishing the command of his Special Forces group. After that, his career would forever take him away from the troops he so loved. There would be no more sudden deployments to places unknown. He would never again have the opportunity, not to mention the thrill and excitement, of pitting his skills and knowledge against impossible situations and wily foes. Though it would be at a much higher level, he would become a staff officer, just like the major before him.

With a simple, "That's all, Major," and a salute, Hightower dismissed Fretello. As soon as the anxious young staff officer had closed the door behind him, the colonel picked up the phone and dialed his home phone number. As the hour drew near, the time had come to say his farewell to the only person in the world whom he loved more than he loved the Army in which he served.

SCOTLAND
21:45 HOURS ZULU, APRIL 8

When Great Britain's Ministry of Defense was presented with the American plan for neutralizing Perimeter, there had been no question about supporting it. While many in the MoD had argued that their island nation would probably not be a target for the handful of missiles dedicated to the Russian doomsday system, the ramifications of any attack on a NATO nation, as well as the subsequent response by the United States, were clear. "Regardless of our personal feeling about the Americans and their rather unorthodox plan," the British Minister of Defense had pointed out, "we have no choice but to support Tempest. Not to do so would make the NATO charter meaningless at a time when it may be needed to protect Europe from a reenergized Russian bear."

This did not mean that the British accepted Tempest in its original form. Like the French, they had some serious reservations. Following General Gérard Rougé's lead, the British insisted upon changes that fit their national policies. And like their fellow European allies, the British were not ready to commit all of their "best and brightest" to this one operation. "Even if Tempest is a hundred-percent successful," the British Chief of Staff pointed out to the Minister of Defense, "we have no way of knowing what will transpire within Russia once all the dust there settles. We may very well need our Special Operations Forces to respond to a renewal of the Cold War."

In light of this opinion, it was decided that only a portion of Britain's Special Operations resources would be committed to Tempest. "Where possible," the Chief of Staff instructed his plans people, "utilize those personnel and elements within the SAS and SBS that are expendable."

When the Chief of the Imperial Staff issued this planning guidance to the officers in the MoD responsible for generating the troop list for Tempest, he did not have Captain Patrick Hogg's name in mind. Senior officers and decision-makers who are part of each nation's Security Council do not think in terms of actual people or personalities. They deal only with "units" or "elements," words that are not tied to faces, or spouses, or children. The commitment of a nation's sons and daughters to combat is hard enough without burdening those initiating the action with actual images of real people. By insulating themselves from the troops who will be sent forth to fight and die for their country, leaders at the national level are thus free to use the word "expendable" without evoking an undue flood of guilt or emotion.

That is how it came to be that Major Thomas Shields and his cadre at Hereford found themselves as part of the United Kingdom's contingent for Tempest, while many of the men they had trained and passed off to the various squadrons of the SAS stood by, idle.

Standing in the center of the three teams he was responsible for, Shields had to look into the eyes of the men who had been deemed expendable. Like Demetre Orlov, Shields knew everything there was to know about the soldiers gathered about him. Though he spent most of his time at Hereford fighting the good fight from a desk, he was not so far removed from the line that he could not read the men's expressions, their moods, or their feelings.

Having finished his briefing, Shields stood back from the table upon which a map of their area of operations lay and looked around. "As the American major stated in his briefing," he stated crisply, "once one of our three teams has placed its device on the silo's hatch, all it needs to do is to withdraw to a safe distance, transmit the standing-by code, and blow the missile to bits when the order to execute is given."

Despite his best efforts to put a positive spin on their mission, the grim expressions staring back at him told him that his men knew that things were not going to be as easy as that. Clearing his throat, Shields lowered his eyes back down to the map and continued: "It will be necessary to inspect the site after the dust and debris have settled, just to be sure that target effect has been achieved."

Hogg chose this moment to interrupt. "Sir, there's one thing I am not absolutely clear on. Does this confirmation mean that we must physically crawl up to the smoking hole in the ground and peek in? Or will we be able to use our best judgment in determining if the ICBM has been rendered non-operational?"

Looking over at the second most senior officer of his group and the leader of one of the teams, Shields nodded. "Yes, I see your point, Captain Hogg. Like you, I would expect that if the shaped charge does its job, there'll be a secondary detonation that will leave no doubt in anyone's mind that the missile has been, shall we say, deactivated."

"Blown to bloody hell is a better way to put it, sir," Hogg replied.

"Yes, of course," Shields acknowledged, doing his best to hide his displeasure over hearing one of his officers use language that he considered unnecessarily colorful. "I will leave it to the discretion of the team commander who is actually executing the target to make that determination. After all, we have all seen enough explosions in our collective lifetimes to be able to judge that sort of thing."

"Yes," Hogg mused as he stared down at the map. "I daresay we have."

Sensing that this was an appropriate time, Sergeant Kenneth McPherson asked a question that had been bothering him ever since they had left the mass briefing for all those with active roles in Tempest. "Sir, if you could, I would appreciate it if you would explain why it is that we are reporting to an American FOCCT team once we have completed dispatching the Russian missile?"

Seeing an opportunity to add a bit of humor to the otherwise grim session, Shields smiled. "That is a very good question, Sergeant McPherson. And as soon as someone explains it to me, I'll be more than happy to pass the reason on to you."

As expected, this generated a spate of chuckles. After allowing the moment to linger as long as he dare, Shields tried his best to provide his subordinate with a reasonable response. "As things were explained to me earlier today, it has to do with which teams are dropped in which areas. Where there is a predominance of one nationality in an area of operation, a Forward Operational Command-and-Control team, made up of personnel from that nation, has been created and charged with the responsibility for all teams within that area. We happen to be fortunate enough to have drawn a target that is in an area of operation populated mostly by Americans."

From across the table, McPherson smirked. "Three cheers for us, eh?"

A chorus of subdued guffaws and snickers rippled through the gathering. Enjoying the moment, Shields related how the commander of the French teams in their area reacted. "Yes, well, the commander of the CRAP team that will be knocking off the missile a few kilometers from ours was somewhat less friendly. Drawing himself erect, the French captain looked the American major who planned this operation, and who is also the deputy of the FOCCT in our area, right in his eyes. 'While I have no say, Major,' the Frenchman said, 'to whomever I report, I must insist that we bring our own rations. Facing the best the Russians have available to throw at them is something that my men will do without hesitation. The idea of having to subsist on your MRE's, however, is completely out of the question.' "

Whether it was the story itself or the manner in which their commander told it, every man present, including Hogg, broke out in uproarious laughter. "Did the French captain happen to say, sir," a corporal asked, "which wine they would be serving?"

Shields didn't miss a beat as he responded to this inquiry with a straight face. "Well, seeing as how we are going into Russia, I would assume that a nice red wine would be apropos."

Again a wave of laughter rippled through the group. Only when it was subsiding did Patrick Hogg attempt to get back to the briefing by pointing to a cluster of buildings marked on the map. "This complex, sir?" he asked in a rather offhanded manner. "Do we know for sure what it is? The German who gave the intel portion of the briefing glossed over it rather quickly."

Refocused on the operation, Shields looked at the

map, then over at Hogg. "It is assumed that this is where the headquarters and support facilities for the Strategic Rocket Force that all these missiles belong to is located."

This sobered up the balance of the assembled SAS men. Hogg considered the major's response for a moment before he continued. "Do we have any reliable idea on how many personnel are there, specifically security and ready-reaction forces?"

While he continued to stare down at the map to the spot that Hogg was asking about, Shields folded his arms. "No, I am afraid I an not privy to that information. As best I can tell, no one is certain of the strength of the security force there. While I expect that some of it will be drawn away to assist in disaster relief, you can be sure they'll leave someone back to mind the store."

Glancing up, the SAS major looked about. He saw the concern on each man's face. "Captain Hogg's point is an important one, one that we must bear in mind at all times. This operation is going to be no walk in the park. We are going into a foreign nation, defended by a force that has but one mission, and that is to defend the very targets we are being sent to destroy. Regardless of what is going on between Moscow and General Likhatchev, those Russian soldiers will defend those rockets with their lives. That's why the Americans insisted on sending three teams against each silo."

"Playing the odds," Sergeant McPherson murmured.

"That's right, Sergeant," Shields responded. "We're playing the odds. So stay alert, and stay focused. We've got but one chance to get this right."

"And if we don't?" Hogg asked.

Shields didn't answer that. He couldn't. Neither the briefings he had received nor his imagination could provide him with a suitable reply.

10

Operational plans, once initiated, have the habit of taking on a life of their own, going forward like a spirited charger carrying its rider into the heart of battle. In part, this is due to the warrior ethic. Since the days when men fought in dense phalanxes on the level plains of ancient Greece, the only honorable course of action once the advance was sounded was to press on until victory was achieved or the combatant was struck down. This philosophy was supported by the myth that a death in battle was a noble thing. To halt before locking shields with one's foe was a sign of weakness that could not be tolerated. To turn and run displayed abject cowardice, which could only be scorned.

As with most things, there is more to this than simple pride. In the days of Homer, turning one's back on an enemy was tantamount to suicide. Most casualties in battle were suffered when one side sensed that things were not going their way and opted to flee rather than continue the fight. In order to make good his escape, the fleeing warrior had to drop the heavy shield he carried, as well as the cumbersome pike that measured anywhere from twelve to sixteen feet long. This left him quite vulnerable to his pursuer.

The potential victor, on the other hand, was presented with a wonderful target, the backside of his enemy. Already fired up with the passions that close combat evokes, it was all but impossible to restrain those in the ranks of the triumphant phalanx. With a bloodlust in their hearts, the winners would rush forth, en masse, to slaughter all before them who were not quick enough to make good their escape. It was because of this practice that Spartan mothers sent their sons off to war with the admonishment, "Return with your shield, or upon it." Since only the victor retained his shield, Mom was basically telling Junior, "Don't you dare run away."

Warfare in the early twenty-first century bears no resemblance to that waged when Greece was the center of the civilized world. But the core philosophy that drives the men and women charged with defending the Western democracies has changed little from the citizen warrior who marched off to battle wearing a bronze cuirass and carrying a great round shield. A tread of continuity runs through the ages, tying the modern Green Beret to those proud Spartans. The Romans adopted the Greek philosophy of "victory or death," spreading it to the four corners of Europe during five hundred years of conquest. As the western Roman Empire faded from memory, the feudal knights who filled the void left by the disappearance of its legions continued the tradition, creating what came to be known as the "chivalric code." When the warlords of the Dark Ages became the great captains of the age of gunpowder, they discarded the armor of their ancestors but not their ethics and traditions. And when nation states rose to prominence and harnessed the energies of their professional soldiers, the code that those officers lived by was based on one that would have been understood by every citizen soldier of Hellenistic Athens.

The stubbornness with which modern warriors cling to such traditions is more than mere sentimentality or slavish dedication to an outdated code of conduct. Unlike most occupations, soldiers are expected to place themselves in harm's way. Neither pay nor benefits alone can induce a sane man or woman to engage in an activity in which death and destruction are anticipated. While every soldier prefers that the death and destruction resulting from the combat in which he engages is visited upon his foe and not himself, the likelihood that he will fall victim to the law of averages cannot be ignored.

Commanders throughout the ages have understood this. Every society that has had to engage in warfare, and history tends to point out that this pretty much includes all of them, has employed those methods that were both socially acceptable and effective in inducing their citizens to fight. Cave dwellers are believed to have created clans and rituals that challenged and tested the young men of their tribes before the aspiring youths were permitted to assume the rights, privileges, and duties of an adult male. Ancient Greeks and republican Romans tied the benefits of citizenship to the duty of bearing arms in the defense of the state. Land and privileges were bestowed upon feudal knights in return for military service to more powerful lords and kings. Frederick the Great implemented a system of discipline and punishment that he hoped would make his soldiers fear him and his appointed officers more than they feared the enemy they faced. And the colonial rabble of 1775 stood their ground against the best army in the world because they were fired up by the radicals of their day to believe in the righteousness of their cause.

In an era when there are no overwhelming threats or external dangers, when prosperity is the norm, and the profession of arms is viewed by the intellectual elite of the nation as a necessary evil to be tolerated but not encouraged, it is difficult to motivate young men and women to become soldiers. The best and the brightest who have an opportunity to attend college do so in order to become captains of industry, not infantry captains. Those entering the workforce straight out of high school, seeking freedom from the educational system and their parents, are not drawn to a profession that requires its members to submit to discipline, endure sacrifice, and adhere to a strict code of conduct. So it is surprising that the armed forces of the United States, as well as those of other Western democracies, actually find anyone to fill the ranks of their armies, man their ships, and maintain and care for their warplanes.

Filling the ranks is only the first hurdle that a modern peacetime army must overcome. Motivating those recruits to actually do what they are being paid to do in combat is something entirely different. To achieve this goal, every opportunity to instill the warrior ethic in the recruit is taken. At Fort Benning, Georgia, this conditioning takes the form of what is called "The Spirit of the Bayonet," which is not only the will to go toe-to-toe with the enemy and engage him in close combat, but the desire to do so. At the armor school at Fort Knox, Kentucky, the "Spirit of the Cav" lives on, imploring young soldiers and leaders of the mounted combat arm to close with and destroy their enemies by the use of fire, maneuver, and shock effect. While there are always a number of prospective soldiers who take to these philosophies with ease, others must work hard at overcoming years of social conditioning that tend to denigrate the traditional concepts of manhood. Some young men find they never can.

Those who do, enter into what the writer W. E. B. Griffith calls "The Brotherhood of War." It is an exclusive clique, one populated by people who take pride in themselves, their chosen profession, and their ability to accomplish their assigned missions no matter how difficult the task or adverse the conditions. Given an order, the modern soldier is expected to do as his ancestors had done generation after generation. The helmet and body armor may be different, but the attitude that motivates the modern warrior has changed little. Like his predecessors, he is trained to salute and press on, no matter the cost, until victory has been achieved.

In a democracy, the warrior is subordinate to politicians, who are guided by different ideals, who adhere to a set of standards that is often at odds with those of the professional soldier. Whereas an officer in the armed forces conducts most of his day-to-day business by issuing orders, democratic leaders achieve their goals through consensus. The popularity of the political figure, or of the program he or she is promoting, is critical. Politicians are skilled in making deals, mustering support from allies, and undercutting their opponents through the use of slander, half-truths, and spin. While they desire to win just as much as the soldier does, a political failure does not carry the same stigma that a military defeat does. The proof of this is borne out in the manner in which the media covers modern politics, turning it into a spectator's sport rather than the serious business of national security. None of this means that the politician is a lesser being, just as the pursuit of a military career does not mean that the professional soldier is a baby-killer. Each public servant, the politician and the soldier, operates in an environment that dictates adherence to certain rules and norms that must be followed if they expect to reach their respective goals.

Under the Constitution of the United States, the American military is subordinate to the popularly elected officials. It has always been this way in the United States and, with luck, always will be. Over two hundred years of operating under this system, however, does not mean that there are not problems. As would be expected when two diverse cultures come together to achieve a common goal, there are misunderstandings that lead to an occasional clash. Professional soldiers, who are appointed to their current rank and position solely on the basis of their previous success and achievements, oftentimes have difficulties in working out solutions with politicians, who know they must maintain their popularity if they hope to be reelected or receive favorable treatment by future historians. The blunt, direct language associated with a "victory or death" mentality tends to unnerve or anger men and women who twist the English language to soften the impact of unpopular measures or to hide the truth.

Another notable difference between these two groups of public servants is the manner in which they make decisions. The warrior, who embraces the philosophy of "victory or death," tends to view the world in terms of black and white. You succeed or you fail. It is that simple. Professional soldiers are comfortable with the idea that once spurred into action, they are expected to continue on, come what may. As one 7th cavalry officer once exclaimed as he rode off to his demise, "It'll be a bullet or a brevet for me."

Politicians, on the other hand, endeavor to conduct their affairs in a manner that permits them to keep their options open, allowing them to dodge that bullet at the last moment if things don't appear that they will work out as expected. Most elected officials and their representatives see no shame in reining in their charger or shying away from a head-on collision with a foe. It is, in fact, often touted as a virtue, demonstrating that the politician is a realist, willing to listen to reason and compromise. These differences do not make one superior to the other. It's simply the nature of the world to which each lives. During times of crisis, politicians can demonstrate the same dogged determination and courage of their convictions as a warrior does, just as the many senior generals who make up the Joint Chiefs of Staff often behave in a manner more befitting a politician.

History has recorded some very notable clashes between these two diverse positions. Douglas MacArthur lost his job when his solution to Chinese intervention in the Korean War went against the policies of Harry S. Truman. While John F. Kennedy listened to his military advisers during the Cuban missile crisis in 1963 and permitted them to prepare for a full-scale invasion of Cuba, in the end, he opted to use the military in a less confrontational manner. The conduct of the entire Vietnam War, from beginning to end, is rife with examples of the military seeking one solution while the President's advisers argued for another. When nothing stood between Stormin' Norman and the administration of a coup de grâce that would have meant the end of Saddam Hussein, his Commander in Chief did what the Iraq Republican Guard could not.

As the hour to execute Tempest drew near, the President's National Security Agency was called together. When General Eric Shepard and the other senior members of the Joint Chiefs of Staff entered the cabinet room, they were under the assumption that everything that had needed to be discussed had been. The only reason they thought they had been brought together was to provide the President's top advisers with a final update on the situation in Russia and to receive the official order to execute.

It therefore came as something of a shock when one of the National Security advisers opened the meeting by stating that the President was having second thoughts about Tempest. "In an effort to avoid the sort of criticism that they endured in the wake of the Kursk incident, the Russians have been quick to solicit assistance from Western nations, including NATO. When briefed on Tempest, the State Department was quick to point out that by the use of these disaster-relief flights to ferry ground troops into Russia, we will not only violate Russian territorial integrity and betray the trust and confidence of the Russian government, but could set in motion a chain of events that may well lead to the collapse of that government. The President has therefore instructed me to come back to you in order to determine if there is a less intrusive option, such as that previously proposed by the Air Force."

Before he could continue, General Smith slapped the polished tabletop with the flat of his hand. *"What?"*

Annoyed that he had been interrupted, the National Security adviser peered over his reading glasses and stared at Smith. "You heard me, General. The President is concerned that exercising the Tempest option could have serious repercussions, not the least of which are the casualties that would be associated with that operation."

"Begging your pardon, sir," Smith countered, "but *not* going through with this *will*, I daresay, result in serious repercussions."

While others sat back and watched in stony silence, Smith and the President's chief adviser began to shout at each other. "Even your own intelligence assessment states that the United States may not be targeted by the missiles under Likhatchev's control.

His disagreement, after all, is with Moscow, not with us."

"Mister Chaplin," Smith shot back, "we've been through this time and time again. A dispute in Russia, whether it is a limited affair or a full-blown civil war that results in the use of nuclear weapons, cannot be contained. In every war game and simulation we've run, eventually things get out of hand and the United States or one of its allies becomes a target."

"Those, General," Chaplin countered with uncharacteristic sharpness, "were just that, war game and simulation. This operation, the troops that will be executing it, and the damage they will create, are real. The President is not sure if he's ready to initiate a chain of events that may spin out of our control."

With each exchange, Shepard watched as Smith's face grew redder. Realizing that things would soon reach a point where he would be unable to restrain his outspoken subordinate, the Chairman intervened. "Mister Chaplin," Shepard stated crisply, "I am afraid we have reached a point where we no longer have the luxury of revisiting this issue. For one thing, once Tempest was adopted as the only practical course of action, all of our resources were funneled into supporting it. The Air Force has marshaled the aircraft necessary for an air strike, and the Navy has moved its carrier task force away from Russia. In short, sir, the only viable options we have left are to either proceed with Tempest or to do nothing."

Being careful to choose his words, the National Security adviser pursued Shepard's comments. "In a worst-case scenario, what is the cost of doing nothing?"

Shepard fought the temptation to roll his eyes. This had been gone over daily since the crisis had broken. Still, he could not resist the urge to snipe at the political appointee sitting across from him. "Worst case?" he asked rhetorically. "Worst case, the President loses five million constituents within the first twenty-four hours." The silence permeating the room as Shepard spoke was oppressive. "Within seven days, that number would triple as the wounded who are beyond help or unable to reach medical assistance died. After ten years, the number would double as a result of increased rates of cancer and birth defects."

Having been responsible for generating the numbers that the Chairman of the Joint Chiefs was laying out, the Chief of Staff of the Air Force added his thoughts. "The people, our fellow Americans, who die within the first few seconds of that holocaust would be the lucky ones, Mister Chaplin. Those who survive are the ones I pity."

Though the tone of the Air Force general's comments angered the National Security adviser, he held his tongue. When he saw that the senior officer in the Air Force did not seize the opportunity to revisit the plan that he had fought for so vehemently on previous occasions, the President's adviser realized that their options were limited to one. "Well, gentlemen, I appreciate your candor," Chaplin mumbled as he struggled to find a graceful way to extract himself from this discussion. "I will advise the Commander in Chief of your opinions and endeavor to get a decision from him soon."

Relieved that Tempest was not going to be scuttled at the last minute, Smith leaned back in his seat. As he ran his fingers along the edge of the table and stared at them, the Chief of Staff of the Army sighed. "When you do see the President, Mister Chaplin, please advise him that he doesn't have much time in which to make up his mind."

This comment caught everyone, including Smith's superior, off guard. "Well, how much time do we have?" the National Security adviser asked.

Slowly, Smith raised his arm and looked at his watch. "Exactly four hours and thirty-seven minutes, sir."

Having gone over the plan in detail, Shepard turned to face Smith. "What's so significant about that?"

Looking around the table at the President's key advisers, Smith shrugged. "Well, ladies and gentlemen, that is when the Tempest teams begin to exit over their targets."

"Wait a minute," the Air Force chief blurted. "It'll take longer than four and a half hours to reach their targets from Scotland."

Unable to resist, Smith sported the smile of a little boy who has just pulled off the perfect prank. "Yes, that's true, provided the aircraft are still in Scotland."

Shaken for the second time that evening, Shepard all but leaped out of his seat. "You mean you've launched Tempest?"

Facing his old friend, Smith nodded. "In your heart, Eric, you knew this would happen. You knew someone would get cold feet at the last minute. So I took the initiative."

Shocked by this revelation, the Chairman of the Joint Chiefs said nothing. Turning toward the National Security adviser, Smith glared at the equally dumbfounded man. "While we can always recall them, Mister Chaplin, I recommend that we don't. The time to act is now. The situation on the ground in Siberia is extremely chaotic. Both Likhatchev and Moscow are permitting international relief·agencies in, a factor critical to us since this will allow us to slip the military transports in with the Tempest teams without raising undue suspicion or concern." Smith paused, looking around at the other members of the Joint Chiefs. "There is not a person here,

Mister Chaplin, who can guarantee that this window of opportunity will remain open. If I were Lik-hatchev, as soon as I had the ability to exercise my authority over the region, I'd start making trouble. While I regret having taken this matter into my own hands, I believe we cannot wait for this to happen. The sooner we de-fang the bastard, the sooner we will be able to settle down to the serious business of rendering aid and assistance to the victims of the asteroid strike, as well as propping up the government in Moscow."

From the back of the room, where the straphangers stood huddled about watching the tumultuous proceedings, a voice broke the ensuing silence. "Thy will be done."

Looking down at his notebook, Eric Shepard finished that thought by adding, "Amen."

With that, the meeting broke up as the participants scattered to the various places from where they would sit out the next few hours and watch, listen, wait, and pray.

11

The task assigned Colonel Demetre Orlov and his men was both simple and straightforward. It was not unlike a dozen or so other missions they had been assigned before. Even with the knowledge that they would be arriving over their target in the wake of a natural disaster unlike anything known to man, the Russian colonel did not let this minor point dominate either his planning or his preparations. There were other, more practical matters that he needed to concern himself with, such as the prevailing weather and the lie of the land, elements over which even the most gifted commander had no influence. Since the Russian colonel could not pick the timing of his assignment, he was obliged to accept the conditions on the ground as they existed when he arrived in the area of operations.

Relying on the best information his nation's foremost experts could supply, he came to the conclusion that the disruption created by the asteroid would do little more than add another element of difficulty to the operation, which would have to be mastered, just as would the armed resistance they would face. Of course, neither he nor the trained experts who had advised him had imagined the true magnitude of the devastation that Orlov's special-response team would face as it sought to bring additional death and destruction to selected inhabitants of the region.

The fallacies of using the Tunguska event as a model from which to estimate damage projections quickly became obvious to all. Unlike the asteroid that struck Siberia in 1908, Nereus 1991 HWC hit the earth like a shotgun blast, scattering multiple fragments through the region in a random manner. Unlike the pellets spewed forth by a shotgun, each of Nereus 1991 HWC's fragments were different. No two pieces weighed the same, were shaped alike, or hit the atmosphere at the same angle. Some of the larger fragments, like the chunk that took out the World News Network team, made physical contact with the earth's surface. These strikes shattered the earth's crust, sending shock waves through the tectonic plates across the region and beyond. While the ground itself was being shaken to the core, millions of cubic tons of dirt and debris, something to the tune of one hundred times the weight of each asteroid fragment that struck, gouged out impact craters, hurling the spoils into the upper atmosphere. Huge amounts of this material was captured by the jet stream, which whisked it away to the east, from where it would either return to earth in Asia or continue on across the Pacific and blanket North America. Some of the superheated debris that was too heavy to be held aloft by the winds fell back to earth, igniting monumental fires.

Not every particle of the asteroid was able to complete its supersonic journey through the dense air of the lower atmosphere. When the extreme heat created by friction became more than a fragment could absorb, it would literally explode, unleashing a burst of energy comparable to the detonation of a nuclear device in midair. Known as airbursts, these events lit up the sky with a fireball that was, for the briefest of moments, more brilliant than the sun itself. Though measured in milliseconds, each touched off a conflagration that devastated the surrounding countryside. Depending on the altitude at which the explosion took place, everything within the tight circle that comprised the zone of total devastation, known as ground zero, was simply incinerated. A bit farther out, all combustible material, including the clothing of those souls unfortunate enough to be caught in the open, burst into flames. The retinas of human and animal alike, those impulsively drawn to view the spectacle, fried as skin and hair were scorched, burned, and destroyed. The lucky died quickly. Those who survived were left to endure indescribable pain and agony, with little or no hope of salvation or relief.

As catastrophic as this was, the shock waves that followed both the airbursts and surface impacts proved to be even more devastating. Traveling at hundreds of miles an hour, trees, structures, and even rock formations, were bowled over, uprooted, or simply crushed. In some cases, fires started by the tremendous release of thermal energy were extinguished by this overwhelming blast of air. That condition, however, was only momentary. With the passing of the shock wave, new fires created by the rupturing of fuel tanks, oil and gas lines, and structures erupted in its wake.

As if all of this were not enough, the sudden release of thermal energy turned the deep snow and thick ice that blanketed the region into billions of cubic gallons of water that needed someplace to go. Within mere minutes, every river in the region was choked with broken trees, tons of soil scoured away by the fury of the onslaught, the remains of buildings, homes, and other assorted structures. Unable to handle this sudden influx of melted snow and ice, the rampaging torrents cut new channels and avenues of escape, changing the landscape forever.

The earth and the creatures who lived upon it were not the only victims of this calamity. The heavens themselves were transformed. Not all of the ice and snow was sent rampaging. Some of it had been vaporized and drawn up into the sky, where it mixed with the dirt, soot, and debris kicked up by blast, impact, and shock wave. Violent drafts of wind and sweeping gusts swirled about as dense black clouds of dirt and ash blanketed Siberia. These dense clouds, pierced by lightning bolts, touched off violent storms that pelted the region with black rain and ash. In some places, breathing without self-contained respirators was all but impossible. The filters on protective masks clogged within minutes of exposure to the worst of these conditions. When one damage-assessment team emerged from its fallout shelter to commence the grim task of measuring the devastation, it was all but wiped out within minutes. The sole survivor of the team, an officer who had never before lifted his voice in prayer, crawled back into the bunker, where he managed to scrawl in a notebook, "God, why have you forsaken us?" as he lay dying alone on the floor.

It was into this hell on earth that Demetre Orlov's special-response team flew. Even before they reached their designated drop zone, it became clear to the Russian colonel that his initial plan to make a drop, under the cover of darkness, right into the compound where General Likhatchev had his command bunker would be all but impossible. Buffeted by turbulence that knew no rhyme or reason, it took every bit of skill possessed by the transport pilots to simply keep their aircraft aloft. A jump into the conditions below would have been suicidal.

One of the favorite truisms of the military is that a plan never survives initial contact with the enemy. Making adjustments to match changes in circumstances is often a military necessity. Good commanders take the unexpected in their stride. Gifted ones use them to their advantage. Sometimes, however, changes in the conditions encountered are so radical that even a military genius is at his wits' end to find a solution.

Like the ancient mariner condemned to wander the seven seas with an albatross about his neck, the command pilot of Orlov's transport roamed the devastated region in search of someplace where he could deposit his cargo of Russian commandos. With the primary drop zone ruled out, the secondary selection just as unacceptable, and the clearing that had been the third choice now turned into a debris-clogged lake, the pilot had no choice but to report to Orlov that he had exhausted his options.

During a hasty conference in the cramped confines of the lead transport's cockpit, Orlov scanned the maps with the aircraft's navigator. "We have no way of knowing," the frustrated Air Force officer explained to Orlov, "what the conditions are on the ground. We've already seen how useless these maps are."

Frustrated, the Russian commander grunted. "There must be someplace where you can deposit us?"

The navigator shook his head. "Putting you down? Yes, we can do that, Colonel. But putting you close to your target . . . well, that is another matter."

"You must put my men near their target as a unit," Orlov explained. "We have no means of ground transportation."

Looking up from his map, the navigator studied Orlov's face for a moment. "May I ask, Colonel, if I was able to get you to where there was ground transportation, would you have the authority to procure it?"

Understanding what the Air Force officer was saying, Orlov nodded. "What I lack in authority, I can more than make up for with audacity."

"Good!" the navigator exclaimed as he flipped the map over to reveal a wider area of Siberia. "There is an airfield located here," he said, pointing at a spot on the map, "reporting that it is open for the reception of relief aid."

"Exactly how far is that from our initial drop zone?" Orlov asked, studying the map for a moment before reaching over the shoulder of the navigator and turning it over in an effort to gauge the distance his team would need to cover.

The navigator allowed the colonel to finish his cursory inspection of the map before lying it down on his small desktop in order to make precise measurements. Finished, he turned to face Orlov. "I make the straight-line distance to be thirty kilometers."

"What about actual distance via road?"

The navigator shook his head. "Like everything else about this trip, Colonel, we have no way of knowing for sure. I would suspect that the conditions of the roads and bridges, if either are still there, are not much better than the foul weather we have been battling or the drop zones we have had to bypass."

Again, Orlov grunted. "I see no other choice. Do you?"

Locking eyes with the commander, the navigator

considered his answer. While neither he nor the pilot had any idea of what Orlov's mission was, the Air Force officer had little doubt that aborting it and turning back was not an option open to the colonel. If that were true, then the navigator appreciated the fact that none of them had a choice. "Then it is decided?" he asked.

Orlov nodded. Not wanting to bother the pilot, who needed to concentrate on controlling his aircraft as it plowed through the turbulent skies, the Russian commander issued his instructions to the navigator: "Inform the pilot of our decision. And tell him not to announce our intent to land at that airfield until the very last second."

"What if they insist that we state our purpose in landing there, or demand to know what cargo we are carrying?" the navigator inquired.

The question was a good one, Orlov thought, demonstrating that the Air Force officers he was dealing with were aware that the mission of the commandos they were transporting required a great deal of discretion. "Make up a story," the commander finally answered. "I am told that pilots are very good at that."

For the first time in hours, the navigator smiled. "Yes, that is true. I have heard that we are almost as good, Colonel, as your commandos."

"I hope for your sake," Orlov responded, "that today you are better."

WESTERN SIBERIA, RUSSIA
03:54 HOURS ZULU, APRIL 9

Were it not for his watch telling him that it was late afternoon, Demetre Orlov would have sworn it was midnight. The airfield where the two transports carrying his assault team had landed was shrouded in a surreal darkness created by forest fires that raged all about the area and debris that had been catapulted into the heavens by the violent impacts of Nereus 1991 HWC.

Like the countryside around it, the airfield was a shambles. There wasn't a single structure that had not been stripped of its roof or sported an intact window. Many of the base's administrative and support facilities were burning. Where members of the garrison were seen to be active, Orlov noticed that they were more intent on salvaging essential items and stores from the devastation than on battling the numerous fires. "We have no water pressure," a young Air Force officer explained to the colonel as the pair headed for the temporary command post. "The underground mains are ruptured in half a dozen places," he stated in a tone that betrayed his frustration. "The best we can do is to save what we will need to survive until real aid can reach us, or . . ."

"Or what, Lieutenant?" Orlov asked when the junior officer hesitated.

Stopping, the exasperated young man threw out his hands in a gesture of utter hopelessness. "Look around you, Colonel. This facility is in ruins! I doubt that I will be able to sustain my own people, let alone support a relief operation. That only one of your aircraft was damaged when landing is nothing short of a miracle."

Though he was still shaken from the near-fatal accident that occurred when the nose landing gear of his transport was snapped while crossing a fissure that had opened on the runway, Orlov did not allow it to show. Instead, he looked about at the devastation. "These are extreme times, Lieutenant," he snapped. "Both the Motherland and the Russian people we serve are depending on us to do our duty."

Out of habit, and unable to find a suitable response, the lieutenant simply mumbled, "Yes, of course, sir. It's just that—"

Reaching out, Orlov placed his hand on the officer's shoulder. Misreading the gesture, the Air Force lieutenant shut his eyes as he braced himself for a slap across the face. Only when he heard the colonel's soothing words, and felt the hand on his shoulder, did the lieutenant open his eyes and permit himself to relax.

"We must rise to meet the challenges we face, Lieutenant." Orlov pointed over at a group of soldiers laboring to fill in one of the many cracks in the runway. "Our soldiers are watching us. They will continue to carry out their duties only if we conduct ourselves as befitting an officer."

"Yes, of course," the nervous young officer stuttered.

Satisfied that he had sufficiently bucked up the rattled officer, Orlov clamped down harder than he needed to on the lieutenant's shoulder and gave it a good shake. "Now, take me to your commander."

The major to whom Orlov was presented was in worse shape than the air base he commanded. Standing before a map that had been hastily tacked to one wall of the room that now served as the base's operations center, the major didn't acknowledge his subordinate or Orlov for several minutes. Rather, with arms tightly folded against his chest, he stared at the map, rocking slowly back and forth on his heels as if transfixed by something neither Orlov nor the lieutenant standing next to him could see. Sensing Orlov's growing impatience, the lieutenant cleared his throat. "Major Kazanski, Colonel Orlov wishes to see you."

While a handful of clerks and other staff personnel shuffled about the room aimlessly, the Air Force major continued to rock back and forth without pause, facing the map as if he were studying it. "Sir," the lieutenant stated a bit louder, "Colonel Orlov is operating under the direct orders of the Minister of Defense. He and his team require ground transport in order to continue their journey."

Pivoting about, the wide-eyed major glared at his subordinate, ignoring Orlov as if he weren't there. "Trucks? He wants trucks? Where in the fuck do you propose I find him trucks? I can't shit them, now can I, Lieutenant? *Can you?*"

While Orlov remained silent, trying to decide whether it was the major's wild expression or his response that appalled him the most, the lieutenant stammered, "There are six available in running order, sir. The colonel requires only four of them."

"Only four!" the major exclaimed as he began to flap his arms about. "Only four. Well, that's bloody generous of him, now isn't it? He's leaving us two whole trucks. Two trucks with which to run this dunghill. Two trucks to haul the relief aid I have been told to expect in the next few hours."

Seeing that the methods he had used to win over the lieutenant would not work here, Orlov reverted to those techniques he was far more comfortable with. With slow, deliberate strides, he closed the distance between himself and the frenzied Air Force major. When he was face-to-face with the man, he leaned forward until the brim of his helmet touched the bridge of the major's forehead. "I will have those four trucks, Major. And if they are not suitable to my purpose," he added in a deep, menacing voice as he reached up and grabbed the major's lapel with his left hand, "I will take the others as well. Is that clear?"

Blinking furiously, the major shook his head. "You cannot," he insisted. "Not without proper authority."

Having exhausted his patience, Orlov reached for the pistol on his right hip. With one smooth motion, he drew the weapon from the holster, shoved it under the major's chin as he slammed him against the wall and jerked the trigger back.

To a man, the staff in the small operations center jumped. Letting the limp body of the Air Force major fall away, Orlov spun about, brandishing his pistol. "I expect cooperation," he screamed. "Full and unflinching cooperation. Is that clear?"

His eyes darting between the blood-splattered map and the pistol Demetre Orlov held in his steady hand, the Air Force lieutenant found it almost impossible to muster up a response. "Ah . . . yes . . . of course . . . sir. As you . . . as you order, sir."

12

The conditions that complicated life for Demetre Orlov were no kinder to the Tempest teams. Like the Russian transports, the inbound NATO aircraft were able to weave their way around the worst of the turbulence and localized storms spawned by the numerous impacts and airbursts. Unlike their Russian counterparts, the NATO teams did not have a great deal of flexibility when they reached their designated drop zones. They *had* to be dropped, and dropped within a reasonable striking distance from their targets.

All across western Siberia, in planes buffeted and tossed about by violent updrafts and raging storms, teams and group leaders huddled together at the front of their respective aircraft, listening to what was going on inside the cockpit. The normally cool and easygoing Special Ops types made no effort to disguise their concerns as they discussed their options, studied maps, or listened to the chatter on the secure radio net that kept them posted on the prevailing conditions across the region. Now and then, one of their number would glance up through the open door and over the shoulders of the pilots in the hope that the conditions they were flying through had somehow miraculously improved since the last time they had looked. In a few cases, the pilots, guided by reports being fed to them from weather recon aircraft combing the region and satellite data, were able to find a break. Sometimes they simply stumbled upon them. Without waiting for or seeking permission, the first pilots who had entered Russian airspace and met the hideous flying conditions had deviated from their meticulously plotted flight plans. Following aircraft benefited from this bold move, as well as from the decision at NATO headquarters to abandon radio silence and open a channel over which current weather data could be fed to the transports. "We had the courage of our convictions to send them into that hell," the senior NATO air commander announced. "Now let's have the balls to give them a fighting chance to do what we sent them in there for."

Just how much of a chance the Tempest teams would have to carry out their assigned tasks was in question. As gallant as the struggle by the pilots to get them to the drop zones was, it would be for naught if prevailing conditions on the ground exceeded minimum safety requirements. Determining if the risk was worth taking no longer lay with presidents or prime ministers, generals, or ministers of defense. That call rested with the captains and young majors who crowded together to discuss the options as their aircraft were pitched and heaved about skies that were as bleak as their outlook.

Using more effort than the simple act of lifting his head should have required, Sergeant-Chef Stanislaus Dombrowski peered through the dimly lit interior of the C-160 to where his commanding officer sat with the other team leaders. The Polish legionnaire was unable to tell if his inability to focus on his captain's face was caused by the queasiness that flying always brought or if the pitching and yawing of the aircraft kept him from seeing clearly. Yet even under these conditions, Dombrowski could tell that his commander was very, very concerned.

"Things are not going according to plan," the Pole stated in a low, somber tone to no one in particular.

"This is the Legion," the ever-cheerful Franz Ingelmann observed. "That is to be expected. Just imagine what it would be like if things always went smoothly for us. We'd have no tradition."

Slowly, painfully, Dombrowski turned his head to face his comrade. "This is different. Normally, they wait until after we are on the ground before things go to shit."

"Well," the unflappable Austrian countered, "this is a special occasion. We're getting an early start. Besides, this might be a good thing."

Struggling to hold his head steady, Dombrowski glared at Ingelmann. "And how could that be?"

"Well, don't you see, my dense Slavic associate?" Ingelmann said with more cheer than the occasion called for. "If we get all this unpleasantness out of the way now, the rest of the mission can proceed without a hitch."

"You're full of shit," Dombrowski growled.

"Oh no, I am not," the Austrian replied, enjoying the exchange as a means of taking his mind off the pervasive gloom. "I'll have you know that I left all of that back in Scotland, where I am sure the English will put it to good use."

Before he could think of a suitable response, Dombrowski felt a bubble deep in his stomach erupt, sending a nauseous stream of acid and gas up his throat. Pitching forward, the Pole brought his hand up to his mouth as he spread his knees apart and dropped his head between them. For several seconds, he remained in that position, held in place by the tightly cinched lap belt that encompassed his waist and the equipment that was strapped to him. All the while, he wondered if it would be better to simply let go and hurl or hold it all back.

The Polish legionnaire was still pondering this question when he felt a hand on his shoulder. At first he thought it was Ingelmann. With a shrug, he attempted to brush the bothersome Austrian away. But the comforting hand didn't budge. "Can you hold on for a few more moments?" a voice close to his ear shouted over the roar of the engines.

Looking up, Dombrowski saw that the hand and voice belonged to his commander, Captain Jules Pascal. Shaking his head in an effort to clear his thoughts, he managed to sit upright and face Pascal. "I am sorry. I didn't know it was you."

Though he had no idea of what Dombrowski was talking about, Pascal shrugged. "That's okay. No problem."

Unable to force even a weak smile, Dombrowski simply nodded. "So, is this thing still on? Are we still going to go?"

Pascal hesitated. This alarmed Dombrowski, for his captain never hesitated. With growing concern, he watched as his commander slowly turned away, looking through the open cockpit door without answering. When he finally did face his troubled subordinate again, the captain's face was as blank as a sheet of clean paper.

Sensing that he was not doing a good job of hiding his concerns from Dombrowski, Pascal drew in a deep breath. "We will know soon, *mon ami*. Soon."

✕

In another part of the turbulent and violent sky, Patrick Hogg listened as Major Shields laid it out for them as clearly as he could: "We have three choices," he stated, as if they were discussing a training exercise at Hereford. "One, we can take our spot and go out into conditions that are well below minimum standards and hope for the best. Two, we can fly on a bit and see if things improve. Or, three—"

A sudden updraft threw the aircraft and everyone onboard upward, preventing Shields from finishing his statement. For several moments, while the pilot struggled to regain control, the SAS officers frantically groped about in a desperate effort to find the nearest strap or handle with which to steady themselves. Only when the aircraft was more or less level again did the SAS major attempt to continue. "Where was I?" he asked rhetorically while he permitted his officers to collect their thoughts and refocus on the matter at hand.

"I believe," Hogg stated dryly, "you were about to present us with a third option, the one in which we tuck our tails between our legs and go scampering back home without accomplishing our mission."

Shields sighed. "Yes, well, something like that." After a lengthy pause, during which no one spoke, it was Patrick Hogg who took up the question that was gnawing at everyone. "Well, Major, which is it to be?"

Looking at each of his team commanders, Shields brought his hands together and shook them. Hogg wasn't sure if he was doing this to steel his nerves or if the man was saying a prayer in an effort to solicit divine guidance. "It's like this," the SAS major finally began. "If we take our spots as planned, there will be casualties. The winds aloft exceed anything any of us have ever faced. They have been that way since we entered the area of operation, and based on reports coming in from other sources, it's not much better anywhere else."

"So then it's rather pointless to go on in the hope of finding a better spot," Captain Abraham, team leader for the Bravo team, said.

"Yes," Shields answered. "That's pretty much the way things are. But not quite." Again he shook his clasped hands before speaking. "Conditions on the ground are, from what I've been told, horrific. It's more than blown-down trees and swollen rivers and mudflats. There are forest fires raging all over the region. The terrain has been rearranged. We have been warned that even the air itself may be toxic."

"Sort of like the cloud of pumice and ash thrown off by a volcano," Abraham added.

Shields nodded. "Yes, exactly. So, even if we do survive the jump, there is no way of knowing for sure if we'll be able to get on with things once we're on the ground."

"What are the chances that our targets are already gone?" Abraham asked.

Shields let his clasped hands drop into his lap as he shook his head. "Those Russian silos were built to withstand everything except a precise hit by a nuclear device. According to the preliminary damage assessment coming out of NATO headquarters, none of our teams have been that lucky."

Again, a silence settled over the small cluster of officers as they absorbed this piece of information and pondered their options. As was his habit, Patrick Hogg spoke up first. "Is this a council of war, Major? Or simply an info brief?"

"A little of both, I suppose," Shields replied weakly. Then, before anyone else could say another word, he sat upright, pulled his hands apart and slapped his knees. "No, that's not quite correct."

Following suit, the other two officers also straightened up as they looked at their commander and waited for him to speak. "We have no choice in the matter, I am afraid. To force you two to share in this decision, one that might very well prove to be fatal, would be wrong. We are going. We have no choice."

Hogg nodded. "I didn't expect that we ever did."

"Perhaps," Shields countered. "But we do have some flexibility about our spots. So rather than all of us blindly going out as if nothing had happened, I propose we drop one team as close to the target as possible, at its designated spot, while the other two remain aloft. If the first team is able to survive the jump, assemble itself and its equipment, and report back its ability to continue with the mission, the other two teams will continue to their designated spots."

"And if they don't?" Hogg asked without any sign of emotion.

"Then the remaining two teams will try to find another place where conditions appear to be better. When we find a place like that, if one exists, the second team will go. Perhaps," Shields added, "this was why the Americans insisted on dispatching three teams to each target."

"Like their baseball, I suppose," Abraham snickered. "Three strikes and you're out."

Though meant to add a bit of humor to the grim discussion, the analogy that the SAS captain used missed its mark.

"Patrick," Shields announced, leaning forward after taking up his map, "as the leader of the second team, once you're pretty sure that I didn't make it, I recommend you instruct the pilot to look for a spot over here, in this region."

Looking up from the map into Shields's eyes, Hogg shook his head. "I won't be able to do that, sir."

Caught off guard, the SAS major looked at his

subordinate and blinked. "And why in the bloody hell is that, Captain?"

"Because I'm taking the first team, not you."

For a moment, the two men stared at each other while Abraham, quite content to sit this one out, looked on. "I'm not going to let you shirk your duties as the senior officer that easily," Hogg said. "I have no desire to stand by waiting to hear from you on the ground as to whether or not we should jump. His Majesty hasn't invested all that money, time, and effort required to train you so that you can play wind dummy. That's what God created the Irish for, don't you know."

"What will they say," Shields asked halfheartedly, "when I come back and tell them I sent my subordinates out to their death before I went?"

Hogg smiled. "They will say you used your judgment, made a jolly good choice, posthumously nominate me for a medal, and promote you."

Unable to resist, the three SAS officers chuckled. Yet they understood that Patrick Hogg's assessment and recommendation were both serious and logical. Though he knew he would never be able to live with himself if, as Hogg jokingly suggested, they died and he lived, Shields saw no other option. "Right," he announced, being as upbeat as he could manage under the circumstances. "Now let's get to it. I'll check with the pilots to see how much time we have and to fill them in on the plan. In the meantime, Patrick, have your team prepare to exit. I don't imagine we have much time."

Rather than face his commander, Hogg glanced down the narrow confines of the transport to where his men sat nestled in the nylon seats. "No, I don't imagine we do."

✕

To a casual observer riding in the rear of the transport carrying the Forward Operations Command-and-Control Team, known as "Team Tiger," the two officers sitting opposite each other just to the rear of the cockpit, their heads bowed, hands clasped and elbows resting on their knees, looked as if they were praying. The only thing that betrayed that notion were the headphones each man wore, tethered by long cords trailing off into the cockpit.

Neither Robert Hightower nor Andrew Fretello said much of anything to each other, or to anyone else. Each concentrated on the command-and-control net he was monitoring. Only when something of particular interest came across the airwaves did either man bother to exchange glances. When they did, only Hightower allowed himself to register his feelings through the expressions he wore. Fretello, unsure of how to take the grim news they were receiving concerning the weather and the status of the drop zones, held to a poker face that served him well during times like this.

Earlier in the evening, when the initial weather-reconnaissance aircraft had begun to penetrate Russian airspace, the initial reports were seen as being good. Radar warning receivers attached to those aircraft failed to pick up any signals. "The electronic-warfare people were right," Fretello had boasted upon hearing that tidbit. "The Russian air-defense network in the region is blind." Intelligence provided by electronic-warfare aircraft following the weather-recon flights were equally encouraging. Those command-and-control networks that did manage to return to the air painted a picture of confusion and panic in the wake of the asteroid's impact. Again, the Special Forces major made no effort to hide his joy upon hearing this. Slowly, however, his attitude began to change as conditions over each of the drop zones became known and it was evident that the operation was in jeopardy.

One by one, the transports reported back to NATO headquarters in Brussels, the decisions being made by the commanders of the assault teams they were carrying. As a staff officer who knew what was expected of him, Fretello kept track of this information for his commander. On a map covered with an overlay displaying the operational graphics, laid out on the floor between himself and Hightower, Fretello marked off a drop zone every time a team leader announced over the Net as to whether he was going to stick with the primary or go for a secondary DZ. In those cases where a team leader came to the conclusion that neither primary nor secondary were acceptable, but that he was going to try to find another DZ near the target into which he could jump with his team, the architect of Tempest placed a question mark over the team's target.

Unlike his superior, Andrew Fretello paid little attention to each of the team leaders' tone of voice as he made his decision known. Having dedicated his entire adult life to the profession of arms, and having been personally involved in some very difficult operations himself, Hightower knew that you could tell a great deal about what was going on inside a man's mind by the words he selected and how he presented himself when using them. When they flew forth in an easy manner, Hightower didn't worry. But when there was a hesitation and the words being used were soft, he became concerned.

After listening to the report sent in by the commander of the French Foreign Legion's CRAP teams, Hightower lifted one of the earphones away and looked up at Fretello. Without being told, the major understood that his colonel had something to say to him. Following suit, Fretello freed up one of his ears so he could hear better.

"You realize that no one is going to back down,

don't you, Major?" Hightower stated dryly in a tone that was almost accusatory.

In all the time he had dedicated to laying out this operation, Andrew Fretello had never allowed himself to take into account many of the human factors that a commanding officer must deal with. Clear and concise instructions, and not the leadership traits and skills necessary to apply those instructions, were the concerns of the staff planner. So the human face that Tempest was just starting to wear was one that Andrew Fretello was least prepared to understand.

Realizing that his well-schooled subordinate had no fitting response, Hightower continued. "We're going to lose a lot of good people during the drop alone. Your number-one job, mister," Hightower stated sharply, jabbing a finger at the silent major, "as soon as we're on the ground and have functional comms, is to find out which ones made it, what sort of shape they're in, and where we have holes that need to be filled."

Fretello didn't need to ask the colonel what he meant by "holes." That, he assumed, meant targets that would not be hit because the teams assigned to them had lost all their equipment, or the teams themselves had not survived the jump. Using phrases such as "didn't make it" allowed professional soldiers such as Fretello to deal with the horrors that those men would face in their final minutes of life, trying to carry out the grim tasks their nations had assigned to them.

Others, like Hightower, could not and would not permit themselves to be so easily dissuaded from the truth of what was actually happening. Hightower was, after all, the commanding officer. He was the man responsible for the survival or death of every soldier under his command. Though those soldiers might meet their end as a result of unforeseen con-

ditions or unexpected enemy activity, Hightower understood that he was the man who set his seal upon
the final plan, who had stood up before those very
men and given the order to go forth and execute
it. Staff officers deal with paper, concepts, and
words. Commanders do their work with flesh and
blood.

13

The driver of the lead truck, seated next to Demetre Orlov, remained silent as he did his best to ignore his commander. Only the sound of the windshield wipers laboring to push aside the heavy, wet ash that came down like snow disturbed the tense silence. With nothing better to do, he stared out into the gloom, watching his fellow commandos as they struggled to clear the road up ahead. It had been like this in the truck cab during the three hours it had taken them to move four kilometers. Ordinarily, such a fact would have evoked a comment by the otherwise easygoing commando. But he knew better than to make mention of their miserable lack of progress. Only the foul, oppressive conditions outside the cab came close to matching his colonel's dark mood.

With little more to do than watch the travails of his men, Orlov was left to brood, fume, and despair. Twisting about in his seat, he looked at his watch. He didn't need an odometer to tell him that they had made little headway since leaving the air base.

As he thought about this, a chill ran down his back. While it was true that the temperature was finally beginning to plummet, the Russian colonel knew that the cold was not the source of this sudden sensation. Rather, it was the realization that he was running out of time. Time and the devastation that blocked their way had become far greater foes than were the units loyal to General Likhatchev, units that the colonel's special-response team would have to face when it reached its objective.

Unable to remained cooped up in the close confines of the truck's cab doing nothing, Orlov grabbed the door handle next to him and gave it a jerk. With more effort than required, he pushed the door open. The driver, though startled by this sudden move, did little more than look over as his commander climbed out. For him, sharing the cab of the truck had been like sitting next to a ticking time bomb that he had no way of defusing. With the impatient colonel gone, the bored Russian commando would be free to relax.

Once on the ground, Orlov hesitated. He wasn't sure of what, exactly, he could do to make things move faster. Mulling this over, he watched his men as they laboriously bulled their way forward. He could clearly see that they were moving as fast as they could. Any efforts on his part to encourage them to redouble their efforts would, he concluded, be pointless. If anything, admonishing professional soldiers such as his to work harder when they were already doing their best could prove to be counterproductive. Nor did they need his supervision. The junior officer in charge of the section and his NCO's were doing well enough. Even in his agitated state, Orlov could see that they were providing all the direction their men required. The only contribution that he could make, he finally determined, was to provide an example to his men. By joining them, he would demonstrate both his willingness to share their labors as well as his resolution to overcome the unexpected and unimaginable devastation that threatened to hold them back.

Before setting out to lend a hand, Orlov drew a deep breath. Quickly, he regretted doing so. The fetid air that coursed through his lungs threw him into a fit of uncontrollable coughing. This became so loud and violent that the men closest to him stopped working and turned to see what was wrong with their commander. Realizing that his error was having an effect opposite of what he had set out to achieve, Orlov struggled with all his might to suppress his convulsions. Reaching out, he grasped the fender of the truck, pulled himself upright, and endeavored to bring his hacking under control. Only when they saw their colonel returning their stare did the work party turn away and return to its labors. Once he was sure that no one was watching, Orlov pulled his scarf up and over his mouth and nose. Though not a very efficient filter, like everything else that day, this improvisation would have to do.

Adversity and an unwavering dedication to duty are powerful motivators. In the past, they had helped Demetre Orlov achieve feats that would have humbled an ordinary man. On this day, however, his single-minded determination seemed to be of little use in the face of the utter devastation he and his small command now faced. The same shattered terrain that had kept them from landing near General Igor Likhatchev's regional command-and-control center was hindering their movement on the ground.

Neither of his previous experiences in Afghanistan and Chechnya had prepared him for this. During operations in those wars, he'd had only to contend with man-made destruction. Though considerable, such efforts had been localized. When faced with obstacles that could not be bypassed, Orlov had found that careful planning, persistence, and a bit of sweat usually sufficed to overcome even the most daunting impediment. In Chechnya, his subordinates had learned how futile it could be to report back to him that they were unable to advance because of a roadblock, a minefield, or rubble. Whenever one was foolish enough to try, Orlov would summarily reject whatever excuse was being offered him. "Any barrier laid down by mortal men," he'd snap, "can be overcome by moral men."

Of course, the premise of Orlov's philosophy on overcoming obstructions on the battlefield was based entirely upon the supposition that mere humans had been responsible for them. But the hand that had wiped away vast sections of the road he was trying to follow now, and had deposited shattered trees, boulders, and thick mud on the sections that remained, was more akin to being divine. Against such odds, even the efforts of a warrior as dogged as Demetre Orlov were for naught. It would take some time for this fact to become apparent to him, since the greatest obstacle facing his small band of commandos was their own commander's stubborn pride.

Over the years, Orlov had labored hard to become the perfect soldier. To him, this meant being impersonal, stern, and uncompromising when dealing with both his men and his mission. He believed that by adhering to these principles, he would be free to assess every situation with the cold, hard logic that a commander needed in order to make informed and proper decisions in combat. But like most professional soldiers, he was unable to shed character traits and flaws common to all humans. While it can be argued that a person's pride in his abilities can be a source of strength, at times it can also cloud his judgment. Nowhere was there a better example of this than along the road leading to the headquarters of General Igor Likhatchev.

At that particular moment, Orlov's pride was preventing him from seeing how futile and wasteful the labors of his men were. Further, an inherent inability to admit failure made it all but impossible for him to appreciate the absurdity of their efforts to bull through to their objective via a road that no longer existed.

Those of his unit tasked to clear a path for the trucks had no such problem. Within the first hour, they had come to the realization that the transportation they had procured was a liability. As they inched their way forward, Orlov's men came to appreciate the fact that they would have to abandon both trucks and strike out cross-country. While even the most ardent of them dreaded the idea of making the long, grueling march across the devastated landscape, the idea of clearing every meter of a road by hand was far more repugnant. So absurd had that effort become that those unfortunate enough to have been selected to clear the debris no longer bothered to mount up when they finished a stretch of road. Instead, they simply trudged on forward to the next stretch of impassable roadway and began to clear it.

As hard as it was on his men, this slowly and seemingly pointless expenditure of effort wore on Orlov's nerves at the same time it was sapping the morale and physical strength of his men. Unable to remain idle and simply stand off to one side and watch, Orlov stepped forward to join them in their efforts. Seeing a single man trying to heft a felled tree, he grabbed hold of the other end. "Get your back into it, man," he yelled to the soldier on the other end. "You hefted loads far heavier than this in training."

From behind Orlov, a voice mockingly called out: "Yes, be quick. We must not keep the President's butcher boy from making his appointed rounds."

Stunned, the Russian colonel let go of his end of the shattered tree and spun about. His eyes quickly scanned the dozen or so men who had been laboring to clear the road. The dust, ash, and grime that filled the air had mixed so well with the sweat that dripped from their brows that it was all but impossible to distinguish one man from another. They had no problem, however, in recognizing the blind fury that manifested itself in their commander's expression. "Which of you bastards said that?" Orlov demanded.

One by one, the soldiers stopped what they were doing, straightened up, and returned Orlov's hard, uncompromising stare. No words were uttered. No steps were taken, backward or to the fore. Surrounded by a cold, hard silence disturbed only by the idling of a truck's engine and the low crackle of burning wood, the two sides warily contemplated one another, waiting for someone to say something.

Stepping out from behind the mute commandos, a figure came forth and made its way toward Orlov, stepping over the debris that littered the roadway. Like the others, this man's uniform had become so permeated with filth and grime, and his face so blackened, that it took Orlov several seconds to recognize that it was his deputy commander. All that he could see with any degree of clarity were the man's eyes, eyes that watched his in the same way one approaches a strange, growling dog.

When there was but a meter between himself and his commander, Major Gregory Petkovic stopped, but said nothing.

"I want you to find the shit who yelled out," Orlov charged.

With a forced calm, Petkovic shrugged and threw out his hands. "And do what, Colonel? Shoot him? Assign him additional duty? Place him on report?"

Unsure of whether his number-two was asking a serious question or mocking him, Orlov said nothing as he clenched his fists and looked past the major before him over to where the men were watching and waiting.

"This is ludicrous, sir," Petkovic stated slowly in a hushed voice. "We are sapping our strength and wasting time to no good end."

Tearing his eyes away from the soldiers, the Russian colonel studied his deputy. Though he knew the answer, he wanted to hear what Petkovic had to say. "And what is your solution, Major?"

"Abandon the trucks," Petkovic stated without hesitation, "and head off cross-country. Though we may be able to make only one or two kilometers an hour, the soldiers will be doing something they understand. They will be advancing toward General Likhatchev's regional command center as a fighting unit, not clearing the road like common laborers, or sitting idle and huddled in trucks like cattle."

Though agitated, Orlov had not missed the fact that his second in command had referred to their objective as General Likhatchev's regional command center. In the past, he and everyone in his special-response team had taken great pains to use terms such as "objective" or "target" when speaking of their intended mark. To hear one of his officers personify their intended victim like this, especially when dealing with a man universally revered by Russia's armed forces, was a bit disconcerting.

Petkovic misinterpreted Orlov's pause, believing it to mean that his commander was seriously considering his proposal. "Colonel," he continued, "you must see that a continuation of our efforts to clear this road is pointless, that we will never make it at this rate. You must give the order to abandon the trucks."

Snapping out of his momentary lapse, Orlov's

eyes narrowed. "Major, do not assume to tell me what I must and must not do. You are not in command here. You will not be held responsible by those in Moscow if we fail."

Though angered by this sudden attack, Petkovic maintained his composure. "Colonel, if we fail, there will be no one left in Moscow."

Again the Russian colonel took a moment to consider his subordinate's words. This time, however, his thoughts stayed on task. With every eye riveted upon him, Demetre Orlov weighed the effect that a failure on his part to carry out his orders would have in Moscow. Would failure in this enterprise be catastrophic? Would General Igor Likhatchev, a man he knew and trusted, really follow through on his threats?

Anxious to get on with things one way or the other, Petkovic disrupted his commander's thoughts again. "Sir, what are your orders for the men?"

Orlov drew in a deep breath. "Tell them to gather their equipment off of the trucks and form up in march column. We move out, on foot, in ten minutes."

Petkovic made no effort to hide the glee he felt in having won over his commander to his point of view as he drew himself up and saluted. This angered Orlov. The idea of allowing a subordinate to think that he'd had a say in what the unit did and how it did it was, to him, a dangerous thing. Orlov reminded himself to redouble his vigilance as they drew closer to their objective.

✕

**WESTERN SIBERIA, RUSSIA
07:50 HOURS ZULU, APRIL 9**

Out of breath and frustrated, Franz Ingelmann took several moments before rendering his report. Squatting next to the panting legionnaire, Stanislaus Dombrowski waited patiently while the Austrian corporal collected himself. "I found no trace of Juan," Ingelmann finally blurted. "Of course," he continued after another moment's pause, "things are so bad out there, I could have passed within a meter of him and not seen him."

"I daresay," Dombrowski stated dryly, "that poor Juan is either hopelessly lost or, like Anton and Kim, hors de combat."

As he reached around for his canteen, Ingelmann looked over to where their captain lay propped against a tree stump. "How's he doing?"

Dombrowski didn't bother looking back at his injured team commander. Instead, his gaze dropped down to the blackened patch of earth at his feet. "Rather well," he mumbled as he repeatedly jabbed at the dirt with a stick, "for a man with two broken legs, perhaps a broken back, and God knows how many internal injuries."

"Isn't that going to make moving him a bit risky?" Ingelmann asked cautiously.

Ceasing his assault on the ground between them, Dombrowski looked up and gave his companion a cold, hard stare. "We are not taking him with us."

Ingelmann blinked. He wanted to say something. He felt the urge to voice his disapproval of this decision. But he knew that such a gesture would be for naught. As a member of les Commandos de Recherche et d'Action dans le Profondeur, the young Austrian knew that the price of being a part of that unit was high. The risks they took during training exercises or in the course of combat operations often bordered on gambling. Yet the sacrifices that individual legionnaires were called upon to pay, no matter how steep, were seldom taken into account when determining if a mission should or should not be undertaken. Only the feasibility of achieving the desired goal of the exercise and the cost of not doing so mattered. Perhaps this is why there is often a wide psychological gulf between staff planners, who deal in the abstract, and ground combat troops, charged with carrying out their plans in a very real and often harsh world.

After taking another sip from his canteen, Ingelmann forced himself to look over to where his captain was slumped. "Is there anything we can do for him?"

The Polish legionnaire didn't answer. Instead, he jabbed the stick he held into the ground, again and again. The question of what they could do for their injured commanding officer had been plaguing Dombrowski ever since he had discovered him twisted about in his parachute and bent backward over a fallen tree. That Captain Pascal was conscious and yet had made no effort to free himself from his harness had told Dombrowski just how severe the man's injuries were. "I've already given him all the morphine in his first-aid packet. Mine as well," the Pole finally stated. After glancing back over his shoulder to where Pascal lay, he looked into Ingelmann's eyes. "I am not sure, but I do not think it would be safe to give him any more."

The Austrian suspected that the look his NCO had just given him, followed by his statement, was meant to convey the thought that now entered his mind. Hesitating, he waited for Dombrowski to say more. But the big Pole just stared into his eyes. Finally convinced that he had read his companion's meaning correctly, Ingelmann replaced his canteen in its pouch, reached around to his own first-aid pouch, and withdrew the small cerates of morphine. Without a word, he offered them to Dombrowski.

After throwing the stick he had been poking the dirt with, using all his might, the Polish legionnaire reached out and took the morphine, then stood up. "Gather the one good charge we were able to recover and prepare to move out," he ordered. "I must go over to the captain and . . ."

And what? Dombrowski wondered. Offer up the morphine he held and say good-bye? He turned and began to make his way to Pascal's side. Was there another way? Was there a chance to accomplish their mission and come back to recover their stricken commander?

The Polish legionnaire was still pondering these thoughts and others, when he reached Pascal. Dropping to his knees, he did his best to avoid eye-to-eye contact.

"I take it," the team commander said, "that Corporal Ingelmann's search was unsuccessful."

"*Oui, mon capitain,*" Dombrowski uttered with little enthusiasm. "If Juan did survive the drop, I fear he is hopelessly lost." Pausing, he looked around. "The asteroid has done a marvelous job of rearranging the terrain."

Gazing past his NCO, Pascal saw Ingelmann readjusting his equipment as he prepared to add the one good shaped charge to his load. "You have done all you can here," the French officer announced, knowing that his subordinate was having difficulty stating what was obvious to both of them. "Take the radio," Pascal said as he waved his hand feebly at the set sitting next to him. "The two of you must press on as quickly as possible. If the rest of the countryside is as torn up as it is here, it will take you twice as long to reach the target as I had estimated."

"*Oui*," the Polish NCO replied weakly as he continued to look around in an effort to avoid facing his commander.

Reaching out, Pascal grasped Dombrowski's arm and gave it a shake. "Stanislaus, you must not concern yourself with my welfare. Your only concern now is the mission. I will manage."

Realizing that there was no easy way to do what he needed to do, the Polish legionnaire looked down at Pascal for the first time. As he struggled to hold back his tears, he stuck out the hand holding the morphine and offered the opiate to his commanding officer and friend.

Slowly a smile crept across the French officer's face. Removing his hand from Dombrowski's arm, he placed it in Dombrowski's hand, which was holding the cerates. "The mission, *mon ami*," Pascal said as he clasped hands with the Pole. "The mission."

Sensing that he was on the verge of losing it, Dombrowski pulled his hand away, leaving the morphine in the possession of his commander. Standing up, he stepped back, came to attention, and saluted.

With a smile and a nod, Pascal returned Dombrowski's salute. "Now, get going."

WESTERN SIBERIA, RUSSIA
08:08 HOURS ZULU, APRIL 9

Captain Patrick Hogg used a simple formula when it came to spacing halts. When he got tired, they stopped. Those following him were expected to keep up. Those unable to do so and falling behind were not given any additional time to catch up. They used the break to do that. No one was given any slack for whatever reason. To drive this point home during training, when Hogg saw the last of his stragglers were just about to catch up, he would pick up his personal gear and give the order to move out. This policy was as effective as it was cruel. No one dared fall out of a march led by the Irishman.

The four men following Hogg at the moment kept an eye on him as he picked his way through the shattered pine forest. Their luck since exiting the C-130 had been rather mixed. While they all had experienced vicious crosswinds and turbulence that surpassed anything they had ever faced before, only one of them had met with a serious problem. That problem had been about as bad as it got. The man's chute had failed to deploy properly. When Sergeant Kenneth McPherson found the unfortunate soul, his partially deployed chute was twisted in a bundle next to him. "As best I could tell," McPherson stated when he informed Hogg of his discovery, "Andrews waited too long to open his chute. Either that or he wasn't stable when he did so. Either way, he didn't have a prayer."

To the good, the drop zone that Major Thomas Shields had selected for them was relatively close to their assigned objective. Unfortunately, even this spot of luck had a down side. The blast caused by a chunk of the asteroid had flattened the trees from left to right along their desired line of march. This meant that the pattern of trees blown down created an unending series of obstructions across their path. Every other step they took required each man in Hogg's small team to climb over or straddle a shattered tree. While the initial wave of thermal energy and the force of the blast that followed had stripped away the pine needles, each freshly felled tree sprouted a dense array of bare, spindly branches that presented a unique challenge to the heavily laden soldiers. To compound this problem, some of these barren branches had been snapped by the blast wave or during the fall. This left a series of sharp, stubby protrusions jutting out at all angles, ranging in length from a foot to a few inches. Quickly, the British commandos found that it was the shorter ones that gave them the biggest problem. The most ingenious combat engineer, with unlimited time and resources at his disposal, could not have come up with a better obstacle course.

Despite this, Patrick Hogg drove on toward his objective. His ears were shut to the yelps of pain coming from the commandos who followed as they straddled fallen tree after fallen tree and were, in the process, impaled by snapped branches and splinters. Even when their swearing reached a crescendo, Hogg kept plowing on, increasing his pace rather than slowing it as he tried to put a bit of distance between himself and those behind him. When he finally raised his hand and shouted over his shoulder that they would halt for ten minutes, the members of his team heaved a collective groan.

While the commandos looked around this way and that in order to find a clear patch of ground upon which to settle, Hogg made no effort to check their condition. Rather, he maintained his distance and eased himself down into a squatting position before leaning back until the pack he carried came to rest upon the ground. Once in this reclined state, he stretched out, closed his eyes, and allowed his head to fall back until it came to rest against the top of the pack. Set, Hogg cradled his Heckler & Koch MP 5 submachine gun snuggly in his arms, cleared his mind of all the thoughts that had been swimming about in it, and did his best to concentrate, instead, on his breathing.

This was not at all as pleasant or as easy as it should have been. Dust, ash, and vapors still permeated the air at ground level. The camouflaged cravat that he wore pulled up over his mouth and nose did little to filter out this odious mixture. Still, it was not quite bad enough to resort to his respirator. That would have been a greater hindrance to his breathing than the fetid air was.

As hard as he tried, Patrick Hogg could not simply disengage his brain as one would the clutch in an auto and let it coast along. There was far too much to think about, too much to consider. Even the simple act of breathing brought new issues to mind. The air he took in betrayed a chill he had not noticed before. The unnaturally high temperatures caused by the asteroid's impact and held in place by the freak atmospheric conditions seemed to be giving way to a more normal temperature. That, he thought, would be a problem, particularly with the amount of moisture that seemed to be coating everything. Ice, added to their trials and tribulations with the blown-down trees, would further hinder their already pathetically slow pace.

He was just about to dismiss this newly generated concern and get back to relaxing when he heard the squish of mud underboot nearby. He didn't need to open his eyes. He knew who it was. "How are the men holding up, Sergeant McPherson?"

"The lads are a bit concerned," the Scottish NCO replied as he settled down next to his commander.

Hogg didn't move a muscle. "I know. We're going to miss our time-mark by a mile. But then I imagine everyone else is going to as well, so that shouldn't be an issue."

"It's not that, sir, that's troubling me."

Hogg knew McPherson well enough to appreciate

by his tone of voice that he was genuinely worried. Opening his eyes, Hogg twisted his head around until he could see McPherson. The pained expression the man wore told him that this was not about the operation. Though he was unsure that he wanted to hear any more, he had little choice at the moment. "Go on."

"You've been preoccupied and a bit off your game since you got back from London. At first we all thought it was because of the manner in which this mission has been thrown together. But then we heard about you and—"

Angered that Thomas Shields had spoken to his men about his personal life behind his back, Hogg propped himself up. "What passes between myself and my wife," he stated as his eyes narrowed and his voice became tense, "is my affair, and my affair alone. Is that understood?"

Now that he was committed, McPherson was determined not to waver. "That's true, sir. Very true. That is, unless it affects your performance in the field."

Though he had done everything he could to separate his difficulties with his wife from his assigned duties, Hogg was able to appreciate that he was not himself. Perhaps, he reasoned, he had tried so hard to behave as if nothing had happened that he was overcompensating. Still, the implication that he was endangering his command annoyed him. "I don't see it that way, Sergeant," he snapped.

"Well, sir," McPherson continued without any hint of trepidation, "with all due respect, that's not how the lads or I see it." With a look in his eyes that seemed to be growing more determined as he spoke, the Scottish NCO went on. "I don't know how else to put this, so I won't bother trying to mince words with you. We've known each other since you joined the regiment. I was with you in some pretty tight spots and have seen you in circumstances that would have humbled a lesser man. You've never let personal concerns, either your own or those of the men under your command, interfere with the mission, whether it be in training or in combat. In that, you've always been utterly ruthless and uncompromising. And yet here we are, in the middle of this hell on earth, following a man who's got a bug up his ass that's bigger than the bloody asteroid that started all this. The men are worried. I'm worried. You're pushing harder than you need to, you've isolated yourself from everyone around you, and you're so caught in your own little world that I'm afraid you may lose sight of what's going on around you."

Pausing, McPherson took a deep breath. Before Hogg could counter, the Scottish NCO plunged on. "Just one second, you always tell the new candidates, is all that separates the quick and the dead. Just one second, one missed opportunity, one misstep. That's all it takes, you tell them. And you know what? You're right. How many times have we waited for those we were tracking to make a mistake? How many times have we come swooping in when our foes were napping and brought their miserable little lives to a quick end? Enough, sir, for you to appreciate that the same can happen to us."

Unable to look his senior NCO in the eye any longer, Patrick Hogg turned his head away. For several long seconds, neither man said a word. Inflamed by his own rhetoric, McPherson continued to stare at his commander. What could he say? The man was right. While the manner in which his senior NCO had presented his concerns bordered on insubordination, McPherson had been right to do so.

No, Hogg reminded himself. It had been the man's duty to do so. Just as it was his own duty, here and now, to pull himself together and put his personal problems behind him. Without bothering to look back at his sergeant, Hogg nodded as he pulled the cravat down from his nose. "You are correct, Sergeant McPherson. I've been off my game by a wide margin." Taking in a deep breath, he looked up at the dark, troubled sky that continued to roil and race by. "The temperature is starting to drop. I expect that once it gets dark, serious freezing will set in."

Turning back to McPherson, Hogg looked into the sergeant's eyes. "Do me a favor and pass the word on to the lads to get themselves ready for that while I collect myself here and . . . well, collect myself."

Sensing that he had achieved what he'd set out to do, McPherson stood up and nodded. "That I'll do, sir. And when you're ready, we'll be waiting."

"Thank you, Sergeant McPherson."

When the Scottish NCO was gone, Hogg again laid his head against his pack and looked up into the turbulent heavens above. Letting go was more than a simple matter of saying good-bye and walking out of a hotel room. He'd need to make a lot of adjustments, both in his life and in the way he thought. But those would have to wait. Every thought save those that concerned this mission would have to be placed on hold. He knew that. He understood that. What he didn't know was if he had the strength to manage it.

14

Seated in a freshly fallen tree, Colonel Robert Hightower looked up from the stick he had been whittling away at and gazed at the low, dark clouds covering the region like a death shroud. Snow was beginning to drift down, heavy flakes that were dirty gray. This was a welcome relief after being pelted by an ice storm, not to mention the freezing rains that had preceded that. It seemed as if the heavens were anxious to rid themselves of all the moisture and dirt that had been thrown their way by the unwelcome intruder from the far reaches of the solar system. How simple, Hightower thought, it was for nature to shed its burden and move on.

The weather forecasts they had been given before departing Scotland were about as useless, Hightower concluded as he scanned the sky. Lowering his head, he surveyed the activities of his diminished command group. Of the eighteen men and women who had exited their transport with him, his executive officer was confirmed dead, three enlisted soldiers had suffered injuries of varying degree upon landing, and one female signal officer was unaccounted for. Fortunately, enough of the communications equipment was recovered in good enough order to establish links with NATO headquarters in Brussels, as well as with most of the Tempest teams.

That they had not been able to contact all of the Tempest teams concerned Hightower. Looking over to where his ops officer was working up their current status on the ground, the Special Forces colonel felt the urge to get up and wander over to see for himself how things were shaping up. To do so, however, would serve no good purpose. If anything, interrupting the ambitious young major would only keep him from completing his task. The colonel knew that as soon as Fretello was ready, he would come scampering over to him and render his report. Until then, Hightower could do little but wait and, quite literally, whittle away his time.

This, he told himself, as he turned his attention back to the stick he was attacking with his Swiss Army knife, was the worst part of being a senior officer. Back in Scotland, when they'd been putting the finishing touches on the plan, coordinating with the Air Force for lift, giving briefings, and conducting precombat inspections, he'd never seemed to have enough hours in the day. Both he and every member of his staff had been going a mile a minute every waking hour. Even when he'd forced himself to lie down in an effort to catch a few hours' sleep, his mind had been so alive with details and the gnawing fear that he was leaving something undone that rest was all but impossible. Back there, it had been the soldiers, the men who would have to execute the plan they were working on, who'd had little to do.

At the moment, the opposite was true. Now he was reduced to hacking away at a piece of Russian pine while the highly trained men he was responsible for were struggling through the maze of shattered forests and across debris-choked streams in an effort to reach their assigned objectives. They were the ones fighting against time. They were the ones who had little opportunity to tend to personal needs or to stop and think about their comrades whom the Fates had not been kind to during the jump. It was moments like this, Hightower thought as he pushed his knife down with all his might, that he longed to be a young officer again, out there in the boonies, fighting the forces of evil and nature for God, country, and the girl next door.

Pausing for a moment, Hightower looked up at the sky again. He chuckled. God, country, and the girl next door. That's what the U.S. Army used to fight for, he thought. That was what he'd joined the Army to do. To him, the principles embodied in his faith and in the Constitution, which he was pledged to defend, had meaning. They were tangible. The idea of going to war to defend corporate America, or to deflect the media's attention from a White House scandal, were as foreign as the very land in which he now sat. He knew that the world changes. He had seen it himself. But the idea that the very meaning of human existence, even if it was a soldier's existence, could change so radically so fast was all but incomprehensible. Only slowly had Hightower come to the conclusion that something was not right, something was out of place, that his own core beliefs were out of sync with the society he was charged to defend. What he could do to adjust things, either of his view of the world or of the world itself, was beyond him. At the moment, though, he had more immediate concerns.

"Colonel Hightower?" A familiar-sounding voice called out, cutting into his dark thoughts. "I have the current status."

Lowering his gaze, the Special Forces colonel looked at Andrew Fretello and blinked as he turned his attention away from his lofty philosophical reflections and refocused his full attention on the mission at hand. "Go ahead, Major."

"Well, sir, there are still a fair number of teams unaccounted for. To the good, we were able to contact Captain Brant. His losses during the jump were minimal."

It always annoyed Hightower when a staff officer giving a briefing equated the loss of life as minimal. Though he knew that such a description was a valid means of conveying an overall picture, minimal casualties were to him akin to saying that someone was only mostly dead. "Exactly how many men, Major, does Captain Brant have with him?"

Pausing, Fretello glanced down at his notes. "Four, sir, not counting Captain Brant."

"So he only lost one man. Any word on his status?"

Fretello shook his head. "Captain Brant did not specify."

Hightower looked down at the stick he held and carved off another chuck. "I guess it doesn't make a difference for now. Continue."

"With Captain Brant and his people, that gives us two teams converging on Alpha Zero Four. We have also managed to contact one of the Foreign Legion teams assigned to hit Foxtrot Zero Two. Their signal was rather weak and the transmission garbled. From what we could make out, they are in fairly bad shape, but retain the ability to hit their assigned target."

Lifting his head, Hightower looked into Fretello's eyes. "Good, that leaves only two holes uncovered."

Though he seemed pleased with this bit of news, the Special Forces colonel did not smile. "We don't know that for sure," Fretello quickly countered. "There's always the off chance that members of the teams assigned to those targets survived the jump but lost their signal equipment. After all, we won't have our backup Comsat until Captain Bell finds us."

Hightower stopped his whittling and gave Fretello a long, hard stare. "You seem to be assuming, Major, that she's still alive and able to walk."

Fretello shrugged. "There's always the hope that she is, sir."

"Hope, Major, is not a good foundation upon which to base a plan of action. You, of all people, should know that."

Unable to frame a suitable response, the young major resorted to the default reply. "Yes, sir."

"So," the colonel stated, as a way of signaling that he was changing subjects. "What are our options as you see them?"

Relaxing his stance, Fretello placed his notepad behind him and grasped it with both hands. "As I see it, we have two options. The first is to divert several of the teams from targets that have more than one team currently converging on them over to hit those that are, to the best of our knowledge, uncovered."

"Not so good," Hightower reasoned out loud. "If your original premise is still operative, Russian security forces at the targets will have to be hit from multiple directions."

"Yes, sir. That is correct," Fretello acknowledged before he went on. "That leaves us with the second-best option. Once those targets that have multiple teams approaching them have been reached and charges have been set, all uncommitted teams will be redirected to those targets currently uncovered."

"How practical is that?" Hightower asked as he took up his whittling again in an effort to work off some of his nervous energy.

"Well, sir," Fretello explained as he reached into

a pants pocket and pulled a map out. Squatting, he opened the map and pointed out the position of the uncovered targets. "Both of them are to our south, ten and twelve klicks away respectively. The teams that will in all likelihood be in the best condition to free up one or more of their subordinate teams are all to the north."

Hightower looked at the locations the staff officer was pointing out. As he did so, something clicked. "It would seem," he stated more to himself than to Fretello, "that the farther south you go, the worse things are."

Having already considered that, Fretello nodded. "Yes, sir. The good news there is that the regional command-and-control complex is pretty much in the heart of an area of near total devastation. Which should mean that their ability to react to our attacks is limited, if they retain the ability to do so at all."

Hightower nodded in agreement as he studied the map. "In the negative," he finally stated, "both of the uncovered sites are on either side of that complex. Which means they are closer to them than we are and will be able to reinforce them faster than we can get to them."

"Well, yes, provided," Fretello countered, "they know we're coming."

Turning away from the map, Hightower whacked away a few chips of wood from the stick he had been whittling as he considered the problem. Without bothering to look up at the staff officer, he began to articulate the decision he had already settled upon. "We'll stay with the plan as it exists, for now. All teams will continue to make their way to their assigned targets and prepare them for execution on order. However, you will put out a warning order that they will hold onto any unused demo packs. On order, they will bring those charges to this location as quickly as possible, together with all personnel that can be spared. Once we have consolidated them, we will resurrect two new teams and set off to hit those targets that have not yet been attacked. Is that clear, Major?"

As he acknowledged his commander's guidance, the young staff officer's mind was already racing with the possibilities of becoming an active part of the operation that this course of action presented. If Colonel Hightower took note of the glint in Fretello's eye and the smile that the major struggled to suppress, he didn't let on. Instead, he stood up, tossed the butchered stick he had been working on as far as he could and took a deep breath. "Get to work on disseminating those orders to all teams ASAP. And have the comms people get Brussels for me. I'll fill them in and brief them on how we're going to deal with the situation."

**WESTERN SIBERIA, RUSSIA
11:25 HOURS ZULU, APRIL 9**

Mechanically, Stanislaus Dombrowski and Franz Ingelmann trudged along. Doubled over by the crippling weight of their packs and the oppressive sorrow each man carried in his heart over the terrible losses they had already endured, neither spoke. Even when the big Pole took time to pause and check their location against his map to confirm their bearings, Ingelmann maintained his silence. Both appreciated the fact that the other was in no mood for the lighthearted banter that often accompanied such a long and arduous trek. There simply were no words in any of the languages either men knew that could erase the anguish they shared.

Just how complete his isolation was to the physical world he was moving through, not really seeing it or allowing himself to feel, didn't hit Dombrowski until it dawned on him that the reason the light was fading was because it was late afternoon. Coming to an abrupt halt, the Polish legionnaire tilted his head back and looked up into the sky. To his utter amazement, it was also snowing. Without thinking, he stretched out his hand and turned his open palm up to catch a few snowflakes in an effort to confirm this astonishing discovery. From behind him, Ingelmann spoke for the first time since they began their grim, silent march. "Is there a problem?"

Dombrowski didn't answer right away. Instead, he lowered his eyes and surveyed the mangled pine forest they had been moving through. As far as the eye could see, which was not very far at this moment, everything was covered with a thin layer of dirty, gray snow. "How long has this been coming down?" he finally asked.

Under ordinary circumstances, the Austrian corporal would have seized upon this statement to poke fun at his oblivious comrade. But these were not ordinary circumstances. The normally jovial and vocal Austrian gave a quick, crisp response. "An hour. Maybe more."

Still in a bit of a daze, Dombrowski continued to scan the scene before him. It was like he had just awakened from a long, fitful sleep. Only, instead of the nightmare ending when he opened his eyes, it was still there before him. A chill from this terrible realization ran down his spine. "We must be getting close," he said, more to himself than to his companion.

Sensing that this would be an excellent time to take a break, Ingelmann gripped a shattered tree that was leaning over at a sharp angle and used it to steady himself as he eased to the ground. Though sitting in the freshly fallen snow sent shivers throughout his body, the relief he felt as the weight on his shoulders lessened caused him to sigh. With his stubby FA MAS assault rifle resting on his chest, Ingelmann closed his eyes, while Dombrowski tried to sort out himself and his circumstances.

Appreciating the fact that this was going to take him a while, he settled down with his back resting against a tree stump. Slowly, almost laboriously, he pulled out the items that he would need. From the oversized cargo pocket on the side of his pants leg he retrieved his neatly folded map, which he spread out onto his lap. Next, he fished the GPS he had taken from his captain out of a pouch on his web belt. Pausing for a moment as he regarded the navigational device, the image of Captain Pascal, forlorn but still sporting a wisp of a smile, flashed before Dombrowski's eyes.

Letting his hands fall to his lap, the big Pole looked around at the snow-covered devastation. Pascal would be dead by now, he told himself. If the overdose of morphine hadn't taken him, then the plunging temperatures surely would have. At least, Dombrowski hoped that was the case. The idea that things might be otherwise sent a shiver down his spine.

With a shake of his head and a blinking of eyes, the legionnaire turned his attention back to his immediate problem. Tapping the location button on the GPS, he watched and waited for the grid-location readout. Memorizing the numbers in the display, he set the GPS aside and took up the map. After finding the spot on the map that corresponded to the given grid coordinates, he made a mark on the map case with a grease pencil before lifting the map so he could study it.

Stunned, Dombrowski looked up from the map

and stared straight ahead. Though he couldn't see it, there was a ridge a kilometer or so ahead. Just on the other side of the ridge, in a valley between the first ridge and another beyond, was their target. Even more incredible was the sudden realization that the very spot they were sitting in was marked on his map as a possible minefield, which intelligence believed was part of the defensive belt surrounding the missile silo.

When he had managed to collect his thoughts and calm down some, Dombrowski looked over to where his companion was resting. "Franz," he called out. "Without moving, look around you."

In an instant, the Austrian's eyes were wide open and his FA MAS firmly in hand. Methodically, he surveyed all around him, first inspecting everything that lay close at hand, then slowly looking farther afield. "What is it I am looking for?" he whispered as loudly as he dared while he continued to scan all around him.

"Mines," Dombrowski stated with greater calm than he felt at the moment.

"Dear God," Ingelmann intoned as he shifted his focus and began to inspect every patch of ground he could see.

"I am sorry. I wasn't paying attention," the Pole replied sheepishly.

"Do not feel badly, *mon ami*. Neither was I."

"Do you suppose that the overpressure that blew down all these trees was enough to set the mines off?" Ingelmann asked without interrupting his search.

"I would expect that is the case," Dombrowski responded without much conviction. "Either that or the information regarding their existence is wrong."

Looking over to his NCO, Ingelmann managed to crack a smile for the first time since exiting their transport hours before. "What? American intelligence wrong? How could that be?"

When he was satisfied that he was not in immediate danger, Dombrowski slowly began to get up. "We cannot be sure of anything, other than the fact that we need to go on." Though the freshly fallen snow made doing so futile, once he was on his feet, the Pole searched the ground about him.

"How far?" Ingelmann asked, without taking his eyes off the ground around him.

"Two kilometers, that way," the Pole stated, pointing in the direction of the unseen ridge. "And if you ask me, I would rather get out of this spot while there is still some light."

"I did not ask, but I do agree. Lead on, *mon* sergeant."

Even though the mines meant to protect the Russian missile silo had been neutralized by the same overpressure that had flattened the surrounding forests, the experience had shaken the two legionnaires. In the final leg of their journey, they exercised a great deal more caution. Because of this heightened awareness, Dombrowski perceived the presence of others in the vicinity of the silo long before they reached it. This caused the pair to redouble their vigilance as they moved forward.

When they had reached a point as close as they could go and still be able to talk in whispers without the fear of being heard, the Polish legionnaire stopped and squatted. With a slight wave of his hand, he motioned Ingelmann to come forward and join him. When his Austrian companion was down next to him, leaning forward so that Dombrowski could whisper in his ear, the big Pole told him to hold in place. "Remain here with the charge," he stated breathlessly. "I will go on and see what we are facing."

"And then what?"

Dombrowski's thoughts hadn't progressed much beyond getting as close as he could and sizing up the situation. Without a functional radio, they had been unable to contact any of the other two Legion CRAP teams assigned to this target. For all he knew, the other teams were totally hors de combat. If that were true, it would be up to the two of them to take out the missile that was now but a couple of hundred meters away.

Lifting his night-vision goggles up onto his forehead, Dombrowski wiped the sweat off his face. He spoke as he reasoned his way through this dilemma. "If it comes to that, then we will have to do the best we can to carry out the mission."

The best response the Austrian could muster was a simple, "I see."

"After I have had an opportunity to check things out," Dombrowski continued, "I will come back here to tell you what I have found. If those are Russians down there, then I will circle around to the other side of the site. Once there, I will open fire. With luck, they will all follow me away from the silo and up over that far ridge. When you hear the gunfire start going down the other side, make your way to the silo cover, place the charge, set the timer for five minutes, and then get the hell out of there."

"What if the order to execute has not been given?"

Frustrated by the situation, Dombrowski snapped, "Damn it! What if the order has been given? What if this is the last missile left?"

In silence, the big Pole waited for an answer. When Ingelmann found he was unable to reply, Dombrowski continued. "We have no choice but to carry on as best we can." Then, after letting his anger subside a bit, he added, "Besides, those are Russians. No one will shed a tear if we should squash a few by mistake."

Not having the innate hatred of that branch of the Slavic people as Dombrowski did, Ingelmann felt uneasy about what his sergeant was proposing. The idea that two lowly legionnaires could trigger a chain of events that would result in a worldwide holocaust flashed through his brain. Still, like Dombrowski, he could see no other option, except one. "I think it would be better," he finally ventured, "if I played rabbit-and-hounds with the Russians while you placed the explosives. You are, after all, the expert in that area and I, as you well know, am far more nimble than you."

The darkness kept Dombrowski from seeing Ingelmann's expression, leaving him to wonder if his comrade was hoping he would turn down his offer. It was only when the Austrian reached out and grasped his arm that the Polish legionnaire realized that Ingelmann was deadly serious. "It must be this way," Ingelmann stated firmly. "You know that, don't you?"

Dombrowski didn't reply. Instead, he repeated his instructions. "Stay here until I get back, is that clear?"

"*Oui, mon sergeant.* Very clear."

The snow on the ground and the debris strewn about made moving forward in silence a painfully slow process. The falling snow didn't help matters either. Still, Dombrowski was able to maneuver himself into a position close enough to the silo cover that he could see most of the shadowy figures. Taking up the best-covered and concealed position he could find under the circumstances, he brought his weapon up and slowly switched the safety to the fire position before settling in to watch and listen.

It didn't take long to figure out that there was a man squatting not twenty meters from him, holding a stubby weapon at the ready and looking in his general direction. Behind that one there were two more figures, standing upright on an elevated mound that Dombrowski assumed was the concrete silo cover. The two were fumbling about with something, but he could not be certain of what they were doing.

Seeing that there was no way of getting closer, the Polish legionnaire was faced with a difficult decision. If he called out the challenge in French and the people he was watching turned out to be Russian, he'd be screwed. His plan of going back to Ingelmann and coordinating their agreed-upon plan would be impossible to implement. Yet if he called out a greeting in Russian and the shadowy figures before him were fellow legionnaires they might shoot before he had an opportunity to properly identify himself. He had too much respect for the marksmanship of his comrades to take a chance like that.

With no other choice, Dombrowski lowered himself behind the thickest tree trunk he could find and removed his gloves. Putting two fingers in his mouth, he let go with a whistle that faintly resembled that of an African bird that almost any legionnaire would be familiar with.

On the other side of the log, in the direction of the silo, Dombrowski heard a sudden shuffling about in the snow, followed by hushed voices, then silence. Finally, a faint whistle, mimicking the one he had just issued, floated through the still night air.

After heaving a great sigh of relief, Dombrowski peered over the tree trunk and gave the challenge as loud as he dared. "Rapière."

From the other side of the tree trunk came the welcome response. "Pélican."

Though all doubt as to who they were had been

erased, the Polish legionnaire still exercised caution as he made his way forward. From somewhere ahead of him in the darkness, a familiar voice boomed out. "Stanislaus! Get your miserable ass over here. We are having problems with this infernal contraption of yours." The voice belonged to Adjutant Hector Allons, leader of Team Bastille.

Before complying with this gruff order, Dombrowski paused and faced about in the direction he had come from. "Franz! *Kommen sie, mach snel,*" he shouted in German.

There was obvious relief in the Austrian's voice when his response of "*Jawol!*" cut through the pitch-black night.

Continuing his advance toward the silo, Dombrowski felt the weight of the world being lifted from him. As he passed the sentry he had first seen, he gave the man a friendly pat on the shoulder. "It is good to see you, my friend."

The legionnaire, a New Zealander named John Dwyer, responded without turning his attention from the sector he was covering. "Believe me, right now we're pissin' all over ourselves with joy at seeing anyone."

"I know, *mon ami,*" Dombrowski stated dryly as he continued to make his way to where the Spanish team chief waited. After reaching the silo and managing to clamber up the slick, steep sides of the concrete cover, the Polish legionnaire tried to determine who was there with Allons. From the man's stature and posture, he guessed it was a fellow Slav by the name of L'udovít Vál. Addressing Allons, the Polish legionnaire saluted and rendered his report. "Sergeant-Chef Dombrowski and Corporal Ingelmann reporting, sir."

There was a moment of silence as Hector Allons waited for the Pole to continue. When he did not, the Spaniard asked in a voice that betrayed his concern. "The captain? The others? Are they—"

Allons didn't finish his question. There was no need to. There was a notable hesitancy before Dombrowski replied, one that none of the men present missed. *"Oui,"* was all he was able to manage.

Again there was silence as the legionnaires who belonged to Allons' team took a moment to reflect upon their most grievous loss. When he was able to do so without fear of displaying any emotion, Dombrowski asked the Spaniard about his team. "Except for some brushes and bumps, we all made it."

Astonished, Dombrowski shook his head in disbelief. "All?"

"I guess," the Spanish adjutant replied quietly, "we were fortunate."

It took a moment for everyone standing on the cover of the Russian intercontinental ballistic missile to shake the pall that had fallen over them and snap back to the reality of the moment. It was Dombrowski, anxious to push the image of a forlorn Jules Pascal out of his mind, who spoke first. "So, Adjutant, what seems to be the problem with the charge?"

With a shake of his head, Allons refocused on the matter at hand. "Both of our devices took some knocking about during the drop. The other was a complete write-off. And this one has several wires that have pulled free. Vál and I were just trying to figure out which one went where when you showed up."

Looking around, Dombrowski asked if the area was secure enough to use the small penlight he carried with him for checking connections. Allons shrugged. "If there are any Russians around, they are the most inconspicuous Slavs I have ever come across."

Taking that response to be in the affirmative, the Polish legionnaire squatted before the device the others had been working on. Cupping one hand over the business end of his penlight, he flipped the ON switch. As he always did during tactical situations, he slowly opened the hand covering the light until there was just enough illumination on the area that required his attention. After studying the tangled bundle of wires, he growled. "What a mess."

"Yes, I know," Allons rejoined. "That is why I am so glad that it was you who came stumbling in here."

Though he didn't share that particular sentiment, Dombrowski said nothing as he surveyed the condition of the device that sat before him. Finally, he shut off his penlight. "The only spot of luck we've had this day is in the fact that one of our two devices survived intact. All we need to do is have Ingelmann bring it on over here and set it up next to this piece of junk."

Allons was quick to veto that idea. "I am afraid that if at all possible, we must save yours and repair this one."

"Save it?" Dombrowski retorted. "What the hell for? Isn't our journey out of this hell on earth going to be bad enough without hauling useless items like that one along?"

Realizing that the Polish NCO had been out of contact and was unfamiliar with the overall situation, the Spanish legionnaire explained the reason why they needed to hang onto his shaped charge device. "By last count, two silos, like this one, have no teams covering them. Either those who survived the jump are out of contact like you were or they are . . . well, gone. Regardless of the reason, we have been ordered to finish up here as quickly as possible and report to the rally point, bringing all unused demolitions along with us. Once there are enough of us there, the area commander intends to organize us into new teams that will be dispatched to take out those targets that have not yet been executed."

Though it was a blow to realize that their work would be far from over when this silo was taken out, Dombrowski hid his disappointment. "It's going to take me some time to sort this mess out."

Pausing, Allons looked down at his watch. "You have forty-seven minutes."

"And then?" the Pole asked.

"We execute."

Though he knew time was pressing, Dombrowski took a minute to gather his thoughts. "So, you're telling me that we're going to blow this silo, and I assume the others, in less than an hour?"

"Correct," Allons replied.

"We're going to hoof it over to the last two and hit them after this?"

"Again correct."

"Don't you think that by the time we reach the other silos we're supposed to hit," Dombrowski asked, making no effort to hide his bewilderment, "the element of surprise will have pretty much evaporated and the Russians will be on to what we're doing?"

Allons nodded. "Yes, I suppose that is also correct."

Rather than continue this line of questioning, the Polish legionnaire grunted and shook his head. "Well, I guess the Americans know what they are doing."

"One would hope so," Allons responded with little conviction in his voice.

Without further ado, Dombrowski settled down to sorting out the ball of twisted wires and leads. One step at a time, he told himself. He had serious doubts that the situation they faced could be sorted out and made right as easily or as neatly as the wires he now held in his hands.

15

The unending series of delays and tribulations that had kept Demetre Orlov and his special-response team at bay was not without its benefits. Darkness had fallen by the time they were within striking distance of General Igor Likhatchev's regional command center. That his former mentor might not be there was always a possibility, one that plagued Orlov as they fought their way across a ravaged countryside. What he would do if that were the case was beyond him. The Russian colonel hated to lose. He would do anything to accomplish his assigned task, which was exactly why he was the darling of the current Russian government.

Reason, however, was quick to silence these nagging doubts almost as soon as they bubbled up. Orlov knew General Likhatchev better than he dared let on. Over the years, he had served this gifted Russian general in many theaters and capacities. When Likhatchev had been named to command the Moscow military district, he had himself selected Demetre Orlov to serve on his personal staff. It had been this assignment that had brought the Russian colonel to the attention of politicians vying for important posts within the post-Soviet government. During periods of internal crises, when the President of Russia or his representatives paid a visit to Likhatchev to sound him out in an effort to gauge the mood of the Army, Orlov was always seated at the right hand of the great general, taking notes and listening with rapt attention. That Orlov survived the purge that saw his superior exiled far from the center of Russian political power was as much a surprise to him as it was to the man who thought he had been nurturing a loyal supporter for the future.

Likhatchev would be there, Orlov kept telling himself whenever doubts began to cloud his exhausted mind. It was eminently logical. The complex had been constructed to ride out everything but a direct hit by a nuclear device. Besides serving as an emergency seat of government for the vast province, the regional headquarters also provided backup command-and-control networks for the Strategic Rocket Force throughout the area. If the National Command Authority were eliminated during a nuclear surprise attack, the regional headquarters could initiate a retaliatory strike, thanks to the Perimeter system. Given the dual importance of the site, a hefty security force, well provisioned with emergency stocks of food, fuel, and other essentials, was also located there. Yes, Orlov repeated time and time again as he struggled through the tangled maze that had once been a vast, peaceful pine forest, Likhatchev would be there, waiting for his chance to bring down the inept system that had plagued Russia since the fall of the Soviet Empire.

As reassuring as his confidence was on this point, the problem of hacking their way through the shield of security that the regional command-and-control center provided Likhatchev presented Orlov with many difficulties. Just how much of the garrison would be situated away from the center, committed to providing emergency services and enforcing martial law in the wake of the asteroid strike, were questions for which he had no answer. He could find himself facing the entire Force. That Igor Likhatchev would be ruthless enough to hold back this Force at such a time would not be at all out of character. The general, after all, was playing for very high stakes and could be expected to follow the Russian military tradition of expending lives freely in order to achieve a designated goal. None of this deterred the commander of Moscow's elite special-response team. Demetre Orlov had faced terrible odds before without flinching. He had been handed missions that others had deemed impossible and executed them with ease. So it was never a question of "if" in his mind but rather, of "how."

Long before they had boarded their transports at the military airfield outside of Moscow, Orlov had developed several approaches to the tactical problems he would face when they reached their objective. In order to decide which approach he would implement, a detailed reconnaissance was required. This he would do personally, since he had taken the precaution of not briefing his officers on any of the options he was entertaining. All they knew was that at some point close to their target, the entire special-response team would occupy a concealed assembly area. From there, he, accompanied by a small number of handpicked commandos, would sally forth to recon the final approach routes into the complex. In his absence, Major Gregory would be left in command. Only when the Russian colonel was satisfied that he had a suitable solution would he return to the assembly area, brief his subordinates on the plan, and then lead them back to execute their assigned task.

Orlov was accompanied by only three men. One of them, Ivan Moshinsky, was a sergeant who often made his personal views on the world they lived in known to his colonel. These views were always unsolicited and very often they made his superior uncomfortable. Orlov allowed this particular man a great deal of liberty, however, for Moshinsky was as close to being a personal bodyguard as a man could be without having been so designated. As big as Orlov, the outspoken NCO was agile and quick. In addition to being a crack shot, he was utterly fearless and had no qualms about sliting a man's throat or eliminating prisoners whom the government in Moscow had no interest in putting on trial. These traits had earned him the nickname of "Great White," since neither creature had anything resembling a conscience when it came to killing.

The second man Orlov took forward with him was a private by the name of Peter Spangen. Young and eager to please, Spangen idolized Moshinsky and revered Orlov as a son would a stern, yet fair father. Spangen had come to the Russian colonel's attention in Chechnya, where his impressive marksmanship had earned him a reputation second to none. Like other snipers in the unit, he normally carried a Russian-made Dragunov SVD sniper rifle that fired a special 7.62mm cartridge. Unlike the others, this young commando had access to foreign-built weapons. His personal favorite was the Barrett 12.7mm rifle, an American-built weapon that fired a Browning heavy machine-gun round. With that weapon, Spangen had no need to get up close and personal, since anything that could be seen within a mile of his location could be hit with ease. He was equally adept when it came to employing the massive 15mm AMR rifle, built by Steyr and capable of penetrating 40mm of armor at a range of 800 meters. On this evening, the young sniper was armed with his Barrett.

The last man in this select entourage was Orlov's senior combat engineer. Slight in stature, Vladimir Kulinsky was responsible for supervising the clearing of a path through obstacles, directing forced entries into bunkers and other hard targets, and marking the route that the entire team would follow once his commander had decided upon an avenue of approach. While his role was not nearly as glamorous as Spangen's or his methods as brutally direct as Moshinsky's, his contributions were more valuable to the special-response team than those of the other two men. Kulinsky's most important skill was his ability to breach any barrier the team encountered. His proficiency in doing this had earned him the honorific of "Orlov's Door Knocker."

More than once, Demetre Orlov had claimed that together with Moshinsky, Spangen, and Kulinsky, he could storm the gates of Hell. On this evening, as the Russian colonel lay on the cold ground just outside the regional command-and-control center that they had been struggling to reach, he imagined that the day had finally come when he would have to make good on that boast.

The last flickering of fires that had consumed the aboveground barracks, administrative buildings, maintenance facilities, and storage sheds showed Orlov more than enough to convince him that this effort was going to be both difficult and bloody. In addition to the reinforced-concrete guard posts that studded the perimeter of the installation, a number of armored fighting vehicles roamed about, making their assigned rounds as they searched relentlessly for intruders such as Orlov and his team. Every now and then a dismounted patrol led by a dog and his handler came into view. After watching all of this through the night-vision sight attached to his sniper rifle, Spangen grunted. "You would think they were expecting us."

"Since when has that stopped us?" Moshinsky replied as he continued to survey the scene before him as a hunter would while picking his killing field. Orlov made no effort to silence this idle chatter. Both men were sufficiently experienced in this sort of operation to know when they could relax their vigilance and when they had to be as silent as the dead. Having seen all they could from that particular vantage point, the Russian colonel returned his handheld night-vision goggles to their carrying case and turned to Kulinsky. The engineer was busily making notes on a sketch map of the installation, using the dim light thrown off by the distant flames. Only when Orlov saw that the man was finished did he speak. "I have seen enough."

The combat engineer nodded in agreement. "Yes, Colonel. By far, this will be the best approach. As long as the patrols maintain the rhythm we have observed, we should be able to slip through this blind spot and make it over to the emergency exit for the bunker. Provided there have been no modifications made to the steel doors, changes that were unrecorded on the plans provided to us by the Ministry of Defense, I will need only a small charge to sever the hinges." Knowing his colonel's concerns, Kulinsky explained the meaning of this. "We will be able to remain right there, on either side of the entrance, when I blow the door."

Though he was pleased with this spot of news, Orlov didn't show it. Instead, he began to back away from the perimeter posts. Always attuned to the actions of their leader and not having to be told what to do, the other members of the team also turned away. Crawling along the ground, Moshinsky fell in behind Orlov. He was followed by Kulinsky. Spangen, his deadly sniper rifle cradled in his arms, brought up the rear. Only when they were well clear of the installation they had been reconning did the men stand up and return to the assembly area. Even then, they maintained the sort of vigilance expected of professionals of their caliber while in hostile territory.

With his plan of execution firmly set in his mind, Demetre Orlov now had to gather his senior personnel, issue his orders, and get on with their mission. As the small, four-man reconnaissance party entered the loose perimeter of the assembly area, where his handpicked commandos were waiting, the darkness hid the anxious stares of his men as he passed by them on his way to the center. Even when he reached the point where his signal detachment was set up, he was totally unaware that anything was amiss. Expecting to find a gathering of selected members of his command there, such as his deputy and those belonging to the signal section, the sound of hushed voices from that gaggle of personnel did not surprise him as he drew near.

It wasn't until he stepped into the center of the group, arranged in a tight circle, did the talking come to an abrupt halt. "I assume things have been quiet here?" Orlov demanded in the brusque manner he usually used when he came upon troops engaging in activities that he was not exactly pleased with. Under ordinary circumstances, the momentary silence would quickly have been broken by the senior man present, stepping forth to offer the most viable excuse he could muster on the spur of the moment to explain away the lapse in discipline their commander had stumbled upon.

The Russian colonel was still waiting for this brave soul to do so when, to his utter horror, one of the silent figures turned a flashlight on and into his face. As he recoiled, shielding his eyes from the sudden and almost painful exposure of this unexpected illumination, Moshinsky surged forward and placed his massive frame squarely in front of Orlov. Flipping the safety of his AK off, he brought it up to his shoulder and aimed at the spot where he assumed the man with the flashlight stood. Spangen, who had pushed Kulinsky out of the way, fell in shoulder-to-shoulder with Moshinsky. Like his companion, the sniper brought his weapon up and prepared to protect his beloved commander with his own life, if necessary. Though not as quick on the uptake as the other two were, Kulinsky managed to fumble about until he had brought his AK up, turned around, and backed up until he felt himself bump into Orlov.

The three commandos encircling Orlov could hear the sound of the safeties on the weapons trained on them being disengaged. Unsure of what was going on, they waited for their colonel to say something, to give an order to them or to their mutinous comrades. Anything would have been welcome at that moment as each man assessed the alarming situation.

The man they were protecting was carefully weighing that situation. Since the day he had assumed command of this special-response team, Demetre Orlov had anticipated that something like this was more than a possibility. He often found himself wondering less about "if" the day came and more about "what" he would do when it did. He had always imagined that when faced with a traitor within the ranks of his own unit, he would instinctively know what to do. Unfortunately, at the moment, his instincts were failing him. For several tense moments, Orlov prepared himself for a death not unlike that which he had meted out to so many other sons of Russia who had become, through no great fault of their own, victims of their times and pawns of forces greater than themselves.

When his mutinous command, holding all of the advantages, did not immediately strike the four of them down, it dawned upon Orlov that he had a chance. His agile mind began to assess the situation. With his self-appointed guardians pressing in on him, he reasoned that the longer this impasse lasted, the better their chance of surviving it. That his command had been whipped up into rebellion by a particularly persuasive instigator, or through some sort of collective agreement among the men he had handpicked, it didn't matter at that moment. What was critical was determining just how far he could go without provoking them. To do this would require both subtlety and diplomacy.

After taking a moment to compose himself, and carefully sling his assault rifle over his shoulder, the Russian colonel wedged his hands between Moshinsky and Spangen. Making sure that whoever held the flashlight saw his every move, he separated the two men and stepped forward. Though the flashlight was blinding him, he forced himself not to blink or to show any sign of weakness. "I would very much appreciate it if you would point your light elsewhere. It makes talking to you a bit difficult."

Without the slightest hesitation, the beam of light dropped to the ground at Orlov's feet. This pleased him, for it was a clear indication that he had an opportunity to assert a degree of control over the situation. "Thank you. Now, would someone be so kind as to explain to me what, exactly, is going on here?"

Now it was the turn of those facing him to hesitate and fumble about. While he waited, watched, and listened, Orlov could detect a sudden spate of whispering and shuffling about on either side of the person holding the light. One of the voices he heard belonged to his deputy, Major Petkovic. Another, though it was quite clear, was unfamiliar to him.

Finally, after he had taken a moment to collect himself, Petkovic responded. "Colonel, this mission is at an end. We are not going to attack the regional command center or assassinate General Likhatchev."

Orlov sensed that his deputy was both nervous and uncomfortable making this announcement. Given that, he decided to ratchet up the pressure on Petkovic by assuming a more authoritative tone. "On what grounds do you presume to make such a decision?"

"Colonel," Petkovic offered in a voice that betrayed a hint of pleading, "General Likhatchev is not our enemy. He is a hero. He is a true patriot."

"At this moment," Orlov countered, "he is in rebellion against the people and state of Russia. He has threatened the very nation that both he and we have pledged ourselves to defend. Eliminating this danger to Mother Russia is not a choice for us. It is our duty."

For the first time, the person possessing the voice that the Russian colonel had not recognized before spoke. Though the tone was both firm and passionate, there was no mistaking that it was a female's. "Comrade Colonel," she stated crisply, "our first duty is to the people. It is for them, and not for the benefit of gangsters and profiteers in Moscow, that we shed our blood. The real traitors are those who sit in the Kremlin."

Despite his best efforts, a hint of a smile crept across Orlov's face. It had been wise of Likhatchev to send out a dedicated and determined woman to rally the special-response team over to his side. A woman presents less of a physical threat, especially to men who are commandos. Not only can a strong woman wield words like a sword, she can do so in a manner that is often more persuasive and always easier for the male ear to take in. Russian history and legends are replete with heroines who rallied their men to overcome daunting adversities and achieve great and noble deeds. "I will not bother asking how it is that you came to find us, whoever you are," Orlov stated as he began his efforts to undo what she had done.

"Zudiev," she said. "Captain Anna Zudiev. I am a member of General Likhatchev's staff."

"Yes, well, Captain Zudiev," the Russian colonel went on, changing his tack to suit the new circumstances. "I suppose you think you are right in what you say, and that rebellion is justified. But I am afraid that no matter how well-intentioned your actions may seem, or how noble your cause is, treason is still treason." While he spoke to the female captain, he made sure that his voice had been loud enough so that the maximum number of his men would hear what he was saying.

Likhatchev's appointed messenger was no fool. She understood the dynamics of the situation and what the Russian colonel was up to. Her superior had warned her that the leader of these commandos was as skilled in the art of persuasion and deception as he was in meting out death, destruction, and mayhem. Rather than risk losing her tenuous grip on the situation by engaging the Russian colonel in a debate, Captain Zudiev decided to play her hand. "Who is right and who is wrong in this matter will be an issue for historians as yet unborn to decide. My mission is to simply bring you and your men a message from General Likhatchev." As Orlov had done before, the woman spoke in a voice that carried beyond the gathering with which she stood. "You can go on and try to carry out your orders without questions, without thinking about the consequences those orders will have on our nation and its people. Or," she added after pausing to catch her breath and let her preceding words sink in, "you can come over to General Likhatchev."

For a long moment, no one spoke a word or moved a muscle as the two parties in this lopsided standoff waited for the other to say something more. In the midst of this awkward silence, Orlov felt Moshinsky ease up against him. He could feel the commando's warm breath as he whispered in his ear. "I can drop her before anyone knows what's going on."

Instinctively, Orlov knew that this would be both foolish and fatal. Raising his right hand, he signaled his self-appointed guardian to back off.

"A wise decision," the female staff officer stated in a tone that was both confident and commanding. "I hope your next one will be just as shrewd."

Again there was a hesitation as Orlov assessed his position. Finally, unable to stand the strain, Major Petkovic spoke. "Colonel, one way or the other, we are all going to die. It is simply a matter of how and when. For myself, I have decided that I if I must do so, I will make my death matter for something that I can be proud of."

"Is not dying for Russia something to be proud of?" Orlov asked, incensed.

Now that he had committed himself, Petkovic's tone reflected his convictions. "Those who sent us out here are not Russia."

"And you think Likhatchev is?" Orlov countered as he struggled to keep this debate going and his chance to turn the situation around alive.

The major did not hesitate to respond. "Ours is a nation that has a habit of placing its people in circumstances in which they have only bad choices from which to pick. Right now, right here," Petkovic stated with the conviction of a zealot, "the choice lies between a government that is incapable of meeting even its most basic obligations to the Russian people, or to a leader who is willing and able to lead us back to greatness."

In the course of this speech, it became obvious to Orlov what had happened in his absence. Petkovic was the one who had fermented the revolt against him. The question that the Russian colonel now had to find an answer to was just how committed the remainder of the special-response team was to this course of action and what he could do to rally those who were not. "You understand what will happen to you if General Likhatchev fails in his bid to oust the government in Moscow?"

Before Petkovic or any of the other commandos could reply, the female staff captain stepped forward. With one hand, she raised the flashlight so that it was once more shining squarely in Orlov's face and blinding him. But he was not so dazzled by this move that he could not see the pistol she held against her hip, at the ready, in her other hand. "I have not come out here to chair a debate," she snapped. "My orders are to bring you back alive. However, if that proves to be impossible, then I have the freedom to take whatever action is necessary to end the threat that you represent."

Behind him, Orlov could feel the barrel of Moshinsky's weapon rubbing up against him as the commando slowly leveled it in an effort to bring it to bear. While the man did his best to conceal what he was about to do, Orlov forced himself to remain as calm as this tense state of affairs permitted.

Unfortunately, there were simply too many eyes watching every move. From somewhere off to his right, Orlov heard a mutineer jerk back the bolt of his assault rifle in order to chamber a round. This sound galvanized those who had been lulled by the exchange between their colonel and the female captain to bring their weapons up again and train them upon Orlov and his small party. For her part, Captain Zudiev took two steps forward, raising her pistol and cocking it as she did so. She pressed the muzzle against Orlov's forehead. "No more discussion," she hissed. "Submit or die."

With his options narrowed to those two extreme alternatives by a person holding a gun to his head and seeming more than ready to use it, the choice was easy. As long as he remained alive, there was a chance.

Reaching around, the Russian colonel placed his hand on Moshinsky's arm and forced it and the assault rifle down. "This is not the time for martyrdom," he whispered to his dedicated companion.

It wasn't until he was seated on the soft, leather sofa in a small room not far from General Likhatchev's office that Demetre Orlov realized just how exhausted he was. How long had it been, he wondered, since he had last slept. Thirty-six hours? Forty-eight?

He was still pondering this when Likhatchev entered the room, carrying a fresh bottle of vodka in one hand and two glasses in the other. Even before Orlov managed to shake off his inattentiveness and roust himself from the sofa in an effort to come to attention, the General was motioning to him to stay seated. "You have traveled a long way to reach us here," Likhatchev stated in his characteristically cheerful voice. "Rest a bit."

Lifting his hand to accept the glass the General offered him took more effort than the Russian colonel dared admit. As Likhatchev filled Orlov's glass, he told the Russian colonel how happy he was to see him there. Orlov waited until after he took a long, hard swig of alcohol before he responded. "Had your staff officer not reached my team before I did,

I am sure you would be singing a far different tune."

Rather than anger Likhatchev, Orlov's statement provoked laughter. As the General stood in the middle of the room, looking down into his glass while swirling the clear liquid about in it, his mood changed. "Would you really have gone through with it?"

Orlov looked up at him. "I expect you know me better than to ask such a question."

Shifting his gaze from his drink to the man on his sofa, Likhatchev nodded. "Yes, I suppose I do. That is why I need you with me again, Demetre."

With nothing more to lose, Orlov felt no compunction about holding back any of his thoughts or mincing his words. "To do what? Go back to Moscow and execute the very men who sent me out here to kill you?"

"No, no, my friend," the General replied as he stepped over to a chair and sat down. "As of late, we have been killing far too many of our own. The old ways of bringing about change in Russia must come to an end. We must stop branding those who oppose us as Reds or Whites, revolutionaries or counterrevolutionaries, traitors or patriots, so that we can justify killing them. We must find a way to pull our people together, under the flag of a truly just and benevolent government that holds the welfare of the nation and its people sacred. Bringing peace, prosperity, and justice is what I need you to help me do."

Now it was Orlov's turn to laugh before taking another sip of vodka.

"What do you find so funny about that?"

Leaning forward, Orlov slammed his empty glass on the table next to the sofa. "I find it funny, my good General, that you are prepared to vaporize the very people to whom you wish to bring peace and justice."

Easing back in his seat, a confident smile lit Likhatchev's face. "Do you really think I would turn such weapons upon our own people?"

"Fine!" Orlov exclaimed, throwing his hands out. "So you don't vaporize Moscow. So instead, you lay waste to Washington, or perhaps to London, which leaves them no choice but to wipe out your beloved people. Either way, you have not accomplished a damned thing."

Likhatchev smiled again as he shook his head. "Demetre, Demetre, Demetre," he repeated in a disappointed tone. "Have I not taught you anything?" Looking back over at the exhausted and bedraggled commando, Likhatchev explained. "It is a bluff, my friend. I would no more launch those missiles than . . ."

Likhatchev hesitated for a moment. Before continuing, he took a sip. As he did so, he eyed Orlov. After wiping a drop of vodka from the corner of his mouth, he reached over for the bottle, picked it up and began to pour the colonel of commandos a fresh drink. "I was about to say," he stated sadly, "that I would no more launch those missiles than you would shoot me."

Taking up his glass, Orlov took a sip. "I see you have not forgotten," he said in a firm tone.

"No, I have not forgotten, Demetre. You are perhaps the best soldier I have ever known. That's including myself," he said, tapping his chest.

For several minutes, neither man spoke. Each sat across from the other, nursing his drink while sizing up the other. Orlov finally broke the deadlock. "If you have your missiles, which you say you don't intend to use, of what use am I to you? Why didn't you simply instruct that female captain of yours to gun me down? You know that leaving me alive is a gamble."

"In order to win big," Likhatchev stated as his previous relaxed and easygoing mood returned, "one has to gamble big. Besides, I would have hoped that you would have figured that out on your own." Pausing, the General shrugged. "Of course, given your trials and tribulations over the past twenty-four hours, I can excuse a momentary lapse of insight. You see," he continued as he leaned forward toward Orlov, "once the government in Moscow realizes that a sizable portion of its own military has come over to me, they will have an excuse to step aside."

"Step aside?" Orlov echoed. "You expect the President to simply step aside and name you as his successor?"

Likhatchev smiled. "That is the way things are done these days. Gorbachev came to power with a mandate to save the Soviet Union. When he saw that he could not do so, he wisely decided to relinquish his hold on power to Yeltsin, the man of the hour. After it became clear that Yeltsin did not have the ability to turn things around, an arrangement was made that allowed him to retire from public life while giving Putin and the hardliners their chance. After he failed, Putin took the wise precaution of leaving office before he was thrown out. Now, with our country on the brink of total collapse, our current President is more than ready to yield. As with those before him, once he understands that he will be allowed to retire to a nice, comfortable dacha, where he will be free to enjoy the wealth that he managed to skim off the top of foreign loans and aid that passed through his hands, he will gladly go in peace."

Aware that the vodka was beginning to take hold, Orlov spoke slowly in order to keep from slurring his words. "Let's just say that you're right. Let's just suppose, for a moment, that the current President uses this crisis as an opportunity to step down. What makes you think that you can succeed where the others have failed?"

Having expected this sort of question, the General leaned forward. "Because, my dear Colonel, I have something that the others did not have. I have a crisis, a crisis unlike anything that this nation has experienced since the Great Patriotic War." Easing back in his seat, Likhatchev waved his glass around. "Our people are a tough people, a people who understand the need to make sacrifices when the times require it. Even the dullest peasants will understand the need to give their all to rebuild Mother Russia, just as they did when Stalin launched his five-year plans."

With the liquor and his exhaustion eroding his ability to think, it took Orlov some time to sort out what he was hearing, to gather his thoughts, and to respond. "This is still a coup. And I am still loyal to those whom you seek to replace."

"It doesn't have to be that way, my friend," Likhatchev countered.

"Out there," the Russian colonel explained as he waved his glass about in a vague gesture to indicate the shattered forest where he had been confronted, "I simply abandoned a hopeless position. I do not recall joining your revolution, General."

Standing up, Likhatchev took a final drink before putting the glass down and starting for the door. Before he left, he turned and looked back at Orlov. "Sometimes the truth is not important," he stated. "For my purposes, simple appearances will do."

With that, he walked out of the room and left his former subordinate alone to sort out where he stood. For the moment, time was on the General's side.

But only for a moment.

16

After having made amazingly good time, delay and frustration became the order of the day for the three SAS teams that were converging on their assigned target. Captain Alex Abraham's team Bravo, approaching from the southwest, had the misfortune of wandering into an uncharted minefield. This incident not only cost Abraham one of the three men with him but the resulting explosion alerted a Russian patrol to their presence. The running gunfight that followed claimed the life of the SAS captain as well as forcing the survivors away from their target.

When Major Thomas Shields discussed this turn of events via radio with Patrick Hogg, both men agreed that engagement was not without its positive aspects. As per their orders, the remnants of Abraham's command were doing all they could to keep the Russian patrol interested and diverting its watch over the missile silo.

While team Bravo did its best, the Russians refused to fully cooperate. Guessing what the unexpected intruders were up to, the commander of the security detachment sent only a small portion of his command to run the survivors of Abraham's team to ground. The bulk of the Russian security force was held back to defend the Perimeter missile the SAS teams were after.

After having gotten as close as he dare, Patrick Hogg, accompanied by Sergeant McPherson, surveyed the situation from a concealed position. The Russian positions encircling the silo stood out against the barren, snow-covered ground. While none of them seemed to be well-dug in, the defenders had more than sufficient cover, thanks to the shock wave that had bowled over the forests. Even more important from the Russians' standpoint, all of the fighting positions were mutually supporting. Rooting them out would take time, Hogg realized, and cost him men that he could ill afford to lose.

From a spot across the way, Major Thomas Shields had come to the same conclusion. In hushed tones, the two men covered the hand mikes of their radios and discussed their options. After comparing notes, they determined that there were probably fifteen or twenty Russians protecting the silo. That gave the security detachment a decided edge, since Hogg had but five in his team, and Shields six, counting himself. While members of the SAS were used to taking on superior numbers, the situation, as it stood, made a successful assault a highly speculative proposition. Neither Hogg nor Shields knew for sure where all the Russians were or their exact number. Ordinarily, a careful reconnaissance would rectify this deficiency, but they did not have time for that. Repeated calls from the American commander in their sector insisted that they execute their assigned target in conjunction with the other teams and upon completion, report to the rally point as quickly as possible.

Having seen all that he expected he would from the spot he was in, Patrick Hogg eased down behind the fallen tree he had been using for cover and continued his discussion with Shields. "Green, this is Blue. They have pretty much gone to ground. Success of an attack from this quarter is highly problematical. I say again, success is highly problematical."

There was a pause before Shields replied in a voice that betrayed just how discouraged he was, "Affirmative, Green."

"It's not like the old man to let something like a dozen or so Russians get him down," McPherson commented as Hogg waited for further contact with his superior.

Hogg, though he meant well, was in no mood to be cheered up. "The major's just lost a fair number of his men," he stated dryly. "Now he's going to have to make a decision that he knows could cost him a good part of what's left."

Sensing Hogg's anger and frustration, McPherson dropped the matter, choosing instead to lean up against the log next to his team leader and take advantage of this opportunity to rest. As he waited in the quiet darkness, there was no doubt in his mind that whatever Major Shields came up with in the next few minutes, it would require a great deal from all of them.

Only after it became clear that his companion had opted to remain mute did it occur to Hogg that this was the last thing he wanted. Unlike McPherson, he could not relax, close his eyes, and let his mind go wandering. To begin with, he was an officer in the midst of a very sensitive operation. Officers could not afford the luxury of disengaging their brains and waiting for someone else to give them a rousing kick in the pants when it was time to pack up and move on. If he permitted himself to relax as McPherson was doing, there was a very good chance that his lack of sleep would catch up and overwhelm him, leaving no one to answer when Shields finally did hail him with a solution to their dilemma.

So the exhausted SAS captain sat there, huddling up as best he could against the growing cold, struggling to stay awake and keep his thoughts focused on the mission.

The darkness that hid him from his foe conspired with the utter stillness and his momentary inactivity to resurrect the personal issues that seemed to be dominating his life as of late. That his Jenny was truly gone was still difficult for Hogg to accept. There had to be another way that he could reach out to her. All he needed to do was to find the right words, he told himself. Hadn't he always been able to do so before? In the past, he had always managed to make her understand just how important she was to him, to see that he needed her and loved her above all else. He couldn't understand how Jenny failed to see that his dedication to duty was simply a calling, while she was his reason for being.

Like a roller coaster that had reached a peak, this last hope hung there for a brief moment before flaring out in the quick and stomach-turning plunge that followed: *She is gone*, a quiet voice whispered from somewhere in the dark recesses of his mind. *You have lost her forever.*

"Green, this is Blue."

With a start, Hogg fumbled about in the darkness as he reached for the hand mike. "This is Green."

"We haven't much time," Shields stated without preamble, "so here's how this will play out. You will engage the Russians in a firefight from where you are. When you have their full attention, pull back, drawing them away from the silo as you go. I'm hoping that they buy into the idea that there are only two teams out here, that you are the last of them, and therefore they'll come at you with everything they have. Do you copy? Over."

With McPherson now fully awake and listening, Hogg acknowledged that he understood.

"Good," Shields replied. "Once you have led them as far as you dare, break contact and make your way to the rally point as best you can with utmost speed."

"Affirmative, Blue," Hogg said without letting his voice betray the apprehension he felt. "Is there anything else?" he asked out of habit.

"This is Blue. Negative. As soon as you're ready, execute." Then, as an afterthought, Shields added, "Good luck."

The SAS captain did not bother to return the sentiment. Instead, he turned to deal with the new situation at hand.

"I always hate this sort of thing," McPherson offered.

His team leader grunted. "I have no doubt that the major's right. The Russians will follow. It's getting them to stop following that's going to be the trick."

"You don't suppose that they'll give up the ghost when they hear the silo go pop, do you?" McPherson ventured.

"Are you willing to bet your life on that?" Hogg countered. When McPherson did not respond, Hogg went back to turning the problem over in his mind. "Do you remember that narrow draw we passed through two klicks back?" he finally asked.

"Yes, of course," McPherson replied. "The place looked like a team of drunken lumberjacks went on a frenzy." Partially shielded from the full force of the shock wave following the impact of the asteroid, the draw in question was choked with shattered trees thrown about at all angles. When he thought he had latched on to his commander's idea, the Scottish NCO articulated his own version: "We lead them back into it, gain the high ground, and chop 'em up while they're mucking about among the tree trunks."

"I'll do you one better," Hogg stated as he began to stir himself off the ground. "I want you to go back there with Jones. Take the two demo charges with you. Set them up on either side of the draw with the business end of the shaped charges angled down into it. Wire them together and into the manual blasting machine. Then find a place from where we can see down into the vale. It has to be far enough away so that whoever executes the demo doesn't go up with it."

McPherson whistled. "Now that will be a neat trick. It's not the blast that I'm worried about. It's the trash that the charges throw up in the air that'll get ya. The splinters from the trees will come down on anyone within a hundred yards of that vale like a hail of arrows."

Hogg gave his NCO a light tap on the shoulder. "I'm sure you'll figure something out by the time I get back there. Now, get going. Send Dunn and Patterson up here to me. We'll give you ten minutes before we open fire."

"That's not much time, sir."

"That's all I can give you. Now go, before the major starts hounding us."

When McPherson was gone, Hogg checked his watch. Ten minutes. An eternity in the SAS. It was ten minutes that he, in truth, didn't have. But having taken them, he needed to make sure they were not wasted. While he waited for the two men who would stay behind with him, he settled into a good firing position. Once he was nestled behind the best cover he could find, he flipped his night-vision goggles down in order to make a final sweep of the area around the silo. Any more thoughts about his wife were for the moment relegated to that place in his mind where all professional soldiers store personal baggage and concerns that have no place on the battlefield.

Making his way up to where McPherson waited for him was an ordeal for Private Jones. Stumbling and tripping, he navigated the maze of fallen timbers that filled the narrow vale as best he could. Born in an area where opportunities for a young man were slim, he had joined the Royal Welsh Fusiliers before volunteering for the SAS. Just how wise a move that had been was, at this particular moment, open to debate. In a pitch-black darkness, he moved as quickly as he could. This effort cost him dearly as he slipped and banged his knees and shins more times than he cared to count. Each time he stumbled he cut loose with a string of oaths. When he was close enough that McPherson could hear him, the Scottish sergeant yelled out to the man, "Stop your bloody whining and get your sorry ass over here, you filthy Welshman."

Between McPherson's exhortations and the echo of gunfire louder with each passing minute, Jones managed to make his way over to McPherson's position. "It's about bloody time," the Scot snarled as he grabbed the lead Jones offered up. "Now, get back to where I told you to go, find yourself a hole to crawl into, and wait there till after I blow this." Knowing enough about demolitions to understand what would happen when McPherson set off the two charges, the young commando was gone in a flash.

When all was set, the Scottish NCO settled down to wait for Hogg to lead the Russians into the kill zone. With nothing better to do, he looked around. As he did so, he began to have second thoughts about the spot he had selected. Though the fold of earth that stood between himself and the charges beyond was quite substantial and would be more than adequate to protect him from the direct effect of the blast, there was little in the way of overhead cover. His warnings to Hogg were spinning about in his mind when he heard the other members of the team enter the vale below.

Carefully, McPherson rose up and called out in the direction from which he had heard his captain's voice. "Up and to your right, sir."

Homing in on the sound of his sergeant's voice, Patrick Hogg ignored the odd burst of AK fire unleashed blindly by one of his nervous pursuers. Like Jones had, Hogg, Dunn, and Patterson found the going both difficult and painful. Unlike Jones, none of them griped. The random fire that continued to gain on them motivated the three stay-behinds to maintain their focus and clear the vale before the Russians caught up.

Huffing and puffing, Hogg managed to reach the hollow where he thought McPherson was. "Sergeant! Where in the bloody hell are you?"

With the Russians now entering the vale below, McPherson had to exercise a bit more caution. Waving only his free hand above the fold of earth he was hunkered behind, he called out as loudly as he dared. "To your right, sir. Over here."

Almost immediately, three heaving, sweating commandos came bounding up over the mound of dirt before McPherson and descended on him. Having no idea of how close they were, one of them landed right on top of the waiting SAS sergeant. Only a display of incredible self-discipline, coupled with a keen awareness of how near the Russians were, kept McPherson from tossing his unexpected assailant off to one side while flailing him with every curse word he could muster.

The assailant, after realizing his error, crawled over McPherson and back onto solid ground. "Sorry about that," Hogg mumbled as he struggled to regain his composure and sort out his jumble of gear that was now in utter disarray.

Glad that he had exercised restraint, McPherson turned to the other two men. "Keep moving uphill till you're clear of the ridgeline. Jones is over there already. You have sixty seconds before I light up the Russians." Then, remembering the vulnerability of his position, he turned to Hogg. "I recommend you go with them."

Sorted out and ready, Hogg shook his head. "I'm staying here with you. Where's there a safe place?"

"Edinburgh, if you must know."

Angered that his NCO would joke at a time like this, Hogg snapped back, "Jesus, man! I'm serious."

McPherson was just as quick and equally adamant, "Well, so am I."

For the first time, Hogg looked around. Even though he could not see everything in the darkness that engulfed them, it didn't take long for him to appreciate just how vulnerable this spot was. "Why in hell didn't you pick someplace farther back?"

Trying to keep track of where the Russians were at the same time he was dealing with his commanding officer, McPherson's answer was to the point. "Not enough wire."

Like most assault units a Special Operations team carries only that which is required to handle the assigned mission and unanticipated contingencies. This is especially true when the team will be expected to cover a lot of broken ground on foot. Although each team had brought two oversized shaped charges with them, the second was meant only as a backup. Each Tempest team had a dual means of detonating their charges. The primary means was a delayed fuse. The secondary was the manual blasting machine McPherson now held in his hand. This machine required a spool of wire in order to function, and only enough wire to prepare one charge for detonation from a safe distance had been included in the demo kit.

Unfortunately, the situation that McPherson faced when setting up his ambush had forced him to make compromises. In order to have the desired effect his captain wanted, he could not get around the necessity of setting off the two charges simultaneously. Since he had to wait until the Russians had entered the kill zone before executing the charges, he could not use the time fuses. When the distance between the two charges was added to this problem, McPherson had no choice but to gamble that his chosen spot, located at the very end of the wire he had on hand, would be good enough.

In an instant, Hogg realized this and started to reconsider his decision to stay where he was. He was in the midst of this deliberation when the sky off to the east of them was suddenly lit up with a brilliant flash. Without thinking, both men turned in the direction of the missile silo. Several seconds letter, a booming report rolled through the vale toward them. Even as this wave of sound hit, the eastern sky lit up again. This time, instead of a bright flash, a sheet of flames that put Hogg in mind of a freshly lit welder's torch shot straight up. "Well, the major's done his job," he said, feeling a sense of relief for the first time that night.

Though he had taken a moment to watch the spectacle in the distance, Sergeant McPherson quickly turned his attention to their immediate problem. "The bastards have stopped."

Without hesitation, Hogg scanned the vale below. He could see that the Russians pursuing them had come to a complete halt. Like McPherson, they were also watching the death of the missile they had been assigned to guard. Near the head of the loose formation, one of them looked up in the general direction that he assumed Hogg had taken, then back at the sky that was being lit as bright as day by the burning of the missile's propellant. With a wave of his arm and a shouted order, this individual signaled to the others that they were giving up their pursuit and heading back.

Without hesitation, Hogg gave the order: "Fire the charges."

The Scottish NCO, who had also been watching, hesitated. "But they're not fully in the kill zone."

Hogg turned on the sergeant and repeated his order. "Fire the charges, *now!*"

Dropping down, McPherson turned away, pushed himself up against the berm that separated him from the vale below, and gave the manual blasting machine a quick, violent twist.

17

When he opened his eyes, Stanislaus Dombrowski was only vaguely aware of where he was. Unlike many of his companions, the Polish NCO was not the type who benefited from brief catnaps or a few stolen minutes of sleep. Once he shut his eyes and went down, he needed to stay down for four hours, minimum. Anything less than that only seemed to exacerbate his fatigue.

Slowly, Dombrowski struggled to rise up off the ground he had thrown himself onto scant hours ago. In the process of prying his eyes open, he noticed that it was considerably lighter. It must be day, he told himself as he finally managed to peer above the level of the fallen trees he had nestled in before drifting off. At first he could not see anything or anyone in the thick arctic fog that clung to the ground. Were it not for the sound of subdued voices piercing the chilly veil, the Pole could almost have convinced himself that there wasn't another living soul anywhere near at hand.

With a shake of his aching head, Dombrowski endeavored to collect himself. Lifting one hand to his chest, he instinctively groped about until he felt his FA MAS assault rifle. Since he could never rely on having enough time to properly wake, he always hung his weapon around his neck when he lay down to rest. That way, no matter what the circumstances were when roused, he'd at least have handy his primary means of defending himself.

Comforted that all seemed to be in order, Dombrowski cleared his throat, forcing up a mass of phlegm in the process. Leaning over, he spit the disgusting wad of mucus out as far as he could. He was still in the process of wiping a bit of drool from the corner of his mouth, when Ingelmann's voice cut through his early morning stupor.

"Ah, there you are, my friend," the cheerful Austrian called out. "If it weren't for that quaint practice of yours, I'd have never found you."

Coughing and clearing his head, Dombrowski grunted. "Ingelmann, you're the only man in the Legion who gets lost going to the crapper."

Emerging from the thick, cold mist, Ingelmann groaned. "Now that happened only once, and only because there was a sandstorm brewing."

Looking up at his companion, the Pole saw that his fellow legionnaire was carefully balancing two steaming mess cups as he navigated the jumble of fallen trees and debris in which they had come to rest. "Twice," Dombrowski countered. "You somehow managed to do so twice."

When he reached his comrade, the Austrian offered one of the cups to him. "Oh, that," he replied dismissively after handing over the cup. "I was drunk."

Not in the mood to carry on this exchange, at least not until after he'd enjoyed some of the warm beverage that he had been handed, Dombrowski brought the cup up to his lips. After taking a sip, he looked down into the black, steaming liquid, then up at the smiling Ingelmann. "Where in the hell did you find this?"

The Austrian chuckled. "The American signal section had a whole pot of it brewing. They were guarding it like it was gold."

Quickly, Dombrowski took another sip, savoring the taste of genuine American Army coffee and relishing the feeling the warm fluid left in its wake. "My friend," he sighed as he closed his eyes and held the steaming cup with the same reverence that a priest would a chalice of sacrificial wine, "this *is* gold." Opening his eyes, he looked over at Ingelmann. "How did you manage to liberate it?"

The Austrian legionnaire pulled back the hood of his cold-weather parka and tapped the unadorned front of his beret. "The Americans are suckers for souvenirs." Then, as if this comment triggered another thought, Ingelmann stuck his hand into a pocket of his parka. When he pulled it out, he was holding a foil packet, which he presented to Dombrowski.

Taking this second gift in his free hand, the Pole turned it this way and that until he could read the label. "English biscuits? You have been a very busy lad this morning."

"Well, you know what the Americans say: The early bug finds the bird."

After using his teeth to rip the package open, Dombrowski set it down on his lap before fishing out one of the biscuits. "I think it's the bird that gets the worm."

Waving his cup about, Ingelmann reached over and snatched one of the biscuits from Dombrowski. "Whatever you say, *mon* sergeant." After taking a bite, he looked down at the remains of his biscuit. "Our SAS friends are far more accommodating than the Americans."

"And how did you manage to pry these from them?"

The Austrian legionnaire looked over at his companion, affecting a long, sorrowful face as he did so. "I told the Brits that we had lost all our rations in the drop, that the only thing we had to look forward to by way of food were American combat rations. After expressing their sincere regrets, one of their officers rummaged around in his rucksack and gave me these."

Dombrowski shook his head in disbelief. "You may be an idiot as far as land navigation is concerned, but you more than redeem yourself when it comes to providing for life's little necessities. Now all we need is a bottle of wine and all will be right with the world."

Looking away from Dombrowski, Ingelmann glanced furtively first to his right, then left. When he was sure that no one was watching them, he reached down inside his parka and began to rummage about for something. When he had found what he was hunting for, he slowly pulled out a metal flask. "Later, *mon ami.*"

After a hearty round of laughter, the two legionnaires settled back to savor their unexpected windfall. Eventually, when he noticed that he had almost drained his cup, Dombrowski tried to recall if he had remembered to bring his beret. "Do you think," he asked innocently, "they would be willing to part with another cup?"

The Austrian gave his friend a sly smile. "I'm sure that if you personally went over there and asked the female sergeant nicely, you'd be able to talk her out of, or into, anything."

"Coffee would be more than enough," Dombrowski replied before enjoying the last sip of his second-most-favorite beverage.

"But, Sergeant, she is just your type. A healthy,

full-figured woman who looks as if she could knit a tank out of steel wool."

The Polish legionnaire gave his companion a dirty look. "Fuck you."

After Ingelmann's laughter died away, the two men sat in silence for several minutes, each lost in his own thoughts as they enjoyed this moment of quiet. It was Dombrowski who finally broke the silence. "So," he said, "we're still in Russia."

Ingelmann shook his head as he looked about. "Yes, we are still in Russia."

Several seconds passed before Dombrowski asked, "Is the adjutant up and about yet?"

"Oh, yes. For some time," the Austrian explained. "He was over with the American command group, sniffing about for information."

"Are they still talking about sending us out on another mission?"

"*Oui.*" Ingelmann's responses had grown uncharacteristically solemn. "When I left the adjutant, he was talking to the American colonel. With the element of surprise gone, the American is waiting until he has enough men and materiel on hand to ensure success."

While Dombrowski knew that this was a wise move, he had no doubt that the longer they waited, the more difficult it would be. No doubt the Russians were scrambling in an effort to muster up every man they could lay their hands on to protect the last of their missiles. As brutal as the operation had been to date, the upcoming phase would be, in the Pole's mind, even more so.

Abandoning that train of thought for the moment, Dombrowski turned his attention to more immediate and personal concerns. Though he knew he didn't want to hear the answer that he anticipated, he had to ask about the third team of legionnaires that they hadn't heard from before he had gone to sleep. "Any word from Team Claire?"

"No." The sad, mournful tone in Ingelmann's curt response was all Dombrowski needed to hear.

Eighteen men had jumped less than twenty-four hours before, the Polish legionnaire knew. Now there were only seven of them left. In time, the names of those lost out there in the frozen wastelands of Siberia would be honored and revered. In the annual ceremony in Corsica during which the Legion recalls its past deeds and fallen heroes, their names would be added to a long and glorious roll. The sacrifice that those men had made would be heralded and held up as an example to the young, unbloodied recruits striving to follow in their footsteps. At the moment, however, Dombrowski could find nothing to rejoice over. First he would need to mourn the loss of so many of those who had become his brothers.

Patrick Hogg was up long before the pitch-black of night grudgingly gave way to a cold, foggy morning. He spent the better part of an hour conversing with Colonel Hightower, going over the operational details of the plan that was being cobbled together to deal with the two remaining Perimeter missiles. Not once during the time Hogg spent with the American did that officer volunteer any hope that one or more of the teams dispatched to eliminate those targets would still, somehow, manage to accomplish their assigned tasks.

It was light when Hogg returned to his teams. By the time he arrived there, the NCO's were in the process of rousting their charges. After pausing only long enough to wolf down a few biscuits and a cup of freshly brewed tea, the SAS captain personally checked each British commando in an effort to assess his condition, inspect his weapons, and provide the sort of command presence that was so essential in a unit such as theirs.

When he was satisfied that all was in order with those who were fully mission-capable, Hogg turned his attention to those who had been wounded. Alone, he made his way over to the American medics, who had set up an open-air aid station. Twice along the way, as he stumbled about in the fog, he had to stop and ask others he came across for directions. While the assembly area in which all the teams were resting was relatively small, the sameness of the broken terrain and the thick fog was disorienting. Only when he came across a bloody pile of discarded field dressings and torn medical packaging did he know he had found the aid station.

The original operational plan for Tempest had not included provisions for a medical team. It had been envisioned that each team, which included its own highly trained medics, would take care of its own. Colonel Hightower, however, had wisely chosen to add a qualified combat surgeon, a physician's assistant, and a pair of medics to the troop list for his forward operations command-and-control team. As Hogg made his way into the spot they had staked out, he came to appreciate the wisdom of this move.

When they had reached the assembly area earlier that morning, the SAS captain had thought that the experience of the other Tempest teams had been like theirs: a few men lost, a couple of casualties, and a lot of bumps and bruises. He was quite taken aback when he found out that the SAS teams had been, in comparison, lucky.

Hogg found Sergeant Kenneth McPherson straight off. A medic was in the process of removing the dressing Hogg had hurriedly applied in the predawn darkness after having picked out the worst of the splinters and shrapnel from his NCO's face.

With the light of day now available, and all those who had more serious wounds tended to, the medics were going back to check work that had been done in haste.

Not wanting to interfere, Patrick Hogg stood off to one side and watched. "Now keep your head still while I change the dressing and clean you up," the medic warned.

The sight of McPherson's face shocked Hogg. Though he had known the man's injuries were bad, he had thought that there had been but one big gash and a few smaller, superficial ones. The light of day, however, revealed that much of the skin on the left side of his NCO's face had been peeled back. Strips of shredded flesh clung to the old dressing as the medic lifted it away. The cavity where there had once been an eyeball was now a torn, bloody hollow. Upon seeing this, the medic gently eased the blood-soaked dressing back into place. "I'm sorry, man, but I'm gonna have the surgeon look at this."

The tone of the medic's voice reinforced McPherson's worst fears. Still, the Scotsman put up a good show. "That's okay, lad. Why don't you run off and tend to some of the others. I'll just rest here a bit and wait for the doc."

Glad that he had didn't have to deal with this particular wound alone, the medic asked McPherson to hold his own dressing in place before heading over to report his observations to the surgeon.

When the medic was gone, Hogg stepped forward and squatted down next to his NCO. "There you are," he exclaimed in a cheery voice, pretending as best he could that he had just happened along at that very moment.

Because of the pain, McPherson was unable to open his one good eye. The best he could manage was to tilt his head in Hogg's direction. "Is that you, Captain?"

Hogg forced himself to chuckle. "Well, I should hope so. After all, how many Irishmen do you suppose are foolish enough to be out and about in Siberia?"

"How'd the other lads make it last night, sir?" McPherson asked. "I sort of lost track of things when that tree came crashing down on me."

Hogg finally managed to gather up the nerve to reach out and lay his hand on the stricken man's shoulder. "Don't you worry about the others. They're all fine. A wee bit tired and sore, but otherwise unscratched."

McPherson did his best to sound cheerful. "I guess I more than made up for them."

For the briefest of moments, Patrick Hogg felt a pang of guilt. It had been his plan, as well as his order, that had resulted in McPherson's suffering. Despite the Scotsman's warning that the spot they were in was too close and the reason for diverting the Russians was gone as soon as the silo had been blown, Hogg had made a snap decision to execute the ambush anyway. That he himself had been less than half a meter away from the Scot during the whole time didn't help. What Hogg was experiencing was akin to what many a survivor goes through when he asks himself, "Why him, and not me?"

It took Hogg a few moments to put things in their proper perspective through the use of hard logic and a large dose of rationalization. They were soldiers, he reminded himself. They all knew what sort of odds they faced during operations like this. Last night, his NCO had paid the price many a man who follows the profession of arms must pay.

The silence that had descended upon them was broken by the appearance of the surgeon. "Looks like you're next on my list of things to do," the

American doctor said as casually as he could while preparing himself to go to work under conditions that were not even marginal. Though he was exhausted after tending nonstop to the wounded cluttered about him, the American managed to give Hogg a wink before starting on McPherson. "Your captain tells me that you can do without the benefit of any sort of anesthetic."

Though it pained him to do so, the Scottish NCO forced a smile. "He's Irish. Don't believe a bloody thing he says."

Giving McPherson a comforting pat, Hogg prepared to leave. "You'll be as right as rain in no time. These Americans are pretty good."

The Scotsman choked out a weak laugh. "No offense, sir, but I hope they'll be a bit more tender when it comes to dressing a wound than you are."

Hogg didn't need to force his laughter. "Well, now you know why I took up arms instead of the scalpel." Then, anxious to check on his major, Hogg stood up. "Is there anything I can do for you before I leave?"

"Yes sir, one thing, sir."

"And what would that be?"

McPherson, swallowed hard as the American surgeon began to peel away the frozen dressing from his face. "Take care of yourself."

Hogg found Major Thomas Shields a few feet away, tucked up against a fallen tree that served as a windbreak. Opening his eyes when he heard the sound of crunching snow nearby, Shields smiled when he saw it was Hogg. "Well, I'm glad to see you're still in one piece."

The same could not be said for the major. With his right arm in a sling and his left ankle swollen to the point where the baggy pants leg of his uniform had to be cut to relieve the pressure, Hogg wondered how his commanding officer had managed to make it all the way to the missile silo, then into the assembly area. Still, Hogg played along with Shields just as he had with McPherson. "I don't recall you telling me," he stated blandly as he dropped onto the ground next to Shields, "that you had been injured during the jump."

Shields shrugged his one good shoulder. "I did mean to tell you, but the topic simply did not come up in our conversations."

"No," Hogg responded, fully understanding the major's point. "I guess we did have other things on our minds." He then proceeded to fill his commander in on what he had accomplished thus far that morning, on the status of each of the men, as well as passing on the gist of the conversation between himself and Hightower. "Our lads will make up the majority of one of the two teams going out after the last two missiles. The rest of our team will be American as well as a handful of legionnaires."

"The American colonel came by earlier," Shields added. "He was hoping that my condition wasn't so bad as to keep me from leading that team."

"I imagine," Hogg enjoined, "he thought better of that after seeing you."

Shields nodded but continued on with the thought that Hogg had interrupted. "I suppose he told you that he is going to lead one of the two teams himself. The other will be led by his major. I'm to stay here as ranking officer."

Hogg found this difficult to believe. "I'm sorry to say, sir, but you're in no condition to be in charge of anything."

"No choice, Patrick," Shields countered. "We're a wee bit short on officers. Everyone who can walk is going after the last of the silos. Only the medical team, the signal detachment, and of course the sick, the lame, and the lazy are being left behind."

The Irish captain look around at the fog that showed no sign of dissipating. "I can't say that I don't envy you. I'm not looking forward to going back out there, stumbling about across this godawful landscape. I never thought I'd say this, but this place makes me homesick for the Scottish moors."

Shields gave Hogg a long, hard look. "Are you sure the tree that bonked Sergeant McPherson didn't hit you in the head as well?"

Even though the major's comment was meant to be lighthearted, the mention of his NCO's name brought a pained expression to Hogg's face. When he saw this, Shields quickly changed the subject. "While we were discussing the new mission, Colonel Hightower asked me about you."

"Uneasy about my credentials?" Hogg asked as he turned his thoughts away from the events of the night before.

"No, not at all," Shields was quick to say. "On the contrary, it's his major he is a bit unsure of. While Colonel Hightower has all the confidence in the world when it comes to him as a staff officer, he admitted that he had not had the opportunity to observe him in a leadership position."

"This is one hell of a time to conduct leadership training," Hogg snickered.

"The colonel told me this in the strictest of confidence," Shields quickly explained. "While he went on to state that he had no reason to doubt his own major's abilities in that regard, he wanted to satisfy himself that if things got a bit hairy out there and his major didn't quite measure up, there would be another officer close at hand who could take up the slack."

Hogg could not believe what he was hearing. As if things were not bad enough, a question of competency on the part of the man selected to lead them was being thrown into the mix. "Since it seems that I have forgotten to bring my copy of *Mutiny on the Bounty* to guide me in this matter, how does the colonel envision me stepping up and lending a hand without causing all sorts of mischief and chaos?"

Reaching out with his good hand, Shields patted Hogg's arm. "Colonel Hightower informed me that he would make sure his major understands that you are a crackerjack SAS officer, one who's opinion is to be taken into account in all operational matters."

"Well," Hogg replied dryly, "that's sure to smooth things out and serve as a foundation for a healthy working relationship."

"You're not going to marry the bastard," Shields snapped. "You're both professionals. Hightower is doing what he can to make sure that his subordinate understands that and conducts himself accordingly. I expect the same from you."

For a moment, Hogg wasn't sure which part of his commander's reprimand cut the deepest, the rebuke itself or the comment about marriage. For as hard as he tried, the memory of his recent separation from his wife was never far from his mind. Seeing that there was little more to be gained by spending time here, he stood up. "If there is nothing else, sir, I need to get back to the men."

Not realizing how personal his remarks had been, Shields smiled. "Yes, of course." Then, just as Hogg was about to turn away, the major called out. "By any chance, do you have a roll or biscuits handy?"

Hogg looked back at Shields and shook his head. "No sir, sorry. I gave my last to a poor legionnaire who was wandering about this morning in search of food."

After waiting while his commanding officer mumbled a response that he did not pay attention to, Patrick Hogg turned his back on the distressing scenes of pain and suffering that permeated the open-air aid station. Lost in thought, he made his way back to where his men were waiting for word of their next assignment. While their thoughts were on what the immediate future held for them, those of the Irish captain were focused on what, for him, lay beyond the completion of this mission.

18

The opening of the door, the sudden rush of noise from outside, and the flood of light were more than enough to wake Demetre Orlov. Even before Captain Anna Zudiev called to him, the Russian colonel was swinging his feet up off the sofa on which he had slept. "The General needs to see you, Colonel," the staff officer said in a voice that was a bit too sweet for a professional soldier.

Before he could speak, Orlov tried to clear his throat. The irritation from inhaling foul air the previous day had left a gritty dryness, making that effort quite painful. Coming to his feet, he took a moment to stretch before looking around the room in an effort to reorient himself.

After Likhatchev left him, Orlov had tried to venture out of the room where he had been sequestered. That effort had been short-lived. Even before he had finished opening the door leading out into the corridor, one of the two armed sentries posted there had moved to block any effort by the Russian colonel to leave. When he asked the man if he was being held prisoner, the sentinel did not reply. While the man was Asiatic, Orlov was sure that he had understood his question. He was simply doing his duty, in the manner the General expected of all subordinates.

Sensing that the direct approach would not work, Orlov tried a different tack in his effort to explore his surroundings. "I need to use the latrine," he stated. While the sentinel still refused to speak, this time he at least acknowledged that he had understood what his charge had said. Keeping one hand securely wrapped around the rear grip of his assault rifle, the mute guard pointed over Orlov's shoulder at a door in one corner of the room. Then, stepping back, the man reached down, grasped the door handle, jerked it away from Orlov, and pulled the door shut.

Left alone again, Orlov had wandered back over to the sofa. Settling down, he poured himself another glass of vodka. While he nursed his drink, he tried to sort things out. This effort soon petered out as his exhaustion, the alcohol Likhatchev had served him, and the inviting softness of the sofa conspired to put an end to all conscious thought.

Without a word, Orlov made his way over to the latrine that the guard outside had so brusquely pointed to the night before. "Colonel," the female captain standing in the doorway stated in a manner that irked him, "the general is expecting you."

Pausing, he turned and faced her. In a deliberate effort to embarrass her, he began to open his fly as he responded: "I do not think the general would appreciate it if I pissed over his boots. Now, if you are in such a hurry, you are free to come along and see if you can squeeze it out any quicker than I can."

His words and gesture had their desired effect.

Red-faced and unable to find a suitable response, Captain Zudiev withdrew from the entrance and pulled the door partially closed. In her haste, she did not hear Orlov's parting shot. Redirecting his efforts, he resumed his leisurely advance to the latrine, shaking his head as he went and mumbling just under his breath, "Silly bitch."

Once in the small, spartan latrine, Orlov went about tending to his needs without much thought. It wasn't until he turned toward the sink to wash his hands that he looked at himself in the mirror. While the reflection was not totally unexpected, it did cause him to pause. The two-plus days of beard was barely visible through the grime and smudges of soot that covered his face. In the field, surrounded by others exposed to the same conditions, a soldier does not notice just how filthy he is until he finds himself in a place where his appearance is the exception and not the norm. It was only after he had taken time to scrub his hands and face twice and look at himself in the mirror again that he noticed just how bloodshot his eyes were.

With water still dripping down his face, Orlov leaned forward in order to inspect his work in greater detail. There was no doubt that he could have done a better job of it, he told himself. That he had tarried here long enough, leaving the staff captain to cool her heels a bit in an effort to put her in her place, was equally clear. Straightening up, he took the thin towel that hung on a ring next to the sink and dried his hands and face. When he was finished, he balled the towel up before tossing it into the bowl of the sink. "Well," he announced firmly as he stared at himself in the mirror, "let us see what our great General has to say."

*   *   *

After leaving the room where he had spent the past few hours, it did not escape Orlov's attention that there were no longer any sentinels outside his door. Nor could he help but notice the extreme sense of urgency with which everyone in the corridor moved. Though he was tempted to ask Zudiev what was going on, he knew better, especially after having treated her the way he had.

The captain escorted Orlov into the main operations center of the regional headquarters complex. The center was like every other operations center the Russian colonel had been in. Every square centimeter of the large room's walls were adorned with charts listing the status of units and facilities, as well as maps of all descriptions. Equally telling was the tension, which was almost palpable, and the near-frantic pace. Without bothering to give any of the maps or charts a close look, Orlov smirked as he mused to his escort. "I see the folks in Moscow have got you hopping."

Captain Zudiev, looking over to where General Likhatchev was busy giving instructions to a handful of staff officers, shook her head while she waited for him to finish. "No," she stated curtly. "Moscow is giving us fits at the moment. NATO troops are active in the region."

Ordinarily, Demetre Orlov could absorb even the most outrageous pronouncements, or listen to incredible news, without showing even the slightest hint of surprise. In part, this was due to the fact that he went to extremes to make sure that he was never surprised. The colonel of commandos was an absolute fanatic when it came to keeping himself abreast of the situation, not only as it existed in his own little sphere of influence, but also ensuring that he was aware of developments within the operational and strategic realms. Before departing Moscow, he had made it a point to personally visit each one of the many contacts he had within Russia's intelligence community. He had specifically looked for evidence of any unusual activities by American or NATO forces, for even the slightest hint that they might be preparing for intervention. That Russia's traditional enemies could somehow launch an attack on them, out of the clear blue without even the slightest warning, was all but unimaginable to Orlov.

He was still reeling from this shocking bit of news when general Likhatchev, finished with his staff, motioned for Orlov to join him. Slowly, the Russian colonel made his way through the crowded room, paying the staff officers little heed. He kept his eyes on the General, trying to gauge the man's mood and, perhaps, his intent.

For his part, Likhatchev greeted his former subordinate as he would any other member of his staff reporting for duty. "I trust you slept well, Demetre."

Conscious that there was more in play than he was aware of and that he needed to maintain his vigilance, Orlov responded with little more than a nod and a grunt.

Sensing that his former protégé's guard was up, and knowing full well that he would insist on some sort of evidence that his claim about the NATO forces was true, the general focused his attention on the wall lined with a battery of maps, each posted with a variety of information. Pointing to red circles on one of the maps displaying the location of the missile silos scattered about the region, the general began by giving Orlov a quick overview of the situation as they knew it. "The NATO transports that appeared in the wake of the asteroid strike brought us more than emergency relief aid. Small commando teams were dropped throughout the region under the most horrific conditions imaginable." Pausing, Likhatchev turned and gave Orlov a once-over. "Of course, I have no need to tell you just how bad things were out there."

For the first time, the Russian colonel felt self-conscious about his physical appearance. Averting his eyes for a moment, he made a halfhearted gesture to brush off his uniform. "Yes," he said in an uncharacteristically apologetic tone. "It was by far the worst that I have ever seen it." Then, catching himself, he straightened and looked into the General's eyes.

Likhatchev made no effort to hide the pleasure he felt in being able to manipulate a man many considered to be impervious to the subtle psychological tricks men use to throw other men off balance. Orlov imagined that it pleased the old man that he had not lost his touch. When Likhatchev turned back to face the map, the Russian colonel reprimanded himself for letting his guard down like that.

"Our damage-assessment teams were the first to discover our unexpected guests," the General continued. "Some of them were already dead, others not far from it. As best we can determine, the force not only consists of the usual suspects, but includes some of the more exotic components of NATO's Special Operations command. We have evidence that members of the Danish Jaegerkorptset, Belgian para commandos, and Hungarians from their Kommando Spezialkräfte are participating in this operation. Even our old friends, the Poles, couldn't resist the temptation to join in on the fun. They threw in some of their finest, commandos belonging to their 1 Pulk Komandosow Specalnego Przezanczenia. All in all, it's a real gathering of eagles."

Likhatchev paused as he reflected on both the magnitude of the operation and the apparent unity among the diversity of the participants. "As you can see, their objectives are scattered through the region."

The Russian colonel, in an effort to gain a psychological advantage over the General, shook his head. "I see that they have been quite selective in regard to their targets," he said in a hushed tone, almost as if he were thinking out loud. "I may be mistaken, but it would appear to me that they are all sites that are part of the Perimeter system."

Now it was Likhatchev's turn to have his composure rattled. He was stunned that a man who was neither a member of the Strategic Rocket Force nor part of the National Command could so easily recognize Dead Hand sites. "Yes, well," he mumbled as he endeavored to recover his composure, "neither their presence nor the targets they are after are a coincidence." Turning, he faced Orlov and drew near until the two were but a centimeter or two apart. "It would appear that our friends in Moscow have been hedging their bets. While they sent you out here to decapitate the threat, they more or less have sanctioned this NATO intervention."

Orlov took this bit of news in stride. "Are you suggesting that our own government is allowing NATO to destroy a key component of our Strategic Rocket Force?"

The general shrugged. "My sources in Moscow are not sure just who approached who in this matter. But," he sighed, "let there be no doubt that the NATO troops out there have Moscow's blessing."

That the men who had sent him out here to kill Likhatchev were capable of such duplicity was easy for Orlov to accept. Equally understandable was the fact that he was never informed about this other effort aimed at ending the General's revolt. Just what he would do now was a question that he had no answer for at the moment. In an effort to buy himself a bit of time to mull this over, Orlov went back to studying the map.

Though the room was crowded, staff officers who

stood between Orlov and the map he was looking at quickly found someplace else to move to when the notorious commander of commandos stepped forward in order to take a closer look. "These two sites," he asked as he tapped each one with the tip of his index finger, "they have been missed?"

Likhatchev grunted as he joined Orlov at the map. "Not through lack of trying. Here," he indicated, pointing to the site nearest the regional headquarters, "we were fortunate in that we had the troops available to defend the silo. The security detachment managed to hold the Americans in check until reinforced by two platoons from here. Through sheer weight of numbers, we were able to wipe out their American Special Forces teams."

"I would have liked to have been part of the interrogation of the prisoners taken from that fight," Orlov commented as he studied the graphics that recorded the ground covered during the pursuit of the American intruders.

Likhatchev bowed his head and sighed. "I am afraid there were no prisoners."

"Not even wounded?" Orlov asked, incredulous.

The general looked up at his former subordinate. "You have engaged in enough close combat to know that when a unit suffers heavily in battle, it tends to show the enemy little in the way of mercy."

"These are NATO troops we are talking about," Orlov retorted, "not Chechen rebels. There will be hell to pay."

Incensed by this criticism from a man who had been sent to assassinate him, the General's eyes narrowed as he drew himself up. "Invited or not, they have invaded Russia!" he bellowed. "No one who has the audacity to lift his hand against our people deserves to be spared."

"Does that include me?" the Russian colonel countered before he forced himself to return to his examination of the map in an effort to demonstrate that he was unaffected by the General's outburst.

The sharp exchange between the two men had brought all activity in the operations center to a complete stand-still. It took Likhatchev a moment before he noticed that his subordinates were gawking in surprise and confusion. Most of them had never seen their commander treated like this by a mere colonel. With a single scathing glance, he brought an end to this embarrassing pause.

The Russian general was still engaged in his silent intimidation of his staff when Orlov, bent over and studying the map, spoke. "I imagine there is a good reason why you have brought me here and taken the time to personally brief me on this situation."

After taking one more spiteful glance at the last of those who had not yet gotten the hint, Likhatchev returned to the issue at hand. "If the goal of the NATO intervention was to disable Perimeter, then it has failed," he announced brusquely, clueing Orlov to the fact that he had managed to best his former superior during their sharp exchange.

Finished with his cursory examination of the terrain and situation, Orlov straightened and turned to face the man he had been sent to kill. "You don't sound convinced."

He wasn't, and he knew it showed. Taking a moment to collect himself, Likhatchev made every effort to soften his tone. "Both you and I know what we would do if we had to deal with the situation NATO now faces."

This brought a smile to Orlov's face, for it reminded him of old times, of desperate missions against foes who meant nothing to him and were, therefore, easy to hate. "We would muster all men who could walk and carry a gun, form them up, and set out to finish the job."

Slowly, Likhatchev's eyes narrowed as he looked

into Orlov's. "Don't you suppose they are in the process of doing that?"

It finally dawned on the Russian colonel what this was all about. But he wasn't going to let on. Playing along, Orlov shook his head in agreement and followed suit by toning down his discourse. "But of course, my dear General. While they may not be Russian, they are still commandos, the best the West has. Despite what some may think of the American military and its weak-kneed European sisters, it is not in their nature to turn their backs on a mission such as this half finished."

"I agree, as does my operations officer. Unfortunately," the General sighed as he turned away and made his way over to a long table running down the center of the room, "I have exhausted my reserves." Stopping at the edge of the table, he rummaged through a stack of papers until he found what he was looking for. After making a show of examining the sheet he held, he offered it to Orlov. "As serious as this particular situation is, I cannot ignore humanitarian relief efforts. Though the forces under my control are numerically impressive, the task they face is daunting."

As he took the sheet the General offered him, Orlov didn't bother looking at it. Instead, he simply stood in silence while Likhatchev went on. "Quite naturally, Moscow has done nothing to assist."

Orlov shrugged. "Naturally. You are, after all, in rebellion, are you not?"

The General, who had taken up wandering about the crowded room as he spoke, paused and looked over his shoulder at Orlov. "Yes, exactly." Then he glanced back at the map that displayed the missile silos and locations of known and suspected NATO forces. "And I suppose it is safe to say that NATO knows what's going on here, even though they continue to send in relief flights."

"Reinforcements?" Orlov asked.

"No. That I am sure of. But I suspect that the NATO aircraft on the ground here are part of the planned egress."

"What will you do if they are, General? With Moscow making no effort to assist by providing disaster relief, and NATO willing to pretend that nothing out of the ordinary is going on, to seize those aircraft, or to block the arrival of still more, would be, in my humble opinion, foolish."

"A perplexing problem, is it not, Demetre?" Likhatchev asked as he shoved his hands in the pockets of his trousers and stared at the row of maps arrayed along one entire wall of the operations center. "This is just the sort of situation that men such as you and I live for."

The Russian colonel could not help but detect the joy in his former commander's voice. Had the asteroid that had set this entire chain of events in motion not been so completely out of the blue, Orlov would have had a difficult time convincing himself that Likhatchev had not been behind the entire crisis. "Since you have brought the subject up," Orlov said slyly, "I am curious as to why you have allowed me to live."

Likhatchev's words lost the somewhat easier tone that had crept into their conversation. "As I said, I have no reserve to dispatch to protect the remaining Dead Hand sites. While it is true that I could pull some of my troops off search-and-rescue, they would be no match for the tough professionals they would be going against. The butchering of the two platoons by a force only a fraction of their size is ample proof of that."

"So," Orlov said, "you want to use my men to do what yours could not."

If Likhatchev was irked by his former protégé's remark, he didn't show it. Instead, tired of their psychological sparring, the Russian general simply nodded. "Yes, I want to use your men. They are available and they are the ideal weapon with which to deal with an elite enemy force."

Folding his arms, Orlov muttered as if in thought. "Huh. Logical, very logical."

For a moment, the two men were silent. Side-by-side, each waited for the other to make the next move. Likhatchev was anxious for Orlov to ask the question he knew the colonel was pondering. For his part, Orlov held back any further comments until his former superior asked the question he knew was coming. In the end, knowing full well that time was not on his side in this matter, it was the General who gave in. Turning to face Orlov, Likhatchev moved as close to the Russian colonel as he could so that no one else could hear him. In a hushed, almost pleading tone, he finally made it clear why Orlov was there. "Will you lead them?"

Feeling a twinge of triumph at having forced his master to ask in this manner, Orlov was now prepared to press his advantage. "I will have no restrictions placed upon me," he stated crisply. "No strings, no political commissars to make sure I behave, and full cooperation from any units under your command that I deem necessary to appropriate in order to accomplish my assigned tasks."

Though he was angered by Orlov's imperious manner, Likhatchev knew that he was in no position to quibble. Drawing in a deep breath, the General nodded. "Yes, yes. Of course. Only," he quickly added, "you understand that I must send an additional signal detachment along with you. The equipment your people brought was configured to keep Moscow informed of your progress. My communications chief tells me you are lacking the sort of short-range tactical sets that will be necessary to coordinate with other friendly forces on the ground."

"Not to mention," Orlov added without hesitation, "keeping you informed of my actions."

Likhatchev managed a sickly grin. "But of course. After all, you were sent to kill me. Only a fool would offer a loaded gun to the man robbing him."

Though he assumed that the general had already taken steps to ensure he didn't have a second chance at accomplishing his primary directive, Orlov decided not to pursue that issue. Based upon his quick study of the terrain he would have to cross and his experience from the previous day, he would need every minute he could find to make it to the sites he was expected to defend. Having finally been given a clear and definitive mission, one that was not contaminated by questions of professional loyalty or patriotism, Orlov found that he had no need to consider the consequences or weigh the alternatives. Snapping to attention, he pivoted about smartly until he squarely faced Likhatchev. "General, I am at your service."

Pleased that his former subordinate was again working for him, the General nodded approvingly, without ever forgetting that this state of affairs could, once Perimeter was secure, change yet again.

19

On the recommendation of his commander, Andrew Fretello dispensed with many of the steps normally taken prior to the commencement of a military operation. This bothered the American major. To an officer trained in the art of operational planning, jumping into something without first making sure that everything was just so went against his nature. But there was little he could do at the moment, since a "recommendation" in the Army carried the same weight as an order, particularly when the person making that recommendation was Colonel Robert Hightower. Never one to ignore reality, Fretello heeded his commander's recommendations with a crisp "Yes, sir" in response.

There was a good reason Hightower insisted on speeding things up. Even the most optimistic of the officers Colonel Hightower had pulled together found it difficult to hold on to any hope that the Russians did not know what their intentions were. The attacks of the previous day, together with the aborted attempt on one of the two remaining Perimeter sites, pretty much laid bare what the NATO Special Ops teams were after. So it was a strong given in the minds of the officers huddled around Hightower that any additional efforts against those sites would be met with stiff resistance. Working on that premise, the American colonel made it clear that every minute wasted by them would give the Russians additional time to reinforce those sites. "Though he's not my most favorite character," he told the surviving leadership, "Nathan Bedford Forest did get it right when he stated that he made it a rule to always get there first with the most men. Well, gentlemen, I have a feeling that today is one of those days when victory will not go to the side with the best plan, but to the one that strikes first and strikes hardest. Do I make myself clear?" None could find fault with this assessment. Intuitively, each officer felt that the sooner they went after the last two sites, the better. They were just that sort of men.

Once that was decided upon, the meeting broke up as each subordinate commander went back to his own people to pass on their new orders and prepare them. During this interlude, Hightower felt no need to go about supervising them as they executed their abbreviated precombat checks as he would have done had this been a training exercise. He understood the psychology of leadership. He appreciated the fact that there were times when a superior needed to make his presence felt, and times when that aspect of military management was a hindrance. He also knew that he had little time with which to prepare his plans-and-operations officer for the task that man would soon be facing. So Hightower spent most of the time he had available with Fretello as he tried to impart as much wisdom and guidance to his headstrong subordinate as possible, while reassuring himself that he was not making a mistake in appointing the major as the commander of the second team. "Those men are every bit as professional and competent as you are," he admonished. "While some of their procedures and practices may seem a bit strange to us, every officer and NCO who will be going with you has proven himself not only according to criteria established by his particular army, but in combat. They know what they're about and how to get the job done. So take care that you don't step in their way."

Listening attentively and nodding at the appropriate times, the young staff officer could not be sure if his colonel's words were simply sage advice or a thinly veiled warning to him to leave the officers who would soon be under his command alone. Having no desire to give Hightower justification to reconsider his selection of him as the commander of the second team, Fretello kept his mouth shut rather than asking for any sort of clarification. He reasoned that once he was on his way, how he did things would pretty much be up to him.

After Fretello gave Hightower the cursory salute that serves to bring most military briefings to a close and he had turned to make his way over to where his own team was assembling, many thoughts ran through Colonel Hightower's troubled mind. Chief among the concerns that plagued him was his decision not to share the full content of his conversations with his superior at NATO Headquarters in Brussels earlier that day.

The failure of Tempest to achieve its assigned objectives set a chain of events in motion that posed a greater threat than the asteroid had. Despite the danger that a fully operational and primed Perimeter system in the hands of General Likhatchev presented to the Russian central government, the

Russian President was having second thoughts about his decision to employ NATO to destroy that system. Those military leaders in Moscow who initially had sided with him found themselves wavering when it was discovered that the man they were supporting had permitted foreign troops to invade Russian soil. To a man, the Russian general staff saw this as an affront, one they felt needed to be redressed. Just how much of this was due to the machinations of Likhatchev and his sympathizers in Moscow and how much of it was the result of patriotic fervor was difficult to gauge. What the Russian President did know was that he was left with little choice. Either he reversed himself on the matter and gave those officers still loyal to him a free hand in dealing with the NATO troops or lose his entire military.

Even before the tremors generated by the demolition charges set off the day before had faded, Russian ambassadors throughout Europe and North America were pounding at the doors of the civilian leadership of NATO's member nations to deliver an ultimatum. Bowing to the demands of his military staff, the Russian President made no effort to dress his warning up with the polite diplomatic language normally used in such communiqués. *"NATO forces,"* his note read, *"will immediately cease all operations and report to the nearest military command loyal to the government in Moscow, where they will surrender all personnel and weapons. Failure to do so, or the pursuit of further operations by those forces against any Russian military installation, will be considered acts of war."*

Within the councils of the NATO member nations, debate sprang up as to what course they should take. With Tempest having failed to achieve its stated goals in the manner in which they had hoped, some saw no sense in risking their already shaky relationship with a Russia in turmoil. They began pushing for complete and immediate compliance with the Russian demands in the hope of salvaging political and economic ties with that country. Others felt that the forces on the ground had to be given the opportunity to finish their assigned tasks. Chief among this faction in Washington, D.C., was General Smith. He advised the other members of the National Security Council to stay the course. In his efforts to convince his civilian counterparts to see the operation through, he pointed out to them what the consequences would be if they failed to do so. "Our people have already paid a staggering price to achieve a ninety-percent solution," he pointed out. "In comparison, the cost for cleaning up those last two sites is negligible."

What the general did not tell the other members seated about the well-polished table in the White House conference room was that he had already discussed the matter with the CinC NATO prior to the NSC meeting. It had been a rather one-sided discussion, with the senior NATO commander doing most of the listening while Smith spoke in riddles whose meanings could not be mistaken. "John, I shouldn't need to tell you how best to deal with a wounded animal."

Though he understood what Smith wanted, CinC NATO was unwilling to translate those desires into orders when he discussed the matter with Colonel Hightower via satellite link. After laying out the political situation in as much detail as he could, CinC NATO ended by giving Hightower his own opinion and views on the matter. "This is not the sort of decision that a colonel in the field should have to make," the general, sitting alone in his office in Brussels, told Hightower. "However," he quickly added, "we are living in strange times, confronted with even stranger circumstances. The order for you to abort may still come down even if you do manage to shake out your teams. I have no way of knowing how things will go as far as that is concerned, but I do know this," he added quickly. "We may never have another chance to de-fang this beast."

The meaning of this encrypted analogy was as clear to Hightower as Smith's had been to the CinC NATO. Though it was not an order, exactly, or even a "recommendation," it was a directive that the Special Forces colonel, standing in the middle of a shattered pine forest in Siberia thousands of miles away, could not ignore. When their conversation was over, Hightower dispatched the radioman on a fool's errand. When that signalman was out of sight, Hightower knelt down in front of the satellite dish and detached the cable that led from it to the main unit. Standing up, he looked around as he slowly coiled the cable up before stuffing it in his pocket. Satisfied that no one had seen him, he turned his back on the disabled unit and walked away.

Movement through the shattered countryside was no easier than it had been the day before. In many ways, the slow and arduous task was even more trying. While the return of subzero temperatures had solved one problem, that of mud, the change generated others equally daunting. In place of the thick, gooey mud, the NATO commandos now found themselves plowing through knee-high snow and skirting around drifts. In addition, the sudden onset of seasonally cold temperatures had created vast patches of ice that made the crossing of open ground hazardous. The moisture that had coated the trees bowled over the previous day by impact shock waves had also frozen. As difficult as the trees had been to climb over before, the addition of this thick coat of ice made matters even worse.

Not all was gloom and doom as far as the environmental conditions were concerned. The snow and the diminishing winds had brought about a considerable clearing in their wake. Though the heavens were still gray and the sky was filled with dark clouds that rolled about, gone were the gale-force winds and dense, choking mist heavily laden with dust, microscopic debris, and fallout of all sorts. The snow had cleansed the air, leaving behind a countryside covered with a strange grayish blanket speckled with flakes of black soot and dirt. To those familiar with military history, the charred, jagged tree stumps jutting out of the tainted snow put them in mind of a scene reminiscent of the fabled Western Front of World War I.

Of this and other matters, no one spoke. Mute and withdrawn, the men of Fretello's ad hoc strike force struggled on toward their new objective. In addition to the equipment they carried and the heavy winter clothing that added its own unique difficulties to their endeavors, most of the commandos were afflicted with a deep foreboding that weighed down upon them like a heavily laden rucksack. This melancholy, exacerbated by exhaustion, so dominated every man's thoughts that it all but radiated out from each of them and overlapped those of their comrades until it cast a collective pall over them all. In light of the horrible losses they had sustained, not to mention their uncertain future prospects, this sad state of affairs was more than understandable. Yet there were those whose spirits could not, or would not, be diminished.

Chief among this fortunate handful was Andrew Fretello. He had listened to the same updates each of the team commanders had rendered to his colonel. Yet the tales of suffering by others did not have the same impact on Fretello as they did on Hightower. In part, this was due to the fact that Hightower was in command, and therefore responsible for everything that happened to the men under him. Even though he was as much a part of the process as a staff officer, he had not, up to this point, had to take on the sense of personal liability that Hightower did. For the moment, the opportunity to command a unit in combat was blinding the young officer to much of the grimness that surrounded him and the awesome responsibilities he would soon be taking on.

Another factor that took the sting out of the words that Fretello heard was the fact that he did not have any personal experiences with which to compare his situation. Never having been in combat before, the reports that were rendered did not evoke any strong emotions, frightening images, or feelings of despair. Though these reports concerned real people and real events, to the young American staff officer, they were not much different than similar reports he had heard countless times before during training exercises. Only a veteran like Hightower was able to relate to what they were being told.

This does not mean that Andrew Fretello was without his own concerns. Many thoughts and questions to which there were no answers ran through his mind as he made his way toward his objective. *He* was a commander now. As such, he had to assume all the burdens that the title carried with it. The speed with which he had been hustled off on his current impromptu mission still bothered him more than it should have. Though he knew in his heart that they did not have time for all the little niceties that both Fort Benning and the staff college at Fort Leavenworth enjoyed, simply throwing a group of soldiers together, pointing them in the right direction, and telling them to go didn't appear to be a sane choice either. While it was true that information concerning current enemy strength, location, activities, and intention in their area of operations was nonexistent, the least Colonel Hightower could have done, Fretello kept telling himself, was to slow down a bit. Speed in combat was a double-edged sword. While haste might get you to your objective before your enemy does, it might also deliver your forces in a state of confusion unprepared to execute the mission they were sent out to perform.

Another worry that dawned upon Fretello as he made his way along was the startling realization that he didn't know any of the people with whom he had been entrusted. A soldier who is knowledgeable about his enemy can make assumptions about its response when combat is joined. A leader cannot, however, comfortably do the same with his own men. The same speed that keeps him from performing precombat inspections also prevents him from obtaining even a passing acquaintance with his newly assigned subordinates. The soldier to his front, as well as the one to his immediate rear, are absolute strangers to him. The sole criteria used in assigning people to Fretello's team had been the order in which they stumbled into the assembly area.

The knowledge that every man with him was a trained professional, skilled in the demanding vocation of special operations, did little to ease this disquieting thought. How, he wondered, would he know who to pick when it came time for him to select individuals to perform the various tasks his team would need to execute once they reached their objective? His ignorance as to who was best qualified to do this or that would reduce his decision-making ability to little more than random luck, something that was against everything in which this compulsive planner believed.

Being the sort of person who was convinced that

there was always a reasonable solution to every problem, Andrew Fretello turned his mind to finding
one for this particular issue. A good place to start
getting a handle on the men in his command, he
reasoned, was to get to know his second in command. Since the British SAS captain had brought a
sizable portion of his own command along with him,
Fretello felt that an open dialogue with him would
provide some insights on the capabilities of the SAS
commandos he would soon be relying upon.

Stepping out of the line of march, Fretello waved
the men behind him on. With little more than a
quick glance at his commanding officer, the overburdened radioman who had been following in Fretello's wake continued walking, making no effort to
close the gap left by that officer. Like his companions up and down the long, slow-moving column,
the radioman mechanically continued to throw one
foot twenty-eight inches out in front him at a time.
Again and again, when that foot came down and
found firm footing in the deep snow, he lifted the
trail foot past the lead foot and threw it another
twenty-eight inches farther along. One foot down,
one foot forward. Each step took him twenty-eight
inches closer to his objective. Each step plunged
him twenty-eight inches deeper into the same unknown that so troubled his commander.

After having spent so much time with his head
bowed down, staring vacantly at the ground to his
immediate front, it took the American major a bit
of effort to refocus his eyes and begin to search out
the SAS captain. While doing so, it struck him as
strange that something as simple as winter camouflage could have so many variations. Though all the
troops in the column belonged to nations that had
been allied with each other for over half a century,
and the outer clothing they wore was meant to conceal them under the exact same climatic conditions,

the snow camouflage patterns that each national army had adopted were strikingly different. For the briefest of moments, Fretello wondered if the uniform-selection boards of the various NATO nations had intentionally gone out of their way to pick patterns that were distinctive and different. Never having given that subject any thought, he found the question quite intriguing.

He was still mulling over this newly discovered curiosity when he caught sight of his deputy. Since he lacked a certain amount of finesse and spontaneity when it came to his people skills, Fretello found it necessary to take time and prepare himself for encounters such as this. It didn't matter if the person he was dealing with was a superior, a coworker, or a subordinate. Nor did it make any difference what the subject to be addressed concerned. To Andrew Fretello, any one-on-one conversation was something of a challenge. Drawing himself erect, the plans-and-operations officer took in a deep breath while he contemplated an appropriate introduction.

Outwardly, there was little to distinguish Patrick Hogg from the other members of his team. With his head bowed low and shoulders pushing forward, he followed the footsteps of the man to his front like everyone else did. As with the others belonging to the diminished SAS contingent, he said nothing as he shuffled along. With so little known about what they would find once they reached their objective, there were no operational plans or details concerning the execution of the upcoming operation to clutter Hogg's brain. So his thoughts were free to wander.

Those thoughts didn't stray too far before they lit upon the subject that he had been dragging along like an iron ball chained to his ankle. Jenny. No matter how hard he tried, no matter what he did, his thoughts always went back to his wife and the sorry state of affairs he had left behind. The wounds caused by her decision to leave him cut too deep and were too fresh to ignore. Hogg found himself recounting, over and over again, all the choices he had made leading up to that fateful moment and how each had led his beloved wife to make the decision she did. Inevitably, his dark thoughts concluded that it had all been his fault, his doing. This evoked a wave of anger and self-condemnation for having been so selfish, so pigheaded and stubborn about the Army. In turn, a sense of loss, unlike anything he had ever experienced, wormed its way into his conscious thoughts, pushing aside the rage that had been building and giving way to an all-consuming grief that muddled his thoughts and blinded him to the harsh realities that surrounded him.

Ordinarily, Patrick Hogg was a practical man. As an SAS officer, he had to be. He was trained to deal with the hard facts of unconventional warfare. His superior expected him to make life-and-death decisions without hesitation. Those who followed him expected him to make the right ones. During his years in the Army, Hogg had never had a problem with meeting either demand. It was in the area of domestic affairs that he never seemed to get it together. Paddy, a close friend of his, once told him over a beer in the officers' mess, "You're a regular contradiction, you are. On the one hand, you can take out a band of terrorists without so much as breaking a sweat. Yet, for some reason, you can't seem to muster up the nerve to lay down the law to your own wife. If it weren't for your choice of mate," his friend concluded, "you'd be the most together individual in the regiment." Though he knew his friend was right on all counts, Patrick Hogg had never spoken to that man again.

Lost in his own world, the SAS captain didn't take note of Andrew Fretello until the American officer spoke. "If you don't mind, I'd like to go over a few things with you."

Doing his best to conceal his surprise, Hogg straightened up and shook his head as he collected his thoughts.

Falling in next to Hogg, Fretello picked up his deputy's pace before speaking again. "I'm not familiar with your men, or with you, for that matter."

As he squirmed about, shifting his load before responding to the American, an old poem came to Patrick Hogg. "You familiar with the poetry of Wilfred Owen?" Without waiting for an answer, the Irishman looked up into the sky, studying the rolling gray clouds for a moment. "He was a Royal engineer in the Great War. Went a bit loony during it. His poetry reflects his attitudes, both before and after that experience, quite nicely."

Now it was the American major's turn to be thrown off guard as he tried to figure out how his statement had led to the topic of poetry. Though he had initiated the conversation with an entirely different purpose in mind, Fretello didn't quite know how to change the subject without offending the British captain who, for reasons known only to himself, had chosen this moment to embark upon a discussion of literature. In silence, Fretello kept pace with the SAS captain, who was searching the clouds above as if looking for his next line of poetry.

"This trek of ours," Hogg finally announced as he continued to stare off into the heavens, "sort of reminds me of one of his more famous pieces." Pausing, he took a moment to modulate his voice before he began to recite, from memory, the opening verse of that poem. "Bent double, like old beggars under sacks, knock-kneed, coughing like hags, we curse through sludge, till the haunting flares we turn our backs and toward our distant rest began to trudge. Men marched asleep. Many had lost their boots but limped on, blood shod. All went lame; all blind; drunk with fatigue; deaf even to the hoots of tired, stripped five nines that dropped behind."

Finished, Hogg's head drooped until he was looking at the ground before him. He stayed like that for a moment before facing his American commander. "He lasted almost until the end. Poor Wilfred was killed in action on November fourth, nineteen-eighteen, seven days before the Armistice."

"That's a pity," Fretello replied.

"Maybe, maybe not. The way I see it," Hogg explained, "it was probably the best thing that could have happened to poor Wilfred."

Surprised, Fretello looked at the Irishman. "How do you figure that?"

Hogg drew in a deep breath and looked up at the sky again. "There's more than one way to die, you know. Sometimes the physical end is a blessing, especially for a man like our friend Wilfred, who had seen so much that his faith in his fellow man had been brutally crushed. I don't see how he could have survived back in England had he lived to see the end of the unspeakable horrors that had become a way of life for him."

The direction that this strange and somewhat surreal discussion was taking made Fretello uneasy. Taking notice of this, Hogg managed to force a smile. "I don't suppose you came back here to chat about a dead English poet."

Glad to be given an out, Fretello shook his head. "As I was saying, I am at a serious disadvantage, not having had time to familiarize myself with my own command."

Knowing that he had made this American staff

officer uncomfortable, Hogg now did his best to ease his burden of command, as a good executive officer should. "My lads are good lads. Like myself, most were levied from the cadre of Hereford for this operation. I've worked with the majority of them for the better part of two years and haven't had a single complaint to speak of as far as their abilities. The only problem I have is that I am a wee bit short on senior NCO's. The ones who started out have become hors de combat. My most senior man, after myself, is a corporal."

With obvious concern in his voice, Fretello asked if that was going to present a problem. Shaking his head, Hogg replied in the negative. "In any other troop unit, one of my corporals would trump the best NCO they have. They'll do just fine. You have my word on that."

"Good, good," Fretello muttered, thankful that the SAS captain wasn't taking advantage of this opportunity to lord it over him like some officers he knew in the American Army would have done.

Hogg looked back toward the legionnaires bringing up the rear. "Though I haven't worked with that lot," he stated as he watched the column wind its way through the shattered landscape of toppled trees and ash-gray snow, "I suspect the CRAP team with us is up to anything we encounter."

The mention of that unfortunate acronym brought a smile to Fretello's normally taut face. "That's one hell of a title to be saddled with, don't you think?"

Looking back at the American major, Hogg also smiled. "If I were you, I wouldn't go out of my way to point that out to them. When it comes to the Legion, they have less of a sense of humor about such things than a bonafide Frenchman. Besides, when we reach the silo, you'll be needing them."

"Yes, I know I'll be needing all of you, I suppose," Fretello countered.

Seeing that his commander didn't appreciate what he was trying to point out, Hogg turned once more to face the legionnaires. "You see that big fellow near the front?"

Fretello looked back along the long line of men until he saw the one he thought the SAS captain was talking about. "Yes? What about him?"

"I am told he's their demolitions expert, a Pole with a knack for blowing things up. He's got one of the two operational packages we'll be needing."

"Oh, I see," Fretello said as he looked closer in order to familiarize himself with a man who would soon become key to the success of their mission. "Thanks. That's good to know," he added as he looked up ahead, to the front of the column. Feeling a bit more at ease as a result of their exchange, Fretello decided to loosen up a bit as he continued to probe into his number two's background. "Married?"

In an instant, the smile disappeared from the Irishman's face. This simple question, one that ordinarily required little more than a yes or no, threw Hogg back into the pits of despair. How did he answer? Not having been asked that since leaving Jenny in London, he had not found the need to sort out an appropriate response. Technically, the Irishman reasoned, he was still married. But in his heart he knew the relationship he so cherished was over. So, he wondered, was he in any sense of the word married?

The sudden change in mood that swept over them like an arctic chill cast a pall on their conversation. That such a seemingly innocent question could affect the SAS captain in this way served as a warning to Fretello. There were topics that professional soldiers didn't allow themselves to become involved in, he quickly reminded himself as he began to seek a graceful way of parting company with Hogg. Politics and personal lives. Both subjects were sure-fire ways of alienating both superiors and subordinates, something that a career soldier like himself did his damnedest to avoid.

Finding the silence that his companions had fallen into intolerable, Franz Ingelmann picked up his pace until he was able to close the gap between himself and Stanislaus Dombrowski. Without preamble, the Austrian legionnaire began to speak. "What do you suppose those two are discussing?"

Having closed his mind to all conscious thoughts other than those necessary to navigate his way through the maze of fallen trees and drifting snow, it took the Pole a moment to respond. As a means of buying himself a bit more time with which to refocus his thoughts and sort out what, exactly, his companion was concerned with, Dombrowski countered Ingelmann's question with one of his own. "Who are you talking about?"

"Them," the Austrian replied, pointing to the American major and the SAS captain marching side by side. "Our two intrepid leaders. They were chatting to each other a moment ago, looking back at us and pointing. What do you suppose they are saying?"

Annoyed that he had been shaken from his semiconscious slumber to discuss such a trivial matter, Dombrowski took the opportunity to poke some fun at his companion. "I would imagine," he stated in a manner that gave the impression he was being deadly serious, "they are asking each other how such a sorry little Austrian shit like you managed to steal his way into the Legion."

Undeterred, Ingelmann persisted with his original line of inquiry. "No, I'm serious, *mon ami.* The Englishman, he was pointing at us, telling the American major something not more than two minutes ago."

The big Pole corrected his friend. "Take care that the captain over there does not hear you call him an Englishman. He's Irish. Very Irish, from what I've been told."

The Austrian legionnaire shrugged. "What different does that make? English, Irish, Welsh. They're all the same, aren't they?"

Looking down, Dombrowski smiled. "You know, I was telling a friend the other day the same thing about the Germans and the Austrians. I told him you really can't tell the difference between them."

Smarting, Ingelmann glared at his companion. "That's not a fair comparison, you know. Austrians are much nicer."

Looking away, the Polish legionnaire's expression changed. "I don't think my father would agree with you on that, not after the last war."

Realizing what Dombrowski was saying, Ingelmann quickly got back to the subject he had first broached. "So, what could those two have been discussing?"

Befuddled by this line of questioning, Dombrowski shook off the gloom that memories of his native land and her sufferings had evoked, and looked down at his friend. "I imagine they are talking about officer things."

Rolling his eyes, Ingelmann threw his hands out in despair. "Why, of course they are talking about officer things. Even I could figure that out!"

"Then why in hell did you bother me with such a stupid question?" Dombrowski roared.

In a gesture of hopelessness, Ingelmann shrugged as he slowly parted company with the big Pole.

"You're hopeless, *mon* Sergeant. Utterly and completely hopeless. Go back to sleep."

Shaking his head as he chuckled to himself, Dombrowski waved his friend away. "Believe me, I intend to as soon as you leave me alone."

Though he heard his young companion say something, the words were muddled and unclear. Without another thought, the Polish legionnaire allowed his mind to drift back into the semi-numb state that made an arduous task such as this tolerable. Only the steady rhythm of the march concerned him at the moment. One foot up and out at a time. Twenty-eight inches ahead, twenty-eight inches farther along. Always forward, ever closer to their objective.

20

Man for man, there was little to differentiate between the two forces of highly trained commandos that were now converging on one point. In numbers and armament, they were about equal. In fact, due to their rather open policy concerning the procurement of weapons, individuals within both commands carried the exact same models. The terrain each unit faced conferred no great advantage to one side or the other. The shotgun pattern with which the asteroid had pelted the region left pockets of devastation that were no less daunting to the Russians. The snow, the ice, and the unending maze of pulverized trees reduced cross-country movement of both units to a virtual crawl.

There was one area in which the Russian commandos did have a decided advantage over their foes. Unlike the NATO troops, who had no option but to catch what sleep they could by curling up in the lee of fallen trees under open skies, the Russians had spent the previous evening at a fixed installation. There they were free to take over the bunks left unoccupied by troops that had been dispatched throughout the region to assist in disaster relief as well as to secure key sites and installations. Some of the bunks belonged to those members of the garrison who had repelled the American Special Forces teams. That they would not be coming back did not bother the Russian commandos who took their place for an evening. Even if they had known the fate of the former occupant with any degree of certainty, it would not have mattered. There wasn't a single man who belonged to Demetre Orlov's special unit that gave such things a second thought. After what they had been through, shelter and a hot meal were all that mattered.

While enjoyable and quite therapeutic, the advantage conferred by this respite from the harsh Siberian conditions was transitory. When the time came, the outcome of any confrontation between the two commands would be determined by other, more traditional factors. Orlov understood this. He also understood that combat is not an exercise in mathematics. The numerically superior force does not always triumph, nor can advanced technology guarantee success. Though they do tend to tip the scales in favor of the side who possesses them, many times it is the will and the confidence of a single man that determines the outcome of a battle. More often than not, this person is the commander.

History abounds with examples of armies that threw away a sure victory because its commander, for one reason or another, failed at a critical moment. Even in the age of digital warfare and precision-guided munitions, the leader must be willing to look his foe in the eye while he drives his sword home in order to prevail. Such a failure of will had never been a problem for Demetre Orlov. He knew of the rumors concerning him spread by those who suspected that he derived a certain pleasure from making the kill. Since his effectiveness depended to a large degree on fear, he did nothing to discourage these stories since they served to enhance his reputation as an uncompromising foe.

As he picked his way forward toward the missile silo he had been assigned to defend, he found himself reflecting on this. While a reputation such as his was impressive to those who knew of it, the NATO troops he would soon be facing didn't have a clue about such matters. There would be no opportunity beforehand to do any psychological posturing. Nor did he suspect that he would be afforded much of an opportunity to size up his opponent. Based upon the situation he had been briefed on before leaving Likhatchev's regional command-and-control center, the best Orlov could hope for was to arrive at the site just ahead of the NATO troops. If that were the case, he would have little opportunity to do much other than take up hasty defensive positions, establish a few outposts, and wait for his foe to make his move.

Of all the uncertainties with which he had to contend, the thought of assuming a defensive posture bothered Orlov the most. His unit was an elite strike force, unsuited for static defense. Everything about it, from its weaponry to its unique organization, was tailored with an eye toward a stealthy approach and the delivery of a swift, decisive blow. They were so wed to this mode of operation that not a single member of his special-response team had a shovel, an item of equipment that had become all but standard issue for ground combat troops since the First World War. It proved to be somewhat of an embarrassment when he had to dispatch his deputy to scare up this simple, yet essential, piece of military hardware.

Thoughts of his deputy triggered another concern that had been nagging the Russian colonel. It was one thing to be ever mindful that one or more members of his handpicked team could, at a critical moment, turn on him. It was quite another to have experienced that and then find yourself marching back into action with the traitorous bastard still with you. As if in response to this apprehension, Orlov turned around and searched the column of soldiers struggling through the snow behind him until his eyes fell upon the major who had led his command in open revolt.

As if on cue, Petkovic looked up and locked eyes with his commanding officer. The two men stared at each other for a moment. Each was too far away to read the other's expression, so they could not be sure of what the other was thinking. But each could guess, and neither was far from the mark.

Ivan Moshinsky, who was in his usual spot immediately behind Orlov, took note of his colonel's expression. After glancing over his shoulder and seeing that Major Petkovic was grimly eyeing his superior, Orlov's self-appointed guardian knew what was transpiring. The veteran of many campaigns kept his thoughts to himself, even after the two officers turned their attention away from each other and back to their tortuous trek.

Good march discipline requires that units halt at regular intervals to allow soldiers to rest. A general rule of thumb many infantry officers follows is a ten-minute break every hour. As highly trained and well-conditioned soldiers, Orlov's special-response team could march on at a rate that would savage just about any other unit. But even the best unit in the world needs to pause every now and then to allow stragglers to catch up, overburdened soldiers to adjust their loads, and individuals to tend to personal needs, whatever they may be.

When he came upon an area that looked as if it would provide a good place to halt, Demetre Orlov stepped out of line, gave a sharp whistle to gain the attention of those who were ahead of him, and waved his hand over his head. "Ten minutes," he called out. He had no need to give any further orders. The lieutenant responsible for the vanguard automatically directed his men to fan out and establish a security screen, just as the senior officer charged with bringing up the rear ensured that some of his men were facing about in order to keep an eye open for anyone who might be following.

Standing off to one side, Orlov watched as his men settled down to take advantage of this respite. Once he was sure that all the appropriate security measures had been taken to protect his command from surprise, he sat down on the ground to rest his weary legs.

This did not mean that he could simply collapse and drift off to sleep as some of his men did at times like this. Even during a rest period, there was too much to do, too many things for a commander to think about. Pulling his map out of his pocket with one hand and his canteen with the other, Orlov laid the map on his lap opened to the section that showed their route of march. He studied it while he slowly unscrewed the cap to his canteen and took a drink of water.

Despite an agonizingly slow pace, they had passed the halfway point. Though they had one more major ridge to climb and a stream that might prove difficult to cross, he was satisfied that they could be at the missile site well before dark. This would give him an opportunity to study the ground by light of day before deploying his troops. With luck, he would even find enough time to send out an ambush patrol or two to cover the most likely avenues of approach leading to the silo. That his foe might

do the same occurred to him for a moment, but he
quickly discounted the thought. They were there for
one purpose and one purpose only: to destroy the
silo. If he had that mission rather than the one he
was saddled with, he reasoned, he wouldn't dilly-
dally with setting up an ambush. He'd swarm over
the objective as soon as he reached it, set his demolitions, and then pull back as quickly as he could.
While he did expect his opposite number to post
security all around the site while the demolitions
party set its charges, the guards would only be concerned with providing early warning and buying
time for the demo party to complete its task, nothing more.

Having finished with his map, Orlov looked
around. His men had already settled in as best they
could to take advantage of the halt. Any thoughts
he entertained about calling his officers together for
a quick meeting was dismissed when he saw Major
Petkovic wandering off away from the column in
search of a place to relieve himself in private. It
would be like that bastard, Orlov thought with a
smirk, to be shy pulling his tiny pecker out in front
of real men, where they could see just how poorly
equipped he was.

Having dropped the idea of an officers' call, Orlov eased his head back until it came to rest on a
tree stump. "Sergeant Moshinsky," he called out as
he closed his eyes, "if I fall asleep, wake me in five
minutes."

From behind him, Peter Spangen, the sniper, answered, "Yes, of course, Colonel. We will do so." Assuming that Spangen was sitting beside Moshinsky
and simply answering in his stead, Orlov let his
mind drift away.

*   *   *

When he was far enough from the column that he was sure he could be alone, Gregory Petkovic looked to his left, then to his right, to make certain that no one was watching. Satisfied that he had some privacy, he unbuckled the snap of his load-bearing equipment, pulled his winter camouflage smock up, and undid his trousers. After pulling the bulky winter coveralls down as far as he could, the Russian major dropped his drawers before slowly lowering himself to a squatting position. When he was sure that all of his clothing was clear of the line of fire, he relaxed as best he could, his bare bottom exposed to the frigid cold, and proceeded to relieve himself.

Like many of those belonging to the special-response team, Petkovic had gorged himself on the freshly cooked rations freely offered them at the command center they had been dispatched to destroy. It had been too long since their last full meal prior to reaching that site, and their efforts to get there had been demanding. Failure to take advantage of the hospitality that had been liberally heaped upon them, as some of the commandos had done out of some foolish notion of pride was in Petkovic's eyes a waste of a marvelous opportunity. That he was having to pay for that moment of indulgence at a time like this didn't bother him. It had been well worth it. Given a chance, he would have stayed behind, where he would have had the use of a decent, well-heated facility instead of being forced to let go while balancing himself on his haunches like a dog being curbed.

When it had come time to make his decision as to whether he would remain or continue on with the special-response team, Petkovic found that he really didn't have a choice. General Likhatchev had gone out of his way to make sure he understood that he did not have an option. As awkward as it would be, given his role in the mutiny against his colonel, Petkovic understood his duty. Despite his decision to turn against his own government, he was a pro-fessional soldier, an officer, and above all, a Russian. So he had saluted the General, as all good soldiers are trained to do, and fallen in behind Colonel Demetre Orlov as if nothing untoward had happened.

At the moment, that issue was the farthest thing from Petkovic's mind. Reaching out, he grabbed the stub of a charged branch with one hand while searching about the pockets of his rolled-up trousers for the tissue stuffed in them for just such an emergency. That he had overlooked placing it where it would be easy to reach annoyed the Russian major. Such laxness, he chided himself, was inexcusable and shameful, especially for an officer.

Gregory Petkovic was in the midst of chastising himself for this when his peripheral vision caught sight of a swift motion descending from above, like a bird swooping down upon him. Before he could do anything but tense up, he felt a hand grab the front edge of his hood and jerk his head back. Caught totally by surprise, he was too busy wildly flapping his arms about in an effort to regain his balance to do anything about the razor-sharp blade that began to bite into the soft, exposed flesh of his neck. He was going to die, Petkovic found himself thinking. Killed taking a shit.

There was no time to carry that thought any farther. With an ease that seemed unreal, the knife at his neck opened a gash that ran from just under the left ear, beneath his jaw, and across to the right ear. Without a pause, the knife was drawn away, the hand holding the front of his hood disappeared, and the stricken deputy commander was left to flop over forward, face-first, into a pile of snow already stained bright red by his gouting blood.

*   *   *

With the same ease with which he was able to give way to a few moment's sleep, Demetre Orlov was able to snap back, fully awake, as soon as he felt a hand come to rest on his shoulder. "It is time, Colonel," a voice called out softly. Thrusting his arms out before him, the Russian colonel stretched before rolling over onto his side to push himself up and off the ground.

Once on his feet, he looked around in the same manner that a mother hen does when counting her chicks. All about him, his men were shaking themselves out and loosening up stiff muscles as they prepared to renew their march. "I don't see Major Petkovic," Orlov announced to no one in particular as he continued to search for any sign of his deputy. When he received no response, he turned to those around him. "Has anyone seen the major?" he asked more pointedly.

There was a moment's hesitation as those belonging to his immediate party looked at each other before turning their attention to Ivan Moshinsky. When he had first cast about to inspect his command, Orlov hadn't taken note of the fact that his self-appointed guardian was off to one side, kneeling on the ground. Now that his attention was drawn to him, Orlov looked closer in an effort to determine what was going on.

Sensing that all eyes were upon him, the Russian NCO looked up from the snow he had been using to clean his bloody hands and into the eyes of his colonel. Without any notable change in his expression, the Russian commando paused. "It is my duty to report, sir," he stated slowly in a deep voice that conveyed not the slightest hint of feeling or passion, "that Major Petkovic is indisposed."

As hardened as he was to such things, a chill ran

down Orlov's spine as he gazed into Moshinsky's eyes. It was not so much what his loyal subordinate had done that bothered him. Rather, as he stood there rooted in place, Demetre Orlov could not help but think that he was looking at a mirror image of himself. The fact that he found this cold and impersonal reflection unflattering only added to his discomfort.

Without a word, Moshinsky fished his knife out of the red-tainted snow he had been using to clean it, gave it a quick swipe on his pants leg, and rose up. All the while, he continued to stare into his commander's eyes. It was, Orlov thought, almost as if the man was daring him to say something by way of condemnation. Yet, that solider knew that his commander would not do so. Besides his past service and unquestioning loyalty, Moshinsky appreciated the undeniable fact that he would be far more valuable in the sort of fight that his colonel had told them to expect than would a major whose loyalty was questionable.

Unable to find an appropriate response, Orlov turned away. It took him a moment to collect his thoughts, and he cleared his throat before he was able to call out to his remaining officers. "Prepare your men to move out."

In silence, the Russian commandos took up their trek. In the strange way that such things are relayed throughout the ranks of a unit, almost without a word being said, the fate of their deputy commanding officer became known. One by one, as the soldiers filed by the place where Moshinsky had cleaned up, each man stared down at the bloodstained snow. The message this sight conveyed was clear and unmistakable, just as Moshinsky had intended it to be.

21

With the grace of feline predators stalking prey, Andrew Fretello, Patrick Hogg, and Hector Allons moved forward in search of a concealed spot from which to observe the object of their efforts. When the three NATO officers found a place that afforded them an unobstructed view of the Russian missile silo, they did their best to become part of their surroundings. Only after the trio was safely tucked away did they commence a visual reconnaissance of their target.

The situation that Fretello beheld was pretty much what he had expected. He knew that the odds of finding the silo undefended were low. Still, the Special Forces major had clung to that hope right up to the last minute that they, and not the Russians, would reach the isolated spot first. While anxious for an opportunity to demonstrate his abilities as a leader during a mission such as this, he would have been just as happy had this foray been a simple matter of walking up to the silo, placing their demolitions on top of it, setting off the charge, and marching away.

That he would need to do more than oversee the placement of explosives was painfully clear. The scene he beheld was not encouraging. From their perch, the three men were able to identify a number of defensive positions ringing the silo. The cover and concealment employed by the Russians made counting them difficult. Still, Fretello concluded that there were, at most, eighteen defenders, armed with an assortment of small arms. It made little difference that all of the positions appeared to have been hastily thrown up and were rather shallow. Nor did the lack of heavy crew-served weapons at the site provide any optimism. Patrick Hogg was quick to point out that those weapons could have been placed just about anywhere in the surrounding countryside, set away, yet able to cover the silo. "We could be looking at bait. Or maybe those are the goalies down there, charged with keeping us from booting in the winning score if their teammates fail to keep us away."

While he never cared much for the use of sports analogies to describe tactical situations, Fretello understood what his second command was saying. Just the thought that they might be looking at only a small portion of the defending force caused him to look closer for any sign of other enemy positions. With that thought in mind and exercising just as much care now as they had while approaching the site, the three withdrew to where their men waited for their return.

Having been sufficiently spooked by what Patrick Hogg had said, the American major dispatched three two-man recon teams to hunt out any foes that may have been overlooked during his personal reconnaissance. One team was led by Hector Allons. Together with the Polish NCO who would be overseeing the placement of the demolitions, he made his way to a location not far from where he had stopped earlier with the American and British commanders. Since his men would have the honor of placing the demolition charges, the Spaniard felt it was important to become familiar with the target area. A second team, made up of two men Hogg had picked from his own contingent, circumnavigated the entire site, just inside of what had once been a thriving pine forest that had concealed the missile silo. The third team, commanded by an American Special Forces captain, also circled about the site, but much farther out than the circuit taken by the SAS. The task of the Americans, like that of their British colleagues, was to confirm or deny the existence of an outer defensive perimeter. Though this took time, no one complained, especially since the three teams were also tasked with the additional responsibility for seeking defensive positions that they themselves could occupy once the site was secured.

When the three teams had returned and finished rendering their reports, Andrew Fretello settled down to the task of deciding how they would execute their mission. Drafting a plan for this sort of thing would be easy for an officer of his training and abilities. As a commander of a Special Forces A team years before, he had faced tactical problems far more complex than this one. During his tour as a staff officer back at Bragg, he had drafted plans that dwarfed his current efforts in every way.

All of those previous efforts, however, had been theoretical exercises or training events. Tempest had been the first major operation he had planned and seen implemented against a real foe. And the assault on the silo that lay but a few hundred meters from where he sat would be the first combat mission that he himself would lead. There would be no after-action review, in which all of the key leaders from both sides would gather and discuss what each of them should and should not have done. The soldiers of the opposing forces would not be able to gather themselves up, dust off their uniforms, and return to their billets, where they would clean up their equipment before calling it a day. Only one side would walk away from the action that Fretello was now planning. Few, if any of those on the losing side would live to see another day. This last fact, together with the understanding that he had but one chance to get it right, created a degree of pressure on the young American major unlike anything he had ever experienced before. With his map laid out and all the information that his scouts had provided scribbled down in his notebook, the staff major began the tedious task of determining how best to proceed.

There were a number of options open to Fretello, each of which entailed its own risks. The presence of the Russians at the silo meant that there would be an assault. How best to go about taking down those defenders was the first problem he addressed. He neither had the numbers with which to overwhelm his foe, nor did he have any interest in throwing away the men he had by simply rushing the site. The advantages Fretello assumed he did have, and which the Russians could not easily match, lay in his superiority in weaponry and the skill with which the NATO troops could employ them. Beside the fact that every man with him was a crack shot, each of the teams had a designated sniper armed with a powerful, large-caliber rifle. Though it would take some time, Fretello was fairly sure that he could deploy the bulk of his command in a manner that would allow them to bring their superior firepower to bear upon every square meter of the site. If he couldn't physically throw the Russians out, he would cut them down one by one.

Having opted to eliminate the opposition by fire, the timing of the attack had to be settled upon. Had his command been an established one, or one that had trained together for an operation such as this, Fretello would have preferred a night attack. But he had serious reservations about initiating an action in total darkness with a group of people who had been thrown together in a haphazard manner. Co-ordination of their efforts during the engagement would be, at best, problematical. If he found that the situation was getting out of control once the assault had been started, Fretello appreciated the fact that he lacked the experience, the procedures, and the means of communication with which to exercise proper command and control under those conditions. Though it meant losing one of the edges that special-ops units often relied on, the risks of striking while it was still light were far less than waiting for darkness and placing his faith in the hope that nothing would go wrong. If there was one thing that Andrew Fretello did know for sure, it was that things always went wrong in battle.

Patrick Hogg watched the American major fret and ponder over what to do next. The SAS officer knew that the Special Forces officer was struggling with decisions that he himself had faced before. For a moment, Hogg considered venturing over to the American and offering his services and advice. That was, he imagined, what the American colonel had in mind when he assigned the SAS contingent to this group.

The idea of interrupting like that, however, went against Hogg's nature. Like most officers who chose

Special Ops over a more conventional military career, the Irishman enjoyed the independence and freedom from oversupervision that the SAS offered. He derived a certain amount of pride in the fact that when handed an assignment, he was only told what he was expected to do, not how to do it. Since the mind-set of America's Special Forces wasn't much different than that held by an SAS officer, Hogg figured that his efforts to assist would be construed as arrogant and insulting. So he let the matter drop. Besides, if there was something about the final plan that the American came up with that he didn't much like, he would have the opportunity to voice his concern when it was briefed to him and the other officers waiting patiently to get on with the task at hand.

When he was finished laying out his concept for the operation they were about to undertake, Andrew Fretello looked up from the map he had been using to brief the three officers gathered around him. After studying the rudimentary graphics Fretello had used to outline his plan, each of those officers leaned back and looked over at him.

Hector Allons was the first to speak. "I do not expect it to take more than ten minutes for my people to place the charge, lay the wire, and be ready to execute the demolitions once you give us the word to go."

Fretello gave the legionnaire a nod. "Good. I hope you can cut down on that some, but I am not by any means rushing you."

"My only concern," the Spaniard continued, "is with the other teams. Once we have neutralized the opposition, I see no need for the English to remain in their positions. I am confident that any Russian who has survived to that point and is foolish enough to attempt to interfere with my demolitions party will be quickly taken out by one of my own men."

"I have no doubts about the ability of your men," Fretello was quick to reply. "It's just that I don't want anything left to chance. Since there will be nothing for Captain Hogg's command to do while your men are out there preparing the site for destruction, I would just as soon leave them in place and cover you." Turning to Hogg, Fretello asked if he had a problem with that.

The SAS captain shook his head. "I see none. Since my lads have to be someplace, staying where they are and covering the legionnaires makes perfect sense to me."

Seeing that he was fighting a loosing battle, Allons shrugged. "Then I guess it is decided." Turning to the Irish captain, the Spanish legionnaire offered him some advice. "Please tell your lads that when they see my men are done and taking to their heels, it would not be advisable to wait around too long before doing so themselves. Otherwise, if the oversized charge my sergeant has prepared does not get them, the secondary explosion that will follow when the rocket blows up will."

After giving Fretello a wink, Hogg looked back at Allons. "No need to worry about my lads. Though there's a good case to support the notion that those who choose to join the SAS are a bit daft, no one has ever accused us of being stupid."

For the first time that day, the leaders of Fretello's small command were able to share a bit of laughter. "Anyone else have a question or comment?" the American major asked as he prepared to leave. By the time he was on his feet, the others were also up and prepared to go their separate ways. "If that's the case," Fretello concluded, looking over at the leader of the American contingent, "since you have the farthest to go, Captain Haynes, you will move out first. Do so as soon as you're ready. The others will key their departure accordingly, with Captain Hogg and his men going next."

"That leaves the Legion bringing up the rear, as always," Allons added.

Again Hogg turned to Fretello and gave the American a sly wink. "Well, I've always said it's a good idea to save the best for last."

With every detail he could think of addressed and his plan about to be set in motion, Andrew Fretello felt something akin to optimism for the first time that day. Using the reaction of the other officers to his concept and their mood as a gauge, the young major was confident that all would turn out well. Now all that remained for him to do was to oversee the deployment of the various elements, give the word to initiate the attack, and let his men do what they were trained to do.

The scene that greeted Adjutant Hector Allons when he returned to where his legionnaires had halted was not what he had hoped to find. Behind the thin skirmish line of men facing out of their small laager and in a spot hidden from view sat Stanislaus Dombrowski, madly fidgeting with the shaped charge.

Stopping short, Allons' shoulders slumped. "Please tell me that you are finishing up and simply putting the damned thing back together."

The Polish legionnaire didn't answer. Franz Ingelmann, who was off to one side making a circuit check on a spool of wire, stopped what he was doing. After looking over at his companion, he answered his team commander's question with nothing more than a pained, sorrowful expression. Allons glanced at his watch before looking back over his shoulder, noting that the Americans were already on the move. Realizing that time was fast running out, he made his way over to Dombrowski and squatted next to him as he prepared to find out just how bad things were.

Knowing what was coming, the Pole stopped what he was doing, leaned back, lifted his frozen fingers to his lips and blew in an effort to warm them. When some feeling had been restored, he rubbed his hands together. "Damned cold," he mumbled as he continued to stare at the tangle of wires he had been working on, half ignoring his commander, half preparing him for the bad news.

Though Allons was a patient man, time was not on his side. "Can you get this thing to work?"

Shrugging, Dombrowski considered the question as he continued to eye the demolition charge. Finally, not seeing a solution to the problem, he looked over at Allons. "If the question is can we make an explosion, the answer is yes. But if you want to know whether or not the shaped charge will function as we want it to, well . . ."

Unable to bear Dombrowski's disappointed expression, Allons looked over at the charge. "One would think that something as simple and robust as that would have withstood the knocking about it took during the landing better than it did."

The memory of their last jump and the image of Captain Jules Pascal's shattered body caused Dombrowski to shudder. "As tough as we would like to think we are," he said mournfully, turning to look back at his damaged device, "there are things that even the best of us are unable to endure."

Though the true meaning of his NCO's comment escaped him, Allons nodded in agreement. "*Oui*, that is very true." Then, using the best authoritarian voice that he could manage under the circumstances, he attempted to reassert himself. "You must find a way, my friend, to make this thing work. The American charge is in worse shape than ours. The liner and high explosives have become separated. When they unwrapped it from its packing, everything just broke up and fell away. Though they tried, their captain said they would not be able to repack the chucks of explosives like they were." With a sigh, Allons shook his head. "I only wish I hadn't switched this charge with the one you had brought along back at the other silo."

Dombrowski grunted. "You did the right thing then. This," he said as he waved his hand at the tangled wires, "is not your fault."

"It was the riggers, you know," Ingelmann stated. "They never use enough padding."

If the Austrian's comment had been an effort to absolve Dombrowski of responsibility for the problem and ease the frustration that was building, it failed miserably. Angered by his inability to correct the problem, the Pole threw down the needle-nosed piles he had been holding. "What the hell difference does it make whose fault it is that this piece of shit won't work!"

Both Ingelmann and Allons recoiled as much from this sudden outburst as from an effort to avoid the piles as they ricocheted off the metal framework of the demo charge. After waiting a moment for his NCO to collect himself, Allons reached over and placed his hand on Dombrowski's shoulder. "Do the best you can. We still have a bit of time."

Added to his already considerable frustration, the big Pole now felt an acute sense of embarrassment over having lost his temper. Without bothering to look up at Allons, he nodded as he turned to search for the needle-nosed pliers he had thrown.

22

The SAS and the legionnaires gave the American teams a head start of fifteen minutes before they moved out. Their movement to occupation of positions from which they could place effective fire upon the Russians huddled around the silo went off without a hitch. The Russians defending the silo, lulled into a state of complacency by boredom and an all-consuming desire to stay warm, remained oblivious to the mortal danger closing in on them.

That the defending troops were not alerted to their presence was, to Andrew Fretello, nothing short of a minor miracle. Rather than gliding swiftly across the broken landscape in absolute silence as he had before, the British commandos and their brethren from across the Channel tromped and stumbled about like a line of Hindu beaters advancing through the bush during a tiger hunt. At least that was how Fretello saw it as he made his way forward between the two assault groups. He could not imagine them making any more noise than they did if they had tried.

Of course, as their leader, he was keenly aware of everything that was going on around him. Fretello was sensitive to every infraction of their stringent noise discipline, whether intentional or not. Only the knowledge that any action he might take to impose greater vigilance would generate even more of a commotion kept him from doing so. With no good choices available, the American major chose to do what all wise commanders do under similar circumstances. He ignored the problem as best he could and hoped for the best.

It wasn't until he received word that everyone had settled into position that Fretello began to feel a sense of relief. To his immediate right were Patrick Hogg's men. At a ninety-degree angle and to his left were the legionnaires. Like the Brits, they were deployed in a line that was more or less straight along ground that overlooked the Russian positions. This deployment allowed Fretello, located between the two teams, to observe the fire of each and its effect on the Russians below. Across from him, on the far side of the clearing in which the silo sat, were two sharpshooters detached from the Special Forces teams that were providing an outer ring of security. Rather then wasting them on the outer perimeter, where there would be no immediate targets for them, Fretello had taken the sharpshooters along with him for the assault on the silo. There they would be able to put their skills and high-powered weapons to good use. From their isolated position, these American marksmen would be free to take out any of the defenders who managed to find cover from the fire directed at them by the main force.

With everything set, all that remained to be done was for Fretello to initiate the action. In a man's life, there is nothing like the feeling of power that this sort of situation instills. It is absolutely intoxicating. It was more than the simple fact that he, as the commanding officer of an elite unit of commandos, was about to unleash a storm of fire that no living creature could survive. It was more than the godlike sense of power that some men experience when they realize that with a single word, they were about to snuff out lives. There is a certain rush a soldier feels when he pulls the trigger or twists the handle of a blasting machine. The smell of cordite, the kick of a weapon, the heat from the blast of air generated by an explosion washing over his face, all this has an allure so incredible that it raises a soldier's senses to a state of exquisite rapture, a feeling that is savored in the same way decent people enjoy those illicit pleasures that tempt them but of which they never speak. It is the feeling that a young boy experiences as he fondles a smooth stone in his hand while eyeing a windowpane that he has set his sights on.

As Andrew Fretello lay on the ground flanked by his command, the tension in the air was all but palpable. The cold, hard fact that he was about to give an order that would end the lives of the Russians before him never came into play. Only later, as many combat veterans discover when the world is once more at peace, would the horror of what they had done return to remind them of the hell in which they had once participated.

"Open fire!"

To his right, he shouted for all he was worth, using every ounce of breath his lungs held. Pausing only long enough to gulp down a fresh breath and turn his head, he repeated the command, this time to his left, to where the legionnaires lay. *"Open fire!"*

No one heard this second command. Even the

British sniper curled up behind a tree stump not more than a meter away from him heard Fretello repeat the order to fire. The eruption of small-arms-fire from rifles, assault guns, machine guns, and grenade launchers was as deafening as it was deadly. All over the patch of open ground that surrounded the concrete silo cover, Russian soldiers were struck down in mid-stride. Some died before they had any idea that they were under attack. Others, who had not been marked for death during the initial devastating volley, ran, stopped, turned, and ran back from where they had come, much in the way a deer caught by an approaching car at night will bolt to safety, only to pivot about and go back toward the danger it so feared. This was panic, pure and simple.

Because he was the commanding officer, charged with orchestrating and directing the action, Andrew Fretello did not fire his weapon. Instead, he watched as his tiny command went about slaying its foe. The scene before him did not form a single, seamless image. Rather, the mind of the American major captured individual, discrete portraits of men in distress. Fretello's eyes fell upon the far end of the field, where the final seconds of a man's life were glutted as he was hit trying to flee. Struck from behind, the Russian threw his arms out and his head back before flying forward onto the ground, face-first and stone-cold dead. Off to one side, another man was literally being chewed to bits by accurate machine-gun fire. Already on the ground but not yet finished, his limbs and torso flopped and bucked about wildly, up and down, side to side, as he was hit repeatedly by a sustained burst of fire. It was like watching a puppet being tossed about by invisible strings. Above all of this was the deafening report of weapons of every sort, manufactured by the leading arms makers of the world with but one purpose in mind: to deliver deadly, accurate fire. As best as

Fretello could see, those firearms were more than meeting that criteria.

Like the American in charge, Patrick Hogg did not personally contribute to the mayhem and slaughter. But he was just as much a part of it as any of his men. With the coolness of a professional and the eye of a perfectionist, the SAS captain kept track of what his men were doing, the effect that their fire was having, and the manner in which the Russians were responding. When he saw a foe preparing to resist, Hogg would glance up and down his line of men, deciding who was in the best position to deal with the threat and direct that man's fire onto the Russian's position. His orders were crisp, clear, and direct. "Jamie! To your right. In the second hole."

There was no need to say anything more to Corporal James Cochran, a man armed with an Accuracy International PM. Known in the British Army as the L96A1, the bolt-action rifle fires a Match-standard 7.62mm by 51mm round. Shifting it in the direction of his new target, Cochran lowered the barrel of his weapon until the bipod at the front of the stock was firmly planted. Once set, he leaned his cheek against the stock, made of high-impact plastic, brought his right eye up to the six-power scope, and laid the crosshairs on the mark his captain had identified for him. Pausing only long enough to take up a good sighting and capture the last of a breath that he was releasing in the same slow and deliberate manner he used when aiming, Cochran squeezed the trigger and waited for the discharge. While he did so, he entertained no personal thoughts. Nor did he struggle to overcome any moral dilemma. He simply executed his assigned duties and then, when he was sure that a second shot wasn't required, moved on.

*   *   *

Off to Fretello's left, Adjutant Hector Allons found that he could not refrain from actively participating in the attack. After ensuring that each of his men had a sector of fire for which he was responsible, the adjutant sized up a target that he had been saving for himself. Allons never heard the American give the order to fire. It was the crack of the first rifle report that cued him. With greater care than one would have imagined given the circumstances, the Spaniard took up a good sighting and let fly with a burst of fire from his assault rifle. The smile that lit his face when he saw the man he had taken under fire crumple into a lifeless heap did not come from a ghoulish sense of pleasure. Rather, it was the pride he took in his work. It does an officer good to know that he is still as competent as the best of his men and is able to prove it to them, as well as to himself.

Situated not more than five meters from Allons, Stanislaus Dombrowski was not concerned about proving anything. He was madly firing away into the target area even when he did not have a suitable target in his sights. Instead of seeking satisfaction or simply doing what was expected, the Polish legionnaire was working off the anger and frustration that was still eating at him over his efforts to restore his precious demolition to a functional state.

Beside him was his ever-constant companion, the corporal who had turned his back on an idyllic home tucked away in a picturesque Austrian valley in order to march through the world's sewers and hell holes. Franz Ingelmann's expression stood in stark contrast to that of Dombrowski's. Where the Polish NCO's face was contorted by an all-consuming rage, Ingelmann's was as inexpressive and impassionate as one could manage at a time such as this. Like his fellow corporal in the SAS, James Cochran, Ingelmann was simply doing what he had been trained to do. Unlike his Polish colleague, the Austrian had no particular feelings one way or another as far as the Russians were concerned. While portions of Austria had experienced the boot of the Red Army during the Second World War, those memories belonged to Ingelmann's grandparents. To him, the soldiers he was shooting at were no different than the African insurgents who had the dubious privilege of being the first foe he had ever faced, or the Bosnian Serbs whom he had been forced to shoot in order to pacify them.

Not a single Russian soldier occupying the kill zone was concerned with the motivations of the men who were in the process of killing them. Few had much of an opportunity to think about anything before their lives were ended with an indifference that was both shocking and brutal. Those who did manage to survive the initial fusillade as a result of luck or of some arduous spadework on their part were now confronted with several choices, none of them good.

In the blink of an eye, they were faced with the choice of fighting or fleeing. The decision each man made was more instinctive than cognitive, since no one can truly purge behavioral patterns that are as much a part of an individual's nature and personality as is the color of his eyes. Training can go a long way toward modeling a person's conduct in combat so as to conform to a desired response. But until genetic engineers figure out how to rewire the brain, men who stare into the face of battle will continue to behave in ways that are at once erratic and predictable, courageous and cowardly, self-serving and sacrificial.

The manner in which Andrew Fretello had deployed his troops made the choice of flight unwise. The fire delivered by his men swept the entire area from multiple angles. An obstruction that protected a Russian from the legionnaires did that man little good against fire coming from the SAS. More often than not, the act of fleeing was itself a death warrant. Rather than a means of escape, the frantic efforts of the panicked soldier doing his best to find safety was a prescription for disaster. The very motion necessary to find a haven in this storm of fire tended to attract the attention of several NATO commandos at the same instant. Those soldiers who found themselves in the embarrassing position of not having a worthy target in their own sector welcomed this unintended invitation. There wasn't a single man in Fretello's command who had any qualms about deviating from the established fire plan in order to take advantage of a target of opportunity that suddenly popped up in another man's sector. The result was a quick death to any Russian attempting to escape death through flight.

The Russians who had resolved to stand and fight lasted longer, but not by much. The exposed positions these stalwart individuals occupied left them open to the same crossfire that was pelting their confused comrades. The act of popping up out of their holes and engaging the NATO commandos all too often triggered a return volley from two or three assailants. Against these odds, the Russians who managed to survive this fire quickly came to appreciate that their situation was well-nigh hopeless.

Since a successful defense was not possible, those who were at heart soldiers resolved to inflict as much damage as they could before they fell victim to the cruel mathematics of war. To some, this was little more than vengeance, the trading of one's own life for as many of his enemy's as circumstances would permit. Others who fought on were less sanguine. They did so because the other option, that of surrender, was unthinkable or, in their judgment, impractical. Surrender requires that the victorious party be open to the idea. The Russians defending the silo, raked by fire and surrounded by death, had no way of knowing just how motivated or how fanatical the enemy they were facing was. Any effort to give themselves up could be just as deadly as trying to flee across open ground, an act that the surviving Russians had come to realize by now was as foolish as it was fatal. So they soldiered on, side by side with their own fanatics.

Other Russians who came to the same conclusion concerning their circumstances sought to preserve life and limb by testing the clemency of their foe. Every now and then, Andrew Fretello caught sight of a Russian in the kill zone suddenly jump up with his hands over his head. These attempts to surrender proved to be futile as each of these wretched souls was struck down without fail as soon as he moved out from behind whatever cover had been protecting him.

In the confusion and heat of the moment, Fretello had no way of knowing which of his subordinate commands carried out what amounted to an execution. Odds were, he suspected, they all were guilty of this heinous infraction of the laws governing the conduct of land warfare. That included himself, since he, as their commander, was responsible for everything his men did, especially when it came to the commission of what some would call a war crime. But since the lawyers and politicians who found it easy to define the fine line between doing one's duty by shooting a foe in battle and outright murder were not present, and Fretello had no idea of what he would do with prisoners, he made no effort to rein in his men. Besides, even if he were inclined to do so, he was unsure of how, exactly, to go about the difficult task of sorting out from the foe those who wished to give themselves up and those committed to fighting on until the end.

In the midst of all this chaos and death, there was one group of defenders who survived simply by doing nothing. Either paralyzed by fear or anxious to ride out the storm in the hope that their attackers would be more charitable when the shooting stopped, some Russians sought safety in the depths of their foxholes. That was, after all, one of the primary reasons soldiers dug defensive positions. And this was the reason why each of the more advanced armies of the world developed weaponry that could nullify whatever advantage an industrious infantryman could gain by going deep. On this day, the countermeasure to the Russian defensive positions came in the form of the grenade launcher, a weapon normally mounted under the barrel of an assault rifle. Both the French and British found the American-made M203 grenade launcher well suited for this particular endeavor. That strange and somewhat awkward weapon allows the grenadier carrying it to engage his enemy with either the standard 5.56mm round or a variety of 40mm grenades without having to make any adjustments or modifications to his piece. Armed with this weapon, a well-trained soldier is able to place the baseball-size grenade through a window at ranges up to 150 meters. Since the distance from where the NATO commandos were situated and that of the Russian positions was considerably less than that, the grenadiers belonging to Patrick Hogg and Hector Allons had no problem in lobbing rounds into each of the pits to their front. Once the initial volley had taken its toll and all the easy targets had been eliminated, the grenadiers began the systematic process of chunking a 40mm round into each enemy position. In the confined space of a foxhole, the effect of even the smallest explosive is magnified, making every round that finds a live victim fatal.

When the attack reached this point, Andrew Fretello carefully rose up off the ground onto one knee in an effort to get a better view of the site below. One by one, the soldiers to his left and right ceased fire, not because they had been ordered to, but due, instead, to the grim fact that they lacked targets. Only the grenadiers, methodically working their way from one pit to the next, continued to engage.

From his position, Patrick Hogg caught sight of his American commander and did likewise. "Hold your positions and keep your eyes open, lads," he called out to his men. "Make sure of your target before you fire."

Sensing that this lull was the prelude to his advance, Allons moved over to where Stanislaus Dombrowski lay on the ground, eyes wide open as he searched for new targets. Coming up behind the Pole, Allons was careful when he placed his hand upon Dombrowski's shoulder so as not to startle the man. "It is time. Prepare yourself, but do not move until I give the word."

Nodding as he pushed himself up off the ground, the Pole continued to observe his sector even as he called out to Ingelmann, "Well, my friend, it is time to find out if all of this has been for naught."

In the aftermath of the one-sided firefight, the ever-cheerful Austrian was unable to muster up little more than a weak "*Oui*" in response. Even if he had been able to quickly push aside his own role in the engagement, the ponderous, steady thump of another grenade being launched, followed seconds later by a dull explosion, served to remind him that the killing was not yet over.

The chatter of small-arms fire in the distance startled Demetre Orlov. Stopping short, the Russian colonel knew in an instant what it meant. The NATO commandos had beaten them to the silo. Though there was still the chance that their attack would fail, such a hope would not be a sound basis upon which to base his actions. Instinctively, he turned and looked back to the rear of the column, where his deputy normally stayed. It took him a moment to remember that Petkovic was no longer with them. That, he told himself, was a blunder that was going to cost them. Though the major may have betrayed him once, he was still a professional soldier who would have been a valuable asset in the circumstances they were about to face.

Without giving the matter further thought, Orlov called out the name of the next officer in the chain of command. "Captain Cherkov!"

From his place near the head of the column, the office summoned made his way over to where his commander waited. Every so often, Cherkov would glance over his shoulder when a fresh volley, sounding like a string of Chinese firecrackers in the distance, erupted.

Even before the anxious young officer reached him, his commanding officer was shouting out orders. "You're to take the first section and continue straight on to the objective."

Winded, Cherkov nodded as he struggled to catch his breath. "Yes, sir. Of course."

"If the NATO commander has done what he is supposed to do," Orlov continued, "you will hit their security screen. You are to maneuver as you see fit, but go after them with everything you have as soon as you make contact. Regardless of the cost, keep up the pressure. Don't let them break off the engagement."

The men who were able to overhear their commander's orders turned and looked at each other grim-faced when the words "regardless of the cost" were mentioned. Since the currency of battle is measured in men's lives, they understood that it would be their lives that would be used to cover the expense of the pending operation.

Orlov paid no heed to what his men were doing, and even less to what they might be thinking, as he went on outlining his plan to his new deputy. "While you are engaging their screen, I will take sections two and three and circle around to the right." Though he expected that Cherkov would have his hands full as the second in command, it was important that the captain know his commander's concept of operations just in case he found it necessary to step up and assume that position as well. "If we are in time," Orlov concluded, "I will hold one of the sections back just shy of the silo to provide a base of fire and use the other to rush in, disable any demolitions the NATO troops have managed to place, and secure the site. Is that clear?"

"Yes. Very clear." Then, having acknowledged his instructions, Cherkov threw a question at his harried commander. "Where do you want me to go with the first section if we manage to overwhelm the enemy?"

Not having thought out any permutations of the problem at hand, Orlov took a moment before he answered, "Go to the left. That way, if I'm stopped, you can come at the enemy from behind. If necessary, I will hold their attention while you clear the site."

Though all of this took but a few minutes, the sound of distant gunfire was already fading. Resistance at the silo, Orlov guessed, was coming to an end. Reaching out, he grabbed Cherkov's shoulder and gave it a shake. "Now go, quickly. We don't have much time."

23

Even before the echoes of the final rounds fired in the one-sided engagement had drifted away, Sergeant-Chef Dombrowski and Corporal Franz Ingelmann were on their feet and bolting forward toward the concrete silo cover. Hector Allons, who had also been quick to scramble to his feet, became alarmed when he saw his demo party going forth. "Stanislaus! Hold up. You need to wait until we have swept the area and secured the objective."

The Spaniard's efforts to rein in his headstrong subordinate were in vain. There was only one thing on the big Pole's mind at the moment. Petty concerns such as enemy resistance were of little concern to him. Though infinitely more attuned to the dangers they were exposing themselves to, Ingelmann did not even break stride when he heard Allons's order. In part, he appreciated the simple fact that the sooner they set up their charge and ran out the wire, the sooner they would be done with this miserable mission. But the main reason the Austrian legionnaire so willingly trotted along in the wake of the big Polish NCO without looking back was the trust he placed in his companion. Nothing anyone said or did could shake a conviction he secretly held that as long as he stayed at Dombrowski's side, everything would work out.

Seeing that his efforts to stop or delay his sergeant had been for naught, Allons lifted his hand over his head, threw it forward, and yelled, "Legionnaires, forward!" louder than he had intended while breaking into a run himself.

Still pumped up with adrenaline from their just-concluded engagement, and taking his shouted order to advance as a call for an enthusiastic charge, the remaining legionnaires found themselves caught in an unintended frenzy. With whoops and yells more reminiscent of a barbaric horde, Allons' command took up their leader's pace and rushed forward into what they thought was an attack.

Over where the SAS commandos stood their ground to cover the legionnaires, there was a mixed response to the sudden and enthusiastic advance. Easing back from his weapon so as to get a better view, a soldier next to Patrick Hogg shook his head, muttering in utter disbelief, "They're bloody daft." The reaction of the man to Hogg's right was just the opposite. Caught up in the moment, he found the urge to join in on the shouting irresistible. "Give 'em hell, Frenchies!"

Concerned that his own men would be swept up in this momentary bout of insanity, Hogg nervously eyed his line. "Steady, lads. Steady. Keep your eyes open and watch your sectors." These words were spoken in a low voice meant to be soothing, yet firm. They had their desired effect. Up and down the line, his men turned their attention away from their NATO partners and back to the kill zone in search of survivors.

Even if Andrew Fretello had heard Hogg's words, they would have done little to calm his growing alarm that was now bordering on panic. As far as he was concerned, not only were the legionnaires totally out of control, they were coming close to endangering the mission. Amazed and angered by the accidental charge, he was consumed by an overpowering urge to chase down the legionnaires in an effort to restore some semblance of reason. Were it not for the steadfast manner with which the SAS held its place, he would have done so. Since the legionnaires were foreign and might not understand his orders, Fretello was quick to dismiss any thought of pursuing those wild men. Besides, he reasoned as he settled in to watch the advance, action now might just contribute to the already confused state of affairs.

The NATO troops and their commanding officers were not the only ones startled by the precipitous and somewhat uncoordinated movement of the legionnaires. Lying on the ground, a Russian who had sought survival by playing dead was completely unnerved by the stampede coming at him. Without thinking, he jumped to his feet, turned away from the howling legionnaires, and tried to flee. Even had he had the forethought to drop the assault rifle he continued to clutch, his sudden and unexpected action brought on a quick and violent response from both the SAS, charged with watching over the Legion's advance, and the legionnaires themselves. The fire directed at the Russian came from multiple sources in close proximity so that individual reports were all but impossible to distinguish. After a quick, vicious chattering of small-arms fire, the ill-fated Russian defender flopped back onto the ground for the last time.

Rather than throw a scare into the legionnaires and cause them to slow their pace and cease their war cries, the renewal of combat served only to raise their enthusiasm to an even higher state. When the drama being played out before him was too compelling for Patrick Hogg to ignore, he found himself mouthing the words of an old poem he had once been forced to memorize in school: " 'Half a league, half a league, half a league onward,' " he whispered, " 'all in the valley of Death rode the six hundred.' "

Looking away from his still-smoking barrel, Corporal James Cochran glanced back at his commanding officer. "I hope we do better than those chaps did, sir."

Caught by one of his men during an unguarded moment, Hogg smiled at his marksman. "Yes," he said sheepishly, "we can hope we do, can't we?"

Long before he felt that it would be safe to make a sharp turn to the right and begin a direct approach to the missile silo, the adrenaline that had spurred Demetre Orlov into action was pretty much used up. Now, as he struggled along he found that he was in no better shape than the fatigued men around him, whom he was suppose to be leading.

What had started out as something of a well-ordered dash, with officers to the front and soldiers maintaining prescribed distances between each other, had degenerated into a test of endurance run by a loose gaggle of winded soldiers. To a man, they were sweating profusely, gasping for breath, and grunting as they clambered over fallen trees and broken ground. Every now and then, one of them would trip and fall, or was suddenly jerked backward as a stray strap snagged a branch and arrested his forward movement. Each man responded to these unexpected occurrences in accordance with his particular nature. Some cursed and berated themselves, or the offending tree limb that had caused the mishap. Others said nothing as they nervously looked about to see if anyone had taken note of their clumsiness.

These calamities were no respecters of rank or position. The commander of commandos found his own forward progress arrested more than once by a misstep or a tangle of branches. Time and again, he bumped into the man in front of him who, for some inexplicable reason, stopped suddenly. Each of these incidents resulted in an exchange that started with the soldier uttering an oath, then mumbling a quick apology after realizing who had rammed him from behind. Only the fact that he himself caused the same sort of run-ins with the man behind him by stopping before an obstruction kept Orlov from losing his temper completely. If anything, he had to be a bit more forgiving, for in his haste to regain the lead, he had found it necessary to step on the back of a man who had fallen and had not had the presence of mind to get up quickly enough.

It was during this mad dash to reach their objective before it was blown up that it dawned upon Orlov that perhaps he had not given the situation sufficient thought. What would the result be, he asked himself as he waited for the man to his immediate front to climb over a fallen tree, if he failed to save the last of the Perimeter missiles? While it was true that a key piece of his nation's nuclear deterrent would be lost, it was equally clear that the most potent weapon in Likhatchev's arsenal would be taken away from him. Without a primed and functional Dead Hand, the rebellious general would be unable to threaten the government in Moscow. They could, if they chose to, dispatch another force to deal with him at their leisure. Or, if they were of a mind to, the duly elected central government could simply let Likhatchev and his loyal band of followers wither on the vine in an area devastated by the asteroid. Though this solution to the problem would not be as quick and direct as an assassination would be, Orlov began to appreciate that in the end, the result would be the same.

Pausing, the Russian colonel looked around pensively. The men with him ignored the strange behavior of their colonel as they continued to scramble past him. None bothered to ask why he was hesitating. Left alone like this, Orlov came to the realization that he could survive this entire affair by simply doing nothing. So NATO blew up the missiles. He could easily explain that to Likhatchev. After all, hadn't it been the General himself who had taken his sweet-natured time about calling him to the ops center and giving him the mission? His commandos, Orlov would explain, just could not cover the ground fast enough. Back in Moscow, after Likhatchev had been muzzled, Orlov could explain to his masters there that he had taken up the mission to save the Perimeter sites, not for the traitor, but in the name of the Russian people. Surely they would understand that, he found himself reasoning as he took up a more leisurely pace. After all, his past performance on their behalf and his unwavering loyalty to the government in all previous matters would be more than enough to convince those idiots in Moscow that he was telling the truth.

Only when the commander of the third section stopped beside him to ask if there was something wrong did Orlov refocus his thoughts on what his men were doing. Facing the puzzled officer, the colonel of commandos smiled. "No. Everything is going as it should."

Though the young lieutenant's gut instinct told him that everything was not going as it should, he didn't have the nerve to challenge his superior, especially in light of the fate that had befallen Major Petkovic.

With nothing to do until the demolitions team had finished setting its charges and was ready to execute, the American major in command of the small, polyglot force of NATO commandos had made his way down into the clearing in which the missile silo sat. He didn't climb up onto the silo cover where Sergeant-Chef Dombrowski was madly fiddling about, reconnecting wires that he had not been able to secure before moving out from their pre-assault assembly point. Standing on either side of Fretello were Hector Allons and Patrick Hogg. None of them said a word. They had no need to. Each understood that the Polish legionnaire, upon whom success or failure now rested, was best helped by being left alone to do his job.

Together, the three officers were anxiously watching Dombrowski's progress when the sound of firing from just over the ridge broke out. They had no sooner heard the chatter of small arms than the small radio Fretello was carrying blared out a contact report from Captain Haynes, commander of the American Special Forces contingent deployed as an outer security screen.

Even as he reached down to snatch the small headpiece and boom mike that he had taken off, Fretello could hear the report that Haynes was firing off to him. "Mike Seven Four. Mike Seven Four. We are under attack. One five to two zero enemy troops armed with small arms coming up from the south are taking the length of my line under fire. Over."

Fretello acknowledged the initial contact report and fired back a few quick questions. "I roger you last, Kilo Seven Four. Can you see any additional enemy forces maneuvering around your position?"

"Negative."

"Is the enemy to your front pressing you?"

"Negative."

"Can you hold them?"

The answer to this last question did not come back as quickly as the others. Hector Allons looked up and over at Hogg just as the Irishman was looking over at him. Both offers knew what was going on. Both had been in circumstances not at all unlike this one. They could sympathize with the Special Forces captain who, in the midst of a violent and deadly firefight, was being asked by a commanding officer, well out of the line of fire, to literally stick his head up, look around and make an assessment of his situation based on fragmented observations and gut instinct. All the while, as the three officers waited in silence, the sound of gunfire continued to reverberate in their ears.

Haynes's response finally broke both the silence and the tension. "Mike Seven Four, this is Kilo Seven Four. I can keep the force in front of me pinned. Over."

Though far from being relieved, the American major was satisfied with the response. "Roger that, Kilo." Then, after giving the problem a moment's thought, he rekeyed the radio. "I am going to be sending Tango Seven Four and his people up to support you. Over."

Judging by Haynes's tone of voice, the news that the SAS team would be coming to their assistance was welcome. "Affirmative, Mike. Advise them to approach from the northwest and around my right. The Russians line ends just shy of that point." Throughout this exchange between Fretello and the Special Force captain, Patrick Hogg said nothing. Instead, he opted to wait before expressing his reservations until his commanding officer was finished.

Satisfied that Haynes had all the guidance he needed, Fretello turned to the next order of business, delivering his instructions to Hogg with the rapidity of a machine gun. "I want you to gather up your men and get over there on Haynes' right. Take the Russians in the flank if you can and roll them up."

After waiting for a moment to make sure that his commanding officer was finished, Hogg looked into Fretello's eyes. "I don't think we should do that, Major."

Anticipating a response different from the one he just heard, it took Fretello a moment to comprehend Hogg's words, stated in a voice low, yet firm. Blinking, the American major cocked his head, maintaining eye-to-eye contact with his subordinate as he did so. "Excuse me?"

Having himself used the posturing and mannerisms the Fretello was now displaying, Hogg understood what was coming. Yet he also knew that the order he had been given was a mistake, one that he was determined not to be part of. "I said," Hogg repeated after drawing in a deep breath, "I think that sending my men gallivanting off over the ridge, away from here, would be a mistake."

Fretello was about to repeat his order in terms that were as clear and uncompromising as possible, when Hector Allons spoke. "The captain is correct, Major. The Russians in contact are probably nothing more than a holding force." Pausing, the Spanish legionnaire looked about at the broken ridgeline that surrounded the missile site as the two Anglo officers continued glaring at each other. "*This* is our objective, *sir*. *This* is what we were sent to seize and destroy, *sir*. *This* is also where the Russian force attacking Captain Haynes *must* come if it hopes to accomplish its mission. So *this* is where the bulk of our force should be concentrated, *sir*."

Having dealt with officers like Fretello many times before, the sharp and cutting emphasis Allons placed on the word "sir" each time he spoke it was no accident. It had the desired effect, for the American major now turned to face the senior legionnaire.

Seizing the opportunity he had been given, Hogg spoke before Fretello had a chance to respond to the Spaniard. "The adjutant is right, you know. This is the *schwerpunkt*, the point of concentration that every asset at our disposal must be concentrated if we are to succeed."

Like a spectator at a tennis match, Fretello's head snapped back toward Hogg as the officer continued to make his case. "The Russian knows that as well. That's why he threw out a portion of his force to engage the screen. They must draw us away from here to succeed." Now, doing as Allons had done, but in an exaggerated manner for the benefit of his commanding officer, Hogg slowly surveyed the terrain dominating the missile silo. "Their main force will do just what you want my men to do. While Haynes and the Russians he's facing keep each other pinned, they will be circling around with a good-sized force to fall on us here." Finished his inspection of the ridgeline, Hogg looked back at Fretello. "I therefore respectfully request that you reconsider your order and instead, deploy my team and the adjutant's command to counter that move."

Andrew Fretello took a moment to study the SAS officer before answering. The Irishman's expression was as firm and uncompromising as his tone. He could have glared at Hogg in an effort to cower him and force him to reconsider his last statement by sheer force of will. Back at Bragg, the young staff officer had won a number of disagreements in that manner. But this wasn't Bragg. The sound of small-arms fire just over the ridge continued without letup, reminding Fretello of this fact. It also served to spur him on to make a decision. He was astute enough to appreciate that any further delay in doing so would deny him the opportunity to issue orders and still leave time for his subordinates to carry them out.

"All right," he finally conceded while continuing to stare into Hogg's eyes. "We make our stand here."

Relieved that they had been spared from participating in what could have been a grand tactical error, Hector Allons, like Patrick Hogg, listened as the American major outlined his plan for defending the site. That they had taken it away from an enemy force that had been in the same position as they now found themselves was foremost in the legionnaire's mind. Nervously, he looked over his shoulder at Dombrowski, still working on the charge. Allons knew that now all depended on that one man. Only his ever-resourceful sergeant had the power to spare them the fate that they themselves had heaped upon the former occupants of this site but a few moments before. Though not a religious man, the Spaniard appreciated that it was at times like this that prayer had been invented.

24

Failure must be engineered with as much care and forethought as success. Unfortunately, circumstance and hesitation did not permit Demetre Orlov enough time to prepare for either. His indecision was confusing to the officers leading the two sections with him and did little to arrest the forward momentum of the commandos under their command. As had happened with their NATO counterparts, the sound of gunfire and the prospect of combat combined to create a volatile mixture that overwhelmed common sense and logic. What little semblance of a formation that they had managed to maintain in their advance through the broken terrain disappeared as they neared the missile silo. With it went all positive command and control.

Caught up in the moment, Orlov's men did what came natural to them. Unlike many of their fellow soldiers, these commandos were tough, self-reliant, and aggressive professionals. Given the sort of missions they were routinely assigned, they needed to be. Yet these traits did have their drawbacks. Instead of pausing as their commander had done just moments before to sort things out, Orlov's crack troops saw no need to. Ivan Moshinsky and the men with him knew what was required of them. It was unnecessary to assess the situation or weigh their options. For them, the situation they faced was quite simple. Somewhere off to their left, their comrades in the first section were engaged in a desperate struggle. Those men were buying them time and the freedom to outflank the NATO forces with their lives. The soldiers of the second and third sections did not have to be told by an officer that only the destruction of the NATO forces at the missile silo would bring an end to this mission and relief to their friends in the first section. With this in mind, they went forward, with or without their officers.

In silence, Orlov watched as the first of the soldiers who had made the rapid flanking march with him crested the ridgeline. Rather than pausing as an officer would have done, the soldier at the forefront of the advance continued over to the other side and toward the missile silo beyond. Without hesitation, his comrades followed suit, even in the face of gunfire that was now directed at them from the far side of the ridge.

Not having shared his conclusion with any of his officers that failure was their best option was proving to be a mistake, but one that was unavoidable. To have done so would have been a gamble, something that was anathema to a man raised in a system where betrayal and deception were seen as useful tools by both politicians and senior military men. Yet his failure to have made his intent known, or at least to have taken steps to ensure that they did not reach their objective in time, placed the Russian colonel in a difficult position. As had happened when the legionnaires had inadvertently followed Stanislaus Dombrowski and taken up the charge, the excitement of the moment had proven to be equally irresistible to the Russian commandos. With or without his blessing, Orlov's men had committed him to a direct assault on the NATO troops, who were doing their best to finish the destruction of Perimeter.

Slowly, Demetre Orlov picked his way forward at a measured pace, listening to the growing volume of gunfire from the ridge before him. Though he could see but a small slice of the battlefield, the sharp sounds that assaulted his ears told him that the engagement was growing and becoming quite heated. The spasmodic nature of those exchanges also indicated that the contest was still rather disjointed. Instead of a continuous exchange of fire, the give-and-take between his men and the NATO troops fluctuated wildly. This muddled trading of salvos was due to the manner in which his men were joining in. Inevitably, as they made they way up and over the crest as quickly as they could, they found themselves fired at. Those who managed to survive the first fusillade instinctively returned a burst of fire before seeking cover. Once having found a suitable spot offering protection, the newly arrived Russians would settle down and begin delivering a more controlled and sustainable rate of fire at carefully selected targets, while more of their comrades came forth and joined the growing fight.

Above the sharp reports of small-arms fire and the occasional explosion of a grenade, Orlov could make out the shrilled orders of section leaders and their NCO's. Drawing closer, he could see that those orders were having little effect on the men. Such a disjointed attack, the Russian colonel concluded as he finally neared the crest, could not possibly succeed against a well-organized defense manned by crack enemy troops. Though it pained him to think that he would lose a good number of his men, their sacrifice would be of some benefit. After all, how could anyone in Moscow question the loyalty of a man or a unit that has suffered staggering losses in battle.

Now, Orlov told himself as he glanced down at his watch, all he needed was for the NATO troops to do their part. That they were taking so long to set up their demolitions and execute their target was puzzling to the Russian colonel. If it had been his operation, he found himself thinking, it would have been over by now. For the first time in his military career, Colonel Demetre Orlov was angered by the apparent ineptitude of his enemy. Since it was not within his power to speed his foe along, he was left with the delicate task of slowing his own people down without making it look like that was what he was doing.

The sound of gunfire near at hand was also angering Stanislaus Dombrowski as he endeavored to reattach loose wires. His anger, however, was not directed at his foe, but at himself. As hard as he tried to maintain his focus on the task at hand, his mind was cluttered with self-recriminations. How in the name of God, he repeated again and again in Polish, could he have messed things up as badly as he had?

The explosive package before him was a simple device. Its main components consisted of high explosives packed around an inverted cone shaped like the front of a trumpet. This cone was more than a simple spacer. It was a device designed to hold the explosive back during primary detonation and precisely direct the full force of that explosion as it developed into a jet stream the width of a pencil. Made from a copper alloy that vaporized during the detonation process, the added weight of the copper molecules contributed to the terminal effectiveness of the charge. In this case, as the jet stream formed by the explosion displaced the molecules of the thin nose cone and payload area of the rocket below, some of the superheated cone's molecules would manage to make it all the way down to the missile's fuel tanks. Exerting well over 100,000 pounds of force per square inch, heated metal debris carried along in the jet stream from Dombrowski's charge would cause what is known as a "sympathetic detonation." Improperly ignited, the volatile rocket fuel would rupture its own containers and, confined by the tight concrete silo, create an eruption that would be truly spectacular.

All of this, however, would not occur if the shaped charge did not function properly. The sequence depended on primers located in the base of the explosives, centered on the tip of the cone. The wires running from those detonators would emerge from the explosive and, on this particular device, be routed in a bundle down the side of the package to a junction box just above one of the three legs that the shaped charge sat on. If the problem facing the Polish legionnaire had been on the outside, the fix would have been easy. Unfortunately, two wires had been pulled out of the primers. This meant that Dombrowski had to carefully burrow into the high explosive in order to uncover the ends of the primers. He then had to open the primers without disturbing their seating, reinsert the wires, then crimp the primers so as to hold the reinserted wires. Even under the best of circumstances, such a feat would be nerve-racking. Under fire, doubly so.

That the gunfire was wildly inaccurate was of little consequence. Dombrowski knew that the SAS and members of his own CRAP team would be able to keep the Russians at bay for only so long. Nor would the concealment provided by the smoke grenades popped by the American major last forever. Eventually, a Russian with a bit of initiative and tactical savvy would manage to find a spot from which he would be able to direct accurate fire at him. While he hoped to be finished before that happened, this thought only added to the distractions under which Dombrowski found himself laboring.

Not every adversity was beyond his control. As he knelt down to connect a wire to the junction box on the leg of the charge, he glanced over his shoulder. Besides Franz Ingelmann, Adjutant Allons, and Major Fretello were watching his every move. Used to being left alone at times like this by his former commander, the presence of these anxious officers, literally breathing down his neck, was a burden the Pole didn't need.

Pausing, Dombrowski looked over to where Ingelmann waited with the spool of wire. Reaching into his pocket, the Pole pulled the manual blasting machine he preferred and tossed it to the Austrian. "Here," he shouted as Ingelmann reached out and grabbed the tried-and-true device. "Take this and start running your wire. Tie the business end off on my leg. I'll connect it as soon as I make this last splice."

Sensing that action was at hand, Andrew Fretello turned his attention from the firefight that was still spreading across the ridge above them. "Are you done?"

Without bothering to face the American commanding officer, Dombrowski continued to run his fingers along the last wire he needed to reconnect. "Almost. Just one more minute, another splice, and all will be well."

As he watched Ingelmann fasten a loop of the wire around the Pole's leg, Fretello looked about nervously. "Is there anything else you need from us?"

Under ordinary circumstances, the question would have solicited a cynical chuckle and a snide remark. But given the straits they were in, Dombrowski responded with a quick, curt, "No."

Knowing his man and his moods, Adjutant Allons took the American officer by the arm. "Come, sir. Let us go with Corporal Ingelmann. We can cover the sergeant from the edge of the clearing just as well as we can here."

Though he was reluctant to leave, Fretello appreciated the fact that he was being told, in a rather circumspect way, that his presence here was no longer appreciated. Since he himself was a loner when it came to his work, he understood how the Pole felt. After popping his last smoke grenade and tossing it upwind of where they stood, Fretello turned and began to make his way back to a point from which they could watch the silo as well as the action along the crest of the ridge.

Upon reaching the crest where his men were hotly engaged with the enemy on the reverse slope, Demetre Orlov found himself having second thoughts about his decision to let the NATO troops blow up the missile. This sudden need to reconsider had nothing to do with the logic of his previous choice, which he knew had been impeccable. But logic in battle is often a rare commodity. More often than not, decisions are based on a simple, primitive response to the sight of the dead and wounded lying scattered about on the ground. For those who have been afforded the opportunity to experience combat, there is nothing quite like the smell of warm, freshly spilled blood, mixed in with the pungent odors of burnt cordite and fear. A whiff of combat has the ability to clear the head and bring into sharp focus only those things that are truly important and relevant. Concerns over Machiavellian stratagems and political intrigue disappear as primeval instincts are triggered by the sickening-sweet scent of death. Even a professional such as Demetre Orlov was not immune to it.

Once more the Russian colonel was hesitant. Those were his men, he reminded himself as he surveyed the situation around him, alternately looking at a corpse, then over to a man actively trading shots with an unseen foe in the distance. They trusted him. As all soldiers did, they depended on their commanding officer to make the right decisions to keep them alive, or when that was not possible, to use their lives well. That he had wasted so much valuable time pondering how best to orchestrate his own personal survival at a time when he should have been bending every effort to exert some semblance of leadership and control over his troops suddenly became a source of embarrassment to the Russian colonel. Even his youngest junior officer, a lieutenant who had recently joined the unit, was doing his part despite a wound that soaked the sleeve of his uniform with blood. "How," Orlov asked aloud to no one in particular, "could I have been so stupid?"

Mired in this trauma of self-condemnation, Orlov wasn't paying attention to the small group that followed him like a shadow. Having been affected by the same sights, smells, and sounds that triggered Orlov's reevaluation of his decisions, Ivan Moshinsky and Peter Spangen left their commander's side and made their way to a place from which they could see what was going on. The remorseless Russian commando, who had dispatched his own deputy commander just hours before without a second thought, was able to catch sight of a party of three men making its way out of a cloud of smoke screening the concrete cover of the missile silo. Excitedly, he thrust his arm out and pointed at them, "Spangen!" he yelled. "Can you drop those bastards?"

Before the sniper was able to direct his full attention and the muzzle of his weapon to where his companion was pointing, a burst of fire from an enemy position below drove the pair to cover. "Damn!" Moshinsky screamed as the rounds unleashed against them smoked the other side of the log he was lying behind, showering the two men with splinters and dirt. As he struggled to compose himself after so narrowly escaping death, Moshinsky's eyes fell upon Kulinsky, the team's combat engineer. In an instant, the Russian put two and two together. "Those men," he called over to where Spangen was lying in wait for the enemy fire directed at them to cease, "they were running from the silo, weren't they?"

Busy doing his best to preserve life and limb, the sniper didn't give the sergeant's question much thought. "How the hell should I know? I didn't even see the men you were pointing at."

Convinced that he was right, Moshinsky continued. "They must have set the charge. They must be getting ready to blow the place up." Then, turning his attention back to Kulinsky he ordered him to his feet. "Kulinsky, you're with me." Turning once more to Spangen, he reached over and grabbed the Russian sniper by the arm. "Stay here. Cover us. We're going down there to disconnect the explosives."

Not sure of what Moshinsky was up to, Spangen answered with a nod, satisfied to remain where he was.

With that, Moshinsky rose to his feet, waved Kulinsky on, and headed down into the maelstrom below.

Belatedly, Demetre Orlov noticed that he was alone. Shaking his head as if to clear his thoughts, he caught sight of Spangen propped up behind a stump busily firing away at something on the far side of the ridge. Rising up, the Russian colonel made his way over to the sniper. "Where's Sergeant Moshinsky?"

The young sniper didn't answer at first. He had a target in his sight and was in the process of letting a bit of breath slip out before pausing, holding what air was left in his lungs while squeezing off a shot. A perfectionist to the core, Spangen didn't let anything interfere with a perfect kill, not even his commanding officer. Only when he was sure that he had hit his mark did he drop down behind cover and answer Orlov. "Sergeant Moshinsky took Kulinsky down there," he stated, jabbing his thumb over his shoulder to indicate the direction of the silo. "He said something about disarming the explosives."

Wide-eyed, Orlov looked at the sniper for a moment, then over the top of the log. Ignoring the zing of return fire that flew to the left and right of his head, he searched for any sight of his wayward NCO. "Which way did they go?"

Exercising more care than his commander had, Spangen raised his head above cover and joined in the search for his comrades before answering. "I don't know, sir. Sergeant Moshinsky just grabbed Kulinsky, told me to stay here and cover them, and zip, they were gone. That was the last I saw of them." Catching sight of the billows of smoke in the center of the clearing, he pointed to it. "I believe they are headed there."

Understanding what they were after, Orlov said nothing as he leaped to his feet, jumped over the log he had been using for cover, and began to make his way toward the silo.

* * *

As in the previous engagement, Patrick Hogg held back from the firing line, concentrating instead on monitoring the actions of his men and the tactical situation before him. Unlike the initial action, which had been as swift as it was one-sided, the current affair was a brutal slugfest, one in which his men were suffering almost as much damage as they were giving out. It didn't take long for the Irish captain to conclude that the forces they were facing were not of the same sorry caliber as those from whom they had taken the silo. Based on the manner in which these men maneuvered and the accuracy of their fire, Hogg guessed that they were elite soldiers, paras perhaps. Maybe even commandos.

Ducking as a well-aimed burst of fire began to chew up the stump he was lying next to, Hogg allowed himself to slip down the slope and away from the spot that had been compromised. Rolling along the ground, he moved about until he found a protected place to hide, close to one of his corporals. Like Hogg, the man was down behind cover, safe from a spray of automatic gunfire that flew harmlessly overhead. The corporal was in the process of fishing a fresh magazine out of an ammo pouch when he took note of his commander's presence. "Can't say I admire your choice of ground, sir."

When he was fairly sure it was safe to do so, Hogg peered over the log he had come to rest behind. "Rest assured, Corporal Allen," the SAS captain said as he continued to scan the terrain to his front, "that if I had my druthers, it would be us up there and them down here instead of the other way around."

The corporal was about to make an additional comment when he noticed a flurry of activity out of the corner of his eye. Turning, he was just in time to see a Russian, holding a knife coated in blood in one hand and an assault rifle in the other, jump up from a position not more than ten meters away.

Even as he fumbled about in an effort to insert a fresh magazine, the SAS corporal yelled out a warning to his commander. "SR! To your right!"

The man's shrill tone was enough to cue Hogg to the danger he had yet to see. In a single swift motion, the SAS officer swung about, bringing his weapon to bear as he did so.

In the U.S. Air Force, fighter pilots call the response an "OODA loop," which is pronounced ou-da. These four letters stand for "orient-observe-decide-act." In aerial combat, the time to repeat that pithy little saying is measured in seconds, because once the pilot acts, his action triggers a whole new set of circumstances that requires him to repeat the process while his foe is doing the exact same thing. This holds true during close combat on the ground. Hogg had to quickly divert his attention in an entirely new direction, take in the situation before him, decide what to do, then do it before the Russian that Corporal Allen had caught sight of did likewise.

Fortunately for Hogg, the foe that came into view was paying scant attention to what was going on to his left or right. Like a shark surging blindly forward for the kill, the Russian with the bloody knife broke into a dead run as soon as he passed the shattered treeline and made for the center of the clearing. The SAS captain didn't need to think about what to do. His decision was as instinctive as it was obvious.

Fate, however, saved that Russian. Just as Hogg was bringing his weapon to bear on him, another figure emerged from behind cover in his wake. This one, unlike his companion, was more acutely aware of his surroundings. So much so that he locked eyes with Hogg, who had just turned his head away from the first man.

A new set of circumstances. Another cycle of the OODA loop. Since the second foe was staring right at him, and Hogg's peripheral vision caught the flash of a gun being brought to bear on him, the lead Russian was quickly forgotten.

The contest between Hogg and his new mark was uneven and over quickly. With his weapon already shouldered, the Irish captain only needed to slue the muzzle of his MP 5 a few inches to the left, aim center of mass, and cut loose. The range between the two adversaries was so short that every round sent his way ripped into Vladimir Kulinsky's chest. Wavering, the Russian combat engineer took one step back before he toppled over dead.

Having been surprised by the appearance of the second Russian, Hogg could not discount the possibility that more would follow. Though he would have liked to have turned his attention back to the one who got away, he maintained his position, waiting to see if more Russians sallied forth from the spot where the other two had. Only after he was sure that the pair had been an isolated threat and his concern about the one who had made off became too overwhelming to ignore, did Hogg turn to deal with him.

This hesitation cost him a clear shot. By the time he caught sight of the charging Russian commando, the man was already disappearing into the smoke that drifted lazily around the silo. Not knowing for sure if there were any friendlies still working on the demolitions package on the far side of the smoke, Patrick Hogg could not simply spray fire at it in the hope of hitting his foe. Seeing no alternative, he took off after the Russian.

All three men, Fretello, Allons, and Ingelmann, saw the Russian emerge from the far edge of the tree-line. No one spoke as they watched him take off at a dead run toward the silo, where Dombrowski was finishing his work. Only Ingelmann responded without thinking. Dropping the blasting machine he had been clutching, the corporal of legionnaires rose to his feet and began to make his way back to the silo. As he picked up speed, he yanked the sling that lay across his chest, bringing his 5.56mm FA MAS assault rifle down to his side, where he grabbed it with his right hand. He gave no thought to the risks to which he was exposing himself. Stanislaus Dombrowski was more of a brother to him than those he was raised with. Running for all he was worth, the Austrian legionnaire started to yell out a warning.

The man didn't have a chance to utter more than his companion's name before a large-caliber slug ripped into his side. In horror, Adjutant Allons watched as Ingelmann was literally lifted off the ground and thrown sideways by the force of the impact. With the might of an explosion, the single fatal round erupted on the far side of the Austrian's skinny frame, unleashing a thick red mist that hung in the air long after the lifeless body had fallen back to the ground.

Before he realized what was happening, Andrew Fretello felt the blasting machine being thrust into his hands. Recoiling, he rolled onto his side and looked up at the Spanish legionnaire who was in the process of scrambling to his feet. "You know what to do, Major," the adjutant yelled as he took off, just as Ingelmann had taken off in a vain effort to stop the Russian who was after his sergeant. Unlike Hogg, who could not fire because of the angle, Allons cut loose with a wild volley aimed at where he thought the Russian had disappeared into the smoke. All the while, Allons yelled at Dombrowski in French, gallantly trying to warn his NCO of the unseen danger about to befall him.

From the treeline, Fretello desperately tried to

take everything in. Besides the adjutant, the American major caught sight of someone breaking away from the SAS position in pursuit of the Russian who was now hidden in the smoke. Seeing that the British commando had a far better chance of success, Fretello started to call to Allons in an effort to bring him back.

Even if he had heard the American, it would have been foolish for Allons to turn around in the open and attempt to return. His only recourse was to go on. If nothing else, he figured, he would be able to cover Dombrowski.

Demetre Orlov was too late to do anything to save Kulinsky. As he continued bounding forward, clearing fallen trees and an occasional corpse, he watched as his favorite combat engineer was ripped apart by a concentrated stream of automatic fire.

Orlov didn't have time to scream in anguish. Nor did the sight evoke sorrow. This was neither the time nor the place for such things. Rather, the Russian colonel brought his weapon up, flipped the safety off, and pulled it tight against his side as he continued on. Instinctively, he cocked his head slightly to the right, in the direction from which the enemy fire had come. Fully aware of the possibility that his foe would still be there, waiting to shoot anyone who might have been following Kulinsky, Orlov intended to open fire just before he burst forth from cover, keeping his finger down on the trigger as he went and sweeping the area to his right with a steady burst. Even if he didn't hit his foe, the Russian colonel hoped the sudden return fire would cause him to duck and seek cover, a move that would buy him a second, maybe two seconds, in which he could take better aim.

He was nearly ready to start shooting, when the

movement of a figure caught his attention and brought him to a halt. Turning to face this new threat, he saw that someone was running away from him, out toward the middle of the clearing, where smoke hid the missile silo from sight. By the pattern of the camouflage, Orlov could tell that the figure was British. Beyond him was a second soldier, this one in a Russian uniform. That man, Orlov realized, could only be Moshinsky. If the Brit was the one who had killed Kulinsky, it didn't matter at the moment. By the look of things, he was after Moshinsky, who was doing his best to reach the silo.

Had he been afforded an opportunity to think things over, Colonel Demetre Orlov would have appreciated that the solution to many of his problems was right there, in the hands of the British commando he was watching chase his NCO. All Orlov had to do was to keep watching. But the Russian colonel was a soldier, trained to seek out and destroy his nation's enemies. While he was well aware that there were Russians who posed a far greater threat to his homeland than this lone Englishman did, at the moment, such distinctions were impossible to make. Demetre was in the midst of a vicious and bloody fight where action, not debate, is the order of the day.

With the ease of a professional, Orlov brought his AK-74M up, took aim, and cut loose with a burst of fire.

Ordinarily, when he finished setting a charge, Stanislaus Dombrowski would step back and carefully examine the entire device, from top to bottom, just to be sure. But the situation was such that this nicety had to be abandoned. The Pole didn't even bother reaching over to pick up the tools that lay scattered about his feet. Instead, he brought his assault rifle down to his side, turned, and prepared to make his way. The only thing he took time to do before heading off toward the edge of the field where the others were waiting was to look around in order to assess the tactical situation.

It was only then that he saw his adjutant running at full speed directly toward him, yelling as he came. It took a moment for Dombrowski to appreciate the danger he was in, a moment that allowed Sergeant Ivan Moshinsky an opportunity to reorient himself as he stormed out of the smoke and turned toward the bewildered legionnaire. Before Dombrowski could do anything to defend himself, the Russian was on top of him. The impact of body against body threw the Pole back and onto the ground, barely missing one of the legs of the shaped charge.

Despite the shock of impact, the two men tore at each other with a viciousness that is often written about but seldom experienced in war. Pinned beneath the big Russian, Dombrowski freed one of his hands, brought it around and covered the face of his assailant. With all his might, he pushed, forcing Moshinsky's head up at an awkward angle. With equal determination, the Russian resisted the Pole's effort to push him away or to snap his neck. Redoubling his effort to hold the legionnaire close to him with his left hand, Moshinsky brought his right hand down and slipped it between them. Then, with a simple twist of his wrist, the Russian tilted the point of the knife he held in that hand downward until he felt the handle against his own midsection. Ready, Moshinsky gave the knife one mighty shove.

The swift, sudden penetration of the Russian's knife was a shock. Dombrowski's body stiffened for a moment, then went limp. Though he could still see and hear, the Pole suddenly realized that he was unable to move. How terrible, he found himself thinking as his field of vision slowly closed in to have a Russian as his last worldly image. How terrible.

In horror, Andrew Fretello watched the drama unfold before him. No sooner had the Russian emerged from the smoke and tackled the Pole than the Spanish legionnaire was dropped by a sniper, just as his corporal had been. As clear as all of this was to the American major, a voice from somewhere in the back of his head was screaming that none of this was happening. It couldn't be! Things had to work out to his advantage. They always did. His plans always succeeded. Always. But the reality of the situation before him could not be ignored, just as the Russian who had made it to the missile silo could not be made to disappear simply by wishing him away.

Setting the blasting machine down, Fretello scrambled to bring his rifle up. The M-16 he carried was his weapon of choice. He had fired it time and time again, never failing to qualify "Expert." But now, when he needed to finally put that skill to work for him in combat, he found that he was all thumbs. The faster he tried to bring his rifle to bear on his enemy, the more he seemed to fumble. It was absolutely unnerving.

Yet, bring it to bear he did. With the weapon finally tucked up firmly on his shoulder, the American major prepared to fire. Easing his cheek against the plastic stock, Fretello looked through the tiny peephole of the rear sight and brought the muzzle of his weapon about until the post on the front sight was superimposed over the figure of the Russian before him. Composed and ready, Fretello held his breath and squeezed once, twice, three times. Each time, he fought the recoil. Each time, he brought the muzzle of his weapon back down and went through the process of aligning its sights before squeezing off the next round. And each time, the round he fired found its mark.

The pain of moving was unlike anything Patrick Hogg had ever experienced. That his wounds were mortal was without doubt. Struggling to prop himself up on his knees, he imagined that he had felt every round as it had hit him. Throughout the whole terrible ordeal, he had never lost consciousness. Instead, he had maintained an acute awareness of what was going on. He not only saw the boots of the Russian who had shot him from behind, he had actually felt the ground shake as his assailant ran past him and on toward the silo. Try as hard as he could, the Irishman was unable to muster the strength to coordinate his arms in time to reach out and grab those bloody damned boots as they passed within inches of his face.

He had also been a hapless spectator to the death of the two legionnaires as they rose up from safety and did their best to go to the assistance of their comrade. Hogg watched now with a strange detachment as the American major, having fired his weapon and discarded it, was madly connecting the wires running from the charge on the silo to a blasting machine he held. Unsure of whether his commanding officer was going to wait or set the charge off from where he was, the SAS captain gathered up all his strength, clenched his teeth, and slowly pushed himself up and onto his knees.

The effort and the pain it sent shooting through his body was staggering. Dizzy, Hogg found that he needed to take a moment to choke back the nausea he felt welling up. Unable to swallow the blood that filled his mouth, he simply let his lower jaw drop so it could spill out. When he had managed to collect himself, he opened his eyes and watched the final act unfold before him.

The smoke that had concealed the silo for so long was finally dissipating. This allowed Orlov to see the three-legged shaped charge far sooner than his NCO had. He paid no attention to the two bodies lying on the ground between himself and the explosive package. With the same determination that Patrick Hogg had mustered in his struggle to get up, the Russian colonel continued on.

Any doubts he had once entertained about letting the NATO troops destroy the missile were gone. Any concern about surviving this combat were forgotten. He had but one more mission to accomplish, one more task to carry out. Stepping over the corpse of a big French legionnaire, Colonel Demetre Orlov prepared to save the missile, not for Likhatchev, and not for the men in Moscow who had sent him to this godforsaken region. Orlov was going to do his duty because he could not do otherwise, not after so many of his men had so freely given their lives doing likewise.

When he realized that there could be no other way, Andrew Fretello dropped his rifle, took up the blasting machine and began to connect the wires. Even as he did so, his nimble mind raced in an effort to find a more suitable solution, another way to succeed without taking the radical step he was preparing to make. There was no such thing as a no-win scenario. He didn't believe in that. He couldn't believe in that. The motto was victory or death, not victory and death.

Still, the reality was there. So too was a new threat he saw as he looked up before attaching the last wire. Where the second Russian on the silo cover had come from was beyond him. But there he was, reaching over to grasp the other end of the very same wire he held in his hand. To stop what he was doing and reach for his weapon would be futile. By the time he took up his rifle, the Russian would have made it to the demo pack. It was now a race, one that Fretello would be unable to celebrate even if he won.

The impact of a boot kicking him in the side was enough to rouse Stanislaus Dombrowski to a hazy state of consciousness. Opening his eyes, he saw what he thought was the leg of the Russian who had stabbed him. Without giving the matter any thought, he reached up, grabbed as much of that leg as he could and gave it a jerk.

Caught off guard, Demetre Orlov pulled back, away from the explosive charge and looked over his shoulder to see who had seized him. Amazed that it was the legionnaire, it took the Russian colonel a moment to figure out what to do about this sudden inconvenience.

This hesitation was all the big Pole needed. While holding on to the Russian with one hand, he searched for a weapon with the other. When his fingers came across a pair of needle-nosed pliers, he wrapped them around that ordinary tool, brought his arm up in a wide, sweeping arc, and jammed the point of the pliers into the Russian's thigh.

The sudden resistance by the legionnaire generated within Andrew Fretello a moment of hope. Perhaps there was another way? Perhaps he could manage to save some of his men and still accomplish his mission? Rising up on his knees, the American major watched and began to reconsider his options.

Patrick Hogg was also watching. He saw the desperate struggle at the silo. He saw the American major, blasting machine in hand, hesitate. He knew what was happening. Though the pain of drawing in a deep breath was unlike anything he had ever experienced, it was the last weapon he had available to him. After spitting out blood that continued to gather in his mouth, Captain Patrick Hogg leaned back before bellowing, as loud as he could manage, his last order. *"Blow the goddamn thing! Now!"*

Startled, Andrew Fretello looked over to where Hogg sat, wavering as he fought the urge to faint. Again, in a voice that somehow rose above the din of battle, the SAS officer shouted, *"Blow the damned thing!"*

It wasn't a suggestion. It wasn't a recommendation. It was an order, something that Fretello understood. Something that he was in the habit of giving and taking.

Without bothering to look back at the silo where a dying Polish NCO struggled to hold back a wounded Russian colonel, Andrew Fretello brought Operation Tempest to a close.

Epilogue

After standing in the doorway without drawing his commanding officer's attention, the young staff officer reached around and lightly rapped on the open door. Looking up from the letter he was writing, Lieutenant Colonel Thomas Shields needed a moment to refocus his tired eyes. "Yes?"

In a hesitant manner, the lieutenant who served as his adjutant advanced into the room. "I was wondering, sir, if there would be anything further this evening?"

Looking over at the window, then up at the clock, Sheilds realized that the normal duty day had ended hours ago without his taking any notice of it. "I didn't realize it was so late. Don't tell me the rest of the staff is still waiting on me to leave before slipping away?"

The young officer took up a relaxed stance with both hands behind his back before answering. "No, sir. The sergeant major chased everyone else out about an hour ago. He tried to toss me out as well, but I held my ground."

His response brought a wry smile to Shields's face. "Bucking for captain already?"

Now the lieutenant smiled as he bowed his head to hide his embarrassment. "Oh, I can assure you, sir, my motives are pure."

"Then what, pray tell, is keeping you chained to your desk waiting for a tottering old fool like me?"

The smile left the young officer's face as he gathered himself up into a position of parade rest. "I was wondering if you've made a decision about the decoration. General Shane's office has called twice today concerning its disposition."

Any vestige of a smile disappeared from Shields's face. "Do you have it with you?"

Slowly, the young officer brought a package out from behind his back and offered it to his commanding officer. Rising, Shields reached across his desk to receive it. "I've been putting this off, you know," he whispered as he took the oversized envelope, carefully laid it in the center of his desk on top of the half-written letter, and slumped back down in his chair.

Once relieved of his burden, the staff officer resumed his position of parade rest. "Yes, sir, I know."

Shields looked at the envelope for a moment. He didn't need to open it. He knew who the medal was for. He knew what the commendation attached to it said. He had no problem with either since he had been the officer who had drafted the recommendation. What was bothering the senior SAS officer was the fact that he would have to deliver it to a person who would have no appreciation of what it meant.

"If you would like, sir," the staff officer finally ventured when he saw that his commander was hopelessly lost in thought, "I can arrange for someone of appropriate rank at MoD to deliver it to her. She lives right there in London."

Shaking his head, Shields vetoed that idea without a word. Again, there was a long impasse as he continued to stare at the package before him. Finally, he looked up. "You know, there's an old Japanese saying that fits this situation quite well."

Not knowing where his commander was heading, the young officer just nodded. "Yes, sir?"

" 'They say that duty is heavy, but death is lighter than a feather.' "

The lieutenant didn't need to have his commander explain the meaning of that saying, or why it applied in this case. Everyone at Hereford knew about the rift that had taken place between Patrick Hogg and his wife just before he'd left for Russia. The officers' wives freely gossiped about how Jenny Hogg refused to return to Hereford to collect her husband's belongings or to attend the memorial ceremony held in September, after the last of the Tempest participants were repatriated. She had made it very clear to anyone who cared to listen to her how she felt about the Army. Which is why, the young officer thought, his commander had put off going down to London to present her with the medal.

"She's done quite well for herself, I hear," Shields finally mused as he continued to stare at the package before him.

"Yes, sir. According to the missus, he's a well-connected barrister who's got his eyes on a seat in Parliament."

Shields sighed. "Yes, yes. A new husband with a real future."

This last comment made the young officer a bit uneasy. "I wonder if she never understood Captain Hogg or what the Army is all about. Seems like that's more common than we'd like to admit."

"Do you understand, Lieutenant?" Shields asked sharply as he looked up. "Does anyone understand?"

Caught off guard, the young officer didn't know quite how to respond. "In truth, sir," he finally answered when it became obvious that the question had not been rhetorical, "I don't much think about that anymore. I, like yourself, just do my duty."

Standing up, Thomas Shields stretched the arm that he had broken in Russia. "Do me a favor, Lieutenant. When you go home tonight, ask yourself that question. If, after careful consideration, your answer is the same, then pick up the paper tomorrow morning on your way in and start looking through the classified ads for a new profession."

Stunned, the young officer did not respond. Instead, he again asked his commander if there was anything else he required from him. When Shields shook his head, the lieutenant scampered out of the office as quickly as he could, leaving Shields alone with his thoughts, the posthumous medal for Captain Patrick Hogg, and a half-written letter to that officer's former wife.

Wandering over to the window, the SAS officer stared out into the quiet evening. In the end, whether Jenny understood or not, it didn't matter. While she and so many of her fellow countrymen could be casual about such things as duty, honor, and loyalty, he could not. Duty, indeed, was heavy.

But, Thomas concluded as he pivoted about sharply and prepared to call it a day, it was something that he understood. On the morrow, he would complete that letter and arrange a time when those who had fallen in the service of their nation would be given their due. That his fellow countrymen did not appreciate the price his men had paid to keep them safe and free was unimportant. Thomas Shields did. He imagined that every man who had ever stood watch over their nation did also. For now, that would be enough.

" . . . that whenever any form of Government becomes destructive of these ends, it is the Right of the People to alter or abolish it, and to institute new Government, laying its foundation on such principles, and organizing its Powers in such Form, as to them seem most likely to effect their Safety and Happiness. Prudence, indeed, will dictate that Government long established should not be changed for light and transient Causes; and accordingly all Experience hath shewn, that Mankind are more disposed to suffer, while Evils are sufferable, than to right themselves by abolishing the Forms to which they are accustomed. But, when a long Train of Abuses and Usurpations, pursuing invariably the same Object, evinces a Design to reduce them under absolute Depotism, it is their Right, it is their Duty, to throw off such Government, and to provide new Guards for their future Security."

—From the Declaration of Independence, 1776

"A well regulated Militia, being necessary to the security of a free State, the right of the people to keep and bear arms, shall not be infringed."

—Article II, (complete text), The Bill of Rights, 1787

"A little rebellion now and then is a good thing."

—Thomas Jefferson, 1787

"Revolution is the locomotive of history."

—Karl Marx

"My Country, may she always be right. But right or wrong, my Country."

—Inscription at the United States Naval Academy

Prologue

The sight of file after file of redcoated soldiers marching boldly onto the green was unnerving. Nestled between his fellow militiamen, a young New England farmer who went by the name of Ned Smith nervously shuffled about as he watched. Every so often he would cast an anxious glance to his left and right in an effort to gauge the response of his companions. Rather than drawing some measure of reassurance, however, the sight of their grim faces and his company's pathetically thin ranks only served to heighten his apprehensions.

Never having been in combat, Ned had no clear idea what awaited them once the British had completed their deployment from a line of march into one of battle. What little his captain had been able to teach them during their musters on this very green did little to prepare him for the sights he now beheld and the sensations they were evoking within him. Never one to be shy about voicing his opinion, Ned wondered if it would make him look cowardly if he called out to his captain and asked if he thought it wasn't a good idea to stand down and disperse. In Ned's mind they had pushed their defiance as far as they dare. To linger here in the face of such overwhelming odds would be foolish.

Yet stand their ground they did. Silently the band of militiamen waited. Across from them the rhythmic tromping of marching feet mixed with the rattle of muskets and gear, stirring the chilly morning air and blood of all present. Every so often this muted cacophony of noise was punctured by crisp commands barked by stern-faced English officers. With machinelike precision the solid phalanxes of the King's troops responded by wheeling about this way and then that in preparation for the pending contest. While few of the rank and file expected they would need to do more than present their muskets and make ready to fire in order to chase away the rabble across from them, none doubted that they would prevail.

This confidence came not from arrogance, but from a simple appreciation of the facts, the same facts that Ned Smith was so keenly aware of. This was not the streets of Boston, where roving mobs felt free to hurl taunts and insults at a handful of British soldiers standing their posts. If it came to it, this would be their sort of scrap, a stand up fight, the sort they had been trained for. Given a chance to play this little drama out to its conclusion, there was not a soldier present who doubted that they would prevail. The only regret that some entertained as they waited was that they would not be given a chance to do so. They would be held back, as they always were, from meting out the just punishment the wretched colonial rabble deserved. After having endured the outrageous treatment that they had been exposed to for so long, all felt the urge to set the record straight and put the colonials back in their place.

*   *   *

Standing before a collection of men who were his neighbors and friends, Captain John Parker was at a loss for words. He found himself unable to muster up a pat response, or find a witty saying that could ease the apprehension that he shared with men he had gathered together in defiance of the orders issued by officers of the King. In time, he knew he would have to yield to the regulars now assembled before him. But he was determined to do so only at the last possible moment, and only after making it clear that they were simply giving ground, and not the principles which had compelled them to make this stand.

Behind Parker, Ned Smith waited with growing concern. Though he could feel the shoulders of his companions on either side rub his as they shuffled about nervously, the young farmer felt very much alone. Absentmindedly, he fingered his weapon's lock as he watched, waited, and prayed.

Ned was no stranger to this piece. He had used it to slay many a squirrel, and, when the occasion presented itself, a rabbit. These little forays beyond the neatly plowed fields of his family farm had been, for him, an enjoyable break to the monotony of daily chores that made those who farmed here as hardy and tough as the land they tended. Whether he sallied out on his own or in the company of friends, the excitement of hunting his prey, and putting his skills to a test, never failed to bring joy to what would have been an otherwise drab and uneventful existence. Perhaps that was why he answered the call by the local militia captain. The militia company was, for Ned, an adventure, a chance to shed the last vestiges of his childhood and stand with the men of his community, for the first time, as an equal.

While such whimsical goals had sufficed to get

him into the ranks then, Ned was quickly becoming aware that it would take more than that to keep him rooted to this spot as he watched as untold numbers of tall grenadiers marshaled before him. This was no longer a game that was being played out by radical politicians. It was no longer a pleasant diversion from the drudgery of farming the rocky plot of earth his father had willed to him. This was a serious matter. These were soldiers of the King, the finest musketeers in the world. Everything from the bayonets that caught the glint of the early morning sunlight to the cold, hard expressions worn by the soldiers who made up the long red ranks told young Ned Smith that trouble was but a hair's breadth away.

On either side of him stood his fellow militiamen, men who had been encouraged by their community leaders, families, and peers to stand up for what they had been told were their rights. Now, like Ned, they stood there in silence, arranged in what passed for a line of battle. Each and every one of them watched the swift, precise movements of professional soldiers arrayed before them. Everything about the English, from the ominous sight of their unsheathed bayonets, to the solid ranks that seemed to stretch across the green and beyond, made Ned and his companions painfully conscious of their own vulnerability. "They're like a machine," the youth muttered to no one in particular. "They'll sweep us aside like so many cinders."

An older man, a grizzly coot dressed in a homespun vest and a coarse muslin shirt, leaned on his musket as if it were a walking stick. He surveyed the scene before them through narrow, squinted eyes. "They're just as nervous about this as we are," he stated bluntly. "See," he indicated with a nod toward the far end of the green, "how their officers are circling and wandering about."

"Well," a gruff voice replied, "their officers may be a bit uneasy, but watch out for their lads. Have you taken note how they eye us with the contempt of Boston thugs. Mark my words, they're spoiling for a fight, lads."

While the gruff voiced militiaman's statement may not have held true for all of the King's men, it certainly summed up Private Robert Johnston's attitude. Like so many of his companions, he was growing impatient with his own skittish officers. Worked up into a near frenzy by the tensions that had been building up, Johnston stepped out of ranks and began shouting oaths for all he was worth. Like many of his mates he ignored his officer's threats to cease yelling and stand to attention. He was tired of standing in ranks like a great bloody statue, forced to endure everything from taunts to stones thrown at them by damned colonists like those across the way without being allowed to respond. "Look at 'em," Johnston hissed as he thrust his fist out toward the line of militia, some sixty yards away. "They stand there, armed to the teeth, in clear violation of the King's law, and dare us when they know there isn't an officer in our regiment with the backbone to give the order." Glancing at a young subaltern doing everything he could to shove the men of 4th Regiment of Foot back in line, Johnston grunted. "I don't know who disgusts me more, our own officers who shy away from a real brawl like a spring virgin, or those damned hooligans who call themselves patriots."

Johnston's companion, a pale, thin fellow named Martin who was also enflamed by the moment, didn't respond to his comrade's comments. Instead, he contented himself with fingering the musket held close to his side as he eyed the gaggle of militiamen gathered opposite them. All that stood between these lines were a handful of mounted British officers who rode between the two lines of armed men in an effort to defuse the situation. Finally, Martin spoke as he eyed a particularly nervous looking colonist who appeared to be backing away from the fray. "One good volley," he finally muttered menacingly. "Let us hit with one good volley and we'll end it right here."

With a grunt, Johnston nodded his agreement. "Aye, that we would. Let 'em see a bit of their own blood spilled. Perhaps that'll make 'em a bit more mindful of the King's law."

"If not the King's law," Martin snapped, "at least we would teach the bastards a bit of respect for his troops."

Shifting his weight from one foot to the next, Johnston was about to hurl a volley of fresh insults when their lieutenant, his face as red as the scarlet coat he wore, passed before him. Sword drawn, he pushed Johnston on the chest with his free hand and shouted. "Hold your place. Keep silent and hold your place, or it'll be the cat-of-nine for you." Without another word, the young officer continued down the ranks until he stopped in front of another offender and repeated his threat. With a sideward glance, Johnston looked at the officer, then over at the rebels. For a moment, the musketeer weighed the merits and risks of continuing with his taunts. Only after considerable thought and the memory of the drummer's lash biting into his flesh did Johnson relent. The release of his pent up anger and frustrations, he concluded, was not worth the punishment. So Johnston pulled himself erect, tucked his musket into his side, and contented himself with watching the confused scene unfold before him in silence.

*   *   *

If it were a simple matter of numbers and demon-
strated abilities with weapons, or logic and common
sense, this strange confrontation would never have
occurred. The armed men who eyed each other
across the flat expanse of village green were, after
all, Englishmen. Both were ruled by the same King.
They shared a common language. The institutions
and practices that governed their day to day life had
sprung from the same roots. In times gone by, they
had fought a common foe under the same banner.

Yet Ned Smith and many of his fellow New Eng-
landers no longer saw themselves and the King's
men as fellow countrymen. Slowly, almost impercep-
tibly at first, the English soldiers who closed Boston
to all commerce had been transfigured into something else. Rather than guardians, they had become
intruders, men from a foreign land sent by a distant
government to deprive Ned and his fellow New Eng-
landers of their rights and their liberties.

Of the many issues that had propelled these two
armed bodies to assemble across from each other in
the cold dawn light, there were but two that compelled the militiamen to stand their ground as long
as they did, and the English soldiers to seek battle
without a hint of hesitation. For the militia, the sight
of the redcoated troops on the ground upon which
they called their own brought home to them the
harsh reality that the issues of freedom and liberty
were no longer abstract thoughts bantered about by
rebel-rousers in Boston's public houses. The agents
who possessed the will and means to deprive them
of both were there before them, but a stone's throw
from their own front doors. While each of the militiamen knew they could capitulate and escape with
their lives, all understood that the price of doing so

would be surrendering the freedoms and right they had come believe were God given.

There was nothing abstract at all about the forces that propelled the regulars. They represented the King. Every English law and every English institution was on their side. As the duly appointed defenders of the King and Parliament, it was their lot in life to follow his orders and enforce the laws of the land. They had been dispatched not to judge right or wrong. Nor were they there to listen to the grievances of the provincials. The soldiers had come across the Atlantic for no other purpose than to carry out their orders and put an end to all resistance, by whatever means. And the means upon which they relied was not a judge's gavel or a lawyer's petition, but a Tower musket, caliber .75 equipped with an eighteen-inch triangular bayonet.

With their own men properly deployed and, for the moment, in hand, mounted British officers rode up and down between the opposing lines. "Disperse," they repeated angrily, spitting out their word as they grew frustrated with the lack of response. "Disperse, you damned rebels, and be gone."

Though it was all but impossible to take his eyes off one mounted English officer who loomed before him, Ned managed to glance to his left and right. Like him, some of his companions were clearly intimidated by the English officers and the solid wall of regulars standing behind them. Twitching and shuffling about in their loose formation, Ned saw more than a few glancing back over their shoulders as if they were making sure there was nothing that would impede their flight if it came to that. Others, however, seemed totally unmoved by the overwhelming might that was arrayed before them. Holding their muskets at the ready, those men simply stood stone cold still, carefully eyeing anything that they perceived to be threatening, which, for Ned, was everything.

Slowly, it dawned upon Ned that they were in an impossible situation, one in which there was no good outcome. If they simply obeyed the King's officer, turned their backs and went home, they would have to face the humiliation and criticism of friends and fellow militiamen. That would have been hard for young Ned to live down, especially after all the bold talk he had bantered about in the tavern. Humiliation, however, could be survived. Standing their ground, as many a crowd had done before in Boston, and hoping that the English would back down, might not. The English, after all, had their pride, too. They had their masters to whom they must answer. What if today was the day, Ned asked himself, if they said, "enough of this" and fired. And if they did, then what? What would he do? What would become of their homes, their families? Where, the young man wondered, had any of the fine gentlemen of Boston addressed *that* in their fine speeches? Why weren't they here? Why, Ned asked himself, was he there in their stead?

That there were others who agreed with Ned's assessment of the situation was obvious. After delaying as long as he dared, their own commander began to make his way down their line. Though nervous himself, Captain Parker at least retained the presence of mind to face the fact that there was nothing that they could accomplish by standing their ground any longer. Even from sixty yards, it was quite obvious that the ordinarily well-disciplined English musketeers were in an ugly mood. With no hope of reinforcement, and ever mindful that the men under his command were his friends, neighbors, and their sons, Parker gave them the order to disperse. To Ned, already on the verge of quitting the field, this was sound advice, advice which he fully intended to follow.

The efforts of the mounted officers riding back and forth along the rebel line seemed to be having an effect when, from somewhere off to one side, a single shot rang out. A quick sweep of the rebel line by every English officer, mounted and afoot, failed to detect any telltale signs of smoke drifting away from it. Leaning forward, despite frantic threats from his officer, Johnston glanced down their own line in an effort to see if he could discover the source of the shot.

He was still looking when, to his surprise, another shot rang out, right next to him. Jumping, Johnston's head spun to his left where he laid eyes on his companion, now enshrouded in a cloud of gray smoke. With an ease borne of long hours of drill and training, the man was bringing his musket down to reload. "DAMN YOU ALL TO HELL!" Martin shouted as he reached behind with his right hand to fish a fresh round from his cartridge box. Then he looked over at Johnston. "Well!" he roared. "You're always griping that we're never allowed to take our measure against those bastards. Here's your chance, man. Take it now or never utter another word of complaint to me."

Johnston was still staring dumbly at Martin, considering what to do, when several more men in the ranks around him brought their pieces to bear on the rebels and fired. Though he hadn't heard an order to fire, Johnston didn't much care. Finally, he realized, he could do what he had wished he could have done for so long. He could lash out and strike a telling blow against a foe that had, for so long, taunted them with impunity.

With the steady, measured steps that were second

nature to him, Johnston brought his musket up to his shoulder, pointed it at the group of men who were, under the King's law, as much an Englishman as Johnston himself. But this little legal nicety didn't matter to Johnston. Not in the least. With great deliberateness, he locked the hammer of his musket back into the full cocked position, steadied his piece, and pulled the trigger. ·

The crack of musket fire was deafening. Even on the ground, where Ned lay, the sound was the most awful noise he had ever heard. For the longest time he stayed there, wondering where he had been hit. It took young Ned a moment before he realized that he hadn't been shot. Only then did he slowly begin to look about. To his front, the English line was half-masked by billowing clouds of smoke their own firing was creating. Off to his right, he watched as several of his fellow militia gamely tried to return the English fire. Feeling embarrassed by the fact that he was cowering instead of standing tall and bold, Ned turned his eyes away to the left.

This, however, brought him no relief, for his eyes were met by the sight of Robert Munroe, lying but a few feet from him. Munroe, with blood pouring freely from an ugly wound, was motionless. Closing his eyes, Ned began to whisper the Lord's prayer.

Only the sound of feet scampering all about him caused Ned to open his eyes. This revealed a most horrible sight. Individually and in pairs, English soldiers, with their bayonets leveled, were rushing forward. To Ned it seemed as if their own officers were trying hard to restrain them, to hold them back. Whether this was so didn't matter to Ned Smith. In a single swift motion he was up, on his feet, and fleeing. What consequences the events he had just witnessed would have on him, on his family, and on his tiny community of Lexington, did not matter at that moment. All that was important to Ned was that he put as much distance between himself and these English soldiers, vicious regulars who had bodly marched into the town where Ned had been born and raised, and who were killing his neighbors.